## Meet the men of
## THE WINTER OF OUR DISCOTHÈQUE

### Tony

"I have *never* spent a week at the baths. A long weekend, maybe. But *never* an entire week. I know that for a fact. Those cubicles are so small I couldn't get a week's worth of luggage *into* one."

### Dallas

"The world we live in, you and I—all gay men—is based and ordered and ranked on one thing and one thing alone: appearance. It is not a plutocracy, but a *beau*tocracy."

### Devlin

"Shouldn't you be cleaning out the gutters of Manhattan with your tongue? That *is* what you do when you're without a man for more than a couple of days, isn't it?"

### Valentine

"When you're as rich as I am, you can *never* be certain your lovers aren't after your money. I stopped worrying about that long ago. It ruins all the fun."

### Connecticut

"I love it when guys don't wear underwear. It's so sexy."

### Tuxedo

"With the type of men you pursue, the kinds of places you're seen in, and your truly extraordinary abuse of drugs and alcohol, you should have been dead long ago."

*Please turn the page for rave reviews of*
*The Winter of Our Discothèque*

# THE WINTER OF OUR DISCOTHÈQUE

## ANDREW W.M. BEIERLE

KENSINGTON BOOKS
http://www.kensingtonbooks.com

This is a work of fiction. Names, characters, places and incidents either are the products of the author's imagination or are used fictitiously, and any resemblance to actual persons living or dead, events, or locales is entirely coincidental.

KENSINGTON BOOKS are published by

Kensington Publishing Corp.
850 Third Avenue
New York, NY 10022

Copyright © 2002 by Andrew W.M. Beierle
A chapter of this novel was originally published as a short story called "Pump Jockey" in the anthology *Rebel Yell* published by The Haworth Press in 2001.

All Kensington titles, imprints and distributed lines are available at special quantity discounts for bulk purchases for sales promotion, premiums, fund-raising, educational or institutional use.

Special book excerpts or customized printings can also be created to fit specific needs. For details, write or phone the office of the Kensington Special Sales Manager: Kensington Publishing Corp., 850 Third Avenue, New York, NY 10022, Attn. Special Sales Department. Phone: 1-800-221-2647.

Kensington and the K logo Reg. U.S. Pat. & TM Off.

ISBN 0-7582-0142-7

First Hardcover Printing: April 2002
First Trade Paperback Printing: March 2003
10  9  8  7  6  5  4  3  2  1

Printed in the United States of America

*To my sister, Maggie*

## Acknowledgments

No one has had a greater impact on my career as a writer than Susan Lowell Butler, lifelong teacher, mentor, and friend, whose love, support, and encouragement have transformed my life. I cherish her.

I also would like to thank Frank Manley and Ivy Fischer Stone for helping make this book a reality. John Scognamiglio has been a patient, creative, insightful, and inspiring editor.

My closest friends have supported me from the very beginning of this process and have sustained me by continuing to believe in my dream. My heartfelt gratitude goes to Katherine Hinds, Emil C. Hines, Grady Chance, Steve Rogers, Richard L. Eldredge, Susan Carini, William L. Baites, and Jameson Currier.

*Virtue is the result of insufficient temptation.*
           —Dallas Eden

*June 21, 1969—the longest day of the year and the first day of the last summer of the 1960s. It was the summer of Woodstock, both zenith and swan song of the flower children; the summer of Stonewall, the Lexington and Concord of the gay revolution. In less than a month, man would view an earthrise from the surface of the moon. It was Sharon Tate's last summer—and Mary Jo Kopechne's. Judy Garland had less than twenty-four hours to live.*

# PART I

# 1

TONY ALEXAMENOS was wet and naked when the pale yellow Cadillac floated into the station, as cool and smooth as a Creamsicle on wheels.

*Damn! Who the hell wants gas at seven-thirty on a Saturday morning?*

In the darkness of the service station bay, he turned off the hose he had been using to sluice the salt water from his body, threw his dripping jams on the back of a battered red folding chair, and stepped clumsily into his oil-stained work suit, hopping from one foot to the other as if he were standing on hot coals. His clean undershorts, glowing like ivory neon in the darkness, lay out of reach on the workbench across the room, where he had left them on his way to the beach.

Outside, the driver laid on the horn.

"Hang on. I'm comin'." *Shit! If the old man wakes up, there'll be no surfing for a week.* He shrugged his arms into the suit and slipped into his flip-flops, shuffling across the gritty concrete until his toes locked into place around the yellow rubber thongs. Crescents of dampness materialized around his armpits and crotch.

The horn sounded again.

"Keep your pants on," Tony muttered, struggling with his own. The overalls' zipper had snagged about two inches below his navel, and he couldn't get it unjammed. But with this horn-happy idiot apparently warming up for a John Philip Sousa march, he decided to abandon modesty in favor of speed and ran toward the garage bay door.

Tony was pissed. The station wouldn't even open for another half hour, and everyone in South Beach knew it. When he'd been in the water not fifteen minutes earlier, he'd had the opportunity to survey the island for signs of life, and he'd seen not a single light in the kitchens or bathrooms of the flat-roofed, Necco-hued houses along the beach, nor in any of the double-wides scattered like jetsam at the Point. And it was way too early for lost tourists, who at this hour would still be snug in their beds, dreaming of their free Continental breakfasts at the Suncoast Quality Inn.

Still, he figured he was lucky. If the waves hadn't been so piss poor, he'd still be in the surf, and if this bastard and his mobile brass section had rolled in here and roused his father from the loving embrace of Jack Daniels, there'd be hell to pay. It wouldn't matter to Demetrios that the damn station wasn't even open. He'd fly into a rage and take a swipe or two at Tony, who long ago had learned to duck and dodge his boozy father's infamous flying fists.

Tony grunted as he hefted the garage door. Outside was a '59 DeVille convertible in showroom condition, twin bullet taillights mounted in silver bezels on the biggest tail fins the world had ever seen.

"Fill 'er up. Hi-Test," the driver demanded in a croaking voice as Tony walked briskly around the car, his fingers thrumming lightly across the sculpted hood of the idling Caddy. Tony didn't make eye contact, just turned and kept on walking to the stern of the land yacht.

"Yessir," Tony said, then added, loud and flat, "Engine off." He was damned if he was going to kiss butt before he was even on the clock. He busied himself at the ancient pump, its red paint scabrous with rust.

The man in the car wore a Panama hat a couple of sizes too big and an oversize pair of sunglasses that effectively masked the upper half of his face. He was huge, a blimp, and it appeared as though all he was wearing was a bathrobe. Tony didn't want to know if there was anything under it. Definite pervert. That explained the hat and glasses. Probably planned on distributing candy to minors.

Sliding his sunglasses down his sunburnt nose, the driver peered into the rearview mirror directly at Tony's reflected image. Sensing that he was being watched, Tony turned his head. Their eyes met on the silvered surface, but the driver instantly looked away, mumbling something indecipherable.

"Sir?" Tony said, anticipating a rebuke. People always did that. They want to complain but don't have the balls to actually say anything, so they mutter into their armpits or elbows for their own sake or the benefit of their passengers.

"Yes?" the man said, returning his sunglasses to the bridge of his nose with his right index finger but not looking back at Tony.

"You said something, sir?"

"No no no, my dear boy. Just thinking out loud."

*My dear boy.* Must be British or something. Yeah, right, *British.* The damn pump pressure was low again and filling the tank on this boat would take an eternity. It gave Tony the opportunity to carefully inspect the car. For ten years old, this one was absolutely cherry—not a single ding or dent, not a trace of the salty residue that blanketed cars every night and ate away at them all day. The white convertible boot was brilliant and supple, free from the green-black mildew that, in the primordial mists of central Florida, attacked anything remotely hospitable. Even the spikes in the car's decorative rear grille looked as if they had been recently flossed.

The interior was a different story. The rear seat was awash to the armrests in boxes, paper cups, and foil wrappers from every fast-food joint in Sugar Mill Beach: Krystal, Kentucky Fried Chicken, Krispy Kreme, even Astro Burger, the mom-and-pop fast-food shack out Highway 1 toward Titusville. Tony could see mustard and ketchup smeared on the white leather upholstery like a child's two-tone finger painting; and on the dash directly below the mirror, five rings from sticky cold drink cups approximated the international Olympic symbol.

"Check your oil, sir?" Tony asked as he screwed on the filler cap.

"By all means!"

*By all means, my ass.* Tony was familiar with that falsetto of exaggerated enthusiasm. It was the same tone of voice the Big Bad Wolf had used on Little Red Riding Hood. *The better to eat you with, my dear.* Tony knew when he was being hit on; it happened to him all the time. All of them were creeps: the skinny Italian guy from Miami with the see-through shirt and iridescent pants, the fat shoe salesman who offered Tony the pick of any of the footwear in his trunk, the pasty-faced man from New Jersey with a station wagon full of wife and kids who lured him into the men's room on the pretext that the john was overflowing and then got down on his knees and begged Tony—*begged* him—to let him have at it. It was pitiful. Each and every one of them said he wouldn't have to do anything but "sit back and enjoy it," but he wondered what on God's green earth made them think he would enjoy anything that involved bodily contact with them. When Tony first declined their invitations, they invariably offered him cash; but he was even more disgusted by the way they humiliated themselves. There was *no* amount of money that would convince Tony to surrender himself to this joker today, should he ask, and he probably would. He'd rather feed his family jewels to a meat grinder.

But, Tony thought, there was still a way to profit from an encounter with this sorry sack o' shit. He could easily scam this dumb fuck by telling him his shocks were shot, which was obvious. He would replace only those on the driver's side but would charge him for all four. He guessed the right shocks were in great shape; anyone could see what the problem was. On the other hand, did he really want to have this bozo hanging around the station all morning? What the hell? A buck's a buck, and he needed thirty more to buy a rebuilt carburetor for his van.

Tony had learned the art of the scam from his father. Much of the station's income was bilked from hapless tourists who rolled in looking for directions to Turtle Mound or the old sugar mill ruins and rolled out with four brand-new tires or a new transmission and a tale of woe that would make the distinguished gentlemen over at the Better Business Bureau of East Central Florida piss purple for a week.

"Everything looks fine under here, sir," Tony called out, leaning his head around the upraised hood. "But you know, it looks like you could do with some new shocks. Leastwise you ought to let me check 'em out."

"I couldn't possibly today," the man said. "But I will come back for a complete inspection under your skilled and capable hands. Now, how much do I owe you?"

"Seven twenty-five, sir." *And I'll be keeping my skilled and capable hands to myself, Dumbo.*

The man reached into his bathrobe pockets and came up empty-handed.

*Great, now I'm gonna get stiffed.*

The poor slob tried to shimmy over toward the glove compartment but succeeded only in rocking the car side to side. His belly was trapped beneath the steering wheel.

"Be a dear and open the glove box, won't you?"

Tony walked around the car and reached into the glove compartment. He found a greasy roll of bills inside a red-and-white striped french-fry box and handed the wad to the man, who peeled off a ten and gave it to him.

"Here you are . . . ? Did you tell me your name?"

Tony squinted off into the distance while turning the ten spot over in his hands. "It's Tony."

"Well, Tony, you are a very fine young man who provides excellent service. I'm sorry I was so impatient when I pulled in. Take this for your trouble." He pressed a second greasy bill into Tony's hand.

"Thing is, we ain't even open yet."

"I understand."

The driver started the car, put it in gear, and fishtailed onto the highway in a cloud of sand, gravel, and broken shells. Tony looked at the bill the man had crushed into his hand. A fifty. "Shit yes!" he said. This was without a doubt the biggest tip he had ever received, if indeed it was a tip and not a mistake. Probably thought the fifty was a five. Better not plan on buying that carburetor for a couple of days, just in case the clown comes back demanding a refund.

Tony went into the station's office, which, despite the fact that two of its walls were floor-to-ceiling glass, always managed to look cramped, dark, and dingy. The eight-by-ten room was cluttered with oil cans and spare parts, and on a ledge along the front window, peppered with dead houseflies, were faded copies of *Popular Science, Field and Stream, True*, and *Reader's Digest* magazines customers had left behind. He banged open the ancient black cash register, made change for the ten, which he pocketed with his fifty—*his* fifty—and, whistling, went out back to hose off his surfboard before the predictable lineup of South Beach sad sacks arrived, wanting a buck's worth of gas and some free air for their nearly bald blackwalls.

Tony never understood how his father put food on the table and clothes on their backs with the income the station generated, though come to think of it, food got to be spotty at times and Tony bought most of his clothes himself with his earnings from his other jobs—lifeguarding and working at the surf shop. As he saw it, the main problem with the station was location. It sat at the dead end of a dead-end road on a dead-end island, with the wide blue Atlantic on one side and Mosquito fucking Lagoon on the other.

Thank God for the students from the college. Every September, when the streets of Sugar Mill Beach filled with bright, shiny new sports cars bearing license plates from Virginia, New York, and Massachusetts, business picked up at South Beach Gulf. Instead of ten-year-old Chevy Bel Air station wagons eaten away by rust, Tony serviced muscle cars: 'Vettes, Goats, and Chevy Malibu SS convertibles, with the occasional racing green TR-6 thrown in. The cars belonged to students at Sanctuary College, the elite Sugar Mill Beach school that was a lesser-known academic rival of such respected Magnolia League schools as Duke, Tulane, and Vanderbilt.

A surprising number of the sports cars ended up at South Beach Gulf for repairs, considering the ten-mile drive to an area that, other than being home to Gator Grove, the second largest mobile home park in the state of Florida, had no points of interest whatsoever. But on the Sanctuary campus, Demetrios Alexamenos had a reputation for cheap, reliable service—cheap mostly because Tony did the work at something less than minimum wage, and reliable because he *never* ripped off Sanctuary students, who were worth a good four years of repeat business and invaluable word of mouth.

Demetrios did not allow the students in the bays while he worked. But if he was out cold, which was more and more the case lately, Tony didn't mind if they stood in the doorway or even came in and talked to him, as long as they didn't touch anything and then complain about getting grease on the starched and monogrammed Oxford broadcloth shirts they wore with oversize khaki or Madras shorts and those damn penny loafers without socks. It was less aggravating to divert them with small talk than to have them whine every fifteen minutes about how long it was taking or repeat that they had better things to do than "hang around this filthy grease pit." He despised them for their money, their privilege, and their snot-nosed attitudes but tolerated them because he loved working on their cars. When they weren't around, he could take joyrides in roadsters he would otherwise never have the opportunity to sit in, let alone drive.

Tony generally could discern which of the customers were straight arrows and which were a little bent. The straight boys talked about nothing but themselves, their cars, their fraternities, and their girlfriends, typically in that order. But the others were interested only in Tony. How old was he? Did he go to school? Was that his surfboard? Ever get in to town? Can I have your phone number? Tony pointed out that the telephone number was on the receipt, but none of them ever called, other than to complain about something. Maybe they were just making up the problem to talk to Tony and were waiting for him to ask them to bring the car back. But Tony was sure of his work and busy enough that he didn't need to waste time checking out, for free, a nonexistent problem for some Sanctuary stud with a hard-on for him. It might be different if they weren't such candy asses, but Tony knew all of them would scream rape if he laid one greasy hand on their pretty pastel polo shirts.

# 2

DALLAS EDEN headed slowly north on A-1-A, his eyes flitting regularly to the rearview mirror, where he watched the silhouette of South Beach Gulf dwindle to a speck and vanish. It was a sorry-looking place, stucco painted beige, sitting on a flat, scrubby lot covered mostly in yucca and mangrove. It seemed more Southwestern than Floridian, like a ginger-bread Alamo left to bake in the sun.

Dallas slowed and spun the wheel to the right, heaving the yellow behemoth onto the roadside dunes. His heart was pounding as he patted away the beads of perspiration on his forehead with a handful of folded white paper napkins from the local Kentucky Fried Chicken franchise. Lust was a bitch. Especially at eight in the morning.

Dallas Eden was obsessed with two things, great physical beauty and prodigious talent, himself possessed of neither. Over the years he had chastely husbanded a number of prodigies from childhood to respected positions in the worlds of art and science. He also had enjoyed a litany of exquisite young men who were intimate with him for three or four months and left considerably enriched. His protégés stimulated and quickened his mind, while his concubines did the same for his body.

This boy was different, although Dallas wasn't readily able to articulate how. Enticing? Yes. The boy oozed sex from the pores of his honey velveteen skin. Everything about him—from his enchanting face to his elegant torso—screamed sex. He probably stank of sex. But this time Dallas felt something more, a sensibility divorced from his gonads that clutched at his heart in a new way. If he were not careful, he would soon do stupid things, make costly mistakes. Just look at him! He was already a mess: rapid, shallow breathing; trembling hands; arrhythmia. And he was sweating like a tall glass of gin in the summer heat. Dallas Eden prided himself on maintaining his composure under even the most taxing circumstances. It had to do largely with his bulk. A silly queen wandering the ancestral manse wailing and gnashing his teeth was one thing, but an overwrought pachyderm was entirely another. It could be lethal, if not to the hired help then at least to the Limoges.

He broke down and wept, his self-control washed away by wave after relentless wave of his implacable self-loathing. He blubbered into his doughy hands, mucus streaming freely from his nostrils, his pale flesh quivering as it reverberated with his gasps and sighs. Never in his life had he been more ashamed of the sodden, shapeless mess of a body he inhabited. He was sick of being nearly forty years old and having to rely on his valet to tie his shoes as if he were a child, sick of being so fat he could not reach his own penis for purposes of pleasure or utility.

Dallas knew he was in trouble the instant he laid eyes on the kid emerging from the murky maw of the service station, struggling deliciously at crotch level with the zipper of some ridiculous baggy garment, torn at one knee and spotted with grease. Dallas had nearly bitten through his tongue. The boy was tall, six-one at least, maybe six-two. Deeply tanned, he had painted a triangle of zinc oxide on his perfectly proportioned nose. His chest was hairless; his nipples, when Dallas could see them flash beneath the fabric, were as dark and creamy as Hershey's Kisses; his stomach as hard and defined as the shell of a horseshoe crab. His hair, long and wet, medium blond, was drying into finger curls and ringlets that clung to his cheeks and temples. For such a beauty to be pumping gas in a leper colony like South Beach was insane, nothing short of criminal.

Sitting by the side of the road, gradually regaining his composure, Dallas wished he had the presence of mind to ask for a lube job or some air in his tires, anything to have kept the boy in view. But he was hung over, unshaven, unwashed, and unclothed save for this tatty beach robe. No, that would never do. He needed time to strategize. He would have to play his cards with *extraordinary* care.

Dallas slowly, deliberately, pulled himself together and eased the car back onto the road, tail first. His heart raced for a moment when the rear tires spun in the sand, the engine whining, before they bit into the asphalt with a sharp yip, a whiff of burnt rubber, and a sudden jerk backward. How on earth, he wondered as he drove north again, could an angel like that end up in South Beach? It was like finding a Caravaggio at the fucking Kmart!

Until this very morning, Dallas had never even set foot in South Beach, although he had grown up a stone's throw away. What brought him there today was that scrofulous hustler, a skinny blond-headed kid he'd picked up hitchhiking on State Road 44 near Samsula last night and dropped off today at his dilapidated South Beach home, with a battered red pickup perched on cinder blocks in the front yard. Dallas had to smuggle him out of the house this morning before his mother woke up. He sighed. This was what he was reduced to—tiptoeing through the manse at dawn like a hippo in a tutu, dragging some pimply redneck goon behind him. Oh, how he missed his harem.

Dallas followed the road where it bore left, then took a hard right across the narrow, singing metal bridge that joined South Beach to Sugar Mill Beach. The scenery improved immediately as the road sliced through the seaside neighborhood of Sugar Mill Estates, where pastel houses sat like decorations atop green squares of cake. He checked the odometer. Ten miles—it was a little more than ten miles from South Beach Gulf to his home. It may as well have been ten thousand, for as much intercourse as there was between the two communities. The gulf between the two towns was far wider than the brackish estuary that separated them. To understand the difference, one need look no farther than the very road on which Dallas drove, the one common element the two shared. In Sugar Mill Beach, A-1-A, known as Tropicana Boulevard, was lined with graceful palms and hedges of hibiscus of a hundred hues, its grassy median dotted with flowering trees: Queen's crape myrtle, bottlebrush, frangipani. But in South Beach, only thickets of mangrove and yucca clung to life along the ragged edges of asphalt known simply as the Old Beach Road, frequently littered with the carcasses of roadkill: possum, armadillo, and the occasional alligator.

Residents of Sugar Mill Beach banished their worst fears to South Beach. It was there the bogeyman lived, there the bodies of drowned fishermen washed up on the shores of Mosquito Lagoon. All the usual prom-night tales were invariably set in South Beach: men with hooks instead of hands, strange thumps on the roof while a couple was fornicating in the backseat of the boy's family car, or long-dead prom queens walking on water surrounded by a phosphorescent chartreuse halo. *And yet,* Dallas thought, *in that grotesque landscape, there exists this bewitching manchild.*

He eased up on the accelerator as he approached the entrance to Edensgate, parting the forbidding black wrought-iron gates with his visor-mounted remote control. Dallas Eden was well known in Sugar Mill Beach, and Edensgate, the home he shared with his mother, silent film star Eve Eden, was a showplace more worthy of Palm Beach or

Newport than the tiny coastal town north of Cape Canaveral where it was secluded at the edge of the Sanctuary College campus. Upon its completion in 1930, one breathless critic declared it, with Biltmore House and San Simeon, "among the most magnificent private residences in America." John Lindsey Dunstan Jr., heir to a vast citrus and cattle fortune and himself founder of the Dunstan's department store chain, had built the mansion as a winter home for Eve Eden, who gave up her career to marry him at the advent of the talkies. He founded Sanctuary College as a private drama school to indulge Eve's theatrical pretenses and used his fortune to make it one of the premier liberal arts colleges in the South. The college was built adjacent to and just north of Edensgate and was screened from view by lush tropical landscaping. A two-mile-long, waist-high wall of natural stone, known simply as the Wall, separated the campus from the Tropicana Boulevard business district in downtown Sugar Mill Beach.

Christened John Lindsey Dunstan III at his birth, Dallas chose to pursue the career his mother had forsaken for the love of his father, taking her last name as his own and adopting her birthplace as his Christian name. He attempted a serious dramatic role in a Broadway play his mother financed, but failed, only to become a popular success on the nightclub circuit. He made his first movie, *The Three Stooges Meet King Tut*, in 1957. Five years later, his role opposite Bob Hope in *This Zulu Is Crazy* earned him an Academy Award nomination for best supporting actor, but he lost to Ed Begley's performance in *Sweet Bird of Youth*. He continued his career as a stand-up comedian in Las Vegas and as a stand-in game show celebrity in New York, wedged between Kitty Carlisle and Arlene Francis on *To Tell the Truth*.

Dallas abandoned the Caddy on the circular drive and, in the foyer, found his chauffeur, Jorge, and handed him the key chain as if it were a dead rat, before heading for the Jacuzzi in the ground-floor solarium. There he summoned his valet, Alfred, and told him to remove the sheets from his bed and burn them, as well as any stray socks or undergarments left behind by his vile nocturnal visitor. Then he called his personal assistant, Gloria Patri, in her suite and told her to join him immediately. She arrived ten minutes later wearing a fluffy white bathrobe and a magenta terry cloth turban. Her face was not made-up.

"I can only imagine what trouble you're in that you had to summon me from my douche," Gloria said as she settled in to a wrought-iron-and-leather chair near the tub. She had worked for Dallas Eden long enough that she spoke her mind without fear of reprimand.

"I'm doomed, Gloria. Doomed. This one will kill me—I know it. You may as well start making the arrangements," Dallas said as he sat in the roiling water smoking one of his malodorous stogies and swilling Dom Perignon from the bottle. "I don't want some tasteful little service, either. I want a *circus!* I want people talking about it from Cape Canaveral to Cape Cod to the Cape of Good fucking Hope."

"What on earth are you talking about? Do you think you caught some fatal disease from that maggot you brought home last night?"

"Oh, God! You *saw* him?"

"I was coming back from my morning swim and saw you leaving."

"He was even more lacking in charm and social graces than is the norm amongst his ilk. And come morning, he had the most hideous teeth—rotted down to little black nubs, indubitably the combined effect of too many Moon Pies and too little Crest. But no, this isn't about him. And mind you, *none* of this would have happened if Alessandro hadn't been on a nookie strike."

Alessandro de Nicotéa, a silver medalist in diving at the Mexico City Olympics the previous year, was Dallas's current inamorata. In return for his companionship, Sandro had been ensconced since March at Dunstan Hall, Dallas's crenellated manse at Fifth Avenue and Seventy-ninth Street, handed a deck of credit cards and told to go play. When his tour of duty was done, he would be given the luxury roadster of his choice and return to Spain. But when Eve Eden's health declined precipitously, he accompanied Dallas to Edensgate. In New York, Dallas maintained a harem of stunning, pea-brained muscle men to satisfy his baser carnal needs, so he was usually content simply to gaze upon Alessandro, nude, reading a book or draped provocatively on black satin sheets. But it was far too big a risk to bring the harem to his mother's home, and ultimately Dallas required intimacy from the almond-eyed champion with considerably more frequency than either could have anticipated. In truth, this required little but Alessandro's physical presence, as Dallas's sexual repertoire consisted mainly of basting his lover's inert torso with spit, kissing him with the brutish ardor of a lifeguard resuscitating a drowning victim, and swallowing whole his genitalia, more often than not flaccid. Only young men with exceptional imaginations could reward his ministrations with an erection, let alone an ejection. Dallas himself had multiple orgasms, his copious ejaculate congealing in the ridges, folds, and furrows of his epic stomach and thighs. But enough was finally enough for the Spaniard, and Sandro had taken to barring his door and had asked for his payoff up-front.

"Why don't you just give him the damn thing and be done with it?" Gloria said.

"The question is moot. Our Miss Nicotéa will be Barcelona-bound this time tomorrow. You brought your steno pad?"

Gloria flourished a pad and pen from her robe's oversized pocket.

"Good. I want you to make plane reservations for him—first class, coach, baggage compartment—whatever it takes to get him out of here today."

"This isn't like you, Dallas. You've never been so unforgiving. You've had some headstrong boys before, and you've always managed to ride it out. He'll come around. This is Sandro, for God's sake. Need I remind you of your authentically Pavlovian response the first time you saw him last summer? What's up?"

Dallas cocked his head back, inhaled deeply of his cigar, and exhaled a perfectly formed, seemingly endless stream of smoke precisely the diameter of a number two pencil. "I had a beatific vision this morning. I'm in love, Gloria. Truly, wonderfully, frighteningly, madly in love."

"Oh really? This sounds serious," Gloria said, demurely uncrossing and recrossing her well-tanned legs. Dallas's romantic exploits were always fascinating, occasionally bizarre, and frequently hilarious in a pathetic sort of way. But a beatific vision? That was one she'd never heard before. "And where, pray tell, did this encounter take place? I'll want to buy real estate there to set up a souvenir stand for all the believers-on-a-budget who can't afford to make the trip to Lourdes. God, I hope there's a grotto nearby."

"It happened at a gas station in South Beach."

"What in the name of God were you doing in South Beach?"

"Taking home that sorry excuse for a trick. I'd thought about having Jorge drive him, but I was so embarrassed by him that I just couldn't. So I took him myself, and no sooner than I'd shoved the pockmarked cretin out of the car and started home, I realized I was driving on fumes. Can you imagine my horror at the prospect of running out of gas in South Beach? Then, in the distance, I saw this huge orange lozenge shimmering like a rising sun. A Gulf station! I pulled in and this *seraphim* emerged from the depths of a service bay. He was a true revelation."

"So what you're saying is that he's trash, but he'll clean up right nice?"

"Once he's been civilized, he'll cause whiplash and coronaries from one end of Fifth Avenue to the other."

"Let me guess," she said, licking the end of her pencil in mock seriousness. "Skin as luminous and unblemished as Carrara marble, lips like Cupid's bow, hair the color of gold spun from straw by Rumpelstiltskin . . ."

"It goes beyond mere physical beauty, though of course he has that. I sensed that this boy would prove to be entirely different. I think he is The One."

"The one *what?* The one who will rob you blind? The one who will invite his thug friends here to murder all of us in our beds?" An errant strand of hair fell over Gloria's left eye; she pushed out her lower lip and blew it away. "If I may be blunt, Dallas, this is what you say every time you see a new piece of meat that's bigger or prettier than the one you've already got in your mouth. God, you are *such* a novelty queen. As soon as it wears off, and I guarantee you it will, you'll give him a couple of greasy C-notes and send him on his way. He's obviously not protégé material. No Nathan Bismarck. No Connecticut Jones. You take this youth and beauty thing far too seriously. You make gods out of these boys. Why don't you forget about this child and have breakfast with Sandro at the pool? Toss back a couple of mimosas. Work things out. He's bored, for God's sake. He contracted for New York and he ends up here, in this mausoleum."

Gloria liked Alessandro immensely. He was sweet and kindhearted. It was unlike him to make demands of any kind. This whole thing must be a misunderstanding.

"No, Gloria, I've made up my mind. I want that little greaseball out of here. *Inmediatamente!*"

"And what do I tell him? I assume, of course, I *will* be the one to tell him."

"Tell him I've taken ill. Tell him the Rapture has taken place and I've gone to my mansion in the clouds. Tell him anything you want. Just get rid of him. Today. I'll write a suitable check. Not enough for a Lancia, but more than adequate to compensate him for his services to date. More than adequate."

"Are you absolutely sure this is what you want to do?"

"Gloria, this new boy is the *most* extraordinarily beautiful human being of either gender I have *ever* seen. There was a certain quality about him, too, a kind of vulnerability he tried to mask with arrogance. He absolutely broke my heart. I was so unsettled, I very nearly threw up."

"Well, why didn't you say so? The ability to induce vomiting has always been high on the list of characteristics *I* seek in lovers."

"Bitch."

"Will that be it, then? Make Sandro go bye-bye?" Clearly irritated, she rose and smoothed the nap of her robe, feigning distraction. "Nothing else?"

"I want you to find out everything you can about this new boy. Tony something or other. Greek last name. It's on the wall of the station if you can't find it any other way. Must be seventeen or eighteen, so I presume he's enrolled at Sugar Mill High, unless he's graduated."

"Or dropped out."

"I want his family history, his school records, his police record if he has one. Everything."

"Shoe size? Or do you already have a rough idea about that?"

"Go."

ALESSANDRO took the news surprisingly well, after the check was proffered, and he left for the Daytona Beach airport at noon for a flight to New York. Half an hour later, at about the same time his plane was turning north over the crowded beaches, Gloria Patri arrived at the Volusia County Sheriff's office, hoping to discover that this new kid was a rapist or had beaten a murder rap on a technicality. Although it was now too late for Dallas to reconsider his dismissal of Sandro, maybe he'd at least learn a lesson about a bird in the hand if this Tony person was bad news. But probably not.

Dusty Rhodes, the sheriff of Volusia County, greeted Gloria in his office, a pine-paneled room accessorized with wanted posters and garishly colored maps of the county and the state of Florida. Thanks to the visibility of South Beach Gulf on the island, he knew immediately who Dallas was curious about and was more than happy to oblige the man who so generously supported county youth services.

"This kid in trouble with Mr. Eden?"

"No. Nothing like that. Dallas—Mr. Eden—just thinks he might be able to improve the boy's circumstances."

"Mr. Eden always has been generous when it came to the young men of our community. He's given many a boy a head start."

*No*, Gloria thought, *he's given many a boy* head.

Sheriff Rhodes went to his files but returned empty-handed. The boy had no criminal record, he said, not even for something as minor as shoplifting or stealing a bicycle.

"No grand theft auto?"

"That what you lookin' for? 'Fraid not. But now his father, *Deme-*

*trios* Alexamenos, has several drunk and disorderlies at the local tavern and three D.U.I.s."

Gloria thanked the sheriff and had Jorge drive her to the home of the Sugar Mill High principal. She found Frank Ferlinghetti in his pool, and he groused about going to the high school to look at the boy's file. But he put his cocktail in a go-cup, threw on a short-sleeved tropical-print shirt over his trunks, and joined Gloria in the backseat of the limousine. It was not until they were inside the school building that Ferlinghetti realized he knew who Tony Alexamenos was. "Got 'im," he said, snapping his fingers. "I know the one. Graduated just this year. Bright, but a pain in the ass—pardon my French."

"Troublemaker?" Gloria asked as she pulled a slender, gold, monogrammed pen out of her tidy purse. *Steals kids' lunch money? Disembowels live dogs? Please, God, let it be something good.*

"Not so much *trouble*, I guess, as truancy. When the waves were good, it was *adios amigos*." Ferlinghetti handed her a buff folder with Tony's name typed on a smudged label.

"So he's a surfer?"

"A pretty fair one, as I understand it. He's not really a bad kid, when it comes to cases. Mostly a laissez-faire attitude. No parental guidance." He gestured toward the file. "You'll see scores well above average on standardized tests like the Iowa and California, but his grades don't reflect it."

Gloria flicked through the pages of the file with the clear-lacquered, business-length nail of her right pinky. His grades were roughly divided between Cs and Bs, with an A in his drama elective.

"His grades aren't *that* bad," she said.

The folder was stuffed with truancy reports on paper the color and texture of air-mail stationery. The secretary who filed them had long ago given up keeping them in chronological order. Among the truancy slips, Gloria found a number of handwritten notes from teachers worried about Tony's attendance record and his home life. One in particular, Gina Marescheno, appeared to submit pleas on the boy's behalf with some regularity.

"There are a lot of notes in here from teachers who seem to think he's worth salvaging. Couldn't you do something for him?"

"Nah," Ferlinghetti said, massaging his unshaven chin. "Don't have the resources. It all boils down to resources."

"But otherwise there were no major problems?"

"Come to think of it, there was a time the Catholic Charities put him in a foster home over in Winter Park for six months or so. Seems like after the kid's mother died, the father apparently didn't bother to properly feed or clothe the boy, who got by, I figure, with whatever he could beg, borrow, or steal. The school nurse over to the junior high on the island could tell he was malnourished after a cut on his finger became grossly infected. She took a personal interest in the kid, tried to get him out of the situation. She had a hard time at first, but then the old man apparently did something really awful and the state welfare people stepped in and packed him off to the foster home. I don't think things improved much by the time they let him go back home."

Gloria discovered yet another note from Gina Marescheno, who apparently was the drama coach as well as Tony's homeroom teacher. It praised Tony's acting ability and suggested that one of the school's guidance counselors attempt to get him into the theater studies program at Sanctuary College on a scholarship.

"Whatever came of this?" she asked, handing Ferlinghetti the pale rose sheet of personal stationery.

Ferlinghetti read it and flipped it over to see if there was a notation on the back indicating a response. It was blank. "Nothing I know of. I do remember now that he was in a school play this spring. *Death of a Salesman.* Not the lead role. One of the sons. He refused to cut his hair, so they tied it back in a ponytail and tried to hide it best they could under his varsity letter jacket. Kept on coming out about midway through. The teachers got to calling him 'Malibu Biff,' because of the hair. Nobody followed up on the Sanctuary thing, I think, because he was a Southie. These days, our counselors barely have enough time for the regular kids, let alone a kid from the island."

"That's a very enlightened attitude, Mr. Ferlinghetti."

"Why thank you, Miss . . . Pastry?"

"Patri, Gloria Patri."

"So what's this kid trying to do, blackmail Mr. Eden or something? I'll bet I could dig up enough dirt to hang 'im if I tried. That is, if that's what you're after."

"I trust you can find your own way home," she said. She handed him the folder without further comment, turned on her heels, and walked tappity-tap down the freshly waxed linoleum floor. She didn't know what this kid was going to be like when they finally met face to face, but to her surprise she found herself in his corner. She was actually *glad* Dallas was going to take an interest in him, although at what price to the boy no one knew.

# 3

A WEEK LATER, Tony was sitting in the gas station office waiting for his best buddy, Charlie Pickering—Pick to his friends. Tony and Pick were going to throw their boards in the back of Pick's '52 Chevy pickup and drive down to Sebastian Inlet. The waves were usually better there, and they went whenever they had the chance. Tony sat with one clunky work boot, loosely laced, on the floor, the other atop the gray metal desk. He was leaning back in the green vinyl–covered chair, snapping his gum and tossing loose screws and washers into the trash barrel across the room. Tony's van was still not running. He had grown uneasy about his windfall in the week since he'd come into it. He wanted to spend it— with fifty bucks he could not only get a carburetor but also a passenger-side window—but was dead certain that as soon as he did, the fat man would pull up and demand forty-five dollars change.

Tony got out of the chair when he heard the Chevy hacking and grinding up the road. Pick, a gangly redhead whose body was dappled with a network of freckles the color of Georgia clay, bounded out of the cab and slammed the door. His face was alight with excitement.

"Tony, I know who your mystery man is!" He was out of breath. "You know—the oinker in the yellow Caddy."

"Shhhhh! The old man don't need to hear this." Tony was expecting his father to relieve him any minute now. "So who is it?"

"Dallas Eden. Dallas fucking Eden!"

"You're shittin' me. Dallas *Eden?*"

"One and the same. I'm surprised you didn't recognize him."

"Me, too, but I couldn't hardly see his face with those sunglasses and that hat. Plus, I didn't think he had gotten that fat. Christ, the guy was disgusting. So how do you know it's him?"

"My cousin Jimmy told me. He works at the ABC Liquor on Tropicana, and some guy's been pullin' up to the drive-through for a couple of weeks in that same yellow Caddy and picking up a couple of fifths of Jim Beam and some paper cups. Anyway, he's got one of them American Express cards, and sometimes he uses it if he don't have cash on him, so Jimmy's seen his name. Figures he drives around looking for nice, juicy teenage boys, gets 'em drunk, and . . . you know, bingo-bango!" Pick snapped his fingers like a lounge singer. "Jimmy says he gives 'em money so they don't squeal to the cops. And Tony boy, it looks like your number has come up! Why else would he give you a fifty-buck tip?"

"Christ, Pick, you make it sound like it's good news. Like I've won the Irish Sweepstakes or something."

"Tony, it *is* good news! Jimmy says if the creep *really* likes you *and* you play hard to get, you could walk away with some major payola. Some guys he wants bad enough he gives 'em cars!"

"I'm not buying *any* of this shit, Pick. Besides, think of what you're asking me to do. The guy's a fucking creep, for Christ's sake."

"Hey, I'm not asking you to marry the guy. Just let the perv do his stuff, and you drive away in a candy apple red Corvette convertible." Pick tried to cover up his exasperation. He knew Tony didn't like to be pressured.

"If you want the car so bad, *you* do it."

"Tony, *you* don't pick this guy, *he* picks you."

"How can you be so sure I'll get a car? And who's to say after five knob jobs I actually get a 'Vette? This ain't the fuckin' *Price Is Right*. What if he ain't feeling all that generous and gives me a fuckin' Dodge Dart instead? I don't care *how* rich you are, you just don't go around giving away free cars like it's some sort of church raffle."

"He's a *Dunstan*, Tony. They *own* Sugar Mill Beach and everyone in it. And he's gonna get *everything* when his old lady kicks. Jimmy said he read in the *Babbler* where she's got one foot on a banana peel and the other on a roller skate right now."

"Yeah, well I wouldn't believe any of the garbage they print in that rag."

"Okay, go ahead and piss on the damn Corvette. But the next time your fuckin' van breaks down—if you ever even get it running again— don't call *me* to come to the rescue. You're makin' a big mistake, Tony, my friend. You have *no* idea what this could mean for you."

TONY KNEW—knew pretty specifically—what this could mean. He knew what Dallas Eden was looking for, and he shriveled at the thought of it.

And he knew a damn sight better than Charlie Pickering what it meant to get a blow job from another guy. Or to give one. For nearly three years he had what he called "an outhouse romance" with Mitch Novak, their old Gulf delivery man, right there in the men's room at the station. Tony had idolized Mitch since the day he first laid eyes on him, when he was just ten. Mitch was from over Ocala way—horse country—and stepping down from the cab of his tanker truck, he could have just as well been jumping from the driver's seat of a stagecoach at some Arizona way station. He wore black stovepipe jeans, a chambray work shirt with the sleeves hacked off at the armholes, and a dirty, sweat-stained cowboy hat. Coiled around his right forearm, stretching from elbow to hand, was a faded rattlesnake tattoo, ending with its mouth split between his thumb and index finger so he could make it open and shut like it was going to bite. It scared the piss out of Tony when he was younger, but in later years he worshiped it.

Once when Mitch put him in a headlock, Tony caught a whiff of his armpit; mostly it smelled of Dial soap and Old Spice deodorant, but there was enough sweat in it to give it a sharp, sour bite Tony never forgot. It was like a pinch in his pants. Nothing *really* happened until three years ago, when he turned fifteen. He'd seen it coming, like an eighteen-wheeler overtaking him on a steep decline, horn blowing, lights flashing, until he just put it in neutral and let the damn thing roll over him.

Tony had been drawn to men since long before he had words for his feelings, before he knew his desires were different, forbidden. As a child, he directed his affections toward his favorite male TV stars. He lived for each weekly episode of *Seventy-Seven Sunset Strip*, *Surfside Six*, and *Hawaiian Eye*, all detective shows in exotic locales, with plenty of opportunities for the leading men to wear bathing suits. In particular, he had crushes on Edd Byrnes and Robert Conrad. He frequently invented situations in which his two friends were shirtless—sometimes in just their BVDs—bound and gagged by villains and desperate for his assistance. He toyed with them, savoring the sight of them sweating, struggling against their bonds, until it became clear that the bad guys were coming back from buying cigarettes and the three of them had better vamoose on the double. When he got a little older, his heart throbbed all the more appreciatively for Bob Conrad as James West, who was, conveniently, stripped to the waist and suspended above quicksand and alligator pits by cheesy Mexican banditos with some regularity.

As near as he could recollect, it was in the eighth grade, when other boys began to notice that girls bulged beneath their sweaters, that he genuinely appreciated how guys bulged below their belts. He wanted to touch and smell other boys; and yet he knew, knew *absolutely*, that he couldn't. But try as he might, he couldn't keep his eyes off the chino-and corduroy-covered crotches of his classmates, even the thugs and bullies. *Especially* the thugs and bullies.

He was fourteen when he accidentally stumbled across a mention of "homosexuality" in an Ann Landers book for teenage girls he'd found in the backseat of a car he was servicing. The book wasn't terribly specific about the consequences of *being* a homosexual, but it didn't make it sound like the adventure of a lifetime. From then on, Tony read everything he could find about the subject in the Sugar Mill Beach Library, which was precious little. A couple of years later, on parts runs to Jacksonville, he made time to search the stacks at that city's public library. What information he could find often came in obscure, dusty books bound in what looked like reptile skin. They were of little help—too dry, too technical. He wasn't interested in charts and graphs of "galvanic skin response," whatever the hell that was. He wanted somebody to tell him what to do with these feelings. None of the authorities gave any indication how widespread a phenomenon it was, and certainly none of them encouraged it. The thought that there might be significant numbers of homosexuals in the world, perhaps even in the state of Florida, did not occur to him at first, nor could he imagine how he would identify such a person.

Tony had dated girls since the ninth grade, with little emotion and no real consequence. Girls were so attentive to him that he felt he had no choice. He'd take them to Daytona Beach, where they'd walk on the boardwalk hand in hand, eat pizza and Italian ices, play a few games of Ski-ball, and ultimately head for the band shell or a deserted stretch of beach, more at her urging than his. He necked without benefit of instruction, and he liked the way it felt to kiss and be kissed. But he was never really interested in much else. Sometimes the girl would guide his hand to one of her breasts, and he instinctively knew to gently rub or squeeze it, to appear surprised and appreciative of the opportunity, and to ratchet up the kissing and the moans. But he might as well have been kneading a pound of Play-Doh. The path of passion, so clearly marked for other boys his age, was a dead end to him. It was his good fortune that he lived in South Beach, because just about the time girls got serious about him, their parents discovered he was an islander and put an end to the romance.

Tony felt differently about boys; they were awesome and beautiful in a way ninth- and tenth-grade girls were not. He'd go to wrestling matches or track meets to cheer on his favorites, and in the process he developed the image of a regular guy, sports-minded, school-spirited—the furthest possible thing from a pansy or a fag, epithets frequently applied to members of the math club or the AV crew. *If only they knew why I was really here,* he'd think as he'd watch one wrestler put a scissors hold on the other so the underdog's face was but an inch from his competitor's crotch. And then with a wink, a smile, and the sliding of the flimsy lock on the men's room door, Mitch Novak answered the questions Tony had been asking himself all these years.

Tony kept his every-other-Saturday trysts with Mitch for three years. And, of course, he thought about Mitch on those occasions, twice or three times a day, when he beat off. Then, just three months ago, Tony was awakened from his reveries of Mitch—permanently. On the first Saturday of March, he was waiting in the office for Mitch with his usual preemptive hard-on. He had leaped out of bed at six, half an hour early, and struggled into his jams with an erection that just wouldn't quit. His pop was in Tampa on family business, and for the first time he and Mitch could actually use a bed—get completely naked and *make love* in his bed.

Mitch knew Tony's old man would be gone—he must have told him three times last trip—and he promised to be there as early as possible. But when the dusty Westclox inside the toy tire, a promotion for the Goodyear store in Daytona, struck eight, Mitch was nowhere to be seen. He had never been late, not once. And this time he said he'd be there early, so they'd have more time to themselves.

There could be only one explanation: he'd had an accident. The rig had jackknifed on I-4 and fallen into Lake Monroe. Or worse, Mitch had struck an abutment, the truck exploded, and he'd been trapped, burned alive, beating against the window with his fist, a boot, a flashlight, anything, until it was too late.

At nearly ten-thirty, paralyzed with fear and anticipating the worst, Tony at last felt the familiar low rumble of the rig coming up through the floor. He jumped up and ran to the door, bracing himself on either side and leaning out for his first glimpse of the blue-and-orange cab and gleaming silver tank. But it wasn't Mitch behind the wheel. It was a small man who didn't fill up the windshield the way Mitch did. Tony flexed his arms against the doorsill and pushed himself back into the office. He sat down at the desk and opened an *Argosy* magazine, ring-stained from where his pop had set his cold beers down. He heard the truck's brakes shiver with a pneumatic sneeze and then the door of the cab open and shut. A pair of boots squinched over the gravel, and a weasely lookin' fella stuck his head in the door.

"I got a delivery here for a Demetrios Alex . . . ?" His teeth were as brown as bark—he chawed all right—and he could hold a stogie in his mouth with his jaws shut thanks to the absence of a couple of his upper teeth.

"Alexamenos," Tony said, trying to sound casual, though he was nearly breathless. "You got the right place."

"Awright then." The man spit into his hands, rubbed them together, and disappeared back out the doorway. Once the gas was flowing, Tony got up and peeked out the window for a better look at this varmint. He'd taken off his cap and was scratching his head and smoothing a few strands of dirt-colored hair across his bald spot, which was brown as a nut, except where it was flaking off, leaving patches of pink and white.

Foremost in Tony's mind was Mitch's whereabouts, but he wondered how was he going to find out what happened to him without letting this hayseed know something was afoot. He thought that no matter what he said, his lust and anxiety would be immediately obvious. But hell, Mitch had been the regular driver for nearly eight years. It was only natural for a customer to inquire about him.

Tony got up and walked outside, real casual-like, feigning an interest in the thermometer hanging on the wall, snapping it twice with his index finger as if it hadn't been broken since dinosaurs ruled the earth. How should he phrase it? Don't ask about Mitch, ask about "the regular driver," as if he didn't know his name. That'll throw him off the scent.

"Say, where's the regular driver?"

"Mitch Novak? Hoo-boy, is his sorry ass in the sling! Let me tell you, I shore wouldn't want to trade places with him today."

Tony felt like someone had stuffed a whole loaf of soft white bread down his throat. "Whatdya mean?" he managed to choke out.

"How old are you boy?"

"Eighteen," Tony said. "Almost."

The runt had his mouth all screwed up and his right hand was holding up his stubbly chin. "Well, I guess you're old enough to be told the truth, which is that ol' Mitchy was caught with his pants down with the Lamar twins over to Sanford, the two of 'em, Matt and Andy, diddlin' Mitch, when their daddy walked in on 'em. Jasper Lamar was s'posed to be off fishin', but there was a big algae bloom on Lake Monroe and he didn't want to put in the boat. Came back to the station and found the 'Out to Lunch' sign in the office window. Guess we know what kind of lunchmeat was bein' served."

Tony had been to the Sanford Gulf on 17-92 a couple of times to pick up some parts. Sanford was a sorry-assed place, like South Beach, with nothing to recommend it but some tired zoo down by the lake that looked more like the county dog pound. Tony'd met Matt and Andy Lamar, but they hadn't impressed him as being queer. They were good-looking, like Ricky Nelson or Fabian with blond hair, and they were jocks—Matt lettered in football, Andy in wrestling, but what the hell was Mitch doing messing around with them?

"You mean he's been fired?" His heart sank.

"Fired? Hell boy, he was damn near kilt!"

"What? How?"

"They say Jasper went berserk. You would too, you see both your young 'uns serving this pervert's twisted needs. Well, Mitch got hisself zipped up lickety split and ran for his truck, but Jasper brought him down with a tire iron to the head. He dragged Mitch back into the men's room and whupped him sumpin' turble. Lost an eye and most all his teeth. Way I heard it, Jasper was about to cut Mitch's balls off when some Seminole County deputies pulled up. Mitch was a bloody pulp lyin' on the men's room floor, and at first the cops thought it was Jasper they was s'posed to arrest! Then Jasper told them Mitch had been having carnal relations with the two boys, and that was another thing entirely. They cuffed Mitch quicker'n you can snuff a match. Then they called a ambulance so's not to get their black-and-white red all over. Pretty funny, eh? Black-and-white red all over?"

"Yeah. Ha-ha." Tony didn't know whether to cry, throw up, or force the gas hose down the throat of this foul-mouthed bastard, who was obviously enjoying every delicious bit of gossip about his coworker. He was scared and sorry Mitch was hurt, but mostly he couldn't bring himself to believe that Mitch would do with other guys the things they did together. He *worshiped* Mitch. What they had was special, not something common and filthy, even though they'd only ever done it in a rest room.

"Now get this: Matt's the one had called the cops—to *stop* the beatin'—and neither one of them snot-nosed young 'uns would stand by what their daddy was saying to the *police*. They said they ain't never done nothin' like their daddy said and didn't know why their paw and Mitch was thrashin' it out. Can you imagine that? Those boys sided with that homo!"

Tony was trembling. He hoped the slimeball wouldn't notice. "So is Mitch going to go to jail?"

"Hell no. Not with both boys sayin' Mitch ain't done nothin'. It's Jasper's word against Mitch's. See, where Jasper went wrong was he went too far. Bunged Mitch up bad, real bad. Anyways, they agreed not to file no sex molestin' charges against Mitch if he agreed not to press charges of assault with intent to kill against the kids' old man. The po-lice said one or two licks to subdue the bastard would have been satis-factory and then call the law in, but Mitch was mighty tore up. Half-blinded like I said." The peckerwood spit into his right hand and smoothed down his flyaway hair, pulled on his cap, and tugged twice on the greasy brim. "Why're you so interested in Mitch Novak anyways? He didn't slip *you* his sausage, did he?"

Tony could barely control himself. He'd as soon kill this freakish lit-tle rodent as look at him.

"It ain't nothing like that. He's just been our Gulf man for about as long as I can remember. He seemed like a nice guy. I never thought noth-ing like this would happen to him."

"He done brought it on hisself."

"So you're gonna be the regular on this route?"

"Looks that way," he said, lifting himself into the cab.

Tony's shift could not end soon enough, and even though Demetrios was only five minutes late, it seemed like five hours. He'd filled the van's gas tank the minute he'd decided to go to Sanford and was ready to leave when his pop walked in. "Hey, Pop. Got somethin' to do," was all he said, and he jumped in the van and laid precious rubber his thread-bare tires could ill afford. He took the back roads through the celery fields and made good time despite the difficulty of passing farm equip-ment on the two-lane blacktop. It was not quite three when he arrived at Seminole Memorial, his dusty face streaked with sweat and tears.

The hospital's foyer was cool and quiet, the burgundy-and-black floors recently buffed, the faintest of medicinal smells in the air. A sign near the front desk indicated that visiting hours were about to begin and would last until 6 P.M. Behind the desk, a plump woman with powdered cheeks answered the phone while sorting large index cards with colored tabs on their edges. Tony approached her.

"I'd like to see Mitch Novak. Can you tell me where he is?" Tony hoped the quaver in his voice wasn't noticeable.

"Let me check," the nurse said, pleasantly. "Are you family? Mr. Novak's visitors are family only."

"Yes ma'am, I am," Tony said, then drew a blank. "I'm his uncle. . . . I mean, he's *my* uncle, ma'am."

She looked at him over her bifocals. "Very well then, your uncle is in room two-twenty. Don't stay too long. He hasn't got much stamina."

Tony had bolted for the elevators as soon as she had given him the number. He kept repeating it over and over. Two-twenty. Two-twenty. Two-twenty. He felt like he was going to crap his pants. Outside the room, he took a deep breath and pushed on the door.

Inside, the blinds were drawn and the room was dark. Tony moved toward the bed. Had he not seen Mitch's name in a little plastic slot on the door, Tony would not have been certain it was him. Mitch's nose, which had been broken in two places, was set and braced; his entire upper face and head was in a cast; and his mouth was held slightly open by metal braces. Tony saw only three teeth in the front part of his mouth. His head was immobilized, and his left arm was in a cast. But the most frightening thing was that his head cast only had one eye hole in it.

"Holy shit, Mitch! What the fuck did he do to you?"

The gritty sound of plaster moving against bedsheets was the only indication that Mitch was conscious and had heard him. Unable to turn his head, he motioned with his good arm for the owner of the voice to come closer. When Tony was within reach, Mitch grasped his T-shirt with his good arm and pulled him closer, almost up to his face. After a few seconds, he grunted and pushed him away.

"Mitch. Jeez. I freaked out when I heard. Christ, it's every bit as bad as he said it was."

With obvious difficulty, Mitch managed to push out a sound, "Oo?"

"The guy who replaced you. He looks like a half-dead old rat."

Mitch convulsed and issued another one-syllable word, but Tony couldn't understand it.

"I swear to God, I'll kill the bastard! I will. I'll kill him tonight!"

Mitch waved his hand back and forth as if to say, "No, that won't be necessary, thank you."

"Mitch, I'll stand by you. I'll see you through this, I swear. I *love* you, Mitch."

Tony could not have been more hurt by what happened next. In the same way Mitch had told Tony not to kill Jasper Lamar, he waved his hand back and forth. *Not necessary. Not interested. Don't bother.*

"But, Mitch, I . . ." His words were swallowed when Mitch grabbed him by the shirt again and pulled him even closer.

"O!" Mitch's mouth smelled rank, like Listerine and shit. He released him with a snap and Tony fell backward. Then he motioned for Tony to give him the pad and pencil on the bedside table. He had trouble writing with one hand until Tony caught on and steadied the pad for him. Mitch released the pad and coughed. The message was sloppy, but Tony was able to make it out. "GET OUT DONT COME BACK."

Mitch made one more grunt-word, which sounded to Tony like either "Out!" or "Now!"

Tony ran from the room, the horrible smell of Mitch's breath clinging to his own nose and lips, still feeling the deathly grasp of his clawlike hand reaching through his T-shirt to crush his heart. Outside the hospital, he was overcome by the sensation, at once familiar and confusing, that he was back in a world in which no one loved him—and no one ever would.

More than anything, Tony was baffled—*stunned*—by the swiftness with which his life had changed. It reminded him of the time eight years ago when he had said good night to his mother, fully expecting her to be there for him the next day, and had never seen her alive again. Just this morning, he had been anticipating the happiest day of his life—to be with Mitch completely and to show him how much he loved him—and suddenly, he was alone, devastated by Mitch's rejection and, worse, by his betrayal. Mitch had been more than Tony's lover; he had been his *life*. Tony had dreamed about escaping the island with Mitch, partnering up with him as long-haul truckers once he graduated from high school. Mitch could quit his job with Gulf and they'd buy a rig and travel the country together, coast to coast. They would never have to be apart, not even for a minute. And now, without warning, without a word of explanation, that dream was over. There was not a soul in the world who loved him, who cared if he lived or died. His pop certainly didn't. He was rarely sober enough to know that Tony even existed; and when he was on a bender, he holed himself up in his bedroom and days passed when Tony didn't even see him. It was like living with a complete stranger. Nothing Tony did, good or bad, made the old man sit up and take notice. So for the past three years, Tony had gotten what he needed from Mitch: a hug, a kiss, an occasional question about what he was doing in school or how his surfing was coming along. For fifteen or twenty minutes every other week, Tony had Mitch's undivided attention. But now, it seemed even *that* was a lie.

On the long drive home, with the late winter sun low in the sky behind him, Tony smoked his last two joints and every damn roach he could find in the van. That night, he and Pick got so drunk that for the first time ever he called in sick to both of his other jobs.

# 4

AS DIFFICULT AS IT WAS, Dallas Eden kept his distance from South Beach Gulf. His seduction was still aborning, and he didn't want to do or say anything that might jeopardize its success. He knew the young men he so adored regarded him as a circus freak; they did not come cheap. They had to be promised something so extravagant they could not refuse his sexual advances. Dallas considered it a game, and he was determined to know *precisely* what each young man desired and how far he would be willing to go to get it. (Invariably, boys and young men who considered themselves heterosexual required inducements several magnitudes greater than those who had homosexual experiences in their pasts.) Gloria was indispensable. The seduction of Alessandro de Nicotéa, until now his favorite, during and immediately after the Mexico City Olympics, would not have been possible were it not for Gloria's fluent Spanish, her understanding of the subtleties of a Latin man's persona, and her skill as a negotiator.

By the end of the week, she had gathered enough information about Tony from a variety of sources and, poolside, was able to report her findings to Dallas. Tony, she reported, had twice been suspended for fighting and several times for refusing to cut his hair (the school administrators, sensing a standoff, ultimately gave up, asking only that he keep it clean). Of the teachers Gloria was able to track down, most appeared to like him, and the women among them expressed what could only be described as maternal feelings. When Gloria visited his drama coach, Gina Marescheno, she called him exceptionally talented.

"He could be anything he wanted in this world, but I get the impression he thinks he can't do anything right," the well-groomed, thirtyish woman told Gloria over iced tea in her Daytona Beach tract house. She was midway through doing her nails when Gloria arrived, and from time to time she shook her right hand in the air as if it were so much dead meat. "That boy is an absolute angel—hardworking, polite to a fault, and *so* good-looking."

"Something significant happened to him five or six years ago, but nobody knows exactly what," Gloria told Dallas. "Frank Ferlinghetti alluded to it, and the school nurse, one Ida Zhinger, verified that the information Frank had was essentially correct. His father was declared unfit by Volusia County authorities, and Tony was placed in a foster home—someplace near Orlando—for about a year. Once the old man cleaned up his act long enough to impress the social workers, he got the boy back.

"The school nurse said Tony was different when he came back to school after the time with his foster family. Something had definitely happened to him. He wasn't as outgoing as he had been. He was sullen; that's the word she used. He frequently skipped school and went surfing. Nobody really seemed to care—at least not the school administrators.

"Now *this* should be of special interest to you, Dal. Miss Zhinger, who had been a friend of Tony's mother, tried her best to look out for Tony's welfare. But he absolutely refused to accept help of any sort from her or anyone else. He wouldn't take anything, even if it meant he had to miss a meal here or there or come to school wearing the same socks and underthings the entire week."

"Ah, what I wouldn't pay for a pair of his oft-worn drawers. Sheer ambrosia," Dallas said, miming ecstasy as he trailed a napkin across his face. "He could name his price."

"This is clearly not your run-of-the-mill sugar daddy gig, Dallas. It's impossible to shop for the boy who wants nothing."

"I suppose a car is out of the question. Too bad. A car usually works right off the bat. Quick and easy. He would look divine in a red Ferrari, no?"

"I doubt he'd take a can of soda from you, let alone a car. That is, of course, unless you can convince him that a shiny red Testarosa is, in fact, widely acknowledged as an even swap for a snootful of his soiled underthings."

"Cheap at twice the price, from my point of view. But don't toy with me."

"Dal, the point of all this is for you to be able to be close to this kid for as long as possible and as frequently as possible, right?"

"*Mais, certainement.*"

"I suspect we're going about this all wrong, this time. The chances are that no matter what enticements we offer him or how cleverly we disguise them, he's not going to take them if he views them as charity. Why don't we make him work for them?"

"Work? At what, for God's sake?"

"I don't know. He sells surfboards, pumps gas, and saves lives. Any of them applicable?"

"He could give me mouth-to-mouth for a hundred dollars an hour."

"I'm surprised you didn't come up with another anatomical configuration. But just the same, couldn't he help Jorge with the cars? Tune-ups and such? Wash and wax?"

"Seeing him all stripped down and smeared with grease *does* sound ever so tantalizing. I'd have Jorge *require* him to go topless. But wait, that won't work. What am I supposed to do, sit in the garage all day and write my memoirs?"

"What do you suggest?"

"I could be at the pool, I suppose, or in the house with a pair of binoculars."

"That means putting him outside. Hmm. Not enough to do at the pool, per se, although that could be *part* of his job. Wait . . . you could let him be Hiroki's assistant. There's always plenty to do on the grounds, and you can sit by the pool and watch him get even more lusciously tan. He probably won't wear anything more than cutoffs and some of those incredibly sexy work boots and big, itchy, dirty athletic socks, which you could eat for dinner every night."

"Damn, I'd forgotten what a genius you can be! Thoroughly twisted, but a genius nonetheless." Dallas felt optimistic for the first time in days. "But wait, what about his other jobs? He won't just walk away from the people he's known and been loyal to for so many years, will he?"

"Oh, Dal, must I do all the thinking? We'll get him fired."

"No, that sounds too prejudicial. We don't want to damage his ego, or his employment record. Let's call it laid off. Of course, I imagine we'll have to grease the palms of his bosses."

"If he is indeed the type of employee he has been described as—punctual, reliable, productive—they won't want to lose him."

"Whatever it takes, Mata Hari," he said. *"Whatever* it takes."

# 5

━━━━━━━━

TONY WAS TEN when his mother died. She'd had a wasting illness and spent nine months in Halifax Hospital in Daytona, during which time her skin became dry and paper-thin and nearly transparent, and she lost weight relentlessly. No one, not Tony's father, not his Aunt Thalia, ever told him exactly what was wrong with her, but as he got older he suspected it was cancer of one sort or another. No one ever told him his mother was going to die, and the thought simply didn't occur to him. He knew she was bad off, but he figured they would find the right medicine someday and she would come home. Instead, she got paler and skinnier and sometimes took on a whitish glow like the luminescent Virgin Mary holy water holder that was nailed to the doorsill in his bedroom. Near the end she said things that didn't make sense to him—talking about his uncle Antinous, for whom he had been named, like he was still alive, or telling him to turn down the volume on the television, when there wasn't a set in her hospital room. In late October of 1961, without notice of any kind, Demetrios brought Helen Alexamenos home from the hospital. Tony came home from school, and there she was, just sitting in the high-backed, red vinyl recliner, looking through a family album. Tony ran over to her and hugged her, and she felt as light and delicate as a bird in his hand.

"Antinous, I want you to sweep in the dining room, wipe the table, and set out four places for dinner," Demetrios said. "Your Aunt Thalia is coming. Then you wash up, a real shower with soap, so you look presentable."

Tony liked his Aunt Thalia, but that night she got on his nerves. She was constantly hugging him and tousling his hair. He wasn't used to such attention, especially since his mother had been sick. All Helen could eat at dinner was the corner of a tiny piece of the baklava Thalia had brought with her. While Tony did the dishes, the grown-ups sat on the rickety back porch facing the water. Demetrios lit up a cigarette but put it out when Helen told him it was making her queasy. Tony joined them when he was done cleaning up. He wanted to sit down in front of his mother, his feet in the sand and his back against her legs, but Thalia made him sit with her on the rusty old glider that made grinding noises when it swayed back and forth on its runners. Demetrios sent him up to his room at nine o' clock.

Early the next morning, when the sun was nothing but a coral scar between the silver ocean and a pewter sky, Tony got up and went to his mother's room. He tiptoed in and climbed onto the bed knees first, as he had done when he was smaller and she let him snuggle with her in bed if Demetrios was gone. Almost immediately, he realized something was wrong. She didn't shift in response to the additional weight on the bed; she looked much sicker than she ever had in the hospital; and as far as he could tell—he held his breath and watched her, counting the sec-onds—she wasn't breathing. He thought she might be in one of those coma things he'd heard talk of at the hospital, which was, as far as he could tell, a deep, deep sleep like Princess Aurora had in *Sleeping Beauty*. Whatever it was, it couldn't be good.

He backed slowly away from her on his knees and got off the bed as carefully as he could. He went and knocked on the door to the spare room. When nothing happened, he opened the door and went in. His Aunt Thalia was asleep. Tony stood by her side and called her name as softly and politely as he knew how until she woke up.

At the age of ten, Tony couldn't be expected to grasp the finality of his mother's death. He sometimes imagined that she would come back for him, restored to her former beauty, and she would take him far away from his father and the damned island in a new white Ford Galaxie 500 con-vertible. But ultimately he realized that his belief in his mother's return was like his belief in Santa Claus: he would have to outgrow it. And he did.

The worst result of his mother's death was the harsh reality of being at home alone with his father, month after month, with absolutely no promise of deliverance. Demetrios was crude and he drank too much. He made noises when he ate, and Tony tried every way he knew to avoid being at the table with him: skipping meals, eating out of the re-frigerator, saying he wanted to watch something on TV. Demetrios belched and farted gleefully and never excused himself. But the worst, the very worst, was the way Demetrios walked around the house when he was on a bender. He wore only a yellowing undershirt that usually reached just short of covering the things that needed to be covered. And he scratched himself like a dog.

During his mom's illness and after her death, all the womanly chores—the cooking, the cleaning, the laundry—became Tony's responsibility. Never mind that he was just ten years old. In addition, he was expected to man the gas pumps from three-thirty until six on weekdays and for a minimum of four hours on Saturday, either in the morning or the afternoon. At the end of his shift, if Demetrios hadn't come to check up on him, Tony slipped a couple of bucks from the cash register. It wasn't much, but it frequently was all that stood between him and basic necessities like lunch money or underwear with no holes.

Once Tony turned sixteen and was able to get a real job, he had to fight with his father to cut his hours at the station. He finally got the old man to put out the honor box at five so he could shower and race over to Cocoa, about thirty miles away, in an unreliable vehicle, to begin his six o'clock shift at the surf shop. On weekends from April until October, he took the early shift at the gas station and manned a Volusia County lifeguard tower in Sugar Mill Beach from noon until five both days and the late shift at the surf shop on Saturday night. Even though Tony's other jobs sometimes meant the difference between eating and not eating—for *both* of them—Demetrios still groused when they kept Tony from finishing work on a particular car or when he realized he had slept through his own afternoon shift and had lost yet another half day's revenues.

Tony had long ago given up trying to understand why his father drank so much or why he was always so sad and angry. His Aunt Thalia had told him the story, but it seemed to Tony that it had happened a long, long time ago—a year before he was even born—and it shouldn't have mattered anymore. His uncle Antinous was just nineteen when he had fallen off Demetrios's fishing boat in Tampa Bay, gotten tangled in the net, and was drowned by the time they hauled him on board with a couple hundred pounds of red snapper. Those were the last fish Demetrios Alexamenos ever caught. He ordered them thrown over the side as soon as Antinous, limp and blue-lipped, had been cut from the net.

Thalia said Demetrios was never the same. He had worshiped his younger brother, who was the baby of the family and sixteen years his junior. Within the family and among friends, it was universally thought that the Alexamenos family had "saved the best for last." It embarrassed no one to say it, except perhaps the one to whom it referred. Antinous was smart. He was the first Alexamenos to apply to college and was working on the boat that summer to help pay his tuition at the University of Tampa. He was always laughing and playing practical jokes on his brother and seven sisters—never cruel or harmful tricks, but ones that would make them laugh at themselves or each other. And he was handsome, with black hair like silk and eyes the color of chestnuts. Every girl in the Greek community in Tampa had, at one time or another, written his name on their notebooks or in the sand at the beach, or embroidered it on delicate lace-and-silk pillows filled with potpourri. They wove crowns of flowers for him on the Orthodox holy days and brought him Greek delicacies almost daily at school. At his funeral, his casket was draped with a coverlet of pink baby rosebuds with an Orthodox cross of white roses in the center, which had been made by the young women in the three days between his death and his burial. They worked on it night and day in the sanctuary of the church, and their fathers trucked in roses for them from St. Petersburg and Sarasota and Naples.

No one really blamed Demetrios, and everyone tried to comfort him. One of the crew said Antinous had been fooling around, joking, when he lost his balance and fell in. "If that was the case," Demetrios said, "then it is my fault for not teaching him the seriousness of this job." Within a month he had sold the boat for a meager profit—sufficient to make a down payment on the house and service station in South Beach, which had come to his attention in the "Business Opportunities" section of the *Tampa Tribune*. His mother screamed when he told her he was moving to the other side of the state. She cried and beat her knotted brown fists on his chest. She had lost her husband nearly fifteen years before and she had just lost her baby boy. Demetrios was the only man in the family and now he was moving across the state to run some gasoline station, some dingy place that reeked of oil and exhaust fumes? What did he know about automobiles? she asked. He told her an internal combustion engine was the same whether it was in a car or a boat, and he had fixed his engine many times in port and out at sea. She begged Demetrios's wife, Helen, whose cool Norwegian demeanor she neither liked nor understood, to convince Demetrios to stay in Tampa. Helen tried, but Demetrios had made his mind up. He had to get away from his guilt and the ghost of the boy he had loved like a son as well as a brother. He couldn't look anyone in the eye anymore, knowing that he had killed what they loved best. So in September of 1950, they drove the six hours across the state to the sandy patch of earth and the dilapidated buildings that would become their universe. When Tony was born, there was no discussion about his name, so he carried the name of a young man he never knew and the responsibility for somehow lightening his father's incomprehensible burden. But it hadn't worked. No matter how hard Tony tried, no matter what he achieved, he always seemed to fall short of his father's expectations. Demetrios was usually sad and almost always angry. Tony came to fear him, to resent him, and to avoid spending time with him at all costs.

Tony particularly dreaded appearing in public with his father and avoided it if at all possible. There was little conversation when the two of them drove anywhere in the faded red '56 Ford pickup with the towing winch rattling away in the bed. If they went to the Publix in Sugar Mill Beach together, Demetrios would spend about five minutes in the produce section "sampling" grapes. Later, his pop would strike up a conversation with the pretty ladies in white aprons who were giving away free samples of cheese and crackers or Jimmy Dean pork sausage, so he could have four or five of the tidbits instead of just one. If he was lucky and there were two or more sampling stations, he could build a meal from the handouts and all he would have to add was the beer, which he would do at home, in spades.

And God forbid there should be a "twofer" sale at the J.C. Penney store in Volusia Mall, where Demetrios could get two ugly cotton shirts for five dollars. Telling Tony it would teach him to be thrifty, Demetrios required him to go to the sales and buy at least one twofer—with his own earnings, of course. Tony frequently spent an hour or more searching every bin, rack, or clothes pole looking for shirts or slacks in the least offensive colors or patterns. There was this one guy, old, maybe fifty, who, if he was on duty, would always follow Tony into the dressing room and insist that he model the clothing for him. This guy was always trying to show Tony how to make the shirt look better by folding the excess material over on itself in back, creating two "darts," whatever the hell they were, and tucking it into the back of his pants.

"It works better, son, if you drop your pants to about mid-thigh, fold over the shirt, and then bring your pants up while simultaneously tucking in the shirt all around. Shall I demonstrate?"

"No thanks, really, I'm okay."

The guy was a major creep. When he didn't smell like onions, he smelled like fish. Sometimes he smelled like onions *and* fish. But Tony never told him to buzz off, for one good reason. If he couldn't find a couple of cheap shirts he could actually wear to school—which was often the case—he'd swing by the store a day or two later and exchange the hideous items for socks or underwear or maybe just one nicer shirt. After a while, Tony realized that Onion Man frequently exchanged his returns for clothes that were worth more than those he brought back, sometimes considerably more.

Tony was generally unaware that people like Onion Man, people he didn't know, treated him differently than any of the other kids at school, but in fact his singular good looks had tangible value. In the shops and businesses in town, he was treated better—by all women and certain men—than any of the other customers. The only reason he figured it out was that friends frequently commented on it. ("You must have some of that charisma stuff the Kennedys are supposed to have," one said sarcastically. "Go figure.") Service was quicker and scoops of ice cream bigger in places like the Howard Johnson's. Waitresses were far more attentive to such things as an empty iced tea glass. Frequently at Astro Burger, where the employees tended to be from South Beach, he would receive a large drink or order of fries while being charged for a small. If he bumped into someone, the aggrieved party usually apologized to *him*, once they saw his face. He could cut into lines at the movies with impunity. And the venerable souvenir-shop adage, "You break it, you bought it," apparently did not apply to Tony Alexamenos. He could upset a whole shelf of conch shells decorated with electric lights, palm trees, and flamingos, and all the slender, excitable shop owner wanted to know was if *he* had been hurt.

When Tony was fourteen, his father caught him beating off on his Mike Nelson poster. Not in the act, per se, but with the gelatinous result of his one-handed passion all too much in evidence. After he had ejaculated, Tony lay down and closed his eyes. He frequently thought about Lloyd Bridges's *Sea Hunt* character and imagined what it would be like to skin-dive with him in just their skins. He conjured up submarine scenarios that would force them to share one bottle of air and one mouthpiece as their naked bodies rose slowly toward the bright ceiling of the sea, chest-to-chest through a column of their own spent air. And then he drifted off, which was his big mistake.

When Demetrios came up from the station, he was pissed that Tony hadn't started dinner yet. They were supposed to have macaroni and cheese from a box and a couple of ears of Zellwood corn apiece, but there on the counter the cardboard container lay unopened, the corn unshucked. When he looked for Tony in his room, Demetrios found his son naked, with his flaccid penis in his right hand and a barely perceptible smirk on his face.

Tony never knew what hit him. One second something was tickling his butt—was it air bubbles or Lloyd Bridges's fingers?—and the next his father was yanking him off the bed by an ear, his greasy thumbnail biting into the delicate skin and cartilage that had bent over on itself.

Tony realized at once what had happened, and in the split second after that he wondered if his father had guessed that it was the face and body of Lloyd Bridges he was thinking of as he brought himself off. It was bad enough to be caught masturbating, but the thought that his father might figure out that men turned him on terrified him. He fully expected the old man to break his neck.

Demetrios said nothing as he dragged Tony, stumbling, down the hallway and out the front door. Tony was so blinded by the pain of his ear that he couldn't see where they were going, couldn't see to stay on the path, and he stepped on stinging needles and nettles and brushed up against the swordlike fronds of low-growing palmettos, which cut into his calves and thighs like the X-acto knives he sometimes used when he built model cars. They stopped, but Demetrios did not let go of Tony's flame-red ear. Tony heard the sound of a Dumpster door being flung open, and then his father grabbed him by the hair and by the balls, threw him in, and closed the door.

"Filth!" Demetrios said. "That's what you are—filth! So now you are finally where you belong, with the rest of the filth, and there you will stay until you have served your penance."

Inside the Dumpster, Tony bent over double in shock and pain. He couldn't see, and he wished his other senses would shut down as well. Even breathing through his mouth, the smell of grease and garbage was overpowering. Every time he moved, he was pricked and scratched and slashed by jagged pieces of metal and glass. When he tried to stand up, he banged his head and fell, unconscious, into a quicksand of empty motor oil containers, soda bottles and cans, oily rags, and rancid food.

Hours later, Tony came to with a start, sweaty and disoriented, his head pounding. The smell of something sour—spoiled milk? rotten meat?—made his nostrils flare. It took only a fraction of a second to re-call his predicament. The Dumpster. He was in the fucking Dumpster. His skin seethed with a blanket of insects—tickling, prickling. "Oh, God! Roaches," he said, and he swatted at the ones on his face. He shuddered and shook off as many of them as possible. He felt a flutter-ing at his mouth and shut it fast, swiping at the air in front of his face with both hands.

Hunched over, he pressed against the metal doors above him with his back. They wouldn't budge. His father must have slid something through the handles, something like a broom, locking him inside. Scooting over to a corner, he curled himself into a ball, providing the roaches with as little surface area as possible and virtually no access to his eyes and mouth.

Tony was scared and sick to his stomach. His ear felt as big as a potato, and it hurt if he moved his head even a fraction of an inch. The Dumpster was stifling, but while he was covered with sweat, he also was shivering uncontrollably. After some time balled up in the corner, he blacked out.

The pneumatic whine of a garbage truck woke him. He jumped at the sound and hit his head again. *Shit!* He pounded on the sides and top of the Dumpster, in vain. Nobody could hear him over the roar of the truck. The Dumpster shivered as the forks of the lifting mechanism threaded their way through the slots on either side of the rusted green box. Tony fell backward into the rubbish as the truck raised the container up and over and upside down. He was now sitting on what was the top of the box, nearly drowning in refuse.

The driver jostled the suspended waste receptacle, but nothing happened. The doors were stuck. He flipped it upright and brought it down to the ground, gesturing to his partner to check the doors. Sure enough, a weathered two-by-four was jammed between the door handles. Tony screamed and pounded on the doors. He didn't hear the wood slide free of the handles, but he felt the doors give way. He stood up, slamming the doors to either side, and climbed into the piercing morning light.

He stood there, naked, covered with oil, spotted with cockroaches, swarmed by flies, his hair plastered down by sweat. As his eyes adjusted to the light, the familiar surroundings of the station and the house swam up from the almost blinding brightness. He looked around at the two garbage men, who could only stare, dumbstruck, at the sight of a naked boy arising from the garbage. He jumped out of the Dumpster and ran toward the house but did not go inside. Instead he grabbed his board, stopping long enough to put on the jams he had left to dry on the deck, and ran toward the water. He wanted to puke from the stench of himself. He didn't think anyone but the trashmen had seen him getting out of the Dumpster. What he didn't notice was Pick, riding his bicycle in circles in the street, taking it all in.

Three weeks later, Demetrios Alexamenos received a summons to appear at the Volusia County Courthouse on charges of child abuse. At the very time his pop was to appear in court, Tony was pulled out of his eighth-grade English class and accompanied to the principal's office, where he was met by a woman who turned out to be a nun in drab street clothes, Sister Mary Catherine of Catholic Charities. Tony's first thought was that his pop had somehow blown the station up and himself with it and he was needed to identify the body. He was only slightly heartened when the actual circumstances were laid out for him.

"Your father has been deemed an unfit parent, Tony," Sister Mary Catherine said. "The Volusia County authorities think it is best that you live with another family until such time as he is better able to take care of you."

"Thank you, Sister, but I'm able to take care of myself pretty good. Is he going to jail?"

Sister Mary Catherine laughed. "Oh heavens, no, Tony. It's not at all like that. The authorities will help him improve his parenting skills, and then everything will go back to the way it was. We're just concerned that during that time you are properly clothed and fed and live in a stable environment."

Tony didn't know what to think. He didn't care much for his pop, but this seemed a little excessive. One of the neighbors must have reported his slumber party in the Dumpster, but he figured he had brought that on himself by being so stupid as to fall asleep after beating off—and with his door unlocked. He'd be happy if his pop just disappeared off the face of the earth, leaving him the house and the station as a way of making a living, but he sure as hell didn't want to go to live with a bunch of strangers.

"How long is this going to take? My pop learning how to be a better parent?"

"Not long, Tony. I think the average is six months to a year."

"A year?" Tony involuntarily jumped out of his chair. It suddenly felt like he was being kidnapped.

"We have to be certain that the delinquent parent has actually reformed. He can't just be putting on an act. In your father's case, he will have to be sober for at least three months, subject to spot-checks by the Volusia County authorities, before we can even consider returning you to your home."

"Jesus, Sister, he's *never* been sober that long," Tony blushed at having taken the Lord's name in vain. "Can't I just go to live with my friend Pick?"

"I'm afraid not, Tony. We find that it is better for the child to be completely away from the home and neighborhood in which he lives. If you lived at the home of a friend, your father could see you at any time. It would defeat the purpose of taking you out of the home, said purpose being to deprive the parent of the love and companionship of the child."

"Yeah, well, he's mostly deprived of that already, so I don't really see how this is going to bother him all that much."

Tony didn't say much for the rest of the afternoon. What was the point? After a trip to Astro Burger (which Tony figured was supposed to be a "treat" for him, though it felt like a condemned man's last meal), they drove to Tony's house, where Sister told him to pack a suitcase and his schoolbooks. He would be allowed to take one personal item with him, and he chose his surfboard, which of course was unacceptable, so he took a framed picture of his mother instead. Sister explained that he was to be placed in a temporary foster home in Daytona until the end of school, which was just a few weeks off, and finish out the year at the junior high there. She told him this home would be like a dormitory for him and several other boys his age, but he was not to worry. His permanent foster home would provide much more of a family environment.

Tony couldn't have been more unhappy with the arrangements. He quickly missed Pick and felt completely isolated at the new school. He didn't understand why they couldn't have waited a few weeks until the term was over before they yanked him out. The way Sister made it sound, he was in real danger, like his father had suddenly turned into some sort of homicidal maniac or something. But Tony knew that nothing was different now than it had been at any time in the four years since his mother had died. He had managed to survive and could continue to do so without the help of Volusia County or the state of Florida, thank you very much. In fact, he felt as if he were being punished, as if *he* had done something wrong. That's what this foster home felt like: a juvenile detention center.

He shared a room smaller than his own at home with three other boys; all of them, he decided, were delinquents. He missed the ocean—this place was well inland, just west of I-95—and he had a hard time falling asleep without the sound of the sea to soothe him. As he lay in his bunk at night, he tried to convince himself that the *whoosh* of cars on the interstate was actually the familiar sound of waves rushing onto shore, but that didn't work. Instead, he found himself thinking about where the cars were going: south to Fort Lauderdale and Miami, north to Jacksonville and whatever lay beyond. It had never occurred to him that he would ever live anywhere but on the island, but his sudden banishment turned his thoughts to escape. Would anyone notice if he didn't show up after school one day, if he simply stuck out his thumb on the interstate and vanished? Would anyone *care*?

The food in the foster home was awful: tomato sandwiches on soggy white bread for lunch, Spam or baloney for dinner, Kool-Aid or powdered milk to drink. One of the kids, Rodney, who was seventeen and had been there awhile, explained to Tony that the people who ran the house got paid a certain amount to feed the boys and every time they cut corners they made more of a profit. Nothing ever went to waste but was turned into leftovers over and over until they were used up.

"You think people in the real world eat corn-and-baloney chowder?" Rodney asked. "I guarantee I could beat off on my plate at dinner and we'd have sperm soup the next day."

A week before the end of the term, Sister Mary Catherine greeted Tony at the foster home when he got back from school. He was actually glad to see her; it meant he might soon be "paroled." Sister waited while he cleaned up and dressed in his best clothes. They were going all the way to Orlando to have dinner at the Robert Meyer Hotel where, Tony knew from watching their commercial on TV, you could eat and watch the fountain in Lake Eola turn colors: red, blue, green, and yellow. Tony's only suit was two years old—it was his Confirmation suit—and he knew he had grown at least three inches taller and an inch in the length of his arms. Sure enough, he looked like a scarecrow, and Sister told him to just wear a shirt and tie and to see if he could wriggle his pants down a little to make up for the length.

It took them nearly an hour and a half to get to Orlando because Sister never went over the speed limit even once. Inside the restaurant, she asked for a table looking out over Eola Park. Tony ordered fried shrimp, which he had picked up a taste for after Pick's dad made them for dinner one night. Over dessert (Tony had a banana split), Sister said they had an errand to do on the way home.

"There is a lovely family I have to visit. The Dombrowskis. They've set aside some clothing for our annual rummage sale. They have a beautiful home on Lake Jasmine and a boy just a couple of years younger than you, I believe."

The Dombrowskis lived in Winter Park, a fashionable suburb just north of Orlando. They owned a split-level home in a neighborhood with lawns as neat and green as stacks of freshly minted ten-dollar bills. The houses were far more modern than anything in South Beach, and they were so well cared for it looked like the set of a movie or television show. Tony expected Beaver Cleaver to come walking down the curb any minute.

"Thirty-one-sixty-five, Tony. We're looking for thirty-one-sixty-five Live Oak Drive," Sister Mary Catherine said. "Thirty-one-sixty-five."

Tony thought she looked nervous or worried, and he wondered why.

"There it is," Tony said. "The one with the horse head things at the end of the driveway. Hey, they drive a Cadillac. '62 Coupe DeVille."

"Oh yes, nothing but the best for the Dombrowskis."

There was plenty of room for Sister to pull up behind the angular black car, but she parked in the street instead. Before shutting off the engine, she took Tony's face by the chin, inspected it, and daubed at it with a handkerchief like his mother sometimes had. Tony squirmed.

"Hot fudge," she said. "Oh dear me!"

The Dombrowskis received them on the deck behind their home, seated on patio furniture that looked brand-new. Stepping stones of blue slate marked a path down to a small dock, to which was tied a small, sleek, burgundy-and-white boat. Tony could see that most of the other homes had boat docks, too, and built-in barbecues in the backyard. Ski boats crisscrossed the lake in the fading light, buzzing like giant insects.

Each of the Dombrowskis reminded Tony of a cartoon character. Mr. Alden Dombrowski resembled Henry Mitchell, Dennis the Menace's father. He was tall and skinny with black hair and a beaky nose, and he still wore a white shirt and bow tie several hours after he must have gotten home from work at Martin-Marietta, the big government contractor down on the Orange Blossom Trail. His wife, Wilhelmina, was a dead ringer for Cruella De Vil: lots of black hair twirled round and round her head, layers of nail polish the color of congealed blood, and a long, slender, gold cigarette holder, almost constantly in use. With his buckteeth and eyeglasses, their eleven-year-old son, Brockton, looked like none other than Rocky the Flying Squirrel.

Sister Mary Catherine did most of the talking, while Tony sipped a bottle of Coke through a straw. She briefly referred to the rummage sale, and Brockton flew into the house to get the box of castoff clothing. Eventually, Sister turned the conversation around to Tony. What a wonderful young man he was: smart, polite, respectful, and an excellent surfer. Until the surfer part, he didn't recognize any of the adjectives. He didn't say much, but smiled at the sound of his name and shrugged a couple of times when Mrs. Dombrowski asked him what his favorite subject was in school and what he liked to do after school—*other* than surfing. It sounded to him like she didn't approve of surfing.

"Quiet little boy. I like that in a child," Mrs. Dombrowski said, exhaling smoke rings. Tony could tell Sister didn't particularly like *that* habit.

Sister asked Brockton to take Tony down to the dock, where he could show him their boat while she talked to his mother and father for just a few minutes. Tony didn't listen to Brockton describing the various features of the boat like an overeager salesman but instead stood rooted to the dock, looking at the three adults on the deck. He couldn't hear what they were saying, but every once in a while one of them laughed. Eventually, Sister clapped her hands to get their attention, the way she must do on the playground at school. Brockton ran up the slope, his arms fixed and spread like an airplane's, swooping from one side to the other. Tony was careful not to step off the slate onto the lawn. He shook the Dombrowskis' hands, except for Brockton, and thanked Mrs. Dombrowski for the Coke. As he stepped into the car, he remembered the box of old clothes they had come for.

"I'll get them," he said, leaping back out of the car.

"That's okay, Tony. It's not important. I'll get them another time."

Tony didn't understand that this was an audition, that he was being peddled like a Hoover vacuum cleaner. In her own way, Sister Mary Catherine was telling Mr. and Mrs. Dombrowski that Tony would be trouble-free and that he came with a ninety-day money-back guarantee, a sort of in-home trial with no obligation whatsoever. She called a week later to tell him the Dombrowskis had been delighted with him and they had asked if they might be his foster parents.

"Of course, I said I'd ask you. This is the chance of a lifetime, Tony. If you move in with the Dombrowskis, your life will be completely changed."

It was. For the worse.

Tony—Wilhelmina Dombrowski called him Anthony even after he told her his real name was Antinous—quickly learned that there was no pleasing "Aunt Mina." Apparently there was an entire world of rules and regulations that Tony had never heard of before. He ate too fast and talked too slow. He wasn't supposed to cut up the meat on his dinner plate all at the same time. He was supposed to say "Sir" and "Ma'am" to everyone, except for the black men who did the yard work. He wasn't even supposed to *speak* to them, let alone offer to help pull weeds, which he had once done, to Aunt Mina's horror. It had been so long since he'd had any adult supervision—between his mother's long illness and death and his father's drunkenness and apathy—that Tony had been forced to find his own way, make up his own rules as he went along. Now, it seemed, he had been asked to play a new, particularly complicated board game, but no one would let him see the instructions.

Once, a neighbor boy, Jerry Welch, was sitting on the porch with Tony, Brockton, and Mrs. Dombrowski, and he asked what year their Cadillac was.

"I have no idea, Jerry," Mrs. Dombrowski said. "Why do you ask?"

If there was one thing that Tony knew, it was cars. He could identify

# 6

TONY WAS BUMMED. He didn't know what the hell was going on. He was sitting on the beach a good half mile south of the house, smoking a very fine joint of Colombian Red from Pick's stash and trying to make sense of it all. Twice in two days he'd been let go from a job. Each time, he'd been told that he was not being fired, just laid off. Yesterday at Ron Jon, Sandy, the night manager, handed him some load of crap about having too many kids under eighteen on the floor at night, in violation of some federal agency's rule. When Tony reminded Sandy that he was going to be eighteen in a couple of weeks, he just shrugged, though he seemed apologetic and actually looked sort of hurt.

At lifeguard headquarters this morning, the story sounded remarkably the same. This time the captain of the lifeguards, Jeff "Hang Five" Edwards (he'd lost the toes on his left foot to frostbite while skiing in France), told him that he had been laid off to make room on staff for a black lifeguard due to affirmative action. What a crock! Tony had never in his life so much as *seen* a black lifeguard. When he brought up the subject of seniority, he was told the layoffs had been by a blind drawing; his name had been picked out of a box. Like Sandy, Jeff was singing Tony's praises as he walked him to the door. And like Sandy, he assured Tony that if the circumstances allowed it, he would hire him back in a heartbeat.

Tony didn't go straight home after he left lifeguard headquarters. Instead he retrieved the Daytona and Sugar Mill Beach papers from trash containers along the boardwalk and drove out a ways on SR44 to the Java Hut coffee shop, with its fake thatched roof and two huge Polynesian heads like the ones he'd seen on *Adventures in Paradise*, which he watched mostly to see Gardner McKay shirtless. He sat at the counter, ordered coffee, and read the help wanted ads. Dunstan's was hiring sales clerks. Dunstan's was always hiring sales clerks, Tony knew, because they treated their employees like shit. The Baskin-Robbins on Tropicana had an opening, but Tony wasn't about to freeze his fingers off scooping out ice cream for Sanctuary boys and their snotty dates from St. Catherine's Girls High. Maybe he could find a job on the boardwalk in Daytona making pizza or handing out change in one of the arcades. A job at J. B. Smith's Texaco on A-1-A in Daytona looked like the best possibility, as long as Pops didn't find out he was working for a competitor. He repossessed the dime he had intended to leave for a tip, called Smith's, and immediately launched into a litany of his skills and experience in the realm of the internal combustion engine.

"Whoa, whoa, whoa, kid. You sound good, but we just hired somebody," said a man, possibly J. B. Smith himself. "These newspaper ads always have 'em crawling out of the woodwork, 'specially now that school's out. You know the story, early bird and all that. But keep your eyes open. Seems like we fire as frequently as we hire."

That was reassuring. The man hung up before Tony could offer his phone number, and he slammed the receiver into its cradle with such force that it jarred a couple of notes out of the ringing mechanism. The waitress looked at him with a kindly expression. She had kept his coffee cup filled for the past forty-five minutes and would have gladly done so for the next three hours. She didn't even mind when she saw what she presumed to be her tip disappear into the battered black telephone by the door. Tony looked at her and she smiled, but he decided he didn't need a fourth cup of coffee and went to see if Pick was surfing off the Point.

# 7

EXULTANT! THAT WAS IT. Dallas Eden was *exultant* as he lumbered through the house in his matching silk jacquard shorts and dressing gown and his custom-made pink bunny slippers. He had offered the boy the job, and the lad had taken it. Cleaning and taking responsibility for the pool. Working with the gardener. All the while half naked and sweating. Dallas nearly swooned when he thought of Tony squatting by the pool, his cutoffs slipping down to reveal an inch of pearlescent flesh as he collected water samples.

And it had been so simple. Two days after the captain of the lifeguards had terminated Tony, Dallas had driven to South Beach late in the afternoon. He was strangely delighted to see that the boy looked terribly downcast. The worse the lad was hurting, the larger a hero he would be.

Tony nearly panicked when Dallas Eden pulled up in the big yellow float. He had spent his fifty-buck tip on his van, and he assumed the guy would want it back, *now,* when he had lost both of his other jobs. But the guy didn't mention the fifty. Instead, he made small talk about the weather and the plan to build a jai-lai fronton in Sugar Mill Beach, where it was largely an unpopular idea.

Tony said nothing as he filled the tank. A grunt or two to acknowledge that Dallas had spoken and nothing more. When Dallas pointed out that the sports facility would bring needed jobs to the city, Tony finally spoke up.

"If Sugar Mill Beach don't want it, we'd take it here in Southie. We could use a hundred new jobs here."

"Slim pickings?" Dallas asked.

"Slim to none."

"But of course, that's not something you have to worry about personally, is it? Your father owns this station, doesn't that give you a guaranteed income?"

Tony hooked the hose back on the pump and walked to where he could make eye contact with Dallas Eden. "Well, this place ain't no gold mine. I had a couple of other jobs, but I lost both of them last week."

"Recession, I suppose," Dallas said, running his fingers around the brim of his hat.

"Yeah, I guess so."

"So you're in the job market?"

"Damn straight. I mean yessir, I am."

"Have you ever done any gardening or landscaping?"

"No sir, I haven't."

"That's too bad. I have an opening myself. An assistant gardener quit last week, just like that." Dallas snapped his fingers.

"Yeah? Well, I'm a real quick learner and a hard worker. And I could get you some damn good references from my old jobs. Or so they said."

"Perhaps we could work something out. Since you have no experience, I would ask that you serve an apprenticeship—a trial period—for a week. At full pay, of course. After that, we can make it official. You'll be working with Hiroki, my gardener—full time during the week and at least four hours each day on the weekends. At time and a half, naturally. I think we can find a few mornings or afternoons on which you can relax or take care of your personal business. All work and no play, you know. But I'm paying top dollar, and I expect to get my money's worth."

"Can I ask what you're paying? I mean, I'm sure it's more than I get here."

"We'll see about that at the end of the week, but you'll start at three . . ."

"Three bucks an hour. That's great."

". . . hundred dollars a week."

"Holy shit! Excuse me, sir. You're kidding, right? That's like . . . forty into three hun . . . seven bucks an hour."

"Seven-fifty, to be precise. To start. As I said, if you successfully complete your trial period, there will be a significant increase."

"Damn, when do I begin?"

"How does Saturday sound? Let's say ten o'clock. You'll be able to spend the day with Hiroki and get the lay of the land. He'll show you around the property." Dallas reached to his visor and pulled out an ivory calling card, gold-embossed with the initial *E*. His name and the word *Edensgate* were engraved in a fancy black script.

"You know how to get here?"

"Yes sir, Mr. Eden, everybody around here knows where you live."
Tony didn't need to look at the card.

"And I see you know who I am, as well."

"Yessir. And Mizz Eden, too. Sorry to hear she's not well."

"Indeed. Then I'll see you Saturday?" He handed Tony a fifty-dollar
bill and put the car in gear.

"Yes sir, ten o'clock sharp."

As he drove off, Dallas could scarcely contain himself. Everything
had gone exactly as planned. He had to hand it to himself: he had given
an Oscar-caliber performance. All the talk about a trial period and getting his money's worth. He would get his money's worth if Tony
lounged in a hammock all day. But he had to make the job offer sound
authentic. Still, he'd have to make sure Hiroki didn't work the boy too
hard. Just hard enough, in fact, to have him glistening.

TONY MUST HAVE DRIVEN past Edensgate a couple thousand times. To get
anywhere from South Beach, you had to drive north on Tropicana past
the black wrought-iron gates with the big, gold, curlicue *E*s on them.
But the house itself was screened from the public eye by dense foliage,
neatly trimmed but nearly impenetrable. Tourists bought picture postcards of the Dunstan mansion at the Eastern News store in town, but
that was nothing like seeing it in person. And now, Tony thought as he
made his way north on Tropicana at an almost ceremonial speed, now
he was going to have the opportunity to really see the big house—maybe
even to go inside it.

An extra lane suddenly appeared on the right shoulder, indicating
Edensgate was not far off. Then he was there, at the massive black,
spikey gates that must have been at least fifteen feet tall. He pulled over
to what looked like a radio mounted on a post and pressed a red button.
Someone answered and he said his name. The gates opened seconds
later.

Edensgate dominated the cul-de-sac of an oak-lined gravel road that
defied perspective. Beginning at the highway that separated it from
Sugar Mill Beach, each tree grew successively taller and broader, so that
from the road those closest to the house looked as large as those at arm's
length. From the steps leading to the house and gardens, the reverse was
true, giving the impression of looking through the wrong end of a telescope. As instructed, he parked his van in a small lot south of the house
for service vehicles and cars belonging to the household staff. A row of

palms that looked like pineapples the size of a man lined a slate path that meandered toward the house through fragrant white blossoms and pale, fingerlike flowers that resembled sea creatures. Elephant ears flapped and nodded in the breeze. When he emerged from the lush greenery, he got his first unobstructed look at the mansion. It was even larger than he had imagined, four stories tall and faced with white marble. Canvas awnings in Venetian black-and-white stripes curtsied over the fragile glass windows and doors of the bulky house, and sprinklers sent glittering diamond fans in lazy waves across the pampered lawn. Two big black dogs gleamed like licorice melting on the flagstones. He was met at the servants' entrance by a distinguished looking if somewhat underfed gentleman, who looked as if he were dressed for a funeral. He said his name was Alfred, and he indicated with a nod of his head that Tony should follow him.

Tony spent nearly three hours talking to Mr. Eden in what Alfred had called the "solarium." It was glassed in and filled with plants. In a more modest dwelling, it would have been called the Florida room. At first, their conversation focused on Tony's job history. When they had pretty much beaten that topic to death, Mr. Eden asked about Tony's schooling. Was he a good student? What were his favorite subjects? Was he involved in any extracurricular activities? After that he wanted a complete family history, including how the Alexamenos family, so clearly of superior stock, happened to settle in South Beach. Then they talked surfing, and Tony found himself demonstrating various moves while standing on a silver tray that had, at the beginning of their conversation, been piled high with cookies and candy bars for Mr. Eden. Tony sure as hell hoped he was getting paid for this. Finally, the gardener knocked on an outside door and entered, carrying a battered fishing hat in both hands.

"Well, Hiroki, you better put this young man to work. I suspect I've been holding you back. But remember, don't wear him out on his first day. We want him to come back tomorrow."

The work was generally pretty easy. Over the course of his first week, Tony came to the conclusion that Hiroki was very cool. Quiet and calm, he took more care with plants than most people did with their relatives. He treated them as though they were alive. Of course, they *were* alive, but he pampered them like pedigreed pets, making sure they got *precisely* the right amount of food, water, and sun. He tested the soil for acidity—to Tony, dirt was dirt—and adjusted it if necessary. Hiroki never got upset with Tony, even when he scarred a hedge with the clippers or set the blade on the lawn mower too low.

Tony saw Mr. Eden several times a day. (Mr. Eden urged Tony to call him Dallas, but that didn't sit right with him.) In the morning when Tony showed up at the staff entrance, Alfred accompanied him to one of several elegant rooms in which Mr. Eden had chosen to "take" breakfast. Mr. Eden always offered him juice and coffee, some sort of pastry that looked like the little Pillsbury crescent rolls his mother used to make, only bigger, and a whole slew of fruit pastries. Tony rarely ate anything. He was always hungry when he woke up, so he ate breakfast at home; and he wanted to get as much work done as possible in the cooler part of the day, so he didn't want to dawdle as his host and employer chowed down. Three or four times a day, he left Hiroki and drove the golf cart up to the house to check the pool chemicals. Mr. Eden was always there under a big umbrella, reading a book and drinking a frozen cocktail. He always stopped reading when Tony showed up and made conversation for half an hour or more, far longer than it took to actually do the work. Tony always apologized to Hiroki when he got back, but the gardener didn't seem to mind. Tony figured he used the time to take a little break, too.

At night, after he'd helped Hiroki secure the garden shed, which was actually bigger than Pick's mobile home, he went in to say good night to Mr. Eden, who was now surrounded by fruits and cheeses and chocolates. He got the impression from Alfred and Hiroki that he somehow was *expected* to make these little morning and evening visits. It was no skin off his nose, except when Mr. Eden wanted to shoot the shit with him for hours. The guy never said much about himself, but he wanted to know everything Tony could recall from his childhood and adolescence. Tony wanted to be polite, but figured he was off the clock and the longer he hung around chewing the fat with the fat man, the lower his hourly rate actually was. It was on these occasions—especially in the evenings—that Tony half expected the guy to reach over and grab his crotch through his dirty cutoffs, and that would be the end of his cash cow. But nothing like that ever happened. He made it a point to tell Pick that Dallas Eden hadn't so much as breathed hard in his direction yet, and his four-hundred-dollar checks (he'd gotten a hundred-buck raise after the first week) were mounting up quite nicely. Pick generally changed the subject.

After Tony had been on the job for a couple of weeks, Dallas Eden started visiting their work sites early in the morning and in the late afternoon, driving a custom-made golf cart that had a small refrigerator where the golf clubs should have been. He'd ask Hiroki about the project they were working on that day, if they needed any supplies, or if Tony would like to come up to the pool for a swim. Perhaps he'd even like to stay for lunch. Tony routinely declined the invitations, but Dallas continued to extend them each time he visited. Tony had seen Hiroki indicating the house with the motion of his eyes and the most subtle tilting of his head. "Go. Make boss happy," he mouthed to Tony. So finally, on a Saturday in late July, he agreed.

Tony thought it was strange—sort of mean or at the very least selfish—for Dallas to entertain guests while his mother lay dying. None of the people he met that day seemed to care about Eve Eden's condition. They were too busy drinking and worrying about whether they were tanning evenly. Sprawled about the pool in groups of two or three, men outnumbered women four to one, but the number of older men was matched by an equal number of younger ones. There was among the guests that day one Mellon Bilonio, a Coconut Grove patron of the arts with steel-wool hair in the style of the bride of Frankenstein. At his side were Amy Cornwallis Bucolic, of the Palm Beach Bucolics, and a couple who looked remarkably like tainted royalty Tony had seen in black-and-white newsreel footage, whom Dallas introduced as Mr. and Mrs. Hamilton Exeter-Fatigue. Beneath a silk cabana, they found Ritzy Ebonettes, the most famous black fashion model of the Sixties. Her smile, her wave, her every pose and gesture seemed to mirror some Esther Williams routine, and she was surrounded by a gaggle of tan white boys in skimpy bathing suits, who took excessive delight in filling a bathing cap with water and, squealing, dowsing one another.

On the far side of the pool, a group of people Dallas said were European kept to themselves, drinking strange dark cocktails and laughing loudly in unison. There were other guests Tony never met. They remained silent white figures on the distant tennis courts or could be glimpsed disappearing into cars on the circular driveway or moving in one of the leaded-glass windows on the upper floor of Edensgate, as aloof as if they were at a summer resort or in a movie.

Tony always wondered if one of those faces belonged to Eve Eden; and after he began working at Edensgate, he went to the Sugar Mill Beach library to find pictures of her. It was easy to do: she was the town's most famous resident and in her day had been as famous as Mary Pickford and Gloria Swanson. She had worked with Douglas Fairbanks, Rudolph Valentino, and even once with Charlie Chaplin. Although many of the write-ups Tony found called her "the most beautiful woman in Hollywood," he couldn't decide if she was really all *that* pretty because the pictures were so old and her hair looked kind of funny, cut short and wavy and sort of plastered down to her head. She was no Marilyn Monroe, that's for sure. In any case, Tony almost couldn't believe that she was Dallas Eden's mother; it seemed impossible that someone as slender and graceful as her could have given birth to a baby destined to become such a large person.

After John Lindsey Dunstan died in 1959, the newspapers said, Eve Eden became as reclusive as Greta Garbo. Rumor had it that she had not set foot off the Edensgate property in ten years, and Tony noticed that none of the cars in the garage were newer than '59s, including Dallas's convertible and a big, black Fleetwood limousine. Five years ago, on her seventy-fifth birthday, she had allowed a reporter from *Life* magazine to interview her, and the way the story ended seemed kind of sad to Tony: "She long ago banished mirrors; there is a room, small and dark, where she stored her mirrors and her vanities when her reflection first betrayed her. She refuses most guests, receiving a chosen few subtly veiled in strategic shadow, and she grows old silently and alone."

Tony couldn't be sure, but he thought he had seen Eve Eden once. He had been trimming some bushes near a window on the north side of the mansion when he saw something flash deep within the house. Standing on tiptoes and bracing himself against the window frame, he tried to see farther into the interior, but it was like looking into a murky pond. Then he glimpsed movement—a metallic flash—and he saw someone sitting in a fancy chair covered in baby blue fabric facing an oil painting of Eve Eden as a young woman, which hung above a marble fireplace. The chair's high back was to the window, so Tony could only see a gem-encrusted hand, a wrist ringed in diamond bracelets, and a pale arm up to the elbow, but he knew that it had to be her.

On the day that Tony had lunch at Edensgate, dark-skinned wait-ers—Tony figured they were Cuban—served gazpacho, fresh poached trout in herb butter, champagne, and lemon cake, and the guests lin-gered over iced cappuccino and conversation until the shadow of their umbrellas—perfect circles at noon—began to stretch eastward to em-brace a larger area of the patio. It was the most wonderful meal Tony had ever eaten, although its subtleties were lost on a palate more accus-tomed to grilled cheese sandwiches and Dinty Moore beef stew. But he could hardly enjoy it for feeling embarrassed and out of place. Each time he lifted a forkful of lemon cake to his mouth, he could see that de-spite his best efforts with the Lava soap and nailbrush, the whorls and ridges of his fingertips were still black with dirt. Sitting next to Dallas

Eden, shirtless, he felt like Tarzan having his first meal at Greystoke Manor. Plus, everyone kept staring at him like his nose was bleeding or something.

Eve Eden died on the fifth day of August. Hiroki called and said Tony could take the rest of the week off, with pay, as Mr. Eden would be traveling to New York for his mother's funeral. Tony didn't understand how Mr. Eden's absence would stop the grass and weeds from growing, but he wasn't going to complain about getting a little paid vacation in the middle of the summer.

DALLAS WAS SURPRISED at how hard his mother's death had hit him. For the first week after the funeral, he went without so much as catching a glimpse of Tony. He thought about him frequently, but without the obsessive edge that typically characterized these infatuations. He remained in bed most of the day, taking his meals there and trying to fathom his relationship with both of his now-deceased parents. As the fog lifted, he realized there were but two weeks left before Labor Day and the commencement of the fall seasons, TV and social. He had commitments for two weeks of *What's My Line?*, a taping of a Perry Como Christmas special in which he played both Santa Claus and Old Man Winter, and the possibility of five segments of *Hollywood Squares*—perhaps more—which would require a trip to Los Angeles. He had invested in several shows, among them *Oh! Calcutta* and *Play It Again, Sam,* and he *had* to be at the openings. What was he going to do about the boy?

The way Dallas saw it, he had three options. The first involved convincing Tony there was enough lawn and garden work to keep him busy at Dunstan Hall, his New York home, which was, of course, absurd. The second was to offer him a scholarship to Sanctuary's drama program. As a bonus, it would provide Tony with his much-needed student deferment, thus negating the need to disappear into the wilds of the Yukon until peace came to Southeast Asia. The final course of action involved flinging himself out the pressurized door of his New York–bound airliner, passing through the blades of a jet engine like a potato through a food processor on "grate," and distributing himself over much of a tri-state area.

He considered his choices carefully. Plan A was implausible, unless he were to invest heavily in bonsai. Plan C was just too messy. And in the final analysis, he was gutless. But Plan B—Plan B had many attractive features. He could monitor Tony's progress as a student, be notified of any of his upcoming performances, and enlist a network of spies among the faculty and staff. They could even take Polaroids of the boy and send them to New York. He called Gloria to his room and told her to contact that raven-haired vixen, as Gloria had described Gina Marescheno. She would be the liaison between Dallas, or more properly the college, and Tony. The idea of him winning a scholarship without so much as having auditioned might be more credible coming from his drama teacher. He would coach her, and he would warn her in no uncertain terms what would happen to her if she breathed a word to Tony.

"Tell her I want to sup with her day after tomorrow," he told Gloria. "And tell her it's formal. We might as well make the experience the most unforgettable of her life. Have her to go to Dunstan's and pick out a new dress, on me. Shoes, hair, bag, the works. It's not often a spinster schoolmarm gets to dine at Edensgate, *n'est ce pas?*"

# 8

IT IS WELL KNOWN that natives of that netherworld known as Dixie are frequently born without benefit of a chin. If they lay claim to being Tennessean, they are blessed indeed to possess so much as a lower lip. Receding jaws are the bane of Southern bloodlines. More prevalent among rural folk, where inbreeding is inevitable, they are not unknown among the gentry, where such behavior is entirely recreational. So it was with some measure of surprise that, upon entering his dorm room for the first time, Tony found himself admiring the sculpturally perfect mandible of his Sanctuary College roommate, Jefferson Davis Shapiro, of Nashville. Jeff Davis, as he insisted upon being addressed, had the exaggerated jawline of a cartoon hero. He had, in fact, the very jaw of Dudley Do-Right of the Royal Canadian Mounted Police.

"Plastic reconstructive surgery," Jeff Davis said, smoothing the skin of his neck with a floral-scented emollient as Tony watched. "I thank God each and every day for allowing me to be born in a time and place where the greatest sculptors work not in marble but in flesh and bone."

Because of its reputation for rigorous academics, Sanctuary College had in recent years become the school to which the leisure class sent their children for a solid education in more agreeable surroundings than New Haven or Cambridge. One half of Sanctuary's campus was old Florida architecture—white and pastel-hued Spanish-style buildings with red-tile roofs, shaded from the intense sun by sprays of Pindo palm and Italian cypress the way a dark-eyed señorita might mask a blush behind her fan. The other half comprised the largest number of Frank Lloyd Wright buildings to be found in one place anywhere on earth. It was half Babylon, half Brave New World.

When Miss Marescheno had driven up to the station and told Tony he had received a full, four-year theater studies scholarship to Sanctuary, it sounded like the answer to his prayers. Tony had wanted to act since he was old enough to understand the concept. From the time he was five or six until she took sick, his mother took him to the college's free summer theater productions, which alternated standing-room-only comedies by the likes of Neil Simon with the works of William Shakespeare and the Greek playwrights, when the chorus generally outnumbered the audience. The shows were presented in an amphitheater that John Lindsey Dunstan had brought to Sugar Mill Beach, stone by stone, from the ancient Roman city of Erratum in an unsuccessful attempt to lure the state theater company away from its home in Sarasota. Tony first saw *Romeo and Juliet* when he was six, and he was inconsolable when Romeo died. His mother wiped away his tears with an embroidered white handkerchief scented with Jungle Gardenia and explained that the striking young man who held Tony in his thrall from his first line wasn't really dead. It was just a story, and she promised him that the boy would reappear on stage with all the other actors, very much alive, to take his bow. Now *that* seemed like magic. Once he understood what was involved, he began to ponder the ramifications of *being* an actor, of pretending you were someone else entirely. When his mother told him that when he grew up he could become an actor just like other boys grew up to become firemen or truck drivers, he decided that was precisely what he wanted to do, to escape not only from South Beach, but from himself, from his life, as well. His mother told him that was a fine idea. But, she said, if his father asked, Tony was to tell him he wanted to run a gas station just like his daddy, so he wouldn't hurt Pop's feelings.

Although the scholarship to Sanctuary now offered Tony the opportunity to pursue his dream, it had not taken him long to realize he was unhappy at Sanctuary, nor had the revelation come as much of a surprise to him. Tony had been reluctant to embrace an institution he had disdained for so long and was particularly wary of fraternizing with the snobbish boys he considered enemies. He had been better able to cope when he had been a grease monkey and the Sanctuary boys were his customers. Then, each of them had a distinct role to play: he fixed their cars; they gave him money. Now that he was a student at Sanctuary, he had hoped that he might somehow be considered their equal, scholarship or not. But with his faded T-shirts and jeans so oft repaired they looked like patchwork quilts, he didn't feel their equal, nor was he treated as such. His fingernails were blunt, chewed down to the quick; and his hands still looked grimy, even after nearly two months without so much as changing a tire. In contrast, the hands of Sanctuary boys were as soft and pink as a fresh piece of Bazooka. Their nails were buffed and rounded, without a hangnail in sight. Tony had never seen so many boys who wore colors from what he considered the feminine end of the spectrum—pink polo shirts and lavender cotton sweaters, all manner of stripes and pastels he wouldn't be caught dead in. Even their boxer shorts, in which they loved to stroll the dorm halls, were pink, some of them, and monogrammed. Their fucking underwear had their initials on it!

Failing to make new friends, Tony concentrated on his course work. His classes were difficult, and he managed to keep up only with extraordinary effort. But despite the amount of time he devoted to studying, he was lonely almost every minute of the day. He really missed Pick, who wrote from Vietnam weekly with descriptions of the war that grew more horrible with each letter. But growing inside him was a need for something more, for a kind of friendship Pick hadn't been able to provide even when he *was* here. His English professor had used the words "soul mate" to describe the way a nineteenth-century poet had felt about her lover, and Tony liked the way that sounded—like Siamese twins joined at the heart.

"I UNDERESTIMATED YOU, Alexamenos," Jeff Davis said as Tony returned from an evening theater class that had run well past ten.

"Huh? What?"

"A dinner invitation from Mr. Dallas Eden." Ensconced in his bed, Jeff Davis waved a piece of paper between two fingers. "Tomorrow. Eight P.M. The Big House."

Tony stopped in place, turned, and lunged for the slip of paper, which Jeff Davis withdrew.

"A *functionary* called about eight o'clock. 'Mr. Eden requests the pleasure . . .' and all the rest. Oh, I called back an hour later to make sure it wasn't some self-aggrandizing prank on your part. It was the Eden residence all right."

"Here or New York?"

"*Listen* to you!" Jeff Davis shrieked as he got off his bed, tugging the tie of his lounging robe tighter. "*Here or New York? Who are you, and what kind of a game have you been playing?*"

Tony snatched the paper out of his roommate's hand. It was the same number he had called this summer. He tossed it into the trash basket next to his bed. Jeff Davis immediately fished it out.

"You're throwing it out?"

"I know the number."

"And you're not going to call back?"

"It's late. I'll call tomorrow." Tony stripped and slipped under the rumpled covers of his bed. "Don't you think that would be the *polite* thing to do?"

"I imagine so," Jeff Davis said, combing his hair back with his fingers. "But just the same."

"Good night," Tony said. He turned his back to his bewildered roommate.

"Wait a minute. How do *you* know Dallas Eden, and why are you putting on this poor-boy act?"

Tony shifted in bed, turning to face Jeff Davis. He had initially been inclined to tell him that all he had been was Dallas Eden's gardener, just some local kid the fat man had a raging hard-on for. But why not fuck with his head? It would be the perfect way to get back at him for all the times he had made him feel like some worthless piece of shit. And maybe it would get him some respect.

Tony sighed. "Do me a favor and just drop the subject. Good night."

Jeff Davis fumed for a good half hour while Tony feigned sleep and listened to his breathless rants. The next day, Jeff Davis was far more excited than Tony about the dinner invitation. He readily offered to outfit Tony from head to toe for his engagement with Dallas, although he didn't understand why Tony was perpetuating his irritating "urchin charade." He asked in return only that Tony provide him with a complete account of the evening.

Tony left the dormitory at seven forty-five, Jeff Davis hovering around him like a mother sending her eldest son to his first prom. He walked the short distance through campus to Edensgate and was greeted by Alfred at the mansion's front door, not the servants' entrance he had used all summer. When Dallas Eden appeared, he looked as if he had recently overexerted himself. Flushed and sweating, he gushed upon seeing Tony. Over cocktails, he told Tony all sorts of gossipy stories about the people with whom he was working in New York—who was sleeping with whom, who had had a botched facelift and had to cancel guest appearances on various TV series, what unmarried starlet was pregnant by which soap opera villain. Tony thought the chatter was stupid, really, but he knew he could parcel it out to Jeff Davis in return for favors for months to come.

Then it was Tony's turn. Dallas asked about everything that had happened since last they had spoken, even though it was just six weeks ago.

Tony was at a loss for what to say, but Dallas just kept asking questions about his roommate, his living conditions, his classes. Had he made any new friends? Was he happy? At the end of the night, Dallas walked Tony to the door, his arm around the boy's shoulders. He said that he would be at Edensgate many times in the coming months tending to his mother's estate and that he hoped to see Tony again soon. He was as good as his word, summoning Tony to Edensgate almost weekly when he returned to Sugar Mill Beach to meet with his mother's lawyers or for meetings of the board of trustees of Sanctuary College.

# 9

IN MID-OCTOBER the drama department announced auditions for the first production of the season, *A Streetcar Named Desire*. Tony had seen the movie and knew enough about the role of Stanley Kowalski to guess he was too young and inexperienced to get the part, but he figured he could use the audition practice. He was more than a little surprised when he made the final cut and was told to return for another reading.

With only four other men there the next night, Tony was able to size them up individually. He paid attention to two in particular as they stood and talked to each other near the exit. They both looked more like the Stanley Kowalski type than he did. One was tall and lean but muscular. Kind of a pug nose. The other was the embodiment of the phrase "built like a brick shit house"—meaty but short. His upper arms were as big around as Tony's thighs, but he had a baby face, with the fullest, most pouty lips Tony had ever seen on a man. Something about the pair excited him—the way the taller one bent down to whisper in the other guy's ear; or how the shorter one kind of leaned into the other guy or straightened the collar on his friend's black leather jacket.

Tony read third. The tall, skinny guy read first and his buddy right after him. Tony thought they were both much better than him. But none of them got the part, which went to the guy who read last—slightly less muscular but more handsome than either of the two guys in leather jackets. Tony shrugged into his tattered jeans jacket and headed for the door.

"Hey, Tony."

Tony turned, puzzled. It was Mr. Shit House, who was walking a few steps ahead of his friend.

"Don't look so shocked—I'm not psychic. The director said your name about a dozen times. You want to get a cup of coffee or something with us at the Sugar Mill Hotel?"

"I don't know. It's late. Thanks, though." The Sugar Mill Hotel, at the corner of Tropicana and Main, was one of the nicest places to eat in town.

"Tonnnny. Live a little. Maybe we can go have a drink at the Boy if you prefer."

Tony was taken aback by the mention of the Boy-O-Boy bar on Tropicana Boulevard. When he lived in South Beach, all he knew was that it had the reputation for being somewhat seedy, a hangout for misfits. There was a strong biker element in central Florida, and Tony figured that, as surprising as it was, maybe the Boy was a biker bar. But since he'd been in Sugar Mill Beach on a daily basis, he'd overheard a number of people mention it. Some were making plans to go; others were putting it down. But it never failed, the words *girl, gay, sister,* and the like were always uttered in the same conversation in which the Boy-O-Boy was mentioned. Were these guys gay? If they *were,* he definitely wanted to get to know them. But he didn't think he really wanted to go to a gay *bar* quite yet.

"I'm underage," he said.

"Never mind. We don't need to go to the Boy. I just thought. . . . But in any case, come with us to the hotel. I'm Duane, and this is my friend, Dick."

"Pleased to meet you," Dick said.

"So how about it?"

"I don't have any money on me."

"Tsk, tsk, tsk, tsk, tsk, Tony. Now you just let Dick and me buy you a cup of coffee and maybe some of that excellent chocolate-mocha layer cake Dick loves so much. We won't take no for an answer."

At the hotel, they were seated in one of the old hand-carved booths looking out onto Tropicana Boulevard. Tony assumed he would sit on one side of the booth and Dick and Duane would sit next to each other opposite him. Instead, Duane motioned for him to slide over toward the window and sat down next to him. Dick sat across from them. Tony was immediately conscious of the pressure of Duane's thigh against his own. It felt as warm as a heating pad.

"Don't be too upset about not getting the part," Dick said to Tony. "The truth is, it wasn't right for you. I do think you'd make an excellent Brick in *Cat,* or Chance Wayne in *Sweet Bird of Youth.* Oh yes, a wonderful Chance. I'm sure in a couple of years you'll be able to have your pick of parts. Unlike us, for whom this was our last hurrah."

"Yeah," Duane said. "We're seniors. Graduate in June. Then it's off to med school for me and an M.B.A. for Dick. We don't know where, but we're only applying to universities with both a medical and a business school."

"Like Harvard and Penn," Dick said.

"We think Penn is our best shot."

Duane did most of the talking. You couldn't shut him up. He and Dick were both from well-to-do families in the North. They liked Florida's weather but thought it was a cultural wasteland. They usually drove to Miami or Fort Lauderdale every other weekend in Dick's Jensen-Healey and were planning a trip to Key West over spring break.

"You should join us!"

"Wouldn't that be a little crowded—three in a Jensen?" Tony asked.

"Not crowded, Tony," Duane said, reaching under the table to pat the inside of Tony's thigh. "*Cozy.*"

TONY GOT BACK to the dorm at 8:30 the next morning. He wanted to shower and try and make it to club breakfast, a self-serve coffee-and-danish buffet for late risers. The dope he'd smoked with Dick and Duane had left him ravenous.

*Dick and Duane.* He shouldn't even think about them unless he wanted to get a hard-on. He had been surprised at how beautiful their bodies were. In their clothes, Dick had looked skinny, Duane almost pudgy. Naked, they were both surprisingly muscular in different ways. Duane's smooth skin was pink and kind of soft, but it was stretched so tightly over his bulging muscles that it practically squeaked when Tony rubbed against it. Dick's body was olive complected, his muscular chest and abdomen covered with fine black hair. Screwing with Dick and Duane had been the most outrageous thing he had ever done. Here he had these two really hot guys lickin', slappin', kissin', suckin', rubbin', and shootin' all over him. There were times he could barely control his arms and legs; they were shaking so much from the intense pain and pleasure his lovers were giving him. Now, as the slippery soap glided across his chest, it was impossible not to think of Duane's hands coming from behind, down his stomach, and into his pubic hair. There, he'd gone and done it. Thrown a bone.

Tony felt a little creepy when he woke up between them this morning—out of place and dirty. He had hoped to pick up his clothes and sneak out the door before they woke up, but Duane's arm was thrown across his throat and he couldn't move without waking him. So he just lay there, feeling the heat radiate off the body on either side of him, smelling a stale but not entirely unpleasant mixture of sweat and bedsheets that should have been washed a week ago. But when Dick and Duane woke up, almost simultaneously, they were really sweet. Dick asked if he had slept okay, and Duane pulled back the top sheet and ran a hand up and down Tony's chest and stomach. When Tony got an erection, they both started in on him again, but he jumped out of bed and said he had to go to the bathroom. When he came out, they gave him a robe and made coffee and acted as if nothing out of the ordinary had happened. Just three guys getting stoned, listening to the Jefferson Airplane on Duane's amazing stereo, and then jumping into bed together and fucking their brains out. It all seemed perfectly natural. Plus Dick and Duane were really funny. Although Tony didn't always understand their jokes about gays and sex, he blew his coffee out his nose twice at things Duane said this morning.

Tony grabbed breakfast on the fly and got to his own class late. He might as well not have bothered. All he could think about was sex. That night, Duane called and asked Tony if he was okay.

"Just checking in. Neither of us thought you'd have a problem, but you are kind of young," Duane said. "Once we made it with a highstrung guy your age who was so freaked out he left school for the rest of the semester. Now he's back, and we can't get so much as a *gesundheit* out of him. Adorable but all eaten up by Catholic guilt."

"I'm not as experienced as you guys, but I *have* done this kind of thing before. I do feel a little weird about it because I don't really know you guys, and the guy I did it with before was someone I'd known for years and really loved. I never thought about just doing it with complete strangers."

"He must have been quite a teacher. You have wonderful technique for someone so young."

"Yeah. I think you both would have liked him."

"Listen, in addition to doing my guardian angel routine, I wanted to invite you to dinner Saturday night. Eight P.M."

"Sounds great!"

Tony walked around in a daze for the rest of the week, constantly fantasizing about Dick and Duane, so he was unprepared for what

Duane told him when he hinted at Saturday's dinner that he'd welcome another roll in the hay.

"No dice," Duane said. "Much as it breaks my heart, you fox. Dick and I are both such sluts our marriage would fall apart if we didn't draw the line somewhere. Trick with someone—anyone—more than once and things are likely to get messy. Feelings are going to get hurt; windshields are going to get smashed. Take it from us. We know. Don't we, dear? But that doesn't mean we don't absolutely adore you and want to be the closest of friends."

Tony was disappointed, but he did sort of understand what Duane was saying. In bed, he had found himself more drawn to Dick, even though he thought Duane was nicer and funnier. He could see how that might cause problems. Still, the three of them quickly became friends. They went to movies, spent weekend afternoons at the beach, and attended the opening night of *Streetcar* to critique the man who had beaten them for the role of Stanley Kowalski. ("Regrettably," Duane said, "I am shocked to discover I have nothing bad to say about his performance.") Some nights they ate dinner at Dick and Duane's apartment and spent the evening talking about gay life, especially in the big cities of the North, where Dick and Duane grew up and where they played on semester breaks and summers. Duane delighted in describing every sexual act, position, or fetish they had seen, heard of, or participated in, including some that left Tony a little shaken. He would never be able to cook with Crisco again.

Despite their entreaties, Tony was reluctant to go to the Boy-O-Boy with Dick and Duane; but on the last Sunday before Christmas break, he agreed to go to Club Capricorn in Daytona Beach, half an hour away. The three of them squeezed into the Jensen, Tony straddling the console and gearshift. Dick glanced at his watch as they pulled up to the oceanfront establishment.

"Good, we're just in time for the four o'clock show," he said.

They sneaked Tony in by jumping a low fence on the beach side and entering through the unattended patio door.

"I can't believe I'm in an actual, real gay bar."

"Color me jealous," Duane said. "I am *so* tired of these flesh pits. But the hunter has got to follow the prey. And here be the prey."

The dim, smoky room was full of college-age men, some a little older. Most wore beach clothes: T-shirts, jeans or shorts, flip-flops, but not one of them looked as if he had actually been to the beach that day. The giveaway was their hair, which had been so meticulously groomed it looked fake, like mannequin hair. Tony recognized certain Sanctuary boys in the crowd and wasn't terribly surprised to see them there. But there were others he had seen on campus—members of the soccer and tennis teams—whom he had not dreamed were gay.

The only table they could find was front and center.

"Not good," Dick said.

"Terrible," Duane answered.

"But I thought you wanted to find a seat I could see from. This one's perfect, don't you think?"

"Well, girls, it's all we've got. Someone flag down a waitress and get me a double Dewar's on the rocks," Duane said.

The room went dark. A single beam trained on a disco ball sent shattered prisms of light through the blackness, and a sort of fanfare, at maximum volume, erupted from speakers throughout the room. When it finally ended, an exceptionally tall and broad-shouldered woman walked on stage in a single spotlight and began to sing "Ain't No Mountain High Enough." As she finished, people banged the tops of tables with their hands or flip-flops. They crumpled dollar bills and threw them on stage. A chant started in the front of the room and spread through the crowd like yellow fever through New Orleans. "Miss T, Miss T, Miss T, Miss T."

The entertainer, who with her craggy features and precariously piled-up black-and-white hair looked like a cross between the Wicked Witch of the West and the Bride of Frankenstein, waved to her admirers as if she had just been crowned Miss America. While the uproar was still strong, she bent down and picked up the bills, stuffing them into her bodice. She quieted the audience and launched into her monologue, a whiny diatribe aimed at, in her words, her "most recent ex-husband."

"Whatever you do, girls, don't *ever* marry a mime! François would fuck me all night, but I never felt a thing! And you all know how I love it when they talk dirty to me! Not this one. Not even when I begged. On the plus side I always had the last word in any argument! But then he left me—without even saying good-bye!"

The crowd roared. Miss T made a show of composing herself, fluffing her hair, smoothing her dress, and taking a long sip of a drink. She walked to the end of the stage, cleared her throat, and looked directly at Tony.

"Girl! Where did you get your wig? It's fabulous. I'll bet it's a Gabor straight from Budapest."

Tony pointed at himself and mouthed the word "Me?"

"Yes, you, darling. Just look at that coif, girls! But never mind, you have the face of an angel. What a specimen! Let's have a little more light over here."

Two spotlights swept through the smoky darkness and came to rest on Tony.

"Turn around and face your admirers. Go onnnn."

Tony reluctantly turned around and was blinded by the spotlights.

"A face to die for!" Miss T shouted. "Am I right or am I right?"

The crowd cheered. She motioned for someone to move an empty chair next to the stage so she could step down to the floor. She descended regally and stepped over to Tony, running her long-nailed fingers through his hair.

"Young man, you are one of the last holdouts of the sixties. A genuine day-old flower child. What's your name, precious?"

"My name?"

"Yes, your name. What do people call you? . . . Other than gorgeous?"

"Tony," he said softly.

"Excuse me?" She thrust the microphone into his face.

"Tony, ma'am."

"Ma'am? A boy with manners. I could get used to this," Miss T said, rubbing her crotch lasciviously. She moved closer to Tony, lifted the hand he had draped across his thigh, and sat in his lap. This close, Tony could smell her perfume, which nearly choked him, and see the heavy makeup on her jaw, already beginning to dry out and crack. "You're *so* young. I guess our doorman was blinded by your beauty and let you in without ID. Let's just hope the ATF boys don't show up. Now, you were just giving me your telephone number and telling me where you were from."

"I was? Well, I'm from South Beach, just down the . . ."

Miss T jumped out of Tony's lap, screaming.

"South Beach? Isn't that the place where nobody ever marries outside the family?"

"No ma'am," Tony stammered. "Not really."

"Nonetheless, I'd wager that your father's sister was quite a striking woman."

The crowd roared, clapping, cheering, and slapping their thighs.

Tony didn't know whether to laugh, cry, or slug the bitch. He wanted to just stand up and run, but the tables were packed so closely together he wouldn't be able to *run* anywhere. By now Miss T was back on stage, and the heat and glare of the spots were off him. The drag queen had blithely launched into another routine.

"Let me tell you, last Saturday night I was cruising an officer of the Daytona Beach motorcycle patrol so hard that I ran right into the rear end of a parked car. Once a cycle slut always a cycle slut, I say. So the officer, who was a dead ringer for Mr. Clint Eastwood, does a U-turn on Halifax and approaches my car. I beg him to frisk me. He declines but decides he'd better take me to lock-up for a closer evaluation. First, he has to read me my Miranda rights. Do you all know your Miranda rights? Show of hands." She walked to the end of the stage and peered into the crowd, blinking into the spots. "I don't know if you are aware of this, but we drag queens have a special set of Miranda rights all our own, our *Carmen* Miranda rights, and the kindly officer read them to me: 'You have the right to do drag. If you choose to do drag, you have the right to accessorize with fruit. You have the right to lip-synch. If you choose not to lip-synch, anything you sing can and will be used against you. You have the right to a hairdresser. If you cannot afford a hairdresser, one will be provided for you.' "

Tony stood up abruptly and said he was leaving.

"You guys can stay. I'll hitch a ride back to campus. I've always been lucky about getting rides."

"Absolutely not," Duane said, rising. "If you're leaving, we're leaving. I'm just sorry you're not having a better time."

Tony seethed most of the way back to campus. He didn't know whether he was more hurt or angry; he wasn't sure it mattered. Nothing Dick or Duane said could make him feel better.

"I can never set foot in that place again, even if I wanted to, which I don't," he said in the car. He crossed his arms over his chest, instead of putting one arm around each of them, as he had done on the way out. "The first time I do, everyone will remember what happened tonight."

"You're exaggerating, Tony," Duane said. "Miss T skewers at least one poor soul every show, and she always picks on the most attractive man she can find. Consider it a badge of honor. Really, I don't see what you're so upset about."

"It wouldn't bother you if someone jumped off your lap like they had just found out you had leprosy?"

"From the look on your face, Tony, I would have guessed that you would have done just about anything to *get* her off your lap," Duane said.

"And if she said your pop had screwed his sister?"

"Tony, she was kidding," Duane said. "Don't take it personally."

But he did take it personally, and by the time he crawled into bed that night, he had placed the blame squarely on Dick and Duane. He stood them up for a dinner they had previously arranged at the Sugar Mill Hotel, and he refused to return the phone calls that followed. When the dorms closed for Christmas break, he went home to live with his father, who wasted no time putting him to work around the house, which was a pigsty, and at the station.

There were no gifts exchanged in the Alexamenos household that year. Tony knew it was Christmas only because the bottles of booze his pop brought home were tied with red ribbons or came in silvery boxes with Christmas scenes embossed on them. What the hell, it never felt like Christmas in Florida anyway, and as he took one of many long, lonely walks along the beach, Tony dreamed about a white Christmas in New York with Dick and Duane. He was sorry he had gotten so mad at them; he knew it wasn't really their fault and that he'd miss them something awful when they graduated. So when they returned for spring semester in late January, Tony called and said he was sorry for being such a jerk about their trip to the Capricorn.

"Oh, no, no, no, Tony. It *was* a mistake," Duane said. "Taking you to that tired place was like asking someone who still uses training wheels to compete in the Tour de France. All our fault. We were both disconsolate during our vacation. I broke down and wept several times at the Continental Baths. No, wait, that was something else entirely."

"Please forgive us," Dick said on the extension. "Let us take you to dinner."

"Sure. But you really don't have to," Tony said.

"For you, anything," Duane said.

During dinner they finally convinced him to go with them to the Boy-O-Boy.

"I promise you, they have no drag queens," Duane said. "But just to make sure we don't have potential tricks fainting dead away at your feet, tell people you're from Sugar Mill Beach, or Daytona, or Cocoa. Any place but South Beach. Got it?"

"Got it."

The Boy-O-Boy bar was unusual in that it catered to both gay and straight crowds. Sugar Mill Beach was too small and provincial to support a freestanding gay bar, yet there was a profit to be made by the businessman ingenious enough to solve that problem, as the owner of the Boy had when he converted some unused storage space in the rear of the building into a somewhat claustrophobic but extremely profitable gay watering hole. Straight patrons used the door on Tropicana Boulevard; gays entered through the alley or feigned heterosexuality and used the front door.

Dick, Duane, and Tony used the back door. Duane took aside the bouncer and whispered into his ear. The man, fiftyish and balding, nodded and looked at Tony approvingly. Finally, he waved them into the bar.

"That was easy," Tony said. "What did you say to him?"

"I told him that in the unlikely event you failed to pick up anyone tonight, it would leave you free to go home with him."

"You didn't!"

"I did indeed. So get busy."

The bouncer's hopes were dashed within minutes.

# 10

IN MARCH, DYING CASCADES of snow-pink azaleas, scarred brown, tumbled to the ground, and the prospect of six months of stifling heat sizzled brightly on the brick streets of Sugar Mill Beach. Dick and Duane had gone to Fort Lauderdale for the weekend, and Tony was uncomfortable attempting to sneak in to the Boy without them, so he was reduced to cruising the Wall along Tropicana Boulevard on a Saturday night. Due to its proximity to the Boy, a curved center section of the Wall—a miniature cul-de-sac—was a favorite haunt of underage gays. After last call, when the unforgivingly bright lights of the bar came on and the last die-hard patrons scattered like palmetto bugs surprised by a sudden blast of light in the kitchen, the Wall got very cruisy.

Going to the Boy with Dick and Duane had become something of a weekend ritual in the two months since Tony's first tentative visit. Even though he turned down most of the offers he got, Tony was getting accustomed to the attention he received from other gay men, and he liked it. Suddenly, it seemed like gay men were *everywhere*. Although he had sex with only a handful of men he met at the bar, Tony could now rarely walk even one block on Tropicana without a complete stranger smiling and greeting him by name. He felt like people were talking about him behind his back. But so far, he had not met anyone he was interested in seeing more than once.

A spring storm had stalled off the coast and was responsible for an irritating type of precipitation—too light to really require an umbrella but heavy enough to dampen clothes and hair over time. Tony hoped the weather wouldn't keep everybody at home. It was just past eleven-thirty—early to be cruising the Wall—so he walked the length of Tropicana Boulevard, window-shopping all the stores he couldn't afford. He continued past the Tavern Restaurant, past the university bookstore and

Chrysalis, the exclusive little gift shop that offered not one thing Tony could ever imagine wanting or needing. He passed the Baskin-Robbins and the Roy Rogers, the pizza shop and the movie theater where *Bob and Carol and Ted and Alice* was playing.

And then he was outside the Boy-O-Boy. He jaywalked across the street and sat down in the shallow horseshoe formed by the curved section of the Wall. His eyes settled on a handsome, dark-haired man seated directly across from him. He was wearing a blue windbreaker with the collar turned up, a plain white T-shirt, jeans, and blue-and-white-striped Adidas. Tony figured the guy was probably close to twenty-five years old. He chain-smoked Marlboros from a crush-proof box, and he even looked a little like the Marlboro Man—tan, with strong, angular features and just a hint of five o'clock shadow. In an instant, Tony was irresistibly drawn to him. He couldn't explain why, but it felt as if someone were taking an electric can opener to his small intestine. It was the way he remembered feeling about Mitch Novak. He knew that he had to meet this man, talk to him. He knew that he would love him.

Something made Tony wonder if the guy was gay. He wasn't picking up any of the subtle cues Dick and Duane had told him to look for—chiefly a sort of telltale, skittish eye movement—and straight people *had* been known to blunder into the gay section of the Wall. As the number of cigarette butts beneath the man's feet approached double digits, Tony decided to make a move. He stood and, looking back over his shoulder, walked up the gradual incline toward campus, past the azalea hedge and into the stand of live oak and pine that partially screened the college from town. He sat down beneath the trees, on pine straw that was barely damp, and could see the man silhouetted against the brightly lit storefronts of Tropicana Boulevard. His head had not even turned when Tony got up and walked away. For a long time he didn't move, except to bring his cigarette up to his lips, inhale, and return it to the protection of his cupped hands. Then, just as Tony resolved to go back down to the Wall and try again, the man stood and walked slowly up the shallow hill, dragging his feet through the wet grass, angling *toward* Tony but not directly at him. He settled down about six or eight feet to Tony's right, still without acknowledging him, and lit another cigarette.

Tony waited thirty seconds before speaking.

"Do you mind if I have one?" he asked, even though he didn't really smoke and hated the taste. "A cigarette."

"Sure. Help yourself." The man stood and offered the pack to Tony, sitting down closer but not so close a passerby would necessarily think they were together.

"My name's Tony." He stretched his arm across the grassy gulf.

"Connecticut," the man said.

"Connecticut?" Tony took a hit off the Marlboro and cringed at the metallic taste. "That's where you're from?"

"No. That's my name. Connecticut Jones. I'm *from* Ormond Beach."

Tony had a hard time talking to strangers under normal circumstances, but it was even more difficult when he was attracted to them. He started a conversation about the weather, eventually turning it to one of the subjects he knew best—the ocean—thus giving him the opportunity to talk about surfing and lifeguarding. This guy wasn't making it any easier. He nodded and smiled a lot—he was definitely paying attention—but his name and hometown were the biggest pieces of information he had parted with so far.

"Listen, I think the damp is finally soaking through my jeans," Tony said. "Whattayasay we hit the S.C.D. for some coffee and a place to keep our butts dry?"

Connecticut agreed and they both stood, whacked at the wetness of their pants, and headed down the slope toward the Sanctuary College Diner, a twenty-four-hour greasy spoon famous for its grilled sticky buns. Students frequently pulled all-nighters in its booths and along its counter, drinking black coffee from pale green Pyrex cups and ordering grilled stickies just frequently enough to avoid being asked to make way for potentially more lucrative customers.

On the way to the diner, Connecticut asked Tony if he were a student and where he was from. Tony said he was a theater studies major but lied and said he was from Winter Park. Connecticut volunteered that he was a graduate student in the biology department. They were lucky to find an empty booth in the back and ordered coffee and stickies. They spent the next half hour complaining about life at Sanctuary. When that topic was exhausted, Tony launched into a monologue on the other subject he knew best, the care and feeding of exotic motor vehicles, until it became clear Connecticut didn't know the difference between lipstick and a dipstick. Just when Tony thought he'd die if he poured another cup of the scorched black liquid down his gullet, Connecticut leaned across the table and spoke in a low voice.

"You're kind of young—do you ever sneak into the Boy-O-Boy?"

"You mean, am I gay?" Tony said, slipping into a corresponding whisper. "Yeah, I guess you could say that."

"Good. I mean, so am I."

Tony thought Connecticut looked tremendously relieved, as if he somehow thought his announcement might have come as a big surprise.

"That's good. I'd have been awfully disappointed if you were just a very friendly straight guy." Tony paused. All he had been thinking about since he laid eyes on this man was how nice it would feel to be held, naked, in his arms, to kiss him, to wake up in bed with him. "Do you want to . . . I mean, do you have some place to go?"

Connecticut shook his head. "I live with my parents. Sorry."

"I have a straight roommate in the dorms."

"Oh, well. Another time then." Connecticut put a crumpled single on the table for a tip.

"Look, we can go to South Beach. . . ." Tony ventured. "I . . . have my van worked on there and I know a couple of places we can . . . park."

"South Beach? Isn't that kind of rednecky? What if we get arrested?"

"Believe me, no one will bother us. I happen to know that South Beach doesn't even *have* a police force. It's served by the Volusia S.O., and then only in emergencies like murders and stuff. They don't even do routine patrols. So if one of us doesn't kill the other, we ought to be okay."

"How reassuring," Connecticut said. "But I'm game if you are. I'm pretty sure I have a blanket in the trunk."

Connecticut owned a new triple-white Cutlass Supreme convertible with custom pinstripes and mag wheels. Once past the Sugar Mill Beach city limits on A-1-A, there were no streetlights, and the glowing of the Cutlass's instrument panel made Tony feel as if they were in a jet hurtling through the empty night sky. He tentatively put his left hand on Connecticut's right thigh. It appeared to go unnoticed, and Tony, feeling awkward, removed it. Connecticut raised his right hand off the gearshift knob and returned Tony's hand to his thigh without comment but placed his own hand on the gearshift again. By the time they reached their destination—an opening in the dunes and palmetto scrub a couple of miles north of Tony's house and the South Beach Gulf station, the mist had turned into a deluge. The two of them looked at each other and simultaneously broke out laughing.

"We're fucked," Tony said. "Unless we do it here."

"Here? In the car? There isn't enough room."

"We don't actually have to do *the deed*, you know. . . . I'm not ex-actly accomplished at that anyway. But we could . . . just sort of mess around." He reached over and undid Connecticut's belt and zipper, then popped the snaps on his own jeans and pushed them to his ankles.

"I love it when guys don't wear underwear," Connecticut said. "It's so sexy."

Soon it was warm and stuffy in the car and the windows fogged up. It took maneuvers worthy of a contortionist to get intimate with each other. Somewhat self-conscious, Tony wished Connecticut had left the radio on to cover the sounds of their passion, but it was still the most romantic thing that had ever happened to him. Something told him he was *really* going to like this guy. But after fifteen minutes, neither of them had come, and Connecticut's erection was becoming increasingly spongy.

"I really think we ought to try this another time" Connecticut said, pulling back from their embrace.

"I wish we'd brought my van, except it's a wreck."

"I'm thinking more along the lines of a queen-size bed in the Sugar Mill Hotel."

"Sounds nice, but to tell you the truth, I wouldn't even be able to split a room at the Quality Inn."

"That's okay, Tony. It's on me. I would have suggested it tonight except I didn't know if we'd be . . . compatible, which I think we are. At least I hope we are."

"Give me your telephone number and I'll call you tomorrow."

"Why don't you give me yours. My mother would be suspicious if you called."

"Suspicious? Of what? Don't you have other friends who call you?"

"No. I mean yes. But she would know the difference."

"You mean you think I'd sound like a queer?"

"No, Tony. It's not that. Honestly. But she knows who calls me, and you'd be somebody new. She'd ask questions. It would just be better for me if we did it my way."

"Sure. Okay," Tony said.

Later, parked in front of Tony's dorm, he wrote his name and phone number on the back of a Walgreen's receipt Connecticut had given him. He would have felt much better about things if Connecticut had given him his phone number; he hated not having a way to get in touch with him. He thought briefly about just looking him up in the phone book, but how many Joneses must there be in the Daytona-Ormond directory? If his father wasn't named Connecticut like him, it would be impossible to track him down.

"Don't you *dare* lose this!"

"I won't." Connecticut briefly touched the piece of paper to his lips as if he were kissing it, then folded it and put it in his wallet. He looked quickly over his right and left shoulders, then leaned toward Tony and gave him a quick kiss on the lips. "Good night."

"Call me," Tony said as he got out of the car. He watched Connecticut drive away, filled equally with joy and dread. He was happier than he had ever been in his life and at the same time convinced that he would never see Connecticut Jones again.

TWO WEEKS PASSED, and Tony had given up all hope of hearing from Connecticut. He was crushed. Finally, around eight o'clock on a Friday night, the phone rang.

"I'm sorry I haven't been in touch," Connecticut said, "but I was unexpectedly called out of town."

"For two weeks in the middle of the semester? What about your classes?"

"I had someone cover them for me."

"Cover them?"

"You know . . . take notes for me. Like that. It's easier when you're a grad student," Connecticut said. He cleared his throat. "Anyway, if you're not busy tonight, I've got a reservation at the hotel—if you still think you'd like to join me. There'll be a whole lot more room than the seat of my car."

"Shit, yeah, I'd like to join you. Damn, I'll have to shave and take a shower. I've been kind of a slob for the past couple of days. Do I have time?"

"Sure. I'm still up in Ormond. Give me an hour, then wait for me in the lobby, okay? Don't ask for me at the desk or anything. If anybody asks why you're there, just say you're waiting for someone. Don't say who. And Tony, after you shower, do you think you could maybe pull your hair back into a ponytail or something? You know, so it's not so obvious? Understand, it doesn't bother me, but the people at the hotel may give you a hard time if you look like a hippie or a deadbeat."

"Sure. Okay. I'll see you . . ." He glanced at the clock. "Around nine. In the lobby."

Tony was hurt, but he did as he had been asked. He got to the hotel at nine sharp, his hair still damp but secured with a fat, red rubber band. Connecticut was nowhere to be seen, so he took a seat in one of the high-backed wicker chairs. Ten minutes later, Connecticut appeared on the landing of the burnished, hand-carved staircase that led to the second-story bar and verandah. He didn't come down, but instead stood at the top of the stairs until they made eye contact. He jerked his head to the right, indicating the elevator, and held up four fingers. Then he turned and, without a word, ascended the staircase. Tony rode the elevator alone and was greeted by Connecticut, somewhat out of breath.

"Geez, Connecticut, why all the hocus-pocus?"

"Need I remind you that you are a minor in the eyes of the State of Florida, at least for the purposes of alcohol consumption," he said, looking around as he put the key in the door. "*And* we are—or at least I hope we are—about to commit a variety of illegal sexual acts with or upon each other in the presence of said alcoholic beverages."

"Far out."

Connecticut opened the door and pointed to a bottle of champagne that was chilling in an ice bucket between two double beds. The nightstand held a votive candle, and several tapers burned in the bathroom, where a bubble bath had been drawn.

"You did all of this for me? And this is only our second date."

"This is our first date. I don't consider that sorry gymnastics exhibition in my car a date. So come on. Let's get out of our clothes and into the tub while the temperature is just right."

The tub was small for two people and initially as uncomfortable as the car had been, but the bubble bath made their skin slippery. They writhed like sea snakes, their bodies making cello sounds as they rubbed against the porcelain tub. Later, in bed, with the candles sending up enormous palm-frond shadows and a breeze caressing them through the open French doors, they made love slowly and seriously, always looking into each other's eyes. Tony knew from the moment they first kissed that what he was doing with Connecticut was different from anything he had ever done with Mitch. Each time they met, the cowboy truck driver had aroused a hunger in him that left him crazed with a raw, almost unquenchable desire. Because Mitch had a delivery schedule to keep, their encounters were hurried and were always over too soon; Mitch frequently had to push Tony away when it was time for him to leave. When he was gone, Tony felt empty and alone, vulnerable, and somehow incomplete, as if Mitch had taken something *away* from him.

With Connecticut, no matter what they were doing in bed, he always held Tony, pulled him close, caressing his hair, kissing him on his lips, his nose, his forehead, the palms of his hands. Instead of arousing a need in him, making him feel somehow empty, Connecticut soothed and satisfied him, made him feel more complete. Tony knew what the difference was: With Mitch, it had been sex, pure and simple. It had been incredible, intoxicating, and it left him breathless. But this was *love*—Tony knew it—and it left him breathless in a different way. Twice Tony tried to speak, to tell Connecticut what he was feeling, and twice Connecticut touched his lips with a single finger to silence him, as if to say words were not necessary. When they had both come, they fell asleep, Tony resting his head on Connecticut's chest, turning as he drifted off to kiss his nipple one last time and nuzzle closer to him.

In the morning, Tony awoke in bed alone to find the room drained of color. Connecticut was asleep in the other bed. Outside it was raining gently. They had forgotten to close the French doors, which had let the damp in. Tony quickly got out of bed to close them, then climbed in beside Connecticut and kissed him until he awoke.

"What are you doing all the way over here?" Tony asked. "Did you lose your way coming back from the bathroom?"

"No. It's nothing," Connecticut said, entwining Tony in his arms and pulling him on top of himself.

"Do I snore?"

"No, Tony. You don't snore. You sleep like a little angel, or maybe more like a little devil. It's just that I have a hard time actually sleeping with someone else, as opposed to having sex, which comes to me all too easily, especially with someone as gorgeous as you. You know, when we met, I didn't realize what a beautiful man you were, in the ever-so-flattering fluorescence of the S.C.D. I'm glad I didn't. I might have been too intimidated to call you if I had."

"Bullshit!" Tony said, reaching down to tickle him. "You're not exactly Bigfoot yourself."

"You go on and take a shower. I'm going to order breakfast from room service."

"Come take a shower with me. I'll wash your back . . . and that nasty old thing between your legs. As long as you promise it won't spit at me like it did last night."

"As I recall, you asked for it. But I've got to answer the door when the food comes. Which reminds me, stay in the bathroom with the door closed until I say it's safe to come out."

"Why wouldn't it be safe to come out?"

"I mean, we don't want the bellboy to see you."

"We don't?"

"No, Tony, we don't. I just don't want to go out of my way to invite trouble."

IT WAS ANOTHER TWO WEEKS before Connecticut called Tony again, something he found a little scary and hard to understand. He already knew he was in love with this man, and their first night together had been so intense and wonderful it didn't seem possible Connecticut didn't feel the same way. But it was late April before they checked in to the hotel again. Each time they were together after that, they had a great time, and gradually the intervals between Connecticut's calls got shorter. By late May, he was calling every other day. Even though they couldn't always get together, Tony liked just being able to talk to him. Every once in a while, Connecticut sent a card to Tony's dorm post office box, usually featuring a teddy bear and a cute, sappy sentiment. Tony saved them in his dictionary as if they were pressed flowers.

This was definitely the happiest Tony had ever been in his life. All the goofy love songs on the radio that he laughed at suddenly made sense, as if they had been translated from a foreign language. It seemed almost inconceivable that there was someone in the world who loved him, who *wanted* to be with him. In high school there had been Pick, of course, but that was different. He liked Pick, loved him like a brother, but when they were together they were really just killing time, waiting for something else to happen in their lives, something real, something *better*. For Pick, it was girls. If Pick had a girl on the line, he'd disappear from Tony's life for a couple of weeks, maybe a month, so he could be with her. He wouldn't even come by the station to surf. When it was over, when the girl started getting too grabby or lovey-dovey, Pick would split and would show up at the station without a word of explanation, and that would be cool. Tony wasn't mad or jealous. He didn't bitch to Pick about it. But he desperately wanted to *be* the person that someone would ditch his friends for, would give up surfing for, or at the very least he wanted to have someone like that in his life, someone he would do those things for. With Connecticut, it seemed like he had finally found that person.

Tony practically failed a class that spring because it was a seminar that met only once a week, on Wednesdays, and somehow it always worked out that Connecticut would call on Tuesday night and they would meet at the Sugar Mill Hotel. Connecticut didn't have class on Wednesday, but Tony's seminar was early, an eight o'clock, and when it came time to get up, shower, and head to class, he just couldn't do it. He couldn't leave Connecticut there in bed. Check-out time was noon, and it was rare that they didn't stay in bed until 11:45. He just didn't care about anything else in the world except being with Connecticut. It wasn't even about the sex part, really, though that was great. He just liked the way it felt to have Connecticut's arm draped over him; the way Connecticut would pull him closer, even though it seemed as though he was still asleep; the way, as the morning wore on, the heat from Connecticut's body gradually made him feel warm and begin to sweat, until he finally threw back the sheet that had been covering them and they lay there, naked and entwined, while outside the sound of traffic on Tropicana Boulevard grew louder, reminding him that this wasn't a dream, it was real. For the first time that he could remember, he felt as though he actually belonged to someone.

Tony figured he had it licked. He had found the man he wanted to spend the rest of his life with. It wasn't *that* crazy. There were guys in the dorms who were dating their high school sweethearts and planned to marry them, even though they were only freshmen or sophomores. The only difference was that Tony was gay and couldn't really tell anybody about Connecticut; but that didn't mean he didn't love him, didn't mean he couldn't be with him forever. It didn't mean he couldn't be happy. Someday soon, they'd live together, and he'd take care of Connecticut, make a home for them. A couple of weeks ago, they had even looked at one of those condominium apartments up in Daytona, and Tony had swiped the soap from the bathroom in the model unit because it was wrapped up all pretty and had a fancy letter C on the paper. C for Connecticut. He figured it was sort of an omen. He'd put it in their bathroom when they moved in together and surprise the hell out of Connecticut.

When classes ended, Tony moved back home. He was sure the old man would make him work six days a week, and he'd never get to see Connecticut. Sure enough, he worked every day save Sunday, but almost every evening after he got off, he and Connecticut ate dinner together. Sometimes they drove to isolated stretches of Playalinda beach on the Merritt Island National Wildlife Reserve. It was out of the way, and not many people stayed much later than six, so they could make out in the car. Tony wanted to go to the gay beach, a mile's walk to the north of the last turnaround, but Connecticut refused. Tony tried to convince him they could have sex in the dunes there, but Connecticut was afraid of being caught by a Park Service ranger. On the weekends, which they spent at the hotel, they more than made up for their blue-ball sessions in the car.

Right after the Fourth of July, Tony told his pop he wasn't working on Saturdays. He said it with such force and certainty that all Demetrios did was mumble and nod. Tony figured his old man had grown accustomed to not having him around the station and would make do. At five-thirty every Friday night, Connecticut pulled the convertible into the station. He never got out of the car, and he didn't even look at Tony until they were well past the first set of dunes along the road. He told Tony he was afraid Demetrios would see something in his eyes and kill them both.

They took trips to St. Augustine, Fort Lauderdale, and Key West, and to tacky tourist traps in central Florida like the Citrus Tower, Gatorland, and Weekee Watchee, where they had their picture taken with their heads on mermaids' bodies. The worse the attraction was, the better they liked it. One night in early August, after having seen *Women in Love*, Connecticut was unusually quiet as they walked along Tropicana Boulevard to the S.C.D. for coffee.

"Heavy, huh?" Tony said. "The movie."

"Mmph," Connecticut said, his face turned away from Tony.

"But didn't you love the nude wrestling scene?"

"Uh-huh."

"And when they found those people after they drained the lake? Curled up around each other like that. That was really sad, don't you think?"

Connecticut stopped walking. Tony was carried forward two steps by momentum before he stopped.

"We've got to talk," Connecticut said, anchored to the pavement.

"We are talking," Tony said, returning to Connecticut's side. "Or perhaps I should say *I'm* talking. Yes sir, lips moving, tongue flapping, a little spit flying out every now and again."

"I mean *talk* talk. We can't talk the way I want to talk in the diner. Let's get the car and go for a drive."

Without another word, they walked back to the Cutlass and drove north on Tropicana and west on SR44 toward I-95. Tony was scared to death and wondered what he had done to bring this on. The only other time he felt this way was when he was eleven and his father told him they would lose the house and station if Tony didn't sign over his savings account, the one his mother had started for him several years before her death. It was not a matter of the money itself—he was not old enough to really understand what five hundred dollars was—but rather the idea that they could "lose" their home; that, somehow, it wasn't really theirs and some people could come and take it away.

Within sight of the interstate, Connecticut pulled over near a shuttered produce stand. He turned off the lights, but kept the engine running to power the A/C. It was so dark, Tony could barely make out Connecticut's silhouette.

"Tony . . . I don't know where to begin," Connecticut said, his voice quavering. He gazed out the car window at the flat, desolate, agricultural landscape. "Jesus, Tony, I don't know how to say this. I'm not . . . I've lied to you. I'm not who I said I was."

"I always suspected Jones was an alias," Tony said, gamely. But he could feel his legs shaking, and he hoped Connecticut wouldn't notice.

"Knock it off, Tony. Please? I'm trying to tell you something important." Connecticut shifted in his seat. He put his back against the door, which enabled him to look directly at Tony, but also put his face as far away from Tony's as possible. "Look, Tony, I'm not a graduate student at Sanctuary. I'm . . . I'm a member of the faculty."

"What?"

"I am the John Lindsey Dunstan Jr. Distinguished Professor of Sociobiology, a member of the faculty senate, chairman of the honorary degree committee, and the second youngest person known to have earned the Ph.D. degree in this country."

"Connecticut, you're barely twenty-five years old. How can you already be a professor?"

"I got my Ph.D. and started teaching when I was twelve."

"Do you really expect me to believe that? I mean . . . isn't that physically impossible or something?"

"No, Tony, it's well within the realm of possibility."

"Okay, say you're telling the truth. We've been seeing each other for nearly six months. Why didn't you tell me before?"

"I didn't want to tell you earlier because I was afraid you wouldn't understand. That you wouldn't want to date a teacher. But now I've got to leave Florida, which means I've got to leave you, too. And I just had to explain things to you."

"You're dumping me?"

"I'm not *dumping* you, Tony. I'm not *rejecting* you. It's just that I have been offered a prestigious teaching and research fellowship at Columbia University. It's the kind of thing one doesn't turn down. But it's only for two years, Tony. I'll be back. You won't even have finished school by then."

"Why can't I quit school and come with you?"

"It's out of the question, Tony. Absolutely out of the question. You have three more years of college to finish—and you're on a full scholarship. You can't throw that away."

"I don't care. I'll bet there are plenty of good acting schools in New York. I could go to one of *them*."

"Not for free, you can't."

"I'm not afraid of working—I had three jobs when I was barely sixteen."

Connecticut shifted back into driving position, leaned slightly toward the steering wheel, and turned on the lights. "I'm not going to discuss this anymore tonight. We both have a lot of think about. We better just sleep on it."

"At the hotel, right?"

"No, Tony. At home. This is a question for the head, not the heart. That's what got us into this mess to begin with."

# *11*

ENVY NOT THE CHILD PRODIGY; there is no one the passage of time treats more cruelly. Connecticut hated the word *prodigy* and never applied it to himself. He thought it had connotations of "dwarf" and "midget" about it. Freak. But by any measure, he *was* a prodigy. He was reading the *Encyclopedia Britannica* by the age of three, devouring it in its entirety within a year. And he retained virtually every word—from *aardvark* to *zygote*. His father, Desmond Jones, a physicist of some note at Krakow Polytechnical University prior to World War II, provided both motivation and discipline, force-feeding him Copernicus and Kepler with his meals and drilling him in mathematics while Beethoven played in the background.

Connecticut's childhood was generally unbearable. He had no friends, no toys—unless a chemistry set and a build-it-yourself shortwave radio could be considered toys. Desmond Jones had been a prisoner in a Polish internment camp—his real name was Janiewicz—and he was convinced it had been his intelligence that had kept him alive, so on the day his son was born, he began teaching the alphabet to Connecticut, whom he had named for the state he had briefly settled in after the war before being recruited to Sanctuary College.

Educated at home by phalanxes of tutors he quickly outgrew, Connecticut mastered mathematics of the highest order with a speed and depth of understanding that left his mentors breathless; he sucked a lifetime of knowledge out of them in weeks. His grasp of the physical sciences—biology, chemistry, physics—was equally remarkable. He had little use, however, for the arts. His interest in music was strictly mathematical; he preferred representational art almost exclusively; and he had no patience with the vagaries of drama or literature. He craved the certainty of fact: black or white, right or wrong. He came to believe that everything that was important could be explained; that which could not be explained was not important.

Connecticut never stopped thinking, not even at the dinner table. Having picked the last meat from a whole frying chicken, he played with the bones, studying their structure, guessing at their function. He demanded an ever-increasing variety of foods, relishing liver, kidney, brain, and tongue, and once swallowing a raw egg, just to see what it felt like. He wondered what made chicken taste different from pork, why beef was universally considered edible and horse meat was not. (He once forced his mother, Mollie, to find and cook horseflesh, christening the result "Belmont Steaks.") He transferred his dinner-table curiosity to books about anatomy, physiology, and chemistry, read all the scientific journals he could get his hands on, and corresponded with researchers in his childish scrawl.

Connecticut passed his high school equivalency exams when he was six and earned his bachelor's, master's, and Ph.D. degrees, all from Sanctuary, before he sprouted a single pubic hair. In the early years, he had been wooed by other institutions. Harvard, Stanford, and M.I.T. all coveted him like some human Manhattan Project. But Connecticut was still a little boy and didn't want to move away from his family. John Lindsey Dunstan, who had taken a personal interest in Connecticut, encouraged administrators at Sanctuary College to establish one of the nation's first departments of sociobiology, with Connecticut Jones as its centerpiece.

When, at the age of twelve, he began teaching undergraduates, Connecticut felt like a refugee from a P. T. Barnum sideshow, a child all gotten up in an oversized lab coat and gigantic black glasses that magnified his eyes to twice their normal size. The circus barker, he thought, would call him "Dr. Egghead" and would display him between the half-man/half-woman and the two-headed boy. He was without peer, in the worst possible way. Sometimes people were condescending to him, sometimes humble and perfunctory, as if they knew a boy with a mind such as his had better things to do than let them prattle on about something as mundane as a new movie or a favorite baseball player.

Connecticut's academic credibility was established with the publication, at the age of fifteen, of "The Effects of Stress on Inversion, Longevity, and Natural Selection in the American Roothog, *Gluttonous venomous*," in *Behavioral Science Quarterly*, the leading journal in its field. The roothog, a remote cousin of the warthog, looks like a guinea pig with miniature tusks. A hardy animal, it procreates at an alarming rate, and the young mature sexually more rapidly than any known mammal.

For his study, Connecticut confined a number of the animals in a too-small enclosure and subjected them to loud noise, chemical smoke, and bright, pulsating lights for up to twenty hours a day. A control group lived in more spacious quarters, free of noise, in natural sunlight. The experiment continued for two years, and Connecticut concluded that such high-stress living created a larger than anticipated rate of sexual inversion among the laboratory animals.

At twenty-five, Connecticut was no longer the novelty he had been at twelve, when his brilliance had defied chronological age. And in a way, that was a blessing; his Shirley Temple days were over. He was older than all of his undergraduates and at least as old as most of his graduate students. And although he welcomed that change wholeheartedly, there were still some demands he resented. While he stood out less at faculty meetings, he still had the feeling he was supposed to do intellectual card tricks for his colleagues' pleasure, to continue to work academic miracles. If he was a genius at eight, people reasoned, he should be *three times* as smart at twenty-five. Connecticut didn't view it that way. For him, it was merely a matter of his body finally catching up with his mind.

Connecticut's social and emotional development did not mirror his intellectual progress. For most of his life, he had been painfully aware that he was an oddity, an outsider. He grew up surrounded by adults who acknowledged him as their intellectual equal but who did not know how to relate to him personally. He could not, after all, drink or smoke with his fellow researchers at the surprisingly licentious late-night parties that frequently followed symposia in New York, Chicago, Paris, and Stockholm. Nor could he sleep with their wives or their female graduate assistants, which his social scientist's eye discerned was frequently the case. Not that he would want to. By the time he was thirteen, he understood that he was different in another significant way: he knew that he was gay.

That he had survived at all was due in no small part to Dallas Eden, whom he had first met eleven years ago, in 1959, at the funeral of Dallas's father, John Lindsey Dunstan. Connecticut was fourteen and had been on the faculty of Sanctuary College for two years. Dallas, who was in his late twenties, had been living in Los Angeles, where he was filming *House of Wax II* with Vincent Price, but had returned to Edensgate during his father's final illness and remained there with his mother for two years following his death.

Initially, Connecticut hypothesized that Dallas gravitated toward him because they were both misfits—Dallas because of his enormous bulk, Connecticut because of his prodigious intellect. After further observation, Connecticut concluded that Dallas used the gravitational pull of his wealth and celebrity to draw to him people who possessed things he did not: intelligence, talent, wit, beauty, youth, innocence. He was something of a fickle collector: those who possessed the most perishable attributes often were consumed in the process and disappeared. But he remained loyal to those (such as Connecticut) whose qualities were more durable, becoming a lifelong ally and supporter who asked little or nothing in return save their continued friendship.

In any event, Dallas was the first person who actually treated Connecticut as an adult. He invited him to dinner and to parties at Edensgate, professed an interest in his research if not a real grasp of its finer points, and was an advocate for him with the Sanctuary College Board of Trustees whenever he requested additional funding (often underwriting the expenses himself).

Connecticut quickly discerned that Dallas was gay. The parties he hosted at Edensgate were, unlike the formal faculty functions Connecticut had endured in previous years, attended almost exclusively by attractive young men. Dallas, who was constantly surrounded by a Speedo-clad entourage of boys he apparently imported from Los Angeles on a regular basis, never made a sexual advance toward Connecticut but offered him a sympathetic ear when, at the age of seventeen, he confessed his personal pain and confusion about his own attraction to men. Soon after, he introduced Connecticut to Nathan Bismarck, a mathematics prodigy several years his senior, with whom Connecticut embarked on a three-year relationship until Nathan, considered a likely Nobel laureate, was institutionalized for manic-depressive disorder. Connecticut had since had one other relationship with a considerably older faculty member, which had ended when he grew frustrated with Connecticut's reluctance to leave his parents' home and move in with him. In their final acrimonious encounter, Connecticut's embittered lover told him in no uncertain terms that he considered him immature and hopelessly inept at human relationships.

Connecticut had not been emotionally involved with anyone in more than two years, and he allowed himself discreet sexual encounters only rarely. Because his previous relationships had not been based primarily on physical attraction, Connecticut was surprised that he was pursuing one that, at least so far, seemed to be based on little else. He was dumbfounded that someone as gorgeous as Tony would even be interested in him, and he was unaccustomed to listening to the demands of his heart, let alone his libido. At first he had tried not to get involved; he resisted calling Tony for two weeks after they met. But he found that he couldn't get him out of his mind. And he realized over the course of the summer that he was in love with Tony in a way he had never been before. He had loved Nathan, yes, but for his brain. When he and Tony were together, intellectual pursuits were the last thing on his mind. After much coercion, he had finally agreed to go to the nude beach at Playalinda, something that previously would have scandalized him, just so that he could see Tony walk in the surf, lithe, golden, naked—a creature of incredible grace. Tony's beauty was *his* genius.

# 12

CONNECTICUT DIDN'T CALL for three days, which drove Tony crazy. He worried that Connecticut had packed up and moved to New York without him. Then, just after he closed at the station, Connecticut called.

"How about dinner at the hotel?"

In all the time they had been dating, Connecticut had never taken him to the restaurant at the hotel. They had always used room service.

"Dinner at the hotel? In the actual dining room? What's the occasion?"

"None of your business, smarty pants."

"Should I bring my toothbrush?"

Connecticut hesitated. "That would be nice."

When Connecticut arrived to pick up Tony, he seemed relaxed. He was smiling a lot and kept turning to look at him. But for the ten minutes it took them to drive into town, they made nothing but small talk. At the hotel, Connecticut asked for a "quiet" table—one away from the large windows that faced onto Tropicana Boulevard.

"So are you going to tell me what the occasion is?" Tony asked after the waiter had taken their order.

Caught in mid-swallow, Connecticut put his glass down, cleared his throat, and ran the tip of his tongue around the perimeter of his mouth once. He cleared his throat again.

"I know that I've hurt you, Tony, and I'm sorry about that. But frankly, I didn't expect the depth of reaction I got from you. After all, we haven't been seeing each other for that long. I thought you might not be *happy* if I went to New York, but I had *no* idea you would be this sad."

*Maybe he wasn't going to take the job in New York after all.*

"It's just that I've just never had to be responsible for anyone but my-self," Connecticut said. "Maybe not even that, since I'm twenty-five and still living with my parents. This move scares me to death, even though I know it's the right thing to do. But I've worried about how I could do it if I had to take care of you, too."

"But you *won't* have to take care of me. I've taken care of myself for nearly ten years. I've had to cook for me and my pop, do the cleaning, *and* work at the station. Plus for the last couple years I worked two other jobs. I'm not some helpless kid."

"Well, when it comes to survival skills, you do pretty much have it all over me."

"See? I can take care of *you.*"

"What about school? What about your scholarship? That's an awful lot to throw away just because you want to be with someone. You know, this kind of a relationship is hard. They don't always work out. Lots of things can happen."

"But I love you, Connecticut, and nothing is ever going to change that."

Tony knew in his heart it was true. He did love Connecticut, *really* loved him. It was different than the way it had been with Mitch. He *thought* he loved him, but he knew it was really only about sex. He didn't even *know* Mitch. He learned *that* the hard way. And Mitch certainly didn't love *him*. But this was different. Connecticut liked him. He *knew* he did. They did things together, made plans, went places. Connecticut always asked about school, knew things about him that Tony's pop had never even thought about. His love for Connecticut was as real and per-manent as if they were brothers. No matter what happened, they would always be connected by that.

"And what about your draft deferment?"

"I never told you? In the draft lottery last spring I got a high num-ber—three twenty-seven. Unless World War Three breaks out, they'll never be able to touch me."

"You're very lucky."

"I know. My friend Pick enlisted and got training to be a medic. Now he's in Vietnam."

"Do you have any money for things like clothes? It gets very cold up North, colder than you've ever been, and you'll need lots of new, warm clothes."

"I've still got most of the money I made last summer." Tony had never told Connecticut for whom he had worked. Dallas Eden had an even bigger reputation in the gay community than he did with the greaser thugs like Pick's cousin Jimmy, and Tony didn't want Connecticut to get the idea he had been one of Dallas's kept boys. "Plus, I know how to live cheap. Really cheap."

"Of course, I'd be responsible for the food and the rent. But I'd expect you to find a job and to find out what kind of acting schools there are in the city."

"You mean you're going to let me come with you?"

"Yes. There are still a few things we need to talk about, but yes, I'd like for you to come with me."

"What changed your mind?"

"I spoke to an old friend, you might even call him a mentor; and he said it sounded like a good idea. I trust his opinion on things like this."

Tony couldn't believe it: he was going to New York with Connecticut! They were actually going to *live* together. He couldn't even begin to imagine what it was going to be like. Everything he knew about New York had come from watching movies at the old Strand Theater on Tropicana Boulevard. He imagined they might live in an apartment like the one Robert Redford and Jane Fonda had in *Barefoot in the Park* and that they would meet glamorous people like Audrey Hepburn in *Breakfast at Tiffany's*. Whatever happened, they would be *together*.

THEIR FIRST GLIMPSE of New York came as they drove over the dead, gray marshes of northern New Jersey, where mammoth green petroleum storage tanks erupted like giant pustules from the apocalyptic landscape. Flames burned ominously atop towers of black scaffolding, and the air was bitter with atomized petroleum. But in the distance, just over the eastern horizon, Tony could see the syringe-like antennae of Manhattan. By the time they reached the banked approach to the Holland Tunnel, the sun was low in the western sky, and the city, now completely revealed, was a relief of hammered silver, copper, and gold. For millions, New York is the Naked City, but for Tony it was arrayed in the emperor's new clothes.

"This is *so* bitchin'," Tony said. "I have never in my entire life seen anything this incredible. I am *so* psyched!"

Connecticut, too, was exultant about their arrival, though for entirely different reasons. He was just glad the trip was over. It had taken them four days to get here, a far cry from his original plan for an eighteen-hour, pedal-to-the-metal marathon on I-95, stopping only to fill their thermos and empty their bladders. But Tony had never been outside the state of Florida, and he wanted to stop in Atlanta to see Underground, Stone Mountain, and the Cyclorama, and to stay at the Hyatt Regency on Peachtree Street; to visit the White House, the Capitol, and JFK's grave in Washington; and to see Independence Hall and the Liberty Bell in Philadelphia.

Connecticut loved the kid—he really did—but he was *always* asking questions. Could the Holland Tunnel spring a leak and drown everyone in it? *No.* Had a plane really crashed into the Empire State Building? *Yes.* Connecticut didn't really want to ignore the questions. They showed a level of intellectual curiosity he would not have guessed was there. The kid was not stupid, but he obviously had not been well served by the public schools of Volusia County, and he had no real-life experience on which to base judgments or opinions. The best example was the current situation. Here he was, giving up a four-year free ride at Sanctuary College, one of the finest private schools in the South, and for what? Because he was in love? He was nineteen years old; what did he know about love? What did either one of them know, for that matter? Connecticut knew he should have left him behind. He reaffirmed it a hundred times on the drive north. But Tony was so goddamned gorgeous, so incredibly sexy, so attentive and affectionate, that he couldn't bear to abandon him.

Columbia had reserved a room in Connecticut's name at the New York Hilton, and once they exited the tunnel, they made their way uptown. At the hotel, Connecticut checked in and went upstairs with the bellhop, while Tony paced up and down the length of the glittering lobby. The longer he stared at the well-heeled women and their dapper husbands, the more self-conscious he felt about the jams and three-day-old Ron Jon T-shirt he was wearing. When Connecticut returned ten minutes later, he suggested they eat dinner outside the hotel. "It'll be cheaper and there'll be more to choose from. We can go to Chinatown if you want. I think you'd like that. Or Little Italy. It's up to you."

"Can I go up to the room a minute and wash? Look at this shit," Tony said. He wiped two fingers across his forehead and held them up for Connecticut to see. They were black and gritty.

"I told you driving through New Jersey with the top down was a mistake. Here, you can use this," Connecticut said, and he handed Tony one of several clean handkerchiefs he always carried. "You can wash your face and hands at the restaurant, and you can take a nice long bath in the room tonight. Let's go."

"Connecticut, you've been doing this the whole trip," Tony said. "It makes me feel like a pervert or something."

"What does?"

"All this cloak-and-dagger stuff. Making me wait in the car or the lobby until you check in and make sure the coast is clear. It sorta made sense when we were back home and you were afraid someone from Sanctuary would see you, but nobody knows you here."

"You're right about one thing, Tony, we're *not* in Sugar Mill Beach anymore. We're in the real world, and frequently it is a very mean-spirited place. How would it look to Columbia if they found out I was shacked up with someone barely old enough to be one of my students? And worse, of the same sex. People lose their jobs every *day* because they're gay. A hotel of this caliber has assistant managers and house detectives prowling the halls day and night. If anybody asked any questions, I just think I could handle things better than you. That's all."

Tony was silent. Connecticut's explanation did little to make him feel better. If anything, it confirmed what he already suspected—that Connecticut thought he was some sort of an idiot who couldn't be trusted to talk to the help in some snotty New York hotel because they would immediately guess he was a fag. All the way up the coast, Connecticut had ordered rooms with twin beds or two doubles. They would have sex in one bed, but Connecticut always slept alone in the other one, just as they had back in Sugar Mill Beach. In Washington, he finally told Tony the reason he did that, and it wasn't because he couldn't fall asleep if someone was in bed with him. The real reason was that if there were ever a fire and they died in their sleep, at least his parents wouldn't find out he was gay at the same time they found out he was dead. That, he said, would be "a double whammy."

When they got to Chinatown, Tony was still so hurt and angry that he didn't want to talk, so he just shuffled along silently all the way to the restaurant. But by the time their meal was served, he perked up. The only Chinese food he'd ever eaten was Chun King chow mein out of a can, which looked like vomit and tasted like library paste. This food was bright and colorful. He could actually taste the individual ingredients—red peppers and mushrooms, green beans that Connecticut called snow peas. After the meal, he was delighted by the fortune cookies. "You shall flower like the cherry blossom," his message said. Connecticut's read: "The road forks." By the end of the evening, after a long stroll though lower Manhattan, he was again excited by New York and the seemingly endless possibilities it offered. Surely there was a place for him *somewhere* in this city. When they returned to the hotel, he discovered that Connecticut had ordered champagne sent up to the room. They shut off the lights, opened the curtains, and made love with the skyline twinkling outside. Once Tony fell asleep, Connecticut carefully slid from beneath the sheet, put on a pair of pajama bottoms, and slipped into the other bed.

The following day Connecticut met with a woman in the Columbia housing office who recommended a number of apartments to him and introduced him to a real estate agent. They eventually looked at five, all as far from campus as possible; Connecticut didn't want fellow faculty members or graduate students dropping in on them unexpectedly. They fell in love with a fourth-floor flat on Grove Street in the Village. Because it was on the top floor, it had skylights in almost every room. It had three fireplaces and a bathtub with *claws*. There was no question about taking it.

As the movers brought up Connecticut's double bed and a new twin-size mattress and box spring still wrapped in plastic and paper, Connecticut took Tony aside. He said he had given their living arrangements considerable thought. Tony, he explained, would keep his things in the smaller of the two bedrooms, and that would be "his" room in the event of visits by Connecticut's parents, colleagues, or other unexpected guests. He was *never* to leave any of his clothes, albums, magazines, or grooming products in the master bedroom, nor was he ever to describe that room as "ours," even when it was only the two of them at home.

"That way, you'll get used to saying it the right way, and you won't make a mistake," Connecticut explained. "One slip of the tongue and all of this careful preparation will go up in smoke."

Tony started to object, but in the end he simply shrugged his shoulders and moved his belongings into the smaller of the two bedrooms. He didn't have much to unpack. All he had brought was his father's World War II duffel bag filled with jeans and T-shirts, a pair of sandals, a moldy-looking pair of Converse high-tops, and a handful of battered albums by the Beach Boys, the Beatles, and the Mamas and the Papas. It was pretty much everything he owned in the world, except his surfboard.

It had been easier to leave South Beach than he might have imagined. Ever since he had been uprooted by Catholic Charities five years before, he felt differently about life on the island. Other than Pick, who was in Vietnam now, he had few friends, just a handful of guys who surfed off

Cocoa or down at Sebastian Inlet, most of whom he didn't even know by name. When he told the old man that he was leaving, moving to New York City, he didn't seem to care much. He didn't even ask why or where he would live. He hadn't asked, the way Connecticut had, if he had enough money to buy some warm clothes. Fucker didn't care if he froze to death. It just didn't seem to matter much to him whether Tony was a thousand miles away in Manhattan or just down the road at Sanctuary College. In either case he wasn't available to pull shifts at the station. The day Tony left, his old man was asleep, or more likely drunk, in his room. Tony didn't even leave a note.

"We've got to keep our story simple," Connecticut said later as they unpacked box after box of books. "We can't make it too complicated or change it too often."

"Why can't I just be your roommate? Straight people have roommates, don't they?"

"Not straight distinguished professors. Once you reach a certain station in life, you don't *have* roommates, Tony. You have husbands or wives or lovers. I'm at that point now. If people find out about you, they're going to know we're more than roommates—unless I come up with a credible explanation for who you are."

"How about your houseboy?"

"God, you really don't get this, do you? Tony, this is a clean slate for me, a new beginning. Ever since I can remember, I've felt different. I've always been a *freak*. But now, at last, I fit in. Sure, the faculty knows I'm a *little* different, a little special, but I'm old enough, I look enough like a *real* faculty member that they treat me like they treat anybody else. I don't want to ruin that. I don't want to suddenly be different again because I'm gay. I love you, Tony. I really do. But can't we do it my way, just for now?"

Tony didn't answer right away. He was hurt and angry, but he didn't really know why. In a way it was kind of nice to have someone tell him what to do. His old man certainly never cared enough about him to tell him how the world worked, to teach him right from wrong. He had never asked if he had done his homework or what kind of grades he got at school. (Tony had eventually given up on him and forged his pop's signature on his report cards.) There had been plenty of opportunities for Tony to have gone wrong. A couple of times, he and Pick had been invited to hang with a group of guys who vandalized cars and broke into houses in Sugar Mill Estates. Sometimes he thought he should have gone with them, gotten caught, and ended up in juvie, just to show the old man. But it would have all been for nothing. Pops wouldn't have cared, and Tony'd still be in the clink. How fucked was that? So he kept his nose clean.

Doing what Connecticut said wasn't so bad. He wasn't being mean about it. He was just being careful. He was looking out for him—for *them*—making sure nobody would start trouble, ask questions, take him away somehow for being a pervert or something, for having sex with an older man. No, Connecticut was smarter than he was—way smarter. Tony knew what was right, and he would do anything Connecticut said if it meant it would make him happy.

GREENWICH VILLAGE was a revelation to Tony, who thought it odd to call any part of a city of eight million people a "village." He loved the family-owned shops and restaurants, the Italian funeral parlors. He savored the smells of freshly baked bread and cut flowers and the exotic aromas of restaurants serving food from all over the world. He had been awed by the glamour and drama of the glass-and-steel towers farther uptown, but now he was glad he didn't live there. In the Village, shade trees grew in tiny brick-paved parks squeezed into the nooks and crannies between buildings or in the triangles of off-kilter intersecting streets. People came to play checkers and cards and some strange ball game that looked to Tony like a cross between bowling and horseshoes. And certain parts of the neighborhood appeared to be populated almost entirely by gay men.

"You can't swing a dead cat here without hitting two fags," Connecticut said on one of their early walking tours of the area. Tony asked why Connecticut would live in a neighborhood with so many obviously gay men if he was afraid people would think he was gay.

"Oh, it's not just fags who live here," Connecticut said. "It's the intelligentsia, too, the writers and painters and poets. People with radical politics. It's like the Left Bank of Paris. *That's* why I want to live here—for the life of the mind."

For the first two weeks, Connecticut spent most of his time setting up his lab, orienting himself to the campus, and moving into his office. Tony wanted to help, if only to be near him, but was told to stay home and clean. Although the apartment was tidy and freshly painted, it was not really clean, not by Connecticut's standards, particularly the kitchen and bathroom. Connecticut expected them to be as sterile as an operating room—or his laboratory. Tony didn't mind all the sweeping and mopping and scrubbing because he felt as though he was making a home for Connecticut and himself, but after four days, there was nothing left to do around the apartment, so he decided to explore the city. He figured he would check out all the sights and figure out which ones Connecticut might like. He left a note on the kitchen counter and made his way to the Christopher Street subway station.

Tony expected the subway to be like the monorails he had seen in pictures of Disneyland and the Seattle World's Fair—clean and quiet, sleek and silvery. Those illusions were shattered the moment he stepped in to the station. It was sort of creepy—loud and dirty and smelly. With its white-tiled walls smeared with graffiti, the station seemed like a big underground men's room. He bought a token and stepped onto the platform without the slightest idea of what he was doing. He approached a young man with unkempt hair and eyeglasses reading a book. He was one of those people whose jaw looked blue because of the density of their beard, no matter how recently they had shaved. On his sweatshirt were the letters CUNY.

"Excuse me," Tony said. The guy looked up. He seemed irritated for an instant, and then he smiled broadly, his eyes traveling from Tony's surf-blonded hair to his high-tops, tied only three-quarters of the way up because the laces had long ago broken. "I'm not from around here, and I was wondering if you could tell me which train to take to get to all the famous places?"

"What?" the young man said, smiling and not taking his eyes off Tony. "What famous places? There are lots of them."

"You know, like the Empire State Building, the Statue of Liberty. And St. Patrick's Cathedral."

"Oh, okay. You're basically sightseeing, right?"

Tony nodded.

"I guess it all depends on which one you want to see first."

"How about the Empire State Building?"

"Okay, that's easy." The man scribbled some directions in the notebook he carried, tore out the page and gave it to Tony just as a train pulled into the station. "You want to go uptown," he shouted as he edged backward toward the train. "You need to get over to the other side of the tracks. I'd be happy to show you myself but I'm late for work. Otherwise I would. Really."

Tony crossed to the other side of the tracks and boarded the first train that pulled in. He didn't look at the instructions until the train was well underway. The stranger's scrawl bordered on unreadable, but written very clearly across the bottom of the paper were the words: Cooper. CALL ME!!! and a telephone number.

"And they say people in New York aren't friendly," he said, folding the paper and putting it in his jeans pocket.

Later, atop the Empire State Building, he spent almost an hour looking out over the city. Again he marveled at the density and compactness of Manhattan and was amazed to see a huge swath of green not far to the north. It looked like a golf course for King Kong, but on the directory next to a coin-operated telescope, it was identified as Central Park. He decided to make that his next destination.

Every day for the next two weeks, Tony made his way around the city with the help of an inexpensive map he purchased at the end of his first day of sightseeing. He had quickly become adept at dealing with the subway system, but for the sake of economy he did a lot of walking, usually riding the train only at the beginning and the end of the day. He liked the idea of taking to the streets. He never knew when he was going to stumble on some place like Times Square or Tiffany's—just like that, out of the blue.

With some trepidation, he tiptoed into the lobbies of the Waldorf-Astoria and the Plaza hotels, waiting for one of the liveried bellmen to grab him by the scruff of the neck and throw him back onto the street, but amazingly none did. An elegantly dressed older gentleman struck up a conversation with him in the lobby of the Plaza, bought him a drink in a place called the Oak Bar, and suggested they retire to his room upstairs, which had a much better view of the park. Tony politely declined and said he had to be going. The man reddened, his right hand crumpling the bar tab, and called Tony "an ungrateful little urchin." The other patrons in the smoky, wood-paneled room looked up from their drinks and chuckled as the man threw a couple of crumpled bills on the table and stormed out.

Except for this man, New Yorkers seemed friendly and genuinely concerned with Tony's well-being. Every time he pulled out his map, three or four men stopped to ask if he needed help. They invariably introduced themselves, asked his name, and suggested that they have a cup of coffee someplace around the corner or maybe—sure why not?—back at their place. Some of them wanted to go sightseeing with him right then, in the middle of the afternoon. Have you seen the Statue of Liberty? they'd ask. Have you been to the top of the Empire State Building?

Although the men seemed harmless enough, Tony declined the invitations for drinks or coffee and for guided tours. He had never been comfortable with strangers, and the incident at the Plaza seemed like a warning to him. Without exception, the men seemed deeply distressed when Tony said no, and most of them offered their telephone numbers or business cards, which he accepted with a big smile but immediately tossed into the nearest garbage can. It was nice of them to take an interest in him, a perfect stranger, but most of them were really old and he didn't think he had anything in common with them. What would they talk about?

When Tony had seen pretty much everything he wanted, he decided to call Cooper, the guy who had given him directions on the subway two weeks before. He at least was young and poor, like Tony. Maybe he knew of some out-of-the-way things to do, some sightseeing sideshows only the natives had heard of.

"Cooper, hi! It's Tony. I wanted to . . ."

"Tony who?"

"Tony Alexamenos."

"Never heard of you."

"Cooper, wait," Tony shouted. "I met you in the subway two weeks ago. I've got really long hair, and I didn't know my way around the city for shit."

"Tony? *That's* your name? This is *you?* Shit, I'd given up on you a week ago. Fuck. The guy from the station?" Cooper paused and, although he covered the receiver with his hand, Tony could hear him shouting to another person in the apartment, who screamed as if he had just seen a mouse. "Sorry, Tony. So how are you? Did you ever find the Empire State Building?"

"Sure did. And all of those other places I said. And Central Park, and lots of museums, and cool little stores full of neat stuff. This city is great! I even walked across the Brooklyn Bridge, but I didn't get off and go in to Brooklyn or anything. I just turned around and walked back."

"That's great, Tony. I'm really glad you like the city."

"I thought maybe you could show me a good cheap place to eat. All I've had for the past two weeks is hot dogs. I was sort of embarrassed to go into restaurants alone. Plus they all cost so much."

"Lunch? Great! Tell you what, meet me at the Christopher Street station like last time, but outside. Stay on the street. We can walk to the restaurant. Say 11:30? I need to take a shower and wash my hair."

"Sure. Cool. I'll see you then."

When Tony first spotted Cooper at the station two hours later, he wasn't sure it was him. His big, ugly, tortoise-shell glasses were missing, and he was much better looking without them. His hair had been cut and was carefully combed.

"Almost didn't recognize you," Tony said, extending his hand as he walked toward Cooper.

"I usually wear contacts. The day we met I had conjunctivitis and couldn't put them in," Cooper said. He shook Tony's hand, then turned and put his left arm around Tony's shoulder, guiding him down Christopher Street. "I hate those old glasses, but since I only use them in emergency situations, I'm not going to spend the money on nicer ones. Really don't have it *to* spend."

"I can identify with that," Tony said. "I've really got to pinch pennies, too."

"You like Indian? I know an Indian restaurant right here in the Village where we can *both* eat really well for under four bucks. You just have to know what to order—the authentic Indian cuisine, not the stuff they put on the menu for tourists."

The restaurant, Kali Ma, was dimly lit and scented with incense, its walls draped in cloth of vivid hues. In the center of the main room was a statue of a many-armed woman, naked to her hips, wearing a necklace of snakes and earrings made out of what looked like tiny human bodies.

"Black mother," Cooper said, pointing to the statue. "That's what Kali Ma means. She's the most bloodthirsty of all the consorts of the god Siva."

"Looks like the patron saint of butchers to me. I imagine all those arms would come in handy in the kitchen."

Cooper laughed and guided him to a booth.

"You really look great, Tony. God, you just have the most extraordinary face. You know that?"

"I don't know. I've been looking at it every day for the last nineteen years, so I guess I'm used to it."

All the waitresses were Indian women in saris, many with jewelry piercing their noses. Cooper ordered for them both and while they waited for the food, told Tony about himself. He was a senior at the City University of New York, a business major, and his biggest worry about graduating was not about getting a job but losing his student deferment.

"Nixon says he's going to cut our involvement by a hundred fifty thousand men, and that's great for *those* hundred fifty thousand,"

Cooper said. "But that still leaves a huge fighting force in 'Nam, and they're going to need people to rotate in and relieve them."

Soon, a waitress in a purple-and-gold sari set two steaming plates in front of them.

"I'm lucky. I've got a high draft number," Tony said, sticking a finger into his food and licking it. "Whew! Hot! . . . My best friend from home is over there right now, some place called Khe Sanh, I think. His letters make it sound pretty scary."

"If push comes to shove, I guess I'll tell them I'm a homosexual," Cooper said.

"You're a homosexual?" Tony was less surprised by the information than by the casual way it was conveyed. Cooper had said "I'm a homosexual" the way he might have said "I'm from New Jersey," or "I'm French," unlike Connecticut, who said it like "I'm a leper," or "I'm a Martian."

"Aren't you?"

"Yeah, I guess so."

"You guess so? What do you mean? You either are or you aren't. Unless you . . . you're not a *virgin*, are you? Someone as gorgeous as you?"

Tony blushed. "No, but I've only done it with about four or five guys and one of them is my boyfriend."

"You have a *lover*? Is he here is the city with you?"

"Yeah. He keeps telling me not to tell anyone about him—about us. He's not real open about it."

"But he doesn't mind if you trick with other guys? That's kind of strange."

"What has that got to do with . . ." Tony stopped eating. Cooper had already done so. "You don't mean you want to . . ."

"You called me up and said let's have lunch!"

"So?"

"Don't you know that means you want to have sex?"

"No. I thought it meant I wanted to get something to eat."

"Tony, this is all a terrible mistake, although I can forgive you because you're young and you're so new to New York. But the next guy you meet might not be so understanding, so let me give you a little advice. Next time someone says, 'Let's have lunch,' don't say okay unless you want to have sex with them. The same with dinner. And when they ask you to come over for breakfast, they mean come over the night before. The only invitation it's safe to accept is Sunday brunch. Brunch is the only celibate meal queens have, possibly because they're too hung over to care, or they got nailed big-time the night before and their butt is too sore."

"Nailed?"

"Screwed, Tony. Hammered. Pounded. Unless you want me to continue with these construction allusions, nod your head."

"So what you're saying is that when some guy says he wants to grab a bite . . ."

"What he wants to bite is *you!*"

"What if he asks me to go to a movie?"

"It'll be an eight-millimeter fuck flick in his bedroom."

"What about the guy who wanted to take me on one of those boat tours around Manhattan?"

"He wanted to put his ship into your slip."

"The beach? A baseball game?"

"Sex, sex, sex. All sex. Tony, when someone is as much of a knockout as you are, anything a gay man says to you is going to mean 'Do you want to have sex?' Listen to me. I promise you, if you ever get a dog and walk it in the park, every queen you pass is going to stop and ask you what kind it is, even if it's perfectly obvious that it's a German shepherd or a French poodle—not that there's any chance of *you* getting a poodle. They'll squat down to pet it, and they'll talk baby talk to it, but really they'll be checking out your box, as if, in your case, that really mattered." Cooper pushed his plate away. "About the only thing somebody could say to you that isn't going to mean 'Let's have sex' is 'Hey, you got spare change?' It's also safe to assume that if someone asks you to go to the opera with him, he's not interested in sex. In fact, he's probably *incapable* of having sex. Opera does that to you. Over time. Puccini in particular. *Beware* of Puccini."

Tony chewed a mouthful of ice slowly, to offset the curry he'd just eaten. "Can't we just be friends, you and me? I could use a friend."

"I'm sorry, Tony, I just don't think I could handle it. I really, *really,* want to jump your bones, and that would always be uppermost in my mind. Christ, I couldn't stop thinking about you for a whole *week* after I met you. I stayed home at night hoping you'd call. I turned down *dates* to sit by the telephone. Maybe if you let me get it out of my system, you know, three or four free throws, maybe *then* we could be friends. Or maybe you'd decide you liked me better than your closet-case boyfriend, and we'd become lovers. But *friends?* I don't think so. You're too young and—forgive me—too *unsophisticated* just to be a friend."

"But I wouldn't be too young to be your . . . lover?"

"Are you kidding? Tony, if you were my lover, everything about you would be *perfect*. I could forgive you your youth and your naïveté. I could forget about poor table manners, extreme lapses of fashion sense, and leaving the cap off the toothpaste. For you I could ignore addictions to drugs and alcohol, grand theft auto, even pyromania. Previous hospitalizations or incarcerations, even homicidal tendencies—out the window!"

Tony shrugged. "Okay. I guess I'd better go, then." He dug into his jeans' pocket. "Here's my two bucks."

"You hang onto it, babe. I've already got egg on my face, lunch might as well be on me, too." Cooper reached out for Tony's hand. "But, how about we go back to my place and blow a little dope?"

"Sure. . . ." Tony caught himself and smiled. "The little dope you want to blow wouldn't be me, would it?"

"Just testing, Tony. Just testing." Cooper got up from the table, made the sign of the cross, and walked toward the door with Tony. "Father, my work here is done."

ONCE TONY HAD SEEN MOST of the high points the city had to offer, he sought out some of its low points, like Forty-second Street, which fascinated and embarrassed him at the same time. He walked up one side of the street and down the other, peeking at the pornography peripherally, but he never mustered the courage to actually enter one of the bookstores or movie houses. Once he stood outside a porno theater for thirty minutes, aching with curiosity. A hundred times he almost stepped up to the ticket window. His center of gravity relocated to his crotch and he felt lightheaded; he was aware only of the filthy, blood-red terrazzo beneath his feet and the nasal, raspily amplified refrain of the cashier: "Foive dawlahs, suh. Thass right, foive dawlahs." Finally he walked away, his heart pounding, his brain screening its own version of what was going on inside that serpent's pit.

Tony decided that if he was reduced to hanging around dirty movie theaters, it was probably time to look for a job. Every morning after breakfast, he bought the city newspapers at a tiny, family-run grocery store just down the block. He decided he would look for work as a waiter or bellboy. Despite having no experience in either area, his smile usually got him in the door, especially if the interviewer appeared to be gay, but his unflinching refusal to cut his hair inevitably got him the boot. Some of the men seemed genuinely distraught when they reached an impasse on the length of his locks: they yearned to see this creature five days a week. More than one gave him his business card, home number on the reverse, "in case you should happen to change your mind—or just want to talk about it."

Connecticut couldn't understand why Tony wouldn't cut his hair if it meant the difference between working and not working. "Tony, you're *so* handsome, but you keep your face hidden under all that hair."

"I thought you liked my hair. You said you did."

"I do, Tony. You do have beautiful hair. But sometimes when you're asleep, I push your hair away from your face, and I imagine what you'd look like with shorter hair. Not short, necessarily. Just short-*er.*"

Two weeks later, just as Tony was looking for the right barber shop—someplace cheap but also liberal enough that he wouldn't have to sit through a lot of Woodstock jokes while his hair piled up on the floor—he got a call. The man on the other end briefly identified himself, then asked for Tony by name. He said there was an open call at the Biltmore Theater at three that afternoon to fill a vacancy caused by an injury to a member of the cast of *Hair*. Tony threw the receiver into the air and whooped.

Tony didn't recognize his benefactor's name, and he was curious about who it might be. He'd met any number of men who, after a few minutes' chitchat during which he had revealed his theatrical aspirations, told him they were Broadway producers (what a coincidence!) and gave him their cards. But he was almost certain he hadn't given any of them *his* name or telephone number.

# 13

"I GOT A JOB CONNECTICUT! I got a *real* job!" Tony had been waiting five hours to speak those words. It was nearly ten o'clock, and Connecticut was just getting in from his lab.

"That's great Tony. Doing what?" Connecticut asked, hanging his tweed coat on a hook near the door.

"I'll be doing *Hair.*"

"You're going to cut hair? Jesus, Tony, do you think you could have possibly come up with a more embarrassing way to make money?"

"Not hair. *Hair!*" He shook his head and teased his blond mane with his fingers. "The musical. The Age of Aquarius. It's a small part, but it's a wonderful show. I can remember reading about it in *Life* magazine when it opened. I can't believe I'm actually going to be *in* it!"

"Isn't that the one where everybody's naked?"

"No. Just one scene. Everybody gets under this huge American flag and then whoever wants to get naked does, and they come out singing."

"Couldn't you get a job in a less controversial show? Like . . . like *Grease.* That's a wholesome, all-American show."

"Much as I'd like to, I'm not able to pick and choose which Broadway show I'll appear in. The guy I'm replacing broke his leg in a fall backstage. Don't you see how incredibly lucky I am to get this? I mean, I really don't have the experience to get a job like this. It's like magic or something—the hand of God. I don't understand it. I can't explain it. But it's *way* too big to say no to. After you've seen the show you'll understand. You *will* come see it, won't you?"

"Okay, I'll go. I suppose if I want to be rational about this I should make some observations before I reach any conclusions."

Connecticut had yet to make an appearance at the theater two weeks later when Tony spied another familiar face in the audience. It was, in fact, precisely at the moment when he emerged from beneath the flag, naked (it had taken him all of the first week to decide to shuck his clothes), when he saw, seated in the first row, none other than Dallas Eden, accompanied by his valet, Alfred. Tony shrank back and accidentally bumped into another cast member, Zen Twigg, an ethereal James Taylor lookalike with whom he had become fast friends.

"Shit, Zen, he's here," Tony whispered.

"Focus, Tony. Tell me later," Zen replied as he skittered away. "Focus."

After the show, he sought out Zen, but his search was interrupted when he ran into Alfred backstage.

"Mr. Eden extends his congratulations on a superb performance and hopes you will be able to join him for dinner this evening. Although it is short notice—he was naturally quite shocked to see you—he fervently hopes you will accept."

"Gee, Alfred, I don't know. I was just lookin' for a friend from the show. We usually grab somethin' to eat and do stuff . . . you know . . . he's showin' me around."

"I'm sure that is quite edifying, Master Tony. But Mr. Eden would be *quite* disappointed if you were unable to join him. Won't you reconsider? He would be most appreciative."

"Well, okay, I guess. But let me at least try and find Zen. He'll be looking for me. Wait right here. I'll be right back."

Tony couldn't believe his bad luck. He and Zen always got stoned after work and went to all sorts of cool bars and coffeehouses and clubs—places Tony would never have found himself or, in some cases, had the balls to go into. He liked Dallas Eden okay, and he appreciated the job he had given him last summer, but all he did was talk about a bunch of people in Hollywood who Tony had never even heard of. Most of them were dead. If he had wanted to suck up to Dallas Eden, Tony could have called when he had gotten to New York. He *had* the number.

As it turned out, the evening wasn't half bad. They ate in the most amazing restaurant Tony had ever been in—very modern, on three levels, with so much glass and so many mirrors that Tony was surprised people didn't walk into the walls. Mr. Eden seemed to know everybody there, and he always introduced Tony as "my friend Tony Alexamenos, currently starring in *Hair* at the Biltmore Theater." *Starring*, he said, as if he were Jim Rado or Gerry Ragni. Tony was embarrassed at first, but he got used to it pretty quick. It felt good. And Dallas Eden never made a move on him the whole time, even in the backseat of the Cadillac

Fleetwood when he drove him home at close to three o'clock in the morning.

CONNECTICUT SPENT MOST OF HIS TIME in the lab at Columbia. He had hired a lab assistant, Joe, a senior who planned to attend Harvard medical school, and set about trying to recreate his experiments with *Gluttonous venomous* so he could test a punishment–reward system of behavior modification in the sexually passive male.

"That will be my *real* achievement," Connecticut said with an enthusiasm Tony found troubling. "That will win me the Nobel!"

Although Connecticut would never say so himself, his work had, scientifically, logically, established homosexuality as a natural biological response to internalized warnings of overpopulation, if only in some overgrown guinea pigs. He refused numerous invitations to address interested gay groups, saying only that his results could not be applied to the human condition with any certainty. But Tony was coming to the realization that, despite his findings, despite the intellectual and professional support his work received, Connecticut was still deeply disturbed by his own homosexuality.

Tony had been pestering Connecticut to let him sit in on one of his classes since the beginning of the semester. Since he didn't go to the theater until late in the afternoon, it would be no problem for him to get up to Columbia on even the shortest notice. Eventually, Connecticut agreed to Tony's request in principle, but he always had a reason why he couldn't attend on any given day. He was giving a test. He was showing a film. Or the students were taking a field trip or making presentations.

"What's the big deal, Tony? You've been to college. You know what it's like. I stand up in front of the room and talk, the students listen. Somebody belches; someone usually falls asleep."

"I just want to see *you* teach. I want to see the part of your life I don't get to see at home."

"I'm not a terribly interesting lecturer."

"I'll hang on every word."

"Don't get smart."

"I wasn't being smart. I meant it."

Connecticut's reluctance stemmed from his belief that it was best if the two parts of his life never intersected. Sometimes he knew he was being paranoid. As Tony frequently pointed out, neither of them had a lavender *Q* tattooed on their foreheads. And he knew several straight faculty members, even one who was married, who were sleeping with coeds. But the thought of having his relationship with Tony revealed filled him with a kind of despair he had never felt before. Tony was always edging their relationship further and further into some sort of openness Connecticut didn't want and couldn't really understand. This insistence on sitting in on one of his classes was just the most recent example.

"All right. You can come to class next Wednesday. But you have to get there before I do and find a seat at the *back* of the room."

"Okay."

"Don't talk to anybody else; don't ask me any questions; and when class is over, leave with the rest of the students. Don't hang around waiting for me. Meet me at Tom's Diner. But I'm warning you, you're going to be sorry you asked to do this."

"How come?" Tony asked.

"The class is about panic and stress. I talk about behavior patterns in stressful situations—accidents, disasters, you know. I show some pretty gruesome slides. Burned people. Dead bodies stacked like cordwood. At Sanctuary, I had two students throw up, and one girl actually fainted."

"Sounds kind of gruesome."

"It is, but it's necessary. The students need to have some conception of the horror of a fire—any panic situation, really—if they're going to understand the behavioral factors that go with it."

Despite Connecticut's admonition about arriving early, Tony showed up five minutes into the lecture. He had missed his train at Christopher Street because at the last minute he decided he needed to be stoned. He saw Connecticut look up with a poker face when the back door squeaked open, and some heads turned instinctively at the noise. The morbid slide show had yet to begin. The room was crowded and the only available seat was in the center of a row, four places in from the aisle. Tony decided to lean up against the windowsill, as several others were already doing, rather than trip over eight feet, two purses, and a gym bag just to reach the seat. He knew Connecticut would be really mad if he caused a commotion, on top of arriving late.

As he prepared to make his transition into the slide show, Connecticut seemed a little nervous. He lost his train of thought briefly once, and his voice quavered uncharacteristically.

"In the past century, fire has claimed the lives of more than one hundred people on seventeen different occasions we can document. Fires in theaters, department stores, nightclubs, churches, and circuses. Fires aboard ship." Connecticut shut off the lights and turned on the slide projector. The first slide showed maybe a dozen corpses jammed against an emergency door. Some of the girls in the room shrieked and shielded their faces with notebooks.

"In Boston, on November 28, 1942, four hundred ninety-two people died when flames swept through the Cocoanut Grove nightclub. Hundreds of bodies were found piled against two doors that could have been used as means of escape. In one instance, panic-stricken revelers knocked a revolving door off its axis, jamming it and eliminating an important avenue of escape. In another part of the club, a door that could have led to safety was hung so that it opened inward, against the crush of people trying to escape. The door jammed, and the bodies just piled up on one another, six and ten deep, and more." Connecticut clicked the slide projector control in rapid succession, each time casting another grim image on the screen.

Most of the students sat transfixed. Some looked away or closed their eyes. A few of the boys smirked or chuckled nervously. Tony thought he heard the words "Crispy Critters." The slides continued—sooty, smudged, black-and-white images: the inside of a blackened movie theater in which the struggle to escape was so strong that whole rows of seats were peeled back like the lids on sardine cans; otherwise unmarked bodies slumped over a table or back in a chair, cocktail glasses still in hand, the victims of poisonous, superheated gas that snuffed out their lives almost instantly; stacks of men's and women's shoes that had been stripped off as their owners were trampled by the same people they had been dancing among only minutes earlier.

"The same thing happens every time fire strikes a public gathering. A conflagration at the Ringling Brothers circus in Hartford, Connecticut, took one hundred sixty-eight lives on July 6, 1944. In Natchez, Mississippi, one hundred ninety-eight died in a dance hall fire on April 23, 1940. Recently, three hundred twenty-two died in a Brussels department store inferno; three hundred twenty-two people who had gone shopping and found themselves in hell. In these seventeen fires, four thousand, six hundred eighty-two people died. That figure could change today, tomorrow, next week; anytime a fire strikes a crowded building. And the next time, the victim could be you."

The screen went black and Connecticut remained dramatically silent. When the lights went up, the class heaved a collective sigh of relief. Girls fanned themselves with their notebooks; one dabbed at her eyes with a handkerchief.

"I know what you're thinking right now," Connecticut began again. "'I'll get out alive. I'll keep my head. I won't panic. I'm too smart for that. If I see a lot of people trying to get out one door, I'll look for another way out. I always check the fire exits when I go into a movie theater. I'll survive.' Well, good luck. Your chances are only as good as the next guy's, and if he panics, you could be dead. It's something you have very little control over."

Connecticut paced the width of the room and halfway up one side, letting the thought sink in. The room was utterly silent. No coughs. No shifting in seats. Not even the flutter of a loose-leaf page. He took up the lecture again.

"Most of these people died needlessly. They died because they panicked or because those around them did. An orderly evacuation of the Cocoanut Grove could have saved hundreds of lives—not every victim, certainly, but many of them. But it's wrong—and pointless—to blame the dead. There was just too much fear, too much anxiety for them to handle. They behaved like a pack of wild animals, like the animals we were in prehistory and still are today, beneath our thin veneer of civilization. In a life-threatening situation, it takes a great deal of self-confidence, self-assurance, to be able to resist the herd mentality. Most people, faced with such a situation, will take the path of least resistance. They will do what everyone else is doing, and in all likelihood they will die.

"There's another phenomenon you should know about. When people are faced with a panic situation and are forced to leave a building, they most often attempt to leave by the same door they came in, regardless of whether that appears to be the best way out under the circumstances. People are creatures of habit, and it's very difficult for them to change their behavior patterns. They are not willing to experiment, to try new things. In a panic situation that's not such a good idea. 'Where does that other exit go?' they ask. 'Does it really lead outside? Or just to the basement? What if it's locked and I've wasted precious time? No, I think I'd better leave by the front door.' Even if the dead are stacked ten deep.

"In closing, I have two words for you: save yourself. In a panic situation—a fire, a plane crash—if you want to live, take responsibility for your own life. If you wait for a friend, even a loved one, if you go back to look for them, if you try to be a hero, you will most likely die. It is better to be alive and alone than dead in the embrace of your lover's corpse. Remember: save yourself."

A bell indicating the end of class rang, and the students slammed their notebooks shut and moved in a pack toward the door more eagerly than usual, trying to shake off the chill horror of the lecture. Connecticut shouted above the shoving and shuffling, "You should be finishing up Salk's *Survival of the Wisest* and starting Selye's *Stress Without Distress* if you want to be prepared for next week's exam."

As the others left, Tony hung back. A large number of students were still inside the classroom, trying to make their way out through the congested doorway. Connecticut, putting his notes into his briefcase, looked up and saw Tony. He nodded toward the back door and mouthed a word Tony could not make out. After a number of repetitions, Connecticut got up, erased part of the blackboard, and wrote the word *diner*. Tony remembered their agreement and walked toward the back door mouthing "Okay" to Connecticut, who wouldn't look at him.

It bothered Tony that Connecticut was reluctant to be seen with him in public. Early on, when Tony showed up at Connecticut's office unannounced, he would lock the door behind him and lick the back of Connecticut's neck or bite him on an ear. Connecticut would try to resist, but eventually he would give in and start making out with Tony. But at the slightest noise—voices in the hall, a shout from a Frisbee-playing student just outside the window—Connecticut would freak out and pull away, wiping his mouth with the back of his hand to remove the evidence of their saliva swap. The ring of the telephone made him jump out of his skin. After such an interruption, Connecticut would straighten his tie and smooth his hair, unlock the door, and open it, to prevent a recurrence.

If they ever ran into another faculty member together, Tony was forbidden to use Connecticut's first name, for fear it would betray their intimacy. Likewise, Connecticut felt awkward calling Tony by his first name on such occasions. In class he always addressed students by their surnames, so he introduced Tony to straight friends or colleagues as "Alexamenos, here," presenting him as Tony only if the third party was also gay. It became a signal between them, letting Tony know just how relaxed he could be or how much formality was required. Even in private conversations, Connecticut never called anyone gay, instead saying they were "a member of the committee," "a member of the royal family," or "a friend of Dorothy." He had no trouble, however, calling someone he disliked "a fag."

Tony waited nearly thirty minutes before Connecticut showed up at the diner. He'd had to order a Coke and fries to justify occupying a table.

"Sorry, I stopped in to the lab after class and lost track of time," Connecticut said. "Is that what you're eating for lunch? French fries?"

"I've got the munchies."

Connecticut frowned. He didn't like to be reminded of Tony's recreational drug use.

"Besides, I had to order *something*."

"The lecture didn't spoil your appetite?"

"No, it was kind of interesting. Maybe a little depressing. I learned some stuff, though. You're a good teacher."

"I was nervous as hell."

"Why? Haven't you given that lecture before lots of times?"

"You made me nervous."

"Me, why?"

"Well, number one, you were late."

"I'm sorry."

"And I've never given a lecture with my . . . *boyfriend* . . . in class."

"Well, it wasn't that hard, was it?" Tony liked the idea that Connecticut called him his *boyfriend*. "And I didn't make a complete idiot out of myself like you thought."

"I never said you'd make an idiot out of yourself."

"I know, but you thought it."

"Tony, can we give it a break, please? I don't think you're an idiot."

"Okay."

"But I would have preferred it if you had shown up on time as I asked."

TONY SAW CONNECTICUT somewhat more frequently at the end of fall semester, when the students—including Connecticut's assistant, Joe—went home for the holidays. Connecticut still spent a lot of time in the lab, but with no students to teach and no office hours to keep, he had more spare time than usual. Instead of going to the lab first thing in the morning, he slept in with Tony and they would go out for a late breakfast, visit the tourist spots Connecticut had not yet seen, and do their holiday shopping. Connecticut spent a fortune on Hanukkah presents for his parents in tiny specialty book and music stores, gourmet food shops, an art gallery, and a travel agency, where he bought them a week-long cruise in the Caribbean. Tony bought nothing for his father and couldn't figure out what to send Pick in Vietnam. When Connecticut mentioned that the deadline for guaranteeing the arrival of packages in the war zone by Christmas had passed, Tony gave up looking. The only gift left for him to buy was Connecticut's.

Connecticut had on several occasions mentioned that he wanted to have a gold fountain pen to sign the doctoral dissertations of his Ph.D. candidates. Tony visited every office supplier, secondhand store, and gift shop in lower Manhattan before he found exactly what he wanted in the window of an antique shop in the Village. He had never seen another pen like it. It was maybe thirty or forty years old, but it had never been used and was still in its original blue satin–lined box. The barrel of the pen was etched vertically and horizontally so that it looked as if its surface was made of tiny gold bricks, and the pocket clip was an elongated S shape, ending with a miniature oak leaf cluster. The price, handwritten on a tiny white tag, was two hundred dollars, considerably more than Tony could afford.

The shop owner, a tall, gray-haired man who Tony figured was at least sixty, was cleaning the crowded shelves with a feather duster when he walked in. He asked if there was something he wanted and Tony described the pen.

"It's a gift," Tony said. "For a friend."

"A very *lucky* friend, indeed. You've made an excellent choice. I was fortunate enough to find it at an estate sale in New Hope."

Tony nodded and smiled, not having the faintest idea what or where New Hope was. The man went to the window, retrieved the pen, and offered it to Tony with both hands.

"Is that the right price?" Tony asked. "I mean, it wouldn't happen to be on sale, would it?"

"I'm afraid not. That's twenty-four-carat gold, young man. It's quite a bargain as is, one of the better buys in the shop today." The man closed the box and laid it on the countertop.

"That's really more than I had to spend."

"And how much would that be?"

Tony hesitated, calculating what he might be able to afford. "Fifty . . ."

"I'm sorry . . ."

"Maybe seventy-five dollars."

The bell above the door jangled and two women walked in. The man moved closer to Tony and turned so that his back was to the women.

"We *might* be able to work out a deal that would make it significantly more affordable," he said in a whisper.

"Really? What's that?"

The man motioned for Tony to follow him into a small room behind the counter. When he got there, the man put his arm around Tony's shoulder and whispered into his ear. Tony jumped back.

"I don't think so. Thanks."

Tony left the store and walked the streets of the Village, SoHo, and Little Italy for two hours, debating with himself, changing his mind with each block he walked. He knew he wanted to give the pen to Connecticut. It was really an exceptional thing. But he just couldn't imagine doing what the man wanted. Not with him. It was disgusting. But the pen was gorgeous. Twenty-four-carat gold. Connecticut would love it. And no one would ever know what he had done to get it. He'd never see the old geezer again. He made his way slowly back toward the store. He stood across the street and watched several people walk in and out. When he thought it was empty, he took a deep breath and went in.

"Yes? Can I help you?" the shopkeeper said, smiling in a way that made Tony think he was making a *big* mistake.

"I . . . want the pen."

"I see."

"I . . . I've . . ."

"I understand. You've come . . . to make a *deposit,* have you?"

Tony looked at him blankly.

"Never mind. It was a little joke. I'll be with you in a moment."

The shopkeeper walked over to the door, locked it, and turned around the hanging sign so the CLOSED side faced the street.

ON THE SATURDAY before Christmas, Connecticut surprised Tony with tickets to the Radio City Christmas matinee and dinner at a well-known steak house uptown. It was definitely the best meal they had together since coming to New York.

"Merry Christmas, Connecticut," Tony said, holding his wineglass aloft.

"Merry Christmas, Tony." They clinked glasses.

"And Happy Hanukkah!"

"Actually, Tony, there's something I've been meaning to tell you. It's kind of about Hanukkah."

"Uh-huh? What?"

"I thought that when we got home tonight, we could celebrate our own little Christmas. You know, open our gifts and all. I have some wonderful cognac that Joe gave me, and we could open it."

Tony was jealous of Joe, who got to spend far more time with Connecticut than he ever did. Connecticut wouldn't describe him to Tony, except to say that he was probably the best graduate assistant he had ever had. Tony had finally seen him a month ago when he had shown up at Connecticut's office early for lunch and walked in on the two of them working at a small, portable chalkboard Connecticut had set up near the window. Connecticut shot Tony one of his famous "not here, not now" looks, so he waited out in the hall. Joe was okay-looking, if you liked Jiminy Cricket. His face was oval and he had normal features, but he didn't have any cheekbones and it looked like his mouth, nose, and eyes had been embroidered onto a stuffed sock. He'd look better if he let his hair grow—it was probably not a quarter of an inch long—and got braces.

"Joe gave you a Christmas present? What did you give him?"

"Nothing, but that's not the point. About tonight . . ."

"Why not wait until the real Christmas? It's only five more days."

Connecticut took another sip of wine and set the glass down. He rested his forearms on the table and leaned forward so he could whisper.

"Tony . . . this is so hard for me to say. I know this is going to hurt you, which I guess is why I've waited so long to do it, but I've decided to go back to Florida—to my parents' place—for the holidays. For Hanukkah."

"Oh. I thought . . ."

"I'm sorry. I would have offered to buy you a ticket so you could celebrate Christmas with your father, but I know there's no love lost between the two of you. It won't be so bad. You'll have the whole apartment to yourself so you can play your music all you want. And don't you have some friends from the show you can spend the holidays with? They all seem like people who wouldn't have much use for families, either."

Tony was staring out into the dining room, decorated with wreaths tied up with red velvet ribbon, with tall white candles on each table, nestled in a small wreath of holly and red berries. It looked like they were the only gay couple there. Every other table had a mother, father, and kids—girls dressed in burgundy or forest green velvet dresses with lace collars and cuffs, little boys in suits.

"Tony?"

"I'm all right. Just thinking. It's okay, go ahead. I never did like Christmas that much anyway, not after my mom died. Sometimes we managed to get over to Tampa to visit my aunts and uncles and cousins, and that was okay. But I'm used to spending Christmas alone."

Tony remembered the Christmas Eve he realized there weren't going to be any presents at the Alexamenos home if he didn't do something about it. It was a little more than a year after his mother died and Tony was eleven. With his father dead drunk in his bedroom, he sneaked in and stole ten dollars from his top dresser drawer, opening and closing it carefully so it wouldn't squeak. He got on his bicycle and pedaled furiously all the way to Sugar Mill Beach with visions of model cars dancing in his head. He would go straight to the Sugar Mill Hobby Shop, buy two car kits and two cans of spray paint, get some homemade fudge on the boardwalk, and still have money left over. It was nearly dark as he approached town, but still warm, the warmest Christmas in years, the radio said. As he got closer, the city seemed deserted—really deserted, like in the movie *On the Beach,* where everybody died from an atomic bomb. As he passed from the residential section of Tropicana Boulevard to the business district, he noticed signs in the windows saying things like "Merry Christmas," and "Closing Early on Christmas Eve," and in Wolf Brothers, the clothing store owned by the Jewish people, "Happy Holidays One and All." Everything had been closed and locked since 5 P.M., and here it was going on six-thirty. Tony continued on to the hobby shop just to be sure, but it was closed, too. A cardboard clock in the window said "Back at" and its hands pointed at the nine and the twelve. "Wednesday" was written on a piece of paper taped to its face. Tony pedaled home slowly. The house was dark when he arrived so he watched TV for a couple of hours and went to bed.

"So when exactly is it that you're leaving?"

"Monday morning, nine-thirty-five."

"You're leaving on Monday? Christ, Connecticut, Christmas isn't until Friday. Why do you have to leave so soon?"

"But Hanukkah begins on *Wednesday*. I've told you how that works. Besides, we've had a wonderful night together, haven't we? Radio City. The finest steaks in town. And we still have our gifts to open. That'll be fun. And I'll build a fire in the bedroom. Won't that be romantic?"

Tony was in no mood for romance. He barely said a word on the ride downtown, just watched all the people Christmas shopping. Some were arm-in-arm; some were holding hands. He was jealous of each and every one of them.

When they got home, Connecticut poured them each a snifter of cognac and laid in a fire. Connecticut went into the closet and retrieved a gift, roughly the same size and shape as a bread box. It was professionally wrapped in gold foil with a big red ribbon and a stuffed felt Santa

Claus with pipe cleaner arms and legs dangling from a gold string. Tony wanted to cry. At the last minute, he had realized he didn't have any wrapping paper and was broke, so he had wrapped Connecticut's present in three tiny scraps of wrapping paper he had found in a dressing room at the theater. They weren't soiled or wrinkled, and they were carefully, tightly folded and taped; but they were still three different kinds of paper.

"Oh, Connecticut, it's beautiful!"

"Go ahead. Open it."

"No, you go ahead and open yours first. I'm sorry about the wrapping, but . . ."

"The wrapping's fine. It looks kind of like a quilt. You did a great job with it. And it was clever of you to make that red rubber band into a bow. Very clever."

Connecticut carefully tore the paper at one end and slid the leather box out into his hand. He looked up at Tony with a confused expression, but smiled. He opened it. For a while, he said nothing. Tony bounced up and down where he sat.

"Tony this is gorgeous, but it's much too extravagant. I can't take this. You've got to get your money back."

"I can't. . . . I can't do that. Besides, it's what you said you always wanted—a gold pen to sign your students' reports with."

"Dissertations."

"What?"

"They're called dissertations."

"Whatever they are. You told me once that's what you wanted. A really, really nice pen."

"We'll talk about this later. Go on, open yours."

Tony tore into the package, revealing a sturdy two-tone blue box.

"A radio?"

"A *clock* radio. An AM/FM clock radio. *Digital.* It's the latest thing. Now I won't have to reset my clock every morning and bring it into your bedroom. Isn't that great?"

"A clock radio?"

"That's right. A clock radio of your very own. Merry Christmas." Connecticut leaned over and kissed Tony on the cheek.

"Thanks," Tony said dully. "A clock radio."

TONY PICKED UP CONNECTICUT at the airport when he returned from Florida on January second. It was a major big deal for Connecticut to let him drive the Cutlass. Connecticut didn't look like he had spent any time in the sun, but he seemed to be in a better mood. He brought home a big pile of gifts from his parents: a dozen identical white shirts, six pairs of trousers, three pairs of cordovan wing tips, enough socks to last a month, and six three-packs of Jockey briefs, all packed in two new pieces of Samsonite luggage.

"You're twenty-six years old and your parents are still buying you underwear? Jeez."

"They know I don't like shopping for clothes, especially underwear. That's too personal for me. I always think the guy at the register is thinking about how I'll look in them. It gives me the creeps."

"Didn't they give you any fun stuff?"

"Oh, sure. They must have given me a dozen books. They were too cumbersome to carry on the plane, so they're shipping them to me later in the week."

"That's it? Books?"

"They also gave me a toaster oven, a coffee maker, and a hot plate, for the office, so Joe and I won't have to spend so much time away from the lab for meals. They're coming with the books."

"Gee, we could use a toaster oven"

"Well, this one's for the office, Tony."

The next morning, when Tony was relatively certain the apartment building was not in immediate danger of spontaneous combustion, he got out of his bed, naked, hopped across the cold wood floors, and crawled in next to Connecticut, who groaned and shifted slightly but otherwise paid no attention to him. Tony fell asleep and when he awoke, Connecticut was out of bed and getting dressed.

"Where are you going?"

"I have to go down to my office for a little while."

"I thought school was closed until the end of the month. I thought we'd have some time to do stuff together. You said I could pick a show to see."

"I did, and we will, I promise. But some animal rights activists in Wisconsin broke into my breeder's lab, stole some animals, and destroyed a good part of the heating system. They got away with about twenty-five of my roothogs, and the breeder has had to store the remaining seventy-five at a veterinarian's office. I wasn't expecting to get them for a couple of weeks, but I authorized a shipment from home, and they could arrive as early as today. I have to go into the lab and get ready for them. I called Joe from Florida, too, and . . ."

"Let me guess, he's coming back to help you. You know, I would have been glad to help you. I mean, what do you have to do, make some new cages or something? How hard could that be? I got an A in metal shop in high school—pretty impressive for a gay guy. And I've worked on a lot of expensive cars."

"We're not building cages; we are setting up a whole new residential environment. These are scientific projects; everything has got to be uniform, precise. You're just not trained or experienced for something like this."

Connecticut drew a perfect Windsor knot up to his Adam's apple. "I may be home late tonight, so you'd better just plan on eating dinner alone."

"I'll wait for you."

"That's okay. Joe and I will order out. Chinese or pizza. I couldn't last until eight or nine without eating. And you shouldn't have to either."

Connecticut shrugged himself into his tweed coat, walked over to the bed and kissed Tony on the mouth, lips together. "You go back to sleep. I'll turn up the thermostat a little so it won't be so cold when you get up. But remember to turn it down after you've showered and dressed."

"Okay. Bye. I love you," Tony said. He could hear Connecticut taking the stairs two at a time, and then the big, wooden door slammed downstairs, shaking windows all the way to the top floor. Pulling the covers over his head, he wished that he were smarter, smart enough to understand Connecticut's work. He'd work for him for free during the day. It would be worth it just to be able to spend more time together. He was just drifting off when he heard the outside door open and close, followed by big, thumping footsteps ascending the stairs and the sound of the key in the door. Maybe Connecticut had changed his mind, gotten horny, and decided to come back.

"Tony!" Connecticut called from the foyer. "Where did we park my car last night after we got back from the airport?"

Tony threw back the covers. "What?"

"The car. The car. Did you move my car?" Connecticut entered the bedroom. His face was flushed and he threw his gloves to the floor. "My car is gone. Gone! You brought up the last of the luggage, and you had the keys. I thought maybe you saw a better parking place, under a streetlamp or something."

"I didn't move it, Connecticut"

"Well, if *you* didn't move it and *I* didn't move it, then who the hell *did* move it?" Connecticut was pacing the room, his big black galoshes leaving lumps of snow on the hardwood floor. "You did *lock* it, didn't you? Christ, you *did* lock it?"

"I did. I'm positive." Tony got out of bed and slipped into his jeans and a flannel shirt that was faintly ripe from four or five days' wear.

"I parked it on Barrow, didn't I?" Connecticut asked.

"I don't remember. I guess so. Yeah."

"It's not where I left it. I could have sworn I parked it on Barrow. Grove was completely full. I know I tried that. I always do. I remember parking it, getting out, crossing Hudson. . . . Maybe I parked on *Christopher.* Come on, put on your boots and coat and help me look."

They scoured the neighborhood for two hours, Connecticut clutching his briefcase the entire time, as if rigor mortis had set in to his right hand. They walked every block from West Tenth Street to Spring, from Hudson to the West Side Highway, with not a glimpse of the Cutlass, not even an empty parking place where it might have been. At home again, Connecticut called the police. When he told the investigating officer the car was registered in Florida, where he used to live, the cop told him to start shopping for a replacement vehicle.

"Not being from the city, you'd have no way of knowing this," the officer said, trying to sound at least somewhat sympathetic, "but chances are your car has already been stripped, chopped, and charred. We'll probably find the chassis in one of the boroughs in the next couple of days, and if we're lucky we'll be able to read the VIN. If that happens, we'll give you a call. In the meantime, you should call my uncle in Mattapan; he's got a lot full of good used cars."

Connecticut was furious and hung up. How dare this guy use his misfortune to help sell his uncle's used cars? Besides, he didn't want to buy another car—not after this little episode. But how was he going to get to work? Not just today, but every day. He came in and left at irregular hours; he needed the flexibility of his own vehicle. Taking a cab every day was out of the question. It would cost a fortune.

"Goddamnit, I'm going to have to ride that filthy subway," he said, pounding a fist against the table.

"Take it easy, Connecticut, I ride it all the time," Tony said. "It's great for people watching, and you actually get where you're going a lot faster than in a car or cab. Trust me. I know my way around real good, and I'll teach you. It'll be fun."

But it was not fun. The cold and the snow were nearing record levels, with a good two months of winter to go. Just as Connecticut was successfully taking to the streets, an arctic air mass very nearly brought the city to a standstill with five days of crippling subzero temperatures, an apparently limitless variety of frozen precipitation, and gale-force winds. Most cars, buses, and cabs wouldn't start. Pedestrians courted frostbite on trips longer than a couple of blocks. And a young man intent on suicide leaped from the eighty-sixth floor of the Empire State Building only to be blown backward, landing on the ledge of the eighty-fifth floor. He crawled to safety through the window of a radio station while a newscaster looked on dumbfounded.

To Connecticut's considerable dismay, their apartment, which had proved to be somewhat drafty in late fall, was barely tolerable in the deep freeze unless all three fireplaces were burning. It gave him yet another reason to spend as much time as possible at his laboratory.

"I hate this city," Connecticut said one night as he meticulously inspected the tip of his nose for cell damage. "I don't understand how people can live like this. But they go on about their business as if they don't notice the weather at all. It's fascinating, really. I'd study them, but I couldn't stand to do the research."

Barely had the weather begun to moderate than a garbage strike began—an ugly disagreement about overtime, safety, and working conditions.

"So they work on garbage trucks, so what?" Connecticut said, angrily swatting the table with the *Times*. "What do they want to do, drive around and put the trash in the trunks of their Coupe DeVilles?"

Tony didn't want to argue. He knew by now that Connecticut had immediate, strong reactions to people or situations he didn't like, and he almost never changed his mind or varied his point of view. Plus, he seemed to be getting angrier and more short-tempered by the day. When Tony didn't say anything, Connecticut sighed loudly. He wanted some discussion. "Really, what do they expect? You're a fireman; you put out fires. You don't hear them complaining about having to enter burning buildings. You're a garbage man; you pick up garbage. By definition. How can you improve the working conditions?"

"Maybe some of the trucks are old or unsafe," Tony said. "It says here that some poor fucker had both legs cut off in a freak accident last year during a blizzard. Don't you think that's reason enough to at least think about safety?"

Connecticut sighed again and tossed the paper into the trash can. "I don't know, Tony. I just feel like everyone's out for a free ride these days."

The effects of the sanitation strike were not noticeable on the first day, or the second. But by the end of the first week, the garbage had become more than an issue. It had become a presence. Limp piles of refuse blossomed next to stoops. Seafood restaurants became the bane of their neighborhoods. In the garment district, cardboard cartons, shirt liners, plastic bags, and hangers were strewn in the streets as if in the bargain basement of a department store. By the end of the second week it became impossible to walk any distance in even the best residential neighborhoods without stepping on coffee grounds, eggshells, or wilted salad greens, in addition to the ubiquitous gifts from the canine population. Early on, the newspapers had been optimistic: "NEGOTIATORS NEAR SETTLEMENT," read the *New York Times*. "OFFICIALS ESTIMATE THREE-DAY CLEANUP." But optimism, too, was soon buried in the fetid mess.

The city took on an apocalyptic countenance. The rich, having more to throw away, suffered most, but they did in fact put their trash in the back of *their* Coupe DeVilles (and Lincolns and Imperials) and had their drivers haul it to New Jersey. Despite such gestures, trash was piled as high as the first-floor windows of many brownstones, and basement dwellers sought higher ground or lived in fear of imminent suffocation. In fact, a forty-five-year-old bum by the name of Nat Gilmore smothered beneath a pile of rubbish that collapsed on him as he slept on a steam grate. All that was visible of him were his battered red Converse high-tops with holes in their soles. Mayor Lindsay was outraged and blamed the strikers for "this insult to human dignity, this triumph of greed." But the strikers successfully turned the tables on him. Two days before the strike finally ended, the *Daily News* ran an editorial cartoon that showed two shoes, one labeled Hizzoner, sticking out of a pile of refuse while gleeful, unionized Munchkins danced in circles around him. The caption read: "He's not only merely dead, he's really most sincerely dead."

# 14

SUNDAY WAS THE ONLY DAY Connecticut slept late. He usually didn't go to the lab until after brunch. Instead he stayed home, reading a new text and listening to classical music. If the weather was good, he'd drag Tony out of bed at ten—early for Tony since he'd done a show the night before—and they would walk around the Village until they found a restaurant that served complimentary mimosas with brunch. Connecticut always did like the idea of getting something for free.

The weather on a particular Sunday in late January offered little incentive to get out of bed, let alone leave the house. It was warm enough, to be sure, and Connecticut was grateful for that. But the warmth brought with it fog and the smell of defrosting dog deposits. Brackish puddles were occasionally brightened by an errant strand of tinsel, still in evidence due to the garbage strike. It was in no way a refreshing or invigorating day. It was, in fact, the kind of day on which one would leave the house in a faux varsity letter jacket and sweater only to return home smelling like a large, damp, dirty sheepdog. Connecticut decided brunch would be served at home. He had become a competent cook, considering he had never done more than put milk on his cereal until five months ago. In a secondhand bookstore, he had purchased a cookbook of basic American cuisine and followed the recipes as if they were scientific equations. The result was flawless, if unimaginative, meals with representatives of the four major food groups. This day he made French toast with raisin bread—a daring departure from the usual Wonderbread—Canadian bacon, and a fruit cup of orange and grapefruit sections he bought in a glass jar at the corner market. The jar contained one lonely maraschino cherry, which he placed on top of Tony's portion.

"You really don't need all this beauty rest, Tony," he said, carrying the precariously overladen tray into the bedroom, where Tony had been sleeping since six-thirty. "If you get any more beautiful, I'd have to give serious consideration to entering you in the Miss America Pageant."

"I'm sure I'd give them a talent performance they'd never forget," Tony said, pulling aside the sheet and blanket to reveal his naked body.

"Sex sex sex. Is that all you think about?"

"No, the rest of the time I think about you you you." He leaned over to give Connecticut a kiss.

"Yikes, watch out! You'll tip over the tray."

Tony sat back and waited for Connecticut to put the tray over his legs.

"Pull up the blanket, Tony."

"Why? This way if I spill the maple syrup, you can lick it off."

"I swear, you are the horniest little boy I have ever met. Now, do as you're told or you'll go hungry this morning, and I'll have to give you a good spanking on your bare bottom."

"Promises, promises."

Tony pulled the covers up and Connecticut placed the tray over his legs.

"I think I have fleas or something, Connecticut. I can't stop scratching. Can people get fleas?"

"What?" Connecticut had been about to take a sip of coffee, but his arm froze midway to his lips.

"My crotch is really itchy. Especially right at the roots of my hair . . . you know, down there." Tony said. "Move the tray and I'll show you how red it is."

"Jesus Christ, Tony," Connecticut said, leaping out of bed and flailing at his bathrobe, as if trying to brush off an ember from a burning cigarette. "You've got crabs! What the hell have you been doing?"

"What do you mean, doing?"

"Sexually. What have you been doing sexually?"

"Oh, I've been masturbating a little. You know me."

"Tony, you don't get crabs from masturbating; you get them from having sex with someone who has them. I can't believe you don't know about crabs." Connecticut had never had crabs himself, but he considered knowledge of them basic personal hygiene.

"You mean I got them from you?" Tony lifted the breakfast tray and kicked the blanket and sheets to the footboard. He got out of bed, using the tray to at least partially camouflage his nakedness. He was flushed red with embarrassment.

"You most emphatically did not get them from me. You get them from low-life hustlers or at places like the baths." Connecticut moved theatrically out of Tony's way as he put the tray on the desk. "And don't spill the goddamned Bloody Marys on my papers."

"Well, I don't know any hustlers, and I've never been to the baths." But in that instant Tony realized exactly where he had picked up the horrid little fuckers.

"There's no other way to get them, Tony. You don't get them from toilet seats."

"What are they, anyway?" He needed to scratch, bad, but he was too embarrassed.

Connecticut lit a cigarette and paced around the room like an interrogator in a holding cell. He ripped open the drapes, letting the anemic sun in. "They're bugs, Tony. Lice. Vermin," he said. "They live on people who don't bathe or wash their clothes regularly." He stubbed out his barely smoked cigarette and stood by the window, looking down into the street. "And if you've brought them into this house, into our bed, I . . . I don't believe this is happening to me."

"Well, what's the big deal? I'm not going to die, am I?" He reached down to the floor to pick up his previous day's undershorts and slipped into them. Under the guise of adjusting himself, he scratched like hell.

"Tony, if you have them, I have them. The sheets are probably full of them. They jump right off one person and onto another." He had turned his back to the window and the fuzzy sunlight created an aura around him. "Which, of course, is how *you* got them. Who have you been having sex with other than me and your right hand."

"Nobody, Connecticut. Honest." He returned to the bed because Connecticut had been giving him such a wide berth each time he passed that he felt like a leper.

Connecticut wasn't sure whether he was more angry about the crabs or the infidelity, but given a choice of infidelity with crabs or without, he'd choose the latter in a heartbeat. "Goddamnit, Tony. These things don't just crawl up your legs and check in to the Crotch Hair Hilton. They are a sexually transmitted disease."

Tony sighed and slumped forward. He pulled his knees up and hugged them with his arms, resting his right cheek on his right kneecap. "Okay, there *was* one person. Zen Twigg—that's not his real name. He's in the show. He's a friend, and he's straight, or bi at least. He lives with a chick. We just sort of started to hang around with each other. We'd go out for coffee or drinks after the show. On our days off we'd go to the movies or something. I knew he lived with a woman, so I didn't expect him to do anything. One day we got stoned and then he started making out with me. I didn't really want to do it, but you know . . ."

"You can't rape the willing."

"Zen told me it was okay, that it's what's called recreational sex. He said people in California do it all the time. Everybody has a good time and nobody gets hurt."

"What a wonderful ethical construct. You act like a bitch in heat and you justify it by calling it 'recreational sex.' How very hip. How totally liberating." Connecticut was furious, as much at himself as at Tony. How could he have been so stupid as to think that a boy of Tony's age, with Tony's face and physique, to say nothing of his charisma, could live in New York, could be in the *theater* no less, and remain faithful to a stuffy, distracted professorial type, with a forty-five-year-old brain housed in a twenty-five-year-old body, with all the prejudices and suppositions that went along with it? Maybe that was why he had been reluctant to bring Tony with him. Maybe he knew all along that it was a no-win situation. Either way he'd lose him, to distance or to the differences in their lives.

"We just did it that one time," Tony volunteered.

"Where?"

"Where?"

"Where did you do it? Here? In my bed?"

"Yes."

"Damn it!" Connecticut grabbed what he could of the Sunday *Times* on the desk and threw it across the room. "How could you possibly do that to me? Do I mean that little to you that you screw your boyfriends in my bed?"

"Connecticut, please don't freak. It happened once. One man, one time. No boyfriends, plural. I liked Zen; I still like Zen. He just caught me off guard is all. One minute we're sitting around blowing a joint and the next he's got his hand on my crotch telling me how he's wanted to get in my pants from the first day he laid eyes on me. He's real smart and he's funny and I *like* him. But I don't love him like I love you. It just seemed . . . *okay*, you know? What harm could it do? I don't think about him all the time or anything, the way I do about you. I mean, it happened, and then it was over." Tony got out of bed, slipped on his jeans, and looked around the room for his boots. "I'm sorry. It won't happen again."

"Is he attractive?"

"Why? Is it okay for me to have sex with ugly people but not cute guys? I was stoned! I was horny! You know how oversexed I am. He means nothing to me—in that way. I was having sex with him. It felt good, but I wasn't feeling what I feel when I make love to you. It didn't *mean* anything to me. I've already forgotten about it."

"How many others have there been?"

"None. I told you. He was the first. And last."

"I'm supposed to believe that?"

"I've told you the truth about Zen. If there were others, don't you think I'd tell you?" Tony put on his coat and headed for the stairs.

"Where are you going?"

"I don't know. Maybe the park, maybe the theater. I just have to get out of here for a while."

"If you want to do something constructive, go to the drugstore and get two big bottles of A-200."

"A what?"

"A-200. It's what we need to get rid of these things. And while you're at it, take the bed linens, both beds, down to the laundromat and wash them twice in hot water with lots of bleach. And all your underwear. *And* mine. All of it. Hot water. Bleach. Twice."

"Connecticut, I'll be there all afternoon if I have to do that."

"Listen, Tony. I don't think you understand how gross this is. And disturbing. You've confessed to adultery and now you're complaining when I ask you to wash the filth out of our personal things? You got us into this, the least you can do is clean up after yourself. It's your moral responsibility. And don't think we won't discuss this when you get back."

But they did not discuss it when Tony returned with the sanitized laundry three hours later. Connecticut was gone—to the lab—and Tony was asleep by the time he got back. This pattern continued for six days. Connecticut was up at five-thirty and left the house at seven. He returned at 9 P.M. and was in bed asleep, or feigning sleep, by the time Tony got home from the theater anywhere between one and three. Tony never got up before eleven or twelve, and although there were a couple of occasions on which he woke up while Connecticut was showering or dressing, he said nothing.

Zen apologized for giving him crabs; he had felt the first symptoms himself the day after their liaison and was able to trace his case to a boy in *Jesus Christ Superstar*.

"What a tight-ass your boyfriend is," Zen said as they dressed after the show. "I mean, it's not like you gave him syphilis or anything."

"Not according to him."

"Look, if he's being such an asshole about it, why don't you come stay at my place for a couple of nights? That'll give him a wake-up call. We don't have to fuck around or anything, although I wouldn't mind, and my old lady *is* gone. I've got a date with the guy from J. C. day after tomorrow—he's clean now, too. I'm sure he'd be into a three-way . . . bring this thing full circle, if you know what I mean."

"Nah. I don't want to play games and get him even more pissed off than he is already. I love him, Zen. I really do. I just want things to go back to the way they used to be. I mean, I got myself into this mess by sleeping with you. I don't think moving in to your place is going to make things any better, even if we don't fuck around."

"You're too romantic, Tony. But it's cute."

Finally, the following Sunday, their waking paths crossed. Connecticut was up at eight and put on some coffee. Tony, who was still a little high from the night before, awoke and followed his nose to the kitchen in his undershorts.

"That's not fair, Tony. You can't go walking around the house like that and expect me not to notice."

Tony scratched himself. "Oops, sorry. Don't worry, those things haven't come back."

"No, I think we did a pretty good job of eradicating them. Coffee?"

"Uh-huh."

Neither one of them spoke until Tony finished his first cup of coffee.

"Tony, I'm sorry I got so out of control over this."

"It's my fault. All of it. I've learned a lesson the really hard way. I swear to God that I'll never cheat on you again. Ever. It's just that Zen somehow convinced me it wasn't wrong. He more or less propositioned me again this week. He wanted me to come stay with him for a while. He even said he could set up a three-way."

"This guy must be a real sex fiend."

"Not really," Tony said, putting down his coffee cup. "He sort of looks at it like exercise, like doing push-ups in a way."

"In a very odd way."

"You know that I love you more than anyone or anything in the world. I felt horrible when this happened. When I realized what I had done . . ."

"You mean when you got caught."

"I just wanted to die. I was so depressed, I had to do speed all week long, just so I could keep up with everyone else in the show."

"That's something I could have gone without hearing."

"I know, I know. You don't like it when I get high. But I had no choice. Everyone is running around and bouncing off the walls in the show."

"I guess we've both had a lot to think about this week. I know I was worth shit most of the time." Connecticut poured each of them another cup. "Listen, why don't we get cleaned up and go out for brunch? Some place really nice."

"Can we shower together?"

"Well, it's nine now, and most places stop serving at one or two. Yeah, I think we can make it if we're fast and keep focused on what it is we're doing."

A week without sex, without affection or intimacy of any kind, had left Tony scared, vulnerable . . . and *horny*. There had been times when he thought he would never again see Connecticut naked, let alone touch him, taste him. In the shower that morning, he made love to Connecticut like it was their first time. This whole thing had been his fault, and he prayed that he could make Connecticut see how much he loved him and vowed never to do *anything* in the future that might make him mad. He thought he would die if Connecticut ever left him.

CONNECTICUT ROLLED OVER on his right side, so his back was turned to Tony. They had had a great brunch at Café Parisian and then whiled away the remainder of the afternoon in book and antique stores. When they got home, Tony practically attacked him on the staircase. For the next several hours they had sex on the floor, the couch, his desk, and finally, his bed. Tony appeared to have learned a thing or two from this Zen character, even in only one session. And while the little tricks were pleasurable, they came as a surprise and Connecticut didn't like surprises. He hadn't really wanted to have sex, but Tony was practically rabid for it. He would have been happy to build a fire in the bedroom and just cuddle.

He had the impression that Tony considered each orgasm today had brought them closer, as if sperm was a salve to his broken heart. But it was not the case for him. He noticed it first in the shower. When they were joined, when Tony was fucking him wildly, his hair sopping wet, all he wanted to do was to force him out and shut his sphincter like a watertight door on a sinking ship. It wasn't that he wasn't attracted to Tony any longer—the best way to describe his attitude toward Tony's physical presence was "worshipful." But he couldn't get this Zen person—what the hell kind of a name was that, anyway?—out of his mind.

He didn't want to get hurt, but that seemed inevitable. Who was he kidding? How on earth did he expect Tony to remain faithful? He'd seen the way people looked at him in the streets, on the subway. Tony created little swirls and eddies as he walked through a crowd and people turned to look at him, even *with* that damn hair. Gay men walked into light poles and tripped on curbs. If the sidewalks were icy, at least one poor sucker would sprawl spread-eagled into the street every four or five blocks. It was embarrassing. But Tony seemed oblivious to it all.

Connecticut shifted onto his back, but he kept his head turned so he couldn't see Tony. At a diner last month, as he came back to the table from the men's room, he saw Tony giving the sexy Puerto Rican busboy a slip of paper. He was sure it was their telephone number, but when he asked, Tony said it was his director's number. Connecticut tried to believe that, but images of Tony and the Latin boy tussling in bed—sweat glistening on their tangled bodies, exclamations of ecstasy *en Español*—kept popping into his head.

No, this thing with Zen might very well have been the first, as Tony said, but it wouldn't be the last. Perhaps they could have made a go of it in Sugar Mill Beach, but Tony was just too good looking and there were just too many goddamned faggot vultures in New York.

But it wasn't just the gay lifestyle that was eating away at him, it was this city, a frozen, pleasureless hole he cursed countless times each day. They called this living? It wasn't worth it. He resolved that tomorrow morning at work he would call his mommy and daddy. They would know what to do.

THE FIRST THING Tony noticed as he approached the Grove Street building was a stack of trash at the curb. Up close he could see magazines and scientific journals and a couple of small boxes—one had once held cigars—in which Connecticut saved things like badges from scientific meetings, business cards, receipts, rubber bands, and claim checks for dry cleaning and photo processing. He lifted the lid of the uppermost box and saw it was still full of those items.

"Must have finally done some housecleaning," Tony said.

A barely discernible trail of random objects—a yellow number-two pencil, a sewing needle stuck in a piece of green metallic foil, a thick red rubber band—led from the curb to the front door and up the stairs. Tony took the stairs slowly, every now and then bending over to pick up something. At the top of the landing, he could see that the door to their apartment was ajar. Tony opened it, cautiously, and stepped in. He hit the light switch. Nothing. He jiggled it like a flipper on a pinball machine, but nothing happened.

"Connecticut?"

As his eyes adjusted to the darkness, he saw why the lights did not come on—the lamps were gone. *Everything* was gone. All he could see was the gleaming expanse of hardwood flooring in the velvety moonlight.

"My God! We've been robbed. We've been cleaned out."

It suddenly occurred to him that the burglar might be lurking in one of the dark corners. And where was Connecticut? Was he hurt? Unconscious?

"Connecticut! Are you here?" His voice echoed in the empty room, but there was no reply.

In his bedroom, nothing had been molested, not even the digital clock radio. He turned on his bedside lamp and took off his pea coat. It was cold. Even colder than Connecticut usually kept the place. In Connecticut's room, nothing had been overlooked. Bed, armoire, night table, mirror, curtains, blinds, and every last stitch of Connecticut's clothing, even his goddamn shoe racks and tie holder, *and* the clothes hook they bought and installed to hang their robes on. His own robe was crumpled in a heap on the floor. Only the red telephone, sitting on the floor in a rectangle of silver moonlight, remained.

Glass crunched underfoot, and he understood why the apartment was so cold: one of Connecticut's windows was broken. *This* must have been how the burglar got in. But in the same instant, he realized this window did not give access to the fire escape. There was no *way* anyone could have climbed in.

In the kitchen, the food was untouched—everything from Kellogg's Corn Flakes to Lea & Perrins Worcestershire Sauce—but the dishes and silverware were gone. The pots and pans, too. And the electric can opener. Even the place mats. But the booze was still there, nearly full bottles of scotch, vodka, bourbon, and whiskey.

Tony went back to his room and sat down on his bed. Something wasn't right. How could a burglar so methodically clean out an apartment without being noticed? It would have taken even two men *hours* to pull it off. And why would they take a clothes hook and leave a clock radio? And booze? That was the first thing he would have expected them to take. It just didn't make sense. And the stuff at the curb. Who ever heard of a burglar sorting through his loot on the premises and politely throwing away the unwanted booty?

He was tired. He was high. He was scared. But the truth was slowly dawning on him. At first it was little more than a taunt, something he was able to rebuff with no effort. But it grew louder, stronger, until it was the only thing he could hear. Connecticut had checked out and left him alone in the Honeymoon Suite of the Heartbreak Hotel. Without, as far as he could tell, so much as a Dear John letter.

Tony stood up and headed for the kitchen. And he wasn't looking for the corn flakes.

TONY AWOKE AT TEN in a room darkened by a sun seemingly delayed in midocean. Outside, the sky was creamy with the threat of snow. He would have gone back to sleep, but it was too cold. Even though he had closed the door between his bedroom and Connecticut's, the arctic air that poured in through the broken window had permeated the apartment. Huddled on his bed beneath a moth-eaten army blanket, five sweaters, and his pea coat, he waited for the courage to face the thick, cold air in the apartment, the frozen floor of the bathroom, the draft in the kitchen that would rattle his teeth the way it had the plates in the cupboard.

It did not take him long to discover a reason to get out of bed. He had to pee, and if he did it where he lay, he would soon have icicles dangling from his dick. He got up and made his way to the bathroom. After he had taken a whiz, he puked, then turned in vain to the medicine chest for aspirin or Pepto Bismol. Connecticut had more or less cleaned it out, leaving behind only a half-used bar of Dial soap and Tony's shampoo, toothpaste, and toothbrush. Tony crawled back into his makeshift den, covering everything but his feet, still shod, with layers of warmth. Without an analgesic, it seemed impossible for him to face the situation, so he pulled the half-empty bottle of scotch in with him, drank the hair of the dog, and, blissfully, passed out.

He awoke sometime later when the telephone rang in Connecticut's bedroom. In the empty room, the ringer sounded as loud as a fire bell, which did little to aid Tony's headache. He got out of bed and answered it, just to stop the noise. It was Dallas Eden. *Dallas Eden?*

"Hell-o, Tony," Dallas said in a singsongy, game-show voice. "It's been awhile, and I just thought perhaps we could get together for dinner. The three of us, if that's possible. Are you free tonight?"

Tony made a noise that could only be described as an oral fart. That would be a no on dinner. And what the *hell* was Dallas Eden doing, calling so early?

"Tony? Is this Tony Alexamenos? It's Dallas. Dallas Eden. Are you all right?"

"Yeah," Tony grunted. "But don't mention food for a couple weeks, okay?"

"Tony, what's wrong? Are you sick? Is Connecticut there?"

Tony didn't know what to tell Dallas. He knew very little about the whys and wherefores of the situation himself, and he hadn't been able to bring himself to believe any of it. He simply told Dallas that Connecticut was gone, that he had moved out. When he finished, he waited for Dallas' reply, but instead Alfred, Dallas's valet, was on the phone. Mr. Eden, Alfred said, was at this moment speeding to Tony's apartment, and he was not to worry. Everything was going to be all right. Tony said nothing, but dropped the receiver to the floor and made his way back to his bed.

"Oh, Christ, Fatman to the rescue." He knew resistance was futile.

# 15

THE FLEETWOOD ELDORADO that delivered Tony to Dunstan Hall for the first time idled with a pleasing throatiness as the Louis Comfort Tiffany wrought-iron gates swung open noiselessly. Dallas Eden's fortress-like manse at Fifth Avenue and Seventy-ninth Street was among the last great homes of turn-of-the-century New York still occupied as a private residence. The others had been carved up into cooperatives or sold to psychiatrists, plastic surgeons, and gynecologists for use as offices; taken over by various foreign consulates; or donated to charitable organizations. Like many of its neighbors, Dunstan Hall was an overblown pastiche of clashing architectural details—buttresses and battlements, turrets and towers, gates and gargoyles—designed first and foremost to intimidate the riffraff and the criminal element.

The drive from the Village had been awkward for both Tony and Dallas. Once Dallas had determined that Tony was indisposed but uninjured, he labored to suppress the ecstasy that overtook him. At long last he would have the boy under his roof. Tony, dazed and disconsolate, was so saturated with alcohol that he had yet to even approach the threshold from drunk to hung over. All he wanted was to go to bed for a week, to see no one, to go nowhere, to feel nothing—to be as close to death as humanly possible without actually passing over to the other side.

As soon as the car stopped, the driver, Jorge, leaped from his seat and walked briskly to the passenger side of the car. Bending slightly at the waist, he opened the door, his left arm stretched toward the house. Tony stepped out and waited beside the car as Dallas Eden extruded himself from its interior, using a walking stick to gain a purchase on the cobblestones. They were met at the top of the stairs by Dallas's manservant, Alfred.

"Sir," Alfred said to Dallas, and he gestured to the open doors as if Dallas had never been there before. "Master Tony."

Once inside, Tony's eyes were drawn to the ceiling some fifty feet above, covered by what appeared to be a 3-D painting. The angels, soldiers, and men on horseback and in flying chariots looked so dizzyingly real that Tony had to close his eyes to regain his balance. Dallas Eden steadied him and moved him forward into a cavernous room, lit from above by a glass rotunda, in which gold-framed paintings encrusted the walls like barnacles.

If Czar Nicholas II and Pu Yi, the last emperor of China, had collaborated on a yard sale, the result might have approached in size and splendor the baubles on display in the Grand Salon of Dunstan Hall. The czar, in fact, would have recognized at least one *objet*, a Fabergé miniature of St. Basil's Cathedral. Worked in red marble, gold, and platinum, its onion domes were inset with diamonds, rubies, emeralds, amethysts, and sapphires.

"Holy shit," Tony said, pointing to a painting that depicted half a dozen voluptuous female nudes in a Turkish bath. "I've seen this picture before . . . in a book somewhere. Is this the real thing?"

"Let's put it this way, Tony," Dallas said, shrugging himself out of the floor-length, black mink coat that made him look like a pregnant grizzly. "It ain't Elvis on velvet."

Dallas stood for a moment behind Tony, his hands on the boy's shoulders. Then he tugged on the collar of Tony's coat to indicate he should remove it. Alfred, behind them at the base of the curving Grand Staircase, cleared his throat.

"You can go up to your room now, Tony," Dallas said. "Alfred will show you the way. He's drawn a nice hot bath for you, so you can just soak your troubles away. And you'll want to give that hair of yours a good scrubbing, too. We'll worry about a manicure later. And one more thing. You'll find a glass, on ice, on a stand near the bath. Drink it. Drink it all, and drink it now while it's at its coldest. It's an absolutely guaranteed purgative, made pleasant to the taste with fresh orange zest and mint harvested from the greenhouse just this morning. It will rid you of the remainder of those spirits you've imbibed."

"You mean I'll puke again?"

"*Puke* is such a harsh word. I personally prefer to think of it as 'praising porcelain.' In any case you'll feel better in no time."

"Maybe I'll just hit the sack and let nature take its course, if that's okay."

"I really don't think that would be advisable, Tony," Dallas said. "We don't know how much you actually drank, and we don't want to risk alcohol poisoning."

"There's really not much I feel like doing right now, and believe me, puking ain't high on the list."

"Trust me, Tony, you'll be glad you did it. It's impossible to describe how much better you'll feel. It will be over and done with in a matter of minutes, instead of hours or days. No more nausea, no repeated trips to the bathroom, and virtually no hangover. Your appetite will even return. That said, would you like anything in particular to eat?"

"I'm not hungry, thanks," Tony said, ascending the stairs behind Alfred with the enthusiasm of a man lost in the Sahara for a week.

"Tony, you simply *must* eat. Now, what's your absolute favorite dish?"

Tony paused on the staircase, looked at Dallas, and shrugged. Nothing sounded appetizing at the moment. "I don't know. I'll eat pretty much anything that's set in front of me, excepting liver and lima beans."

"What did your mother make for you when she wanted to cheer you up or you stayed home sick from school?"

"I forget. . . . Tomato soup? With pieces of toasted Wonderbread kinda floatin' in it. And a grilled cheese sandwich. And some Nestlé's Quik with a scoop of vanilla ice cream in it."

"Done," Dallas said. He stood at the base of the staircase, smiling unceasingly until Tony was out of sight, then headed for the kitchen to give the news to his cook. What a ghastly selection of victuals, he thought. And where on earth does one find Nestlé's Quik on the Upper East Side?

Tony looked pale when he came down for lunch more than an hour later. The pleasant-tasting elixir, upon encountering alcohol and stomach acid, brought forth the most disgusting stew of liquids Tony had ever seen. But he did feel considerably better, if a bit winded. His rib cage ached. Amazingly enough, the brew had tasted almost as good on the way up as on the way down. Rich people, he thought, even know how to puke better than the rest of the poor slobs.

Tony's abundant hair was damp and uncombed, and as he walked into the dining room, he was rubbing his scalp vigorously with a thick navy blue towel bearing the Dunstan crest. He was barefoot and wore a bathrobe so big, white, and fluffy it looked as if he had been enveloped in a cloud of shaving cream. Dallas was already seated when Tony entered. He had instructed Alfred to burn everything Tony had arrived in,

save his undershorts (which would provide Dallas with hours of hitherto unfathomable pleasure), and a small canvas knapsack containing
his personal belongings. Even now the ashes of the boy's tatty blue jeans
and Navy surplus coat were twirling up the chimney of the incinerator
and blowing eastward toward the sea.

"I can't find my clothes. Alfred gave me this when I got out of the
bathtub." Tony pinched the robe's lapel and lifted it from his chest.

"I am afraid your garments have come to an unexpectedly tragic
end," Dallas said, gesturing to Tony's place setting. He was imagining
Tony naked within the caress of the robe. "We have a new Norwegian
laundress, and when I asked her to wash your things, she understood me
to say that I wanted them burned. Entirely my fault, I'm sure. I suppose
I should spend more time with Mr. Berlitz if I don't want to experience
similar disasters in the future."

"What am I supposed to wear?" Tony asked. He sounded panicked.
A red rose and a sprig of baby's breath lay diagonally on his plate, and
a chafing dish kept his soup and sandwich warm. Tony brushed the
flower aside.

"As we speak, my personal assistant, Gloria, is selecting some emergency off-the-rack garments, using the measurements I gave her. I have
an uncanny eye for sizing men up. They can tide you over until we can
pull together your tailored wardrobe. Until she returns, you'll find slippers and lounging pajamas in a variety of sizes and colors, all in your
room. Did I mention slippers?"

Beneath the table, Tony rubbed his bare feet together self-consciously.
"I don't know about wearing clothes that I haven't bought myself."

"You'll love your new clothes, Tony. And I can guarantee they'll be
the most comfortable you've ever worn, because they will be tailored
just for you from the finest materials available—and all natural fibers.
None of this polyester crap the rabble seems to be embracing. Imagine!
Couture by Goodyear."

"Comfortable isn't what I'm worried about. I don't like taking handouts from people. It's embarrassing."

"These are extreme circumstances for you. Your clothes have been
burned. Am I to turn you out onto the street naked?" Dallas imagined
Tony, teeth chattering, balls blue and shrunken to the size of marbles,
pounding on the door.

"Okay, but I'll only need enough clothes for a couple of days—a pair
of jeans, a couple of shirts, some underwear. Is my coat gone, too?"

"Yes it is, Tony. Gone with the wind." Dallas fluttered his hands skyward.

"Anyway, just enough clothes to last until I can figure out this thing with Connecticut and how to get back home. I think he's still mad at me for something I've done, but I hope I can convince him that it won't happen again."

"The plot thickens."

"If it's all the same to you, I'd like to call him. I have the money to pay for the long distance."

Dallas roared. "Tony, *angel,* it's not the long-distance charges I'm worried about. It's you. He's gone, sweetie. There is nothing you can say that will bring him back. Absolutely nothing. The faster you learn that little lesson, the better off you'll be. You stay here with me awhile. Rest up, put some meat on your bones; you're as skinny as a rail. Then get on with your life."

Tony said nothing for so long that Dallas could see a skin developing on the tomato soup as it cooled. He watched as Tony swallowed hard twice, then, with obvious reluctance, broke into tears. Hiding his face in the crook of his arm, he let go entirely, uttering unintelligible words between the gasping and sucking noises he made. Dallas was aghast. He would have never expected such an outburst from a hard-boiled street kid. Tony had fought to conceal it, but Dallas could see now the boy was devastated.

"Tony, Tony, dear boy. Your life is not over. You're young; you're not yet twenty-one, are you? There will be other men. *Many* other men, I can assure you. Countless hordes at your feet."

"I don't want whores at my feet!" Tony blew his nose in the linen napkin. Dallas shuddered in disgust. Mucus was one of the few bodily secretions for which he could not find a recreational use.

"Tony, listen to me. . . . Are you listening? Monogamy is a heterosexual virtue and a questionable one at that. These days it's not working all that well for straight people, even *with* society's approval. With all the other problems we in the homosexual community have, do you really think it's going to work for us?"

"It's just that everyone I've ever loved has left me. My mom died; this older guy, Mitch, told me to fuck off—after we had been friends for years. And now Connecticut. What is so wrong with me that people always dump me?"

"My dear, sweet boy, your mother *died.* She was sick and she died. I am sure there is no other way she would ever have left you. There is nothing wrong with you, Tony, nothing at all. You are a beautiful young man—incredibly handsome, highly desirable. And I promise you, *I* will never leave you."

"That's another thing, everybody's always telling me how fucking gorgeous I am. What does it get me? I'd gladly have a face that looked like a bowl of oatmeal with raisins for the eyes and peanuts for teeth, if only one person I loved loved me back, forever and always."

"You don't mean that, Tony. Someday you will understand. The world we live in, you and I—all gay men—is based and ordered and ranked on one thing and one thing alone: appearance. It is not a plutocracy but a *beaut*ocracy. It is a world in which the exquisite hustler is the peer of a bank president, if not his superior. And you, you are one of the anointed. The world is yours for the asking, your currency a mere nod, a wink, a smile. You don't understand this yet. But if there is one thing I want to do in this world, it is to make you see that, make you believe in the magic of your own creation."

"I don't care. I hate myself, just like everyone hates me. I'm nothing. I'm nobody. And I hate everybody. Everybody!"

Dallas was, for once in his life, speechless. His heart was breaking. As he watched Tony, something tugged at his heart, or perhaps his conscience. He knew then that in one respect the boy was lost to him. He would never ask Tony to have sex with him, not even in the purely passive way in which his transitory paramours submitted to him. It seemed to him that this conversation was infinitely more intimate than having the lad's dick in his mouth. He knew he would probably have to wage a full-blown war with his carnal impulses, but if he could maintain this level of connection with this boy, it would be worthwhile. For Tony Alexamenos, he was prepared to offer everything and demand nothing.

"It looks to me like you're not going to eat anything," Dallas said finally, patting Tony's right hand. "Why don't you go upstairs and dry your hair. Gloria should be back any minute with your clothes, and then we can go out, stop in at the tailor, and do some real shopping."

Tony numbly assented. He was still faintly queasy, but in just the past hour he was learning that objecting to something Dallas Eden wanted was hopeless. He went upstairs, dried his hair, and threw himself down on his bed, trying to make his mind a blank.

Tony missed that night's performance of *Hair,* but Dallas forced him out of bed—and out of the house—for every curtain call thereafter. For the first couple of weeks, Tony thought he might actually die of grief right there onstage. His arms and legs felt so heavy, his breathing was so labored, that it seemed as if he were underwater. And despite the obvious disappointment of certain members of the audience, who had paid premium prices for seats with an especially good vantage point, he could not bring himself to emerge from beneath the flag naked, which he had always considered something of a celebration. He wasn't celebrating much of anything, thank you, except perhaps the fact that he had made it through another day without having done a handstand on the third rail of the IRT.

What he hated most in those first few weeks was his constant state of awareness. Before he even opened his eyes in the morning, at the precise moment he realized he was awake, an emotional freight train roared through his head: boxcars of memories behind a dream-driven locomotive. Against Dallas's advice, he kept a silver-framed picture of Connecticut on the night table. It was the first thing he saw each morning, and it prompted him to think about Connecticut all day in a continuing, circular, obsessive pattern, as persistent as the last song he heard on the radio before he left the house and could not get out of his head. He frequently would taste Connecticut when he touched his tongue to his upper lip or smell him faintly as he showered, as if his body were slowly releasing the essences of his lover it had absorbed during their time together. As the ghostly scents and sensations fled, so too did the memories of what they had said and done together. For a time there were reminders—a crumpled ticket to *Sleuth* he had used as a bookmark, the matchbook from the Chinese restaurant at which they had eaten on their first night in New York—but they too were slowly discarded.

Tony called Connecticut every day, at almost every time of the day, for three weeks. Much of the time the line was busy or the ring went unanswered. On six occasions he left a message with Connecticut's parents—four with his mother, Mollie, two with his father, Desmond. But the calls were never returned, and he eventually was forced to accept Dallas's point of view—that Connecticut no longer loved him and it was time to move on.

It seemed inconceivable to Tony that he would ever love anyone—anyone in the world—ever again. What was the point? He could love people with all his heart and they still left him. He loved his mother more than anything on earth and she died on him. He had loved Mitch for years—*years*—and he had told him, more or less, to go to hell, just like that. GET OUT DON'T COME BACK. And now Connecticut had left him the same way—in the blink of an eye. There could be only one explanation: There was something wrong with Tony, something so ugly, so horrible, that once somebody saw it, they ran for their lives. He had no idea what it could be, why it was that nobody saw it for a while, or how it finally revealed itself. If he knew what it was, he might be able to hide it better, fool people longer, maybe even reveal it to them gradually so they wouldn't freak out when they finally saw it.

And then he remembered what his foster mother, Wilhelmina Dombrowski, had said the day he left her house for the last time: "You know, Anthony, you've been with us for six months and these pants still have the Alexamenos stink in them."

*The Alexamenos stink.*

That was it. The Alexamenos stink. He had inherited it from his father, the drunken bastard. He had to find a way to get rid of it, to wash it away or cover it up. Maybe, if he took enough perfumey baths in Dallas Eden's Jacuzzi tub and wore enough of the expensive colognes that lined the marble shelves in his bathroom, just *maybe* he could fool people into thinking that he didn't stink. And he'd have to get rid of the Alexamenos name. Yeah, someday he'd have to change that, too.

Before he knew it, the winter's accumulation of snow had ebbed, leaving behind satin tatters of ice on bare branches and the sharp edges of buildings. He reluctantly removed the silver picture frame from beside his bed, as distraught as if he were sending Connecticut to the guillotine. Every day thereafter became a wedge between Connecticut and himself, between memory and reality. It was slow going, and Tony frequently fought it. And he knew, without Dallas or anyone else telling him, that it was a process that might never be completed.

Three mornings a week, Tony went to acting classes at the studio of Stella Adler, an old friend of Dallas. On Tuesdays and Thursdays he attended accent reduction classes with a renowned speech therapist. Because neither of his parents was a southerner, Tony was not as bad off as he might have been, but he had picked up many of the cadences and colloquialisms of his schoolmates. These were soon enough lost, and Tony was subsequently drilled in the rhythms and intonations of upper-class American English. He also received instruction in music appreciation from a member of the faculty at Juilliard, and because Dallas was on the board of trustees of several of the city's art museums, he was able to arrange personal curatorial tours for Tony.

Every couple of weeks, they spent a day shopping for clothes and jewelry for Tony, even though he protested that he had worn but once only a fraction of the booty they had plundered previously. Tony had given up objecting to these trips, partly because he knew it was pointless

and partly because he was falling in love with fashion. He was beginning to get acquisitive, and it was extraordinarily easy to do so when
someone else was paying the bills. He now owned two dozen Swiss
watches, thirty or forty rings, gold money clips, identification bracelets,
and even a delicate golden anklet, which at first he thought was kind of
"faggy," as Connecticut would have said, but later came to find somewhat sensual.

BY THE TIME *Hair* closed on July 1, 1972, Tony had been a member of
the cast for a year and a half. At Dallas's urging, he invited the entire
cast to a huge blowout at Dunstan Hall. He was apprehensive at first;
none of his fellow actors had any idea of the luxury to which he returned in the wee small hours of the morning. He felt guilty. He'd heard
stories about friends eking out a living as waitresses or delivery boys
while looking for acting jobs and trying to find or maintain a relationship. But for well over a year he had been living in a house that could
well be a museum, with servants and a limousine, and a genuine celebrity in residence.

Scarcely had the last guest left than the household sprang into action.
Dallas wanted to spend the rest of the summer at his home in the Pines,
and this was the perfect time to arrive, the next day being the Fourth of
July. Tony was delighted to be going to the beach. He figured two
months in an oceanfront house might allow him the opportunity to figure things out. Between parties. Except there *was* no between parties.
The island house, though a fraction the size of Dunstan Hall, managed
to attract nearly as many guests. It was hard to keep track of who came
with whom, who belonged, and who did not (Dallas told him, "Everyone belongs, darling. That is, *if* they are attractive. The plain ones, alas,
require invitations"). Tony walked into orgies on the huge round bed in
his room three times before he called a locksmith to install a lock to
which only he had the key. Tony knew the boys didn't mean to be rude;
they just assumed the whole house was one big party. In fact, they repeatedly invited Tony to join them and were visibly disappointed when
he declined to do so. Although Tony was titillated by the boys on the
bed—such a jumble of heads, arms, and legs that it looked like the spare
parts department of a mannequin factory—he had yet to become comfortable with the notion of sex as a team sport. He did manage a handful of liaisons in the dunes, mostly as the passive partner in oral sex, but
they left him feeling sad and empty and—even eighteen months later—
thinking about Connecticut.

When they returned to the city on Labor Day Sunday—Tony nut brown, Dallas pale as calamari—Dallas revealed his plans for the immediate future: two weeks at a famous upstate health spa, a visit to Malone Models to introduce Tony to Tuxedo Malone, and an appointment with Rudy, the sorcerer of scissors at Flagranté.

"We're cutting my hair?" Tony said in alarm. Tony had visited Flagranté weekly since he had moved in with Dallas, to receive conditioning treatments. His mane had become even more magnificent in that time, thanks to the frequent application of exotic herbs and oils, the essences of fruits and flowers Tony had never even heard of, and the five hundred brushstrokes it received from Ivan, the salon's comber. Ivan encouraged him to follow up on the practice at home, but like a dentist's urging to floss, it fell on deaf ears. Tony's split ends had been judiciously trimmed by Rudy's obsequious subordinates, but he knew he would have no control over length or style at the hands of the most famous tonsorial artist since the Barber of Seville.

"Tony, Tony, Tony," Dallas said, shaking his head. "We're in the third year of the nineteen seventies, darling. The hippies and the Nehru jackets have long ago gone to their respective rewards—and wouldn't it be a hoot if they all ended up in the same place? Richard Milhous Nixon is president, for God's sake. If that doesn't tell you the sixties are over, I don't know what will. Besides, you'll adore Rudy. Such a gorgeous Italian, and when he cuts you wearing only that hot little tapestry vest, nothing could be more tantalizing. Plus, when he gives you your scalp massage, your face is right at crotch level."

"What's this supposed to be, a haircut or a blow job?" Tony asked.

Dallas knew Rudy was a miracle worker, but the first time he saw Tony after his cut, he could barely believe his eyes. It was like witnessing the vines being cut back at Angkor Wat, illuminating beauty unseen for decades, centuries.

# 16

TUXEDO MALONE'S OFFICE was on the top floor of a glass-sheathed Park Avenue skyscraper that had been at the cutting edge of architectural modernism when it was erected twenty years before. Its windows were tinted deep green, and when it rained, as it was doing on the day of Tony's first visit, the street thirty floors below resembled an aquarium: the cars, cabs, and busses swimming up and down the avenue, occasionally gobbling up people like bits of plankton.

"His real name is Thomas," Dallas told Tony in the limo on the way over. "Thomas Andrew Malone. Apparently, he got the nickname Tuxedo when he was studying at the Rhode Island School of Design, because he always managed to look like a million dollars, even though he was practically broke. When Tux was a junior photography major, he worked part-time for a commercial photographer in Boston. On one of his assignments, he was asked to stand in for one of the models who didn't show up. Of course he was to die for and could have made a career out of it, but the Fates had something else in mind for pretty Tommy Malone.

"When his father died in 1962, he inherited the family business, a small portrait studio here in the city. Seventy percent of the business came from the senior class picture market, and Tux quickly tired of doing 'pimple magic' in the darkroom. His father owned the building the studio was operating out of, so Tux, who had already been living off the rental income, closed the studio and undertook a project to photograph Hollywood and Broadway stars whose lights had long ago flickered out. He paired the new photographs with publicity stills from their heydays and wrote a couple of hundred words about each of them. One poor gay devil, whose profile had been synonymous with elegance in the twenties, was now sweating over a sewing machine at the Bike athletic supporter factory."

"He was making jock straps?"

"Yes, Tony, a cautionary tale if there ever was one. For ten years he made jocks and for thirty-five he made jock *straps*. Tux published the book under the title *Night and Day*, you know, like the old Cole Porter tune, and it was quite well received. Big, big seller. It gave him an idea. What if it were possible to resuscitate the careers of some of these ghosts of glamour?

"Within a year Tux was back in his father's studio. He opened a talent agency named Come Again, specializing in recycling celebrities. He rescued child stars of the 1950s from the ignominy of such jobs as parking lot attendants and saved little Monica Kruger, the freckle-faced, pigtailed star of *Mama's in the Kitchen*, from a life in the porno business. Some of his clients rose only to the level of soap opera characters, but that was better than the condition in which he found them—lonely and poverty-stricken. Others found their second careers more lucrative than their first, their fame more widespread, their past virtually forgotten. For all of them, it was as if they had been raised from the dead.

"In 1968, he opened Malone Models, and his instincts and photographer's eye virtually guaranteed his success. A year later, he launched Malone Men, which is, as you know, the top male house in the city these days. In less than ten years, he had transformed a dusty storefront photography studio into a modeling agency of the caliber of Ford, Wilhelmina, and Elite.

"Tux's lover, Parker Kensington, is the heir to the founder of Kensington Mills of Maine—darling of the flannel-shirt-and-parka-set. They've been together since their freshman year at RISD, where Parker was studying fashion design. When Parker's father suffered a heart attack and retired, Parker succeeded him as head of the family business. With Parker at the helm, Kensington Mills evolved into Parker Kensington International, purveyor of upscale sportswear. The menswear line competes with LaCoste, Ralph Lauren, and other high-end brand names. Their logo is a little figure composed of waistcoat, black tie, top hat, and cane appliquéd over the left breast, where everyone else put their alligators and polo players. It's an homage to Tux, of course. Those two are *so* in love."

When Tony entered Tuxedo's Deco anteroom, a line of five heads turned in unison to look at him, each perfect nose tilted upward at a twenty-five-degree angle. It looked like a scene from a thirties musical review. Dallas looked to Tuxedo's longtime secretary, Nola Lemmons, for a sign. She smiled and tipped her head gently in the direction of two large mahogany doors.

Tuxedo Malone hadn't modeled in ten years, but his consciousness of himself was still as acute as it once had been, so when Dallas and Tony entered his office, he looked up from his desk in a pose of surprise, stood and moved toward them in a pose of welcome, and settled back into his high-backed chair in a pose of contemplation. Tuxedo gave Tony a polite smile, then turned and gave Dallas a reassuring look. He asked Tony a few questions about his background and experience, less for the information he received than for the opportunity to evaluate Tony's speaking voice. For a long while, he reclined and observed Tony with the critical eye of a judge at a gymnastics or diving competition. He awarded points for technical merit: the symmetry of the features and their relationship to one another, the clarity of the eyes, the fullness of the lips; and for artistic achievement: the way his smile seemed to linger long after it was gone, the winsome shyness of his downcast eyes. He asked Tony to turn his head slowly to the right and then to the left. Which was his best side? Were there any hidden flaws? Can he sell it? Will it last? Tuxedo got up from his chair, walked around his desk, and took Tony's chin in his right hand like a crystal Tiffany apple. He balanced Tony's head on the tips of two fingers and steadied it with his thumb, angling the chin upward to better illuminate the exquisite geometry of this remarkable face.

Tuxedo returned to his desk and for a moment supported his chin on his interlaced fingers. Then he leaned forward. "Tony, you don't look like the flighty, self-absorbed type I usually see. Dallas has told me, on the contrary, that you are quite down-to-earth, an attribute as refreshing as it is rare. But there are rules in this business as there are in any other, and I feel I must articulate them."

Tony shifted uneasily. It seemed as if the room's temperature had dropped twenty degrees.

"You should never forget that, by and large, the reason you are sitting in that chair today is something you've had very little control over—your looks. Depending on what you believe, you either have God to thank or you have your parents' genetic legacy. Either way, you didn't do jack shit to get where you are today, so don't get a swelled head about it. If you're smart and work hard, you can make enough money in the next five or ten years to comfortably set yourself up for whatever it is you want to do with the rest of your life, if you have enough brains to figure out what that is. But if you're stupid and piss away all your money on fast cars, drink, and dope, and suddenly it's ten years down the line and your career is over, don't come crying to me. This is a business, and I am a businessman. If you remember that, we'll get along fine. I'm fair and I'm honest, but I have an extremely low bullshit tolerance level, and I can't abide prima donnas.

"That said, I'm delighted to be working with you and will probably labor for years to work off my debt of gratitude to Dallas."

The next day, Tony felt silly and embarrassed as people swarmed over and around him as he sat in what looked like a dentist's chair, beneath a navy blue plastic cape. His attendants (he counted six at one time) trimmed, shaped, and buffed his fingernails and toenails; slathered his face with some cold, yellow-green substance, which then turned into Silly Putty; tweezed his eyebrows, nose, and ears; and flossed his teeth.

"Surprisingly good mouth," the flosser told Tuxedo, who stood by watching as if his car were being detailed. "I expected much worse, given the history."

The result of these ministrations was the casual but polished look that invariably characterized Malone men. Through choice and cultivation, Tuxedo had earned a reputation for providing clients with an array of men who were handsome and elegant but accessible. He was pleased with the way Tony looked; he thought he saw more subtleties in the face and hair today than he had yesterday.

After a light lunch, Tony arrived by cab at the Greenwich Village studio of Victor Panache. He rang the doorbell once. Twice. He waited uncomfortably. It opened. Towering over Tony was a man in a black turtleneck and black pants, a face like five pounds of raw ground round, with two black olives for eyes, a nose like a gourd, and two rows of Indian corn teeth. *This guy sure as hell picked the right side of the camera to work on,* Tony thought. Dallas had told Tony that Panache was gruff, a tyrant to work with, but that he had every right to be. The man was one of the top fashion photographers in the country, with cover credits on every major magazine from *Playboy* to *Gentleman's Quarterly* to *Cosmopolitan*. He was also a master of erotic male photography, and his four books of young male nudes could be found on the coffee tables of lascivious gay men throughout the United States and Europe.

Victor Panache was a Hungarian emigré who fled Budapest in 1956 after the Communist crackdown, traveling to London and Toronto with counterfeit documents and arriving in New York with nothing but his

Leica camera. He changed his last name from something that sounded exactly like Panache but was twelve letters long, all but one of them consonants. For ten years he pursued a career in photojournalism until a land mine in Vietnam shattered his left leg and led him to less rigorous work.

In his studio, the photographer fluttered around Tony for a few minutes, studying his face from a variety of positions, moving a light here, adjusting a reflector there. Then, suddenly satisfied he could do no more, he retreated behind his cameras.

"Do you see that painting on the wall?" Panache asked, pointing to a still life. "Without being painted, that bowl of fruit would have merely been eaten or spoiled. Cézanne made it a masterpiece, and now it belongs to the ages. What he did for those apples, I will do for you. So be a good fruit and do exactly what I tell you."

Panache told Tony to relax, but each attempt at informality looked studied, not spontaneous.

"If you can't look casual, goddamnit, look bored!"

Tony sighed and shrugged his shoulders.

"That's it. Perfection. Hold that."

Tony froze, afraid to blink, to breathe.

"That's wonderful. Good." The camera had come alive, clicking and whirring like a cicada on an August night.

That was Tony's first face. Panache taught him to memorize his facial expressions from the inside out, without having to use a mirror. As the day went on, Tony learned how to snap a smile on his face like a visor on a suit of armor.

"Less teeth, boy. Less mouth. I distrust anyone who smiles with more than half of their face."

A WEEK AFTER HIS FIRST MEETING with Tuxedo Malone, Tony was summoned to his office. The faintest hint of fall was in the air, and Dallas delighted in coordinating an autumnal ensemble for him. Tony's salmon-hued turtleneck matched exactly the color of the pinstripe accents in his sport coat. He sat self-consciously in Tuxedo's waiting room, reluctant to make eye contact with any of the other half-dozen young men, who looked impossibly poised and polished. When Nola Lemmons showed him in to Tux's office, several young supplicants who had been there before him glared as he walked past them.

Tuxedo Malone rose and walked toward Tony, his right hand extended, his left poised to cradle Tony's right elbow when they shook hands.

"How has the portfolio shoot been going?"

Tony said he thought things were going well, but that he just couldn't believe the number of rolls of film Victor Panache had used.

"He probably used more film in an hour than my father bought in my whole lifetime. I think I've only got about six pictures of me as a kid."

"That *is* a shame. I'll bet you were absolutely adorable at fifteen or sixteen. Not that you're not gorgeous now—I think we've established *that* for one and all—but those last ripe months before your hormones kicked in full tilt and your beard started to come in must have been magical. Although I suspect you even wear stubble well."

Tuxedo guided Tony to a chair.

"Coffee, Tony? Coke? Seven-Up?"

"No thanks. I'm fine."

"The reason I asked you here today is that there's someone I'd like you to meet. His name is Valentine Rittenhouse, and I want you to spend a lot of time with him over the next week or two. He's quite an experienced model, and he'll take you to all his go-sees and introduce you to some of the client reps and photographers you'll be working with. He'll also be more than happy to point out the wolves and vultures, which are in abundant supply. Perhaps a bit *too* gleefully, for my taste. But you'll like Val. He's very nonthreatening and he's not insecure, which as you can probably guess is the main ingredient in all the cat fights that take place around here. He's in the business because he likes it and he's good at it. He likes to see his picture in print, too. He has fun, and he could care less about the money."

"Why's that?" Tony asked.

"Family money, more than he could spend in three lifetimes. Something silly like paper clips or dental floss. Low cost, high volume, virtually no competition. Apparently, his family's been at it since the day God got into the spare-rib business, and they virtually have a lock on the market. They've got more money than the Kennedys or the Rockefellers combined, but because they've had the good sense to stay out of politics and the tabloids, nobody's heard of them."

"And he's not a snot? I really hate rich kids."

"I guarantee you'll like Val. No, you'll *love* him. He's got a highly developed sense of noblesse oblige, but he's not condescending. He graduated summa cum laude from Yale, knows everyone in the city, and is very big on the charity circuit. In short, he's got a life away from the camera. He's able to keep things in perspective, which would be an especially good trick for you to learn."

There was a knock at the door. It swung open, and a long, delicate, oval face peeked into the room.

"Am I early? Late? What? I do so lose track of time when I'm unemployed." Swirling his coat off his shoulders like a matador's cape, Valentine Rittenhouse flung it on the couch. He approached Tony with both hands extended in a gesture of familiarity.

"You're right on time, as usual," Tuxedo said and turned to Tony. "Val is only unemployed because he wants to be. He's just back from two weeks in Newport, where he was an extra in *The Great Gatsby*. You know the one—Robert Redford and Mia Farrow."

"Really? Cool. Did you meet Robert Redford?"

"Did you say meet or eat, darling? I know I did one of them, but I can't remember which. In any case, I'm pleased to *meet* you, Mr. Anthony Alexander," Valentine said.

Tuxedo had insisted Tony adopt a new professional name.

"Call me Tony, okay? Anthony's not even my real name. Alexander, either."

"Tony it is. And I'm Val." He took a gold cigarette case from his jacket pocket, removed a slender, dark cigarette, and tapped it against the case three times. "Clove. From Turkey. Infinitely more satisfying than mere tobacco. Care for one?"

"I don't smoke."

"And bully for you."

Valentine Rittenhouse was long-limbed and lithe, like the Christ in the El Greco *Resurrection* that hung in Dallas's library. He was thinner than most of his fellow models and found his greatest success in the pages of *Homme* and *L'Uomo Vogue,* wearing high-fashion Italian menswear that would look ridiculous on a typical corn-fed American model. His face, too, looked European, with a long, narrow nose and clearly articulated nostrils that were perfectly designed for flaring in the event of righteous indignation. His hair was thick and brilliant, razor-cut to a virtually seamless finish, and two shades darker than the color of copper wire. Valentine Rittenhouse had grown up viewing life through the crosshairs of a Lincoln Continental hood ornament, and he always looked as if he had just received a compliment. He could afford to be more serene, less bitter and competitive, than those models who had been forced to use their beauty to deliver them from less pleasant circumstances. It was these traits, Tuxedo thought, that would make him the perfect mentor for Tony. Val walked slowly around his protégé, pausing to suck in smoke from his cigarette so deliberately that his cheeks went concave.

"He's hardly unpolished, Tuxedo," Val said as if Tony weren't there. "But it is *quite* obvious that he is only very *recently* polished."

"Thanks a lot. That makes me feel good."

"No slight intended, my dear. I am most certainly not here to dish you, but to act as your spirit guide through the treacherous world of high fashion. Suffice it to say you are an exquisite creature, and I would be delighted to be your patroness until you get your feet on the ground." Val turned and spoke directly to Tuxedo. "Pray tell, how *is* a queen supposed to get her feet on the ground when she's always got her legs in the air?"

Tony winced.

"Are you free Saturday night?" Val asked. "I do hope you don't think it presumptuous of me to ask. It's just that I need a date for the big Cancer Society bash."

"Don't you think that would look funny? Two guys going together."

"Oh, don't worry dear, I'll provide the seafood. But I need someone pretty like you to sit next to me and keep me awake. There will be lots of fabulous entertainment and tons of the most eligible ineligible bachelors, meaning of course that they're married to fish but continue to cast their nets for mermen. And I don't mean *Ethel* Mermen. That reminds me, did I mention Frank Sinatra's the headliner? Black tie, of course. I presume Miss Eden has provided you a tux by this time?"

"Miss Eden's dead."

"How charming. I was talking about *Dallas*. I'm such a gender bender. It's a habit I just can't seem to break. But you do have tails?"

"Yeah. I mean yes."

"Good. We can discuss the details at the Russian Tea Room."

Tony stood up, turned his back to Val, and looked at Tuxedo with a pained expression on his face.

"Go ahead, go," Tuxedo whispered, conspiratorially. He put his arm around Tony's shoulder. "Don't worry, just slip a Valium in his coffee. He'll be fine."

"But I don't *have* any Valium."

"That's okay, borrow one from him. He won't mind."

Fifteen minutes later, at the restaurant, Tony kept turning his head to stare at someone who could quite possibly be David Niven. "Tuxedo tells me you're stinking rich," he said.

"It's not polite to stare, Tony. Really. It's not," Val said, laying his napkin across his lap. "That is who you think it is, and you'll be meeting him and others like him soon enough."

*Not polite to stare, my ass.* This guy was a pushy S.O.B. They'd known each other for less than an hour and he was already telling Tony what not to do. And *swishy*. Connecticut would call it faggoty, and for once Tony would have to agree. He wondered if all models were this way and if it might be contagious.

"So are you? Stinking rich that is. Or is that not polite either?"

"Oh yes, we Rittenhouses *are* stinking rich. *More* than stinking rich, really. We're rancidly rich. Deliciously, odoriferously rich."

"How rich?"

"Now that, my dear Tony, *is* impolite," Val said. "And would you please put your napkin on your lap. You're making me nervous."

"Sorry." He obliged.

A waiter approached. Val ordered for both of them—one raspberry tartlet each and two cups of cappuccino.

"You'll love the pastries, Tony, but now that you're a model you're going to have to watch your waistline. Of course, there are several gentlemen in here who are already watching it for you." Val locked eyes with one of Tony's would-be suitors and mouthed the words "Dream on, queen." Then he closed his eyes and took a deep breath. He had to slow down. He was always this way in public, especially with people he didn't know, always trying to show off his intelligence and sense of humor so people wouldn't think of him only as rich. But he had the feeling it wasn't working with this kid, who was one of the most strikingly good-looking people he had ever met—perhaps the *most* good looking—but so reluctant to crack a smile. Val reached into his jacket pocket and removed a small gold pill case. He took out a single Valium and, under the guise of a cough, tossed it onto his tongue and washed it down with some water. He didn't know how cool this kid was with drugs, but he suspected he'd be a fast learner. These fresh-faced types usually were. Yes, he'd be a real party girl, given the opportunity, of which there would be far, far too many.

"So where does your money come from?" Tony asked.

"Toothpicks," Val said, casually inspecting his fresh manicure.

"Excuse me. Did you say toothpicks?"

"That's right. You pick your teeth with them, hence the name."

"And you make money at that?"

"Just think of it this way: if every man, woman, and child in America used just one toothpick a day, just one, that would be something close to two hundred million toothpicks. Per day. And that's a conservative estimate. Imagine how many canapés, in this city alone, require toothpicks to hold the bacon and water chestnuts together, the prosciutto and cantaloupe. Think of finger sandwiches, fondue, fruit salad. And of course we make more than twice as much profit per pick when we attach that awful colored cellophane garní on top, as revolting as that is. But profit is profit. Rittenhouse Freres pioneered the rounded toothpick, the colored toothpick, the flavored varieties. We are proud to provide eighty-five percent of this nation's toothpick needs."

"That's bullshit," Tony said, looking Val dead-on, trying unsuccessfully to see even a flicker of a grin.

"Of course, we're not in toothpicks *exclusively*. My grandfather diversified when he saw the floss movement about to flower. He always did have wonderful timing. He got in to the tongue depressor market just as Americans were able to afford regular medical care. And then there are popsicle sticks. After all, somebody's got to make them. And cotton swabs. Do you think those little sticks grow on trees? Sorry, bad example. And what about the wooden spoons you get with your cup of black-and-white Good Humor ice cream, the ones that look like flattened peanuts?"

"So you are seriously telling me that you got rich off of toothpicks and popsicle sticks and shit like that."

"Why not? It's no harder to believe than making millions on corn and callus removers. Somewhere there's an heir to the Dr. Scholl's foot fortune. In fact, I think I went to Deerfield with him."

At that moment the waiter arrived, placing their frothy cups and diminutive tartlets on the table. Tony stuck his finger into the cappuccino.

"What kind of coffee is this? It's all foam. And this thing—it's smaller than a ladyfinger, for God's sake."

"With one important exception, Tony, you will discover that bigger is not necessarily better. You're going to have to learn to appreciate the finer things in life, and many times those things are doled out in very small portions. You wouldn't want to overdose on them."

Tony bit into the tartlet. It was delicious. "Can I get another one?"

"All things in moderation, Tony. We wouldn't want any extra padding on those magnificent cheekbones of yours, would we?"

"You know, I'll bet there are plenty of things you haven't done precisely because you were born rich."

"Such as going to bed hungry?"

"No, I mean fun stuff. I'll bet you never had a yard sale."

"I grew up on Fifth Avenue. I never had a *yard*. I once tried to sell my sister, Mac, on the street in front of our building, but my brother, Billy, told Mother about it and I was sent to my room, which was, of course, a loathsome torment, filled as it was with books and toys and such. Yes, I suffered that day."

"You have a sister named Mac and a brother named Billy? How did you get stuck with a sissy name like Valentine?"

"I was born on February fourteenth, and Vera couldn't resist. I think she hadn't fully emerged from the anesthesia yet. By the time she came to her senses, the ink was dry on the birth certificate and I've since had to suffer under the yoke of a foppish moniker. My siblings did not escape. Mac and Billy are really Mackenzie and Billington."

"So anyway, I'll bet your mother never yelled at you for leaving the refrigerator door open and letting out all the cold."

"I was never in the kitchen as a child."

"Okay, have you ever eaten leftovers?"

"At the Continental Baths, maybe."

"Tuna casserole?"

"I can honestly say that, to the best of my knowledge, I have never eaten casserole of *any* type."

Tony laughed. Grudgingly, he was warming up to this guy. Yeah, he was stinking rich, but he was *so* rich that it no longer mattered. Unlike the boys at Sanctuary, he didn't feel the need to broadcast his net worth, or that of his family, every day on the tennis courts or in the dining hall. He didn't have to be insecure about where it came from or concerned that it all might disappear. There was just too damn much of it. Maybe there was hope for this little collaboration after all.

TONY'S ARRIVAL on the modeling circuit created the biggest gossip juggernaut since Ted Kennedy took a wrong turn at Chappaquiddick. Invitations for Tuxedo and Tony arrived daily by mail, phone, and courier. Lunch. Dinner. The Hamptons. Suddenly, every agency head, designer, and photographer was planning the "Party of the Year," often on the same weekend. Tuxedo judiciously sifted through the entreaties and selected only those that might result in appropriate exposure for Tony and financial gain for himself.

Tony was never without work, even though Tuxedo turned down as many offers as he accepted on Tony's behalf. After several of the most successful months for a single model at his or any other agency, Tuxedo cut Tony's schedule by half, fearing overexposure. Tony himself was admittedly "having a blast." He lolled in the Caribbean for Eastern Airlines and romped in the surf off Diamond Head for Hang Ten Sportswear, making more money than he ever imagined possible.

Tuxedo managed Tony's career with foresight and precision. Always conscious of the long-range image he had planned for Tony, he was exacting about the go-sees he sent Tony to, because in most instances, showing up was tantamount to getting the job. He wanted to make sure Tony was never the college student with a dandruff problem or a case of bad breath, never the character with an Excedrin headache or "ring around the collar." He was always the man with the plan, the trusted friend, the well-groomed wonder boy, providing in each instance the best possible solution to the problem at hand. Tux speculated that Tony was the most highly evolved all-American boy in the history of advertising.

# 17

WHEN DALLAS WAS OFFERED the role of Caligula in a big-budget Italian film directed by Franco Piselli, he couldn't turn it down, even though it would mean being away from Tony for nearly three months. Piselli was well known on the Continent for his violent, bawdy historical epics, all with a decidedly homosexual bent. *Caligula* was to be his first English-language production, and its sheer scope and scandalous nature promised to make it the Italian director's crossover film. Dallas hoped it would jump-start his own stalled cinematic career.

"In many ways it will be like playing myself—with a bad case of menstrual cramps," Dallas told Tony. "And I am, frankly, titillated by the fact that for a significant portion of the film, neither I nor the promised legions of young greaseball extras will be clad in anything more than a few strategically placed G-strings and an occasional fabric swatch of the most diaphanous nature. Piselli insists it's an artistic statement, but I think he's just too cheap to spring for costumes. So what do I care? My favorite lunch meat *is* hard salami."

"Sounds more like a bunch of baloney to me," Tony said as they had a final cup of coffee in the breakfast room. "Are you sure this is something you want to be associated with, Dallas? It just seems so . . . I don't know . . . *cheap.*"

"It *is* cheap, dear boy. Cheesy is an even better way to describe it. And I fully intend to wallow in every sordid minute of it."

"Well, then have a blast," Tony said, standing. He had a shoot in less than thirty minutes. Tony leaned down and gave Dallas a quick kiss on the cheek.

That night, alone in Dunstan Hall save for the help, Tony felt adrift—for about half an hour. After that, he was drunk with liberation. For the first time in two years, he was free to make his own plans; without a doubt, it would mean more sex. Tony had not tricked frequently since he had moved in with Dallas, and it was mostly on the road at that. That led to some hot times but no new boyfriends. Occasionally, he would get picked up on the street, but he could never spend the night because he knew Dallas would get worried if he didn't come home. Now he could spend every leisure hour with Val, flitting from one fabulous club to the next like a pair of colorful migratory birds and doing whatever he wanted with whomever he pleased for as long as he liked.

Two days after Dallas left, Tony and Val went to Lune Noir for dinner to celebrate Val's birthday. Afterward, they dropped in at Fusion, one of the most notorious of the self-consciously exclusive watering holes that competed for the attentions of the city's celebrities and beautiful people while reveling in the humiliation of the huddled masses. Tony and Val marched past lines of half-frozen supplicants and were waved in by what amounted to an honor guard of Fusion security lackeys. The interior of the club resembled a set from the film *Forbidden Planet*, with tubes of neon blinking and glowing in sequence, giving the impression of the production of nuclear power. There were few tables or chairs, just endless red leather banquettes undulating around the perimeter of the dance floor, and the occasional king-size water bed "playpen," all still unoccupied at this relatively early hour.

"I forget how amazing this place is," Tony said.

"Frankly, I think it's past its peak," Val replied. "You just don't get out enough. Why do you let Dallas keep you on such a short leash?"

"He says it's in my best interest, that I'm vulnerable and easily seduced."

"That's bullshit, Tony. He's just afraid he'll lose you."

"It's not like we never go anywhere or see anyone. We practically live at Lincoln Center. And we're always going to an opening or to one party or another. I've met a lot of people."

"Any of them even remotely close to your age?"

"A couple, maybe."

"All pretty boys on short leashes, too, I'd wager. Has he ever let you bring anyone home from one of these parties?"

"I couldn't trick with anybody in that mausoleum. Not with Dallas practically in the next crypt."

"Just remember I have about a dozen guest rooms *chez moi*, so you're always welcome to use my place if the opportunity should arise."

"He'd still want to know where I was."

"I'd handle that. I'd tell him we were having a pajama party."

Tony was not particularly attracted to anyone he saw. They were all too dazed or too outrageous for him. A lot of queens wore heart-shaped pins or buttons in honor of St. Valentine's Day. Val nudged Tony and pointed to a man on the dance floor who was wearing only boots, chaps, and a red jockstrap with a stuffed satin heart pinned to it. Embroidered on the heart were the words "Your face here." Tony immediately perked up. He had never before seen someone who on the one hand was so muscular—his arms looked like the coiled cables of a suspension bridge—and on the other so graceful. But most curious was the fact that he was either totally bald or had shaved his head. The dancer's features were strong and sharp, and sometimes, when the pulsating red lights caught his head just right, it looked more like a skull than a face, with his eye sockets blackened by shadow and his lips pulled back to reveal two rows of big, square teeth. The way the man moved was a revelation. His movements were fluid and unstructured; it looked as if he were swimming instead of dancing. Still, Tony found it hard to say whether, when it came right down to it, he was attracted to or repelled by this man whose alabaster ass cheeks protruded through his chaps, alternately tightening and relaxing as he gyrated to the bass line.

Val tugged on Tony's sleeve, leaned over, and yelled over the music, "He's not dancing with anybody."

Tony turned back to the dance floor. It was true. Four couples danced around him, but he had no partner, nor was he part of any group. Tony shrugged, and Val indicated with a nod toward the door that he was ready to move on. Tony followed him to the coat check. Val put out his hand and motioned for Tony to give him his ticket.

"I'm gonna stay," Tony said. "If that's all right. I mean, it *is* your birthday."

"Taken a shine to Mr. Clean, have we? How very *outré.*" Val took his coat from the attendant and folded it over his arm. "And don't think twice about me."

"He's certainly interesting. And he moves great. But I need to take another look at him in better light. You don't think he's loony tunes, do you?"

"He's a bit intense, even for this place, but who knows? At any rate, be careful. What worries me most is this dancing alone business. It speaks volumes. He's unusually self-absorbed. That could be a danger signal. Possibly a sociopath. So take him home with you instead of going to his place, which more than likely is in some tenement with manacles on the walls. Lead him to believe there are Dobermans behind every door."

"There *are* Dobermans behind every door."

"I'm serious. People who shave their heads have always been suspect. It borders on the antisocial. They usually do it because they're going bald. But why they think it's better to be smooth as a cue ball instead of just having a little divot missing is beyond me. Oh, and call me the minute you exile him from Xanadu—*whatever* the hour."

After getting another drink, Tony circled the dance floor, looking for the man who wore his heart on his jock. To no avail. He ascended one flight to gain a better vantage point. Still nothing. Could the guy have left in the short time he and Val were at the coat check? He hated that about these monster bars. An incredible face could float by on a cloud of smoke and you might never see it again.

He needed to use the men's room and headed for the third floor. The facilities on the first and second floors were always crowded, with as many queens smoking joints or snorting as pissing. Because of its location, the third-floor john was less high-density, but it had the reputation for becoming an orgy room with the slightest provocation, which bothered Tony. He couldn't pee if there was a lot of slapping and sucking going on. It wasn't that he was modest; it was just that he got an immediate hard-on, which naturally cut off the waterworks.

Tony swung open the men's room door. Both urinals were occupied, but Tony could tell neither man was pissing. They looked at him over their shoulders, and each took a half step backward simultaneously to display their semi-flaccid wares. He wasn't interested and was about to suggest that they do each other; maybe all they needed was a matchmaker. Walking quickly to the first of three stalls, he yanked on the door. Inside, one man was standing astride the toilet seat, head down, bracing himself against the tile wall with his muscular arms, while a second man stood behind him, his face buried in the proffered ass, alternately groaning and slurping. The top man raised his head at the intrusion and looked over his left shoulder. Mr. Clean.

"Line forms at the rear," he said and laughed so hard he nearly lost his footing. "Get it? At the rear?"

"Try locking it next time, asshole!" Tony said, slamming the door and leaving the room.

He headed for the second-floor bar, ordered a Johnny Walker Black straight up, and tossed it back. His heart was pounding. He asked for another. He thought he should have been disgusted by what he had seen, but instead he was incredibly turned on. He wanted to go back to the third-floor john, grab the ass kisser—a homely son of a bitch with bad skin—yank him aside by the collar, and take his place. And he thought about Mitch, Mitch in that stiflingly hot, rancid men's room, and the impulses he had then that he'd buried out of ignorance and fear. He had not felt this good—or this *bad*—since. Connecticut certainly had never aroused this kind of lust in him. He tossed back his drink and ordered a third.

"Yo, man, you need to slow down," the bartender said as he set down the drink. "You are much too gorgeous to be getting drunk and risk passing out. What a waste!"

Tony said nothing, took the drink, and walked away. His dick pointed up, but his head steered him downstairs to the main floor, out of harm's way. A couple more drinks, he thought, and he wouldn't be able to climb the stairs even if he wanted to. As the night wore on, he stumbled around the dance floor, increasingly wobbly. He spilled a drink on a fairly hot guy, who nearly decked him. But when the stranger saw Tony's face, he asked him to come home with him instead. "You can lick it off me," the man said. Under other circumstances, Tony might have acquiesced, but all he could think of were the pearly hemispheres of Mr. Clean's butt. He sat down on the edge of a roiling playpen and flagged down a waiter. He lost track of his drinks—and the time—until he was startled by the cool, dry back of someone's hand stroking his left cheek. Tony jerked involuntarily, his heart racing from the surprise contact.

"Like what you saw, pretty boy? I like what I see. Very much."

He turned to see Mr. Clean, grinning and gleaming, his torso a waterfall of sweat. Of course he liked it. He fucking loved it. But did he have the balls to say so?

"Cat got your tongue?" the man asked. "Better get it back, 'cause you can't have no fun without it." He pulled Tony to his feet, linked his fingers behind Tony's neck, and pulled him toward him. Their lips touched and tangled. Tony let his drink fall to the floor and put his hands on the man's leather-sheathed hips. God, he was hot. They didn't come up for air for an eternity, not until after Mr. Clean had slipped Tony's sport coat and shirt off and ripped his undershirt to shreds and let it flutter to the floor. Their hairless chests glided over each other, tinted chartreuse and purple by the quavering lights. Tony finally pulled back.

"Listen, why don't we go back to my place?" he said. "I've got great pot, acid, coke—anything you want."

"All I want is you, babe. Hot and wet and begging me for more."

"Then let's get the *hell* out of here."

They bypassed the coat check, and Tony had lost track of his dress shirt, so he threw his sport coat over his glistening torso, knowing his nipples would freeze the moment he stepped out the door. All the better. In the cab they stopped kissing long enough to introduce themselves. Tony's companion, who had produced a leather vest from somewhere but was still wearing no jeans, said his name was Devlin DeSchuys. Tony was sure they almost had an accident when the driver turned to watch them writhing in the backseat. When the cab finally lurched to a halt, Devlin didn't stop his assault on Tony's mouth.

"Hey, Romeo and Juliet, we're here," the cabbie said.

Tony put a crumpled bill in his hand as they got out of the cab. "Keep the change."

"You *live* here?" Devlin asked, looking up at the forbidding facade of Dunstan Hall in the moonlight. "You know, I think I've seen this place before, but I always thought it was the Transylvanian consulate or something. You rent out a room in the carriage house?"

"No, I live in the house."

"Sugar daddy?"

"Not exactly."

"What does *that* mean?"

"I don't have to have sex with him."

"And he lets you stay here? Out of the kindness of his fucking heart?"

"Uh-huh."

"How did you manage that? He must be fucking head-over-heels for you. You're not pimping me for a voyeur scene with some troll, are you?"

"He's in Rome. It's just you and me."

"Rome, *Italy?* So who is this guy?"

"I'll tell you later. Right now, we've got better things to do than talk."

Devlin whistled under his breath as they made their way though the darkened house and up the curving stairs. Tony slipped once, and Devlin caught him. "This place is unfuckingbelieveable. You're not shittin' me about living here, are you? You're not really the upstairs maid or something?"

"No, I really live here," Tony said as he opened his bedroom door and switched on the lights. He retreated to the bathroom to piss and to get a sense of whether he was going to throw up. He stripped, turned off the lights, and slipped under the sheets. After Devlin got naked but before he joined Tony, he performed a series of warm-up exercises on the two-hundred-year-old Bukhara rug at the foot of the bed. He stretched and did handstands and slow-motion cartwheels that made it appear his arms and legs were spokes in a wheel as they cut through a shaft of moonlight from a mullioned window. Tony thought it was a bit showy, but he was thoroughly aroused.

Once in bed, Devlin used his strength and suppleness to bring Tony to plateaus of pleasure unlike any he had experienced previously. They were locked together, thrusting, rolling, spinning until they lost their orientation to anything but each other's eyes. At one point they almost fell out of bed. Tony had been with some hot men in the two years since Connecticut had left him, and especially in the six months he had been with Malone Men—an insatiable Navy SCUBA instructor in Hawaii, a ski bum in Innsbruck, the cowboy who followed him from The Monster to Delmonico's and back in Key West until they hooked up—but he had never experienced sex of this intensity. Devlin was half animal, half machine. He growled as he yanked Tony's head back by his hair and kissed him violently; he purred as his hips rolled against Tony's ass in a fluid rhythm. When they finally collapsed, breathless, their bodies glowed with the hot red blood pumped to the surface by their straining hearts.

"Oh my God," Tony gasped. "We've got to remember what we did so we can be sure to do it again."

"Don't worry, I've got it memorized."

They lay there, not touching, until their chests stopped heaving and their sweat ran cold. The sheets were so wet they were uninhabitable, so Tony took Devlin by the hand and led him to the adjoining guest room.

"Christ, this is amazing," Devlin said. "Fuck up one bed, just go to another. I guess you've got servants to clean up after you?"

"Yeah, but I try not to get used to it. I don't want to become a completely useless slob."

They lay on the bed, Tony on his back, Devlin on his side with his right leg thrown casually across Tony's abdomen. Devlin traced figure eights on Tony's chest.

"So how did you connect with this guy anyhow? You really hit the jackpot."

Tony related his first meeting with Dallas in Sugar Mill Beach and the move to New York with Connecticut. He gave a somewhat vague account of Connecticut's departure and how he had come to live at Dunstan Hall.

"And this whole time there has been absolutely no sucking or fucking of any kind? No Super-8s? Not even any j.o.?"

"Nope, nothing. I was suspicious at first because back home he had a reputation as a pervert. Word was he paid good-looking young guys to have sex with him—and in fact that's true—so I thought I was just the new kid on the block. But he's never laid a finger on me. For a while I was almost insulted, like I wasn't good enough for him. But then I figured, hell, maybe the guy really does just want to be my friend." Tony pulled Devlin down and they kissed. "So how the hell did *you* end up in New York City?"

Devlin DeSchuys was the product of a Dutch-Irish marriage. His grandfather had sailed from Amsterdam to New York at the turn of the century, then headed west to Chicago on his way to California. He took a job in a meatpacking operation for what he thought would be only a few months but stayed until he died of a heart attack on the slaughterhouse floor at age sixty-three, face down in a two-inch sludge of cow entrails. Devlin's father, Piet, worked in the packinghouse his whole life as well and vowed that his son would not set foot into the bloody business.

The key was to get Devlin a football scholarship to Notre Dame. Devlin was a scrappy kid, smallish but solid. He played j.v. his freshman year in high school and made the varsity team as a sophomore. He was a reliable, hardworking player, but he endangered no school records. As football camp geared up before his junior year, he announced his intention to quit football in favor of gymnastics, for which he thought he was better suited. (He knew then, but didn't let on, that he wanted to become a professional dancer.) Piet DeSchuys was flabbergasted. Gymnastics, he said, was a sissy sport, if it was a sport at all.

Devlin was undeterred. A low-waisted boy who was all torso, like a centaur, he was a natural-born gymnast. Shirtless, he erupted like a geyser from the constraints of his size twenty-eight Levis. His massive pectorals helped him conquer the still rings, and his powerful thighs propelled him to record-breaking vaults.

Devlin had come to New York straight out of high school, waiting tables, hefting crates of fish on ice at the Fulton Fish Market, and picking up nonunion construction jobs when he could. He took dance classes at night in a little hole-in-the-wall studio in lower Manhattan, which he partially paid for by letting the owner give him blow jobs. While danc-

166 / Andrew W.M. Beierle

ing with a gay troupe, Modus Vivendi, he was discovered by the artistic director of Möbius, a company that combined dance, gymnastics, and acrobatics with form-fitting costumes, kaleidoscopic lighting, and atonal music. Everyone, male or female, danced bald as an artistic statement, a kind of common denominator and a way to minimize the differences between the genders.

"It's not everyone's cup of tea—the shave, not the dance," Devlin said, rubbing his head. "But I kind of like it. And let me tell you, some guys really groove on it. They can't keep their hands off my head, can't stop kissing and licking it. It drives those suckers wild, especially when I'm in full leather. What do *you* think?"

"Honestly? At first I thought it was a little weird, but once we got home and you took your clothes off, it seemed perfect. Your body's so smooth and hairless, it seems completely natural."

"You know what I'd like to do now?"

"Gee, give me three guesses."

"Not that. Although that is a close second. I want you to show me this place."

"Now?"

"Sure, why not? You've got the run of the place, don't you?"

"No. I mean yes. I mean okay. It's just that I feel funny about it. This place kind of gives me the willies at night, if you know what I mean. It almost feels like it's haunted."

"Ahh, don't be a sissy. I'll protect my baby from the big, bad bogeyman."

"Okay, I guess. Just let me get us a couple of robes."

"Don't bother. I think it would be hot to walk around a place like this buck naked. And then later I'm gonna split your ass wide open in the biggest, darkest, spookiest room in the whole damn place."

THE DAY AFTER THEY MET, Devlin sent Tony an extravagant floral arrangement—probably costing a lot more than he could afford. That night Tony met Devlin at the theater in the Fleetwood, and they drank champagne and made out while Jorge drove them back to Dunstan Hall. Their second night's lovemaking was as explosive as their first, if not more so. After that, Devlin called at least once a day, and he usually spent the night at Dunstan Hall. At Tony's request, they always had sex at least once before Devlin showered off the night's dance sweat. Devlin's natural body odor was an unusual but not unpleasant blend of sour milk and baby powder.

On the night of their first month's anniversary, they took a bubble bath in the Jacuzzi with two bottles of Dallas's best champagne within reach on ice.

"God, Dev, this has been the best month of my life," Tony said as Devlin gently gnawed one of his nipples, made plump and pliable by the hot water. "I think I've had more sex since I met you than in my entire life. And better. Much better."

"The feeling's mutual, guy." Devlin said, lifting his head from Tony's chest. "You know, babe, something's been on my mind, and I'd like to get your opinion."

"Sure. Is something wrong?"

"Nothing, really. It's just that I realized today that the lease on my place runs out in a couple of weeks, and I have to decide what I'm going to do."

"Don't you like living there?"

"Yeah, I do. But what I like isn't the question here. It's what *you* like that concerns me."

"What *I* like?"

"Sure. See, times are tight down at the theater. We didn't get a big arts grant we were counting on, and we might have to cancel part of the season because ticket sales haven't been as good as we anticipated. With that kind of uncertainty, I really need to watch every penny. I don't think I can really afford to renew my current lease. It's too nice a place, too pricey. I might have to move to the boroughs—Brooklyn, probably—and that would make it really hard to be with you as much as I have been. The commute would really be a bitch, especially at night."

"What commute? Jorge can pick you up anytime, anywhere."

"That's cool, Tony, but it seems like such an imposition. I mean, while the boss is away, the chauffeur should play. Right? He's a good-looking guy, he ought to be out on the streets sowing his wild oats."

"So you want me to move in with you?"

"Actually, I was thinking more along the lines of *me* moving in with *you*. Just temporarily, of course. Until we were confident enough in our relationship that we could go out and get our own place. You *do* think that's where this is headed, don't you?"

"Shit, yeah. I've been thinking about that a lot. I just didn't want to look too pushy. Only thing is, I don't know what Dallas will say about you moving in. He *is* just a friend, but he's sort of protective of me. Jealous, even. I could always call him in Rome. We've got his hotel number, but it's been a bitch trying to get him, what with the time change and all. Plus, I figure when he's not working he's chasing Italian tail."

"It was just a thought, guy. If it's a no-go, it'll take me some time and effort to find a place I can afford, so I won't be able to see as much of you as I'd like. But maybe it'll be good for us. Things have been a little intense."

Tony barely slept that night, torn between his fantasy of having Devlin come home to him every night and his concern that he was taking advantage of Dallas's hospitality. But Dallas had always said he was happiest when Tony was happy, and he had never been as happy as he was right now. That would have to make Dallas happy, right? In the morning, while Devlin slept with his face pushed deeply into a pillow, Tony went downstairs in his bathrobe.

"I think I'll have my coffee in the breakfast room, Alfred. Devlin's probably going to sleep late. He danced a new role last night, and he said he was really exhausted."

"As you wish, sir."

"Maybe you could have a cup with me?"

"Is something bothering you, sir?"

Tony told Alfred about his conversation with Devlin, explaining what he wanted and what he was feeling.

"Master Devlin seems like a nice enough young man, although his tonsorial regimen is a bit extreme. Why don't you just call Mr. Eden and ask?"

"I thought of that, but what if he says no? I couldn't lie to him or disobey him, but I really want to be with Devlin. This way we could at least buy some time until Dallas actually comes home. And it seems sort of rude for me to just move out of here without even saying good-bye to Dallas. What would he say when he got back?"

"I think of all your choices, the one that would cause the most damage would be if you left Dunstan Hall. Mr. Eden would be apoplectic."

"Apple what?"

"In street parlance . . . hit the roof, go around the bend, see red."

"You'd be in deep doo-doo, dude," Devlin said.

Tony looked up to see his lover entering the breakfast room wearing only his undershorts. Devlin didn't take to robes much. Tony wanted to melt into a puddle out of sheer embarrassment and simultaneously mash his face into the aromatic and faintly yellow cotton pouch.

"Morning, guy. What's for breakfast?" Devlin placed his hands on Tony's shoulders and kissed him on the top of his head. He reached over and picked up a white ceramic pot of citrus marmalade. He pulled out the spoon and licked it."Mmmm. How about a little dick a l'orange?"

"Dev," Tony said, managing to make it into a three-syllable word. "Not in front of Alfred."

Tony was not inclined to criticize Devlin's propensity for walking around Dunstan Hall nearly naked. It was an incredible turn-on. His lover's naked body was not merely an invitation to sex, it was a full-blown provocation. Even if he was already dressed and running late for a shoot, Tony would always stop to mess around with Devlin, who frequently splayed himself across the bed suggestively. Sometimes Tony thought he was testing him—seeing how late Tony would allow himself to be. It seemed so natural to have Devlin around. He practically lived at Dunstan Hall already. What would it matter if he moved his few possessions in? Besides, Dallas would be gone another two months at least. There was a good chance Devlin would have long ago moved out by the time Dallas returned.

Tony never regretted his decision. With their conflicting schedules, there would have been many nights on which they would have slept alone, had Devlin not come back to Dunstan Hall from the theater. Tony had several unexpected overseas shooting assignments, which lasted from four days to more than a week: Rio, Morocco, Ixtapa. Upon returning, he was frantic that the lapse in physical contact had somehow deflated the relationship, that the momentum had slowed, or even that Devlin had pulled up stakes. But each time Tony arrived at Kennedy, Devlin was waiting for him with flowers, Jorge in tow. And, amazingly, the sex kept getting better, something Tony hadn't thought possible. It was far better than the best dope he had ever done.

A week before Dallas was due home, Devlin started acting a little strange. He was distracted, jumpy, and sexually unresponsive, a first in their relationship.

"What's wrong, Dev?" Tony said after using, in vain, every possible technique to arouse him.

"I was just thinking. What if Dallas *is* jealous that I'm here? What if he throws me out?"

"I don't think he'd do that."

"Anyway, I been thinking. Maybe we ought to break it to him gently—you know, about you and me."

"What do you have in mind?"

"I was thinking maybe I should move into the room next door."

"What's that gonna do?"

"We'll tell him that we're just friends, that I'm an old buddy of yours who's down on his luck, and you invited me to stay here until I could get on my feet again."

"I still don't understand."

"You may not think so, but any queen who would let you live in the lap of luxury without making you put out must have the world's biggest hard-on for you. And if it ain't physical, it's got to be emotional. This guy probably thinks he loves you. He's not going to want to come home after three months and find you shacked up with some stud, namely me, who has quite obviously been tickling your tonsils and other less accessible portions of your anatomy with his exceptionally large and well-trained prick. My way, it wouldn't look like we were dicking each other. But don't worry, I'd still fuck you in every night. Did I say fuck? I meant tuck. Tuck you in. With that common door, it will be easy to pull off. After he's gotten to know and love me, as he surely will, we could start dropping hints that maybe we were becoming more than just friends. It would be a lot easier on the old geezer if we didn't just spring it on him all at once."

"But what about Alfred and the staff. They know the truth. What if they . . ."

"Said something to the boss man? I don't think so. First of all, I can tell that Dallas has surrounded himself with the cream of the crop, real Old World types, right down to the stinking laundress. They know their place. Seen but not heard and all that shit. From what you've told me, I'd guess that he's no Ebenezer Scrooge, either. Probably pays them pretty well. They know that it's not good to upset the applecart."

"Not even Alfred? He's like a brother to Dallas."

"That's where you're wrong. Alfred is *not* like a brother to Dallas and never will be. He's an employee, subservient in every way. He won't talk. Besides, I honestly think Alfred feels he serves *you* as well as Dallas. I can see it in his eyes. He's deferential to you. He'd do anything you asked. Christ, he still calls you 'Master Tony' and 'sir,' even after he found us fucking in the big guy's room. So all you have to do is tell him to keep his lip zipped and we're home free."

Three days later, they arrived at JFK in a small caravan. Tony and Devlin rode in the Fleetwood. Alfred rode in the new Mercedes limo with a handful of the staff, who would help load Dallas's luggage and his "souvenirs" into a black J. L. Dunstan van appropriated from the midtown store. Dallas's attorney, Mordecai "Mort" Saloman, pulled up the rear in his gold Lincoln Continental. He was along to ease his client's way through customs. Dallas had apparently ransacked several villas and at least two small museums in Rome looking for trinkets to add to his collection.

Dallas was easy to spot in the International Arrivals waiting area. He stood dead center in the crowded, noisy room, scanning the crowd for Tony. They both waved simultaneously.

"*That's* him?" Devlin asked. "Christ, I knew he was big, but you never told me he was being considered for fuckin' *statehood*."

"Devlin, I swear to God, if you say anything to Dallas that embarrasses me or hurts his feelings, I'll . . ."

"You'll what? Never let me fuck you again? I very much doubt that. But don't worry. I won't bite the hand that feeds you, even if it does look more like a bloated udder."

"It's cracks like that I'm talking about."

"Keep your girdle on, girl. I'm not stupid."

Tony winced at Devlin's tone, but said nothing. Dallas did appear to have gained weight. He was so fat now that it was impossible to get close enough to kiss him on the cheek, even on tiptoe. But his hair was cut in a flattering Caesar style, and he looked *imperial*.

Tony thought he noticed something flicker in Dallas's eyes when he introduced him to Devlin, but he didn't know what. Jealousy? Surprise? Disapproval? When Dallas extended his hand, Devlin took it in his, bowed, kissed it, and said, "*Enchanté*." Tony blushed, but Dallas gushed.

"What a delightful young man," he said, beaming. "Thoroughly Continental."

"May I say, Mr. Eden, that I have long admired your body of work. I think *The Three Stooges Meet King Tut* is a camp masterpiece."

Tony glared at Devlin.

"You're familiar with it? But that was *so* long ago."

"Your seminal work. It's been on the bill at every Stooges festival I've ever attended."

Dallas was beguiled by Devlin in the terminal, but once they got into the limousine, he turned his attention entirely to Tony, commenting on his ensemble and his new, slightly shorter hair; breaking out the first of many extravagant baubles; or just heaving a sigh, sitting quietly for a moment, and reveling in his presence. Tony said little and tried to look placid, but he worried that he was making the biggest mistake of his life. If Dallas didn't like Devlin or thought he was a phony—which seemed certain if Devlin tossed off many more pissy foreign phrases—he would probably kick both of them out. That might not be all bad. Sure, he'd never again live like royalty, but he'd have Devlin and that's all that mattered. He'd still have his career, and he had money in the bank. It's not like they'd have to live in the Bowery. And God, wouldn't it be great to get away from Dallas's possessiveness, his curiosity about every detail of his life, his inevitable, if somewhat labored, presence in any room Tony chose to retire to? While Dallas was in Rome, Tony had forgotten how claustrophobic it could get, but in the cramped passenger compartment of the limousine, it was all coming back to him.

During the course of Dallas's first weeks at home, Tony offered him plenty of opportunities to express an opinion about Devlin. But his host had little to say, although he once mused aloud about what it would feel like to run his hands over Devlin's gleaming pate, grab him by the ears, and force his lips to do his bidding. Tony was horrified.

When Dallas's larger purchases—sculptures, reliefs, and friezes—arrived and were uncrated, he announced his plans for a weekend bacchanal, a Roman carnival of the flesh. He had spent some time in the Eternal City researching ancient sexual arcana, and he promised live sex acts long unseen in modern times. Tony wanted nothing to do with the revelry. He made a brief appearance at the party in the centurion uniform Dallas had created especially for him, but while Dallas was preoccupied with a blond nymph who appeared to be not more than seventeen, he escaped to his bedroom. He packed a bag for him and one for Devlin and called to reconfirm the reservations he had made at the Plaza. Dallas would be too distracted to even know he was gone.

Devlin had other plans. When he got home from the theater, he hopped into the shower, toweled off, and slipped into a torn and "bloody" tunic that came equipped with an authentic-looking mace and trident. Tony, no longer in his costume, had been downstairs arranging transportation with Jorge. He stepped into his room to see Devlin flexing and posing.

"What the hell are you doing in that costume?"

"There's a costume *party* downstairs. I saw it with my own eyes. There's not a soul in street clothes."

"I thought we agreed to check out of here for a couple of days and have a nice romantic weekend without having to worry about what we said and did in front of Dallas. Maybe have some actual sex."

"Are you nuts? There's all the sex you could possibly want downstairs. It's like a night at the baths except better decor and some incredible food. Have you seen those guys carrying on? The jizz is already an inch thick on the floor, and if they keep on going at this rate, we'll be able to play Slip 'n' Slide on that Oriental runner outside the smoking room."

"That's not exactly what I had in mind, Dev. I was thinking more like some dope, a bubble bath, and a visit from the Plaza masseur. Relaxing. Intimate. Besides, we can't go downstairs and have sex. Dallas would know we were lovers."

"I wasn't talking about *us* having sex. In case Dallas *does* suspect we're more than friends, this is the perfect chance to prove to him that we're not. He'll see us having sex with different people, and it will put his mind at ease. I really think he's beginning to suspect. This little festival couldn't come at a better time. Now slip into your cute little leather skirt and let's get down and party."

Devlin was gone before Tony could say anything. He sat on his bed awhile, then figured it would be less depressing to get drunk at the party than to do it here, alone. He put on his red tunic, his breastplate, and various studded leather accessories, secured his sandals, which laced up nearly to his knees, strapped on his sword, and looked at himself in the mirror. "You look just like Ben Hur, you fool."

To Tony's anguish, Devlin made a spectacle of himself at the orgy, doing naked cartwheels across the marble floor and ejecting grapes from his ass into the mouths of his many admirers. Tony retired at 2 A.M., early for an event of such cinematic proportions, but only after getting sucked by an athletic, dark-skinned boy for thirty minutes directly in front of an apparently oblivious Devlin. As Tony left in disgust and frustration, the boy ran after him and begged Tony to fuck him, if not with his own cock than with one of the myriad rubber devices he carried with him. He did not stop until Tony slammed the bedroom door in his face.

Dallas was still not sated at sunrise. With some effort, he had saved his own eruption for an encounter with Tony's spectacularly sexual friend, Devlin. Oh, he had been wary of the boy from the moment he met him at the airport on his return from Rome. He was too glib, his spirit as slick as his scalp. And he worried that Devlin might be a bad influence on Tony. But soon thereafter, Devlin began making visits to Dallas's sleeping quarters. The first time, he arrived swathed in a white, gold-trimmed towel, "innocently" looking for a certain brand of analgesic, an item Alfred could have easily provided. Devlin's pretense and his towel dropped simultaneously as Dallas invited him into his suite. Thereafter, Devlin visited Dallas nightly, and Dallas showered the boy with gifts on each occasion. He saw no harm in it. Though he was initially afraid Devlin and Tony might be lovers, Devlin assured him that was not the case. The two seemed close, but their physical contact appeared to be limited to a kind of friendly roughhousing. Dallas was mesmerized by Devlin, but his feelings were in no way similar in form or magnitude to those he held for Tony.

Tonight, seeing Devlin being attended to by the youngest and most attractive men and boys, watching him plow boisterously through a chorus line of asses with speed and brutal power, Dallas was more aroused by the boy's sexual potency than ever before. He could not wait another minute; he had to have Devlin squatting over his face, offering him that arctic blossom, that tight, fragrant, heavenly blue flower. Those nether lips appeared able to do anything but speak a foreign language. When most of the gasps and cries had quietened and Devlin was not in evidence, Dallas pulled on his silk toga and made his way slowly out of the Grand Salon, up the elevator, then down the hall to Devlin's room. Devlin had always been the one to come to him, but he saw no problem with pursuing him. He would simply awaken the inevitably naked beast and take him back to his room.

The door was not locked. Why should it be? He opened it and inched in sideways. Devlin's bed was empty, and the door adjoining Tony's room was open, admitting a weak, wavering light, as from a candle. Curious, Dallas moved carefully toward the connecting door, sweating, an electric tremor rising from his sphincter to his scapulae. He heard voices, not speaking but uttering guttural animal noises. Loud, rhythmic breathing. Sudden spikes of anguished pleasure screams. . . . The floor creaked under his weight, and he froze. Had they heard him? He could not risk being discovered, but he had to see what was taking place.

When the bucking of the bed grew more intense, the cries louder, he hurried, as only he could hurry, to the half-open door and looked in. By candlelight he could see Tony, on his back, arms tied to the bedposts, legs in the air. Devlin's left hand appeared to be pulling and twisting something in a way that made Tony shriek and then laugh and wail. It was his nipple. Devlin was torturing Tony's nipple.

"Let's hope I don't have any bathing suit shoots this week," Tony said, chuffing the words out to the rhythm of Devlin's hips.

"Are you ready for me to start on the other one?"

"Fuck *yes*. My only regret is that I have but two nips to give to my lover."

Dallas nearly swooned, recalling the silken bites of cherubim on his own gigantic eraser heads. He backed away from the door, into the darkness. He was still able to see but was less likely to be seen. He didn't know how long he stood there as the springs sang and the candles flickered. It seemed like forever. He knew he should get out now, while they were still conjoined, but he couldn't pull himself away. He wanted desperately to burst into the room and lick every sweaty crevice of Tony's body. He thought he might cry. Then the air was rent by familiar exclamations in two distinct voices, one erupting a heartbeat after the other. A few echoes of springs, a few loud exhalations. Then nothing. Then exhausted laughter. Giggles of the most intimate nature.

"God, you're good, Devlin. I love it when you fuck me."

"Do you want more?"

"Do you have to ask?"

Devlin straddled Tony and took a hit of poppers. As the rush took hold, he bent his body backward until his head touched the bed. All Tony could see were Devlin's oiled, soiled cock and balls and beyond them his swelling pectoral muscles.

"Dancers are the best sex," Devlin said. "Dancers and gymnasts. We can make our bodies do things other people can't even imagine."

"So come on, fuck me again."

Devlin drew his arched body up, smoothly, gracefully, one vertebra at a time. Halfway up, his right arm extended, he looked like an art deco interpretation of Helios.

"I want to come in your mouth this time," Devlin said, his slick dick throbbing an inch from Tony's lips. "Suck it, pretty boy."

"Devlin, it's got lube and shit all over it. Go wash it off."

"Suck it, you little fag."

"Forget it," Tony said and strained against his bonds. Instantly, Devlin was kneeling on Tony's shoulders.

"What's the matter, too good for a taste of your own shit?" He grabbed Tony by his hair and pulled his head sharply back. "Suck it, you little pussy, or I'll jam it so far down your filthy cocksucking throat my cum will ooze out your ears."

Dallas shrank back into the shadows, stunned. He was outraged. Horrified. For an instant he thought of giving himself away, of confronting Devlin and throwing him out into the street in what he was wearing: two alligator tit clamps connected by a slender chain and a studded leather cock ring. But he knew that if Devlin was capable of carrying off the scene he had just witnessed, he was capable of telling Tony about his sexual encounters with Dallas, which, while sordid enough, could approach the grotesque with the least embellishment.

Tony would despise him. And the boy had been savagely humiliated. If he knew Dallas had been watching, he would be devastated. What kind of a pervert was he, Tony would ask, sneaking around the house at night and spying on them? No, if he kicked Devlin out, Tony would follow, and he might never see him again.

He backed out of the darkened room carefully, his heart breaking as he listened to Tony's now-muffled objections. He dared not dwell on the precise details, but once safely in the hallway, he allowed himself to cry, noiselessly. Instead of returning to his room, he headed for the ormolu elevator and descended to the library. The incunabula were stored under archival conditions, and he pulled a pair of white, acid-free gloves onto his puffy hands with some difficulty before removing two volumes from their shelf: *The Devil's Delights* and *Lost Secrets of the Spanish Inquisition*. He turned the brittle pages slowly, lingering over some of the more gruesome woodcuts. He knew where he would first use the radiant poker on Devlin. Or would that be the last orifice he would cauterize?

Dallas knew, of course, he wouldn't actually inflict these punishments on Devlin, but it was cathartic to imagine them. Still, he knew just as certainly what he wanted to accomplish and what he could reasonably expect to carry off without any unpleasant repercussions. It would cost him, dearly, but when had that ever mattered? All he needed now was a minion to carry out his orders.

# 18

TONY SAT AT THE HEAD OF DEVLIN'S BED, holding his hand, alert for the strident bleat of the limo's horn that would signal the last possible moment to leave for Kennedy and still catch his flight to Australia. He would be gone for nearly three weeks, with shoots at Sydney, Melbourne, and the Great Barrier Reef, and in the Outback, which also happened to be the name of the cologne for which the trip was being made. Val, who was there to see him off, had been baiting him for the past two weeks about having a go at the infamous Aussie lifeguards—jacks, they were called. "You'll be eighteen thousand miles away, Tony. Have a fling with a jack-o. There's no reason not to kick up your heels. Devlin won't be any the wiser."

But Tony insisted he was not interested. "The only jack-o I'll be doing is Mr. Jack *Off*."

In fact, Tony couldn't think of a worse time to consider adultery. A month ago, while crossing Park Avenue at Seventy-ninth, Devlin had been hit by a cab. Tony, who had by chance been walking just three steps behind, had never seen anything like it. The taxi appeared out of nowhere and threw Devlin to the ground with a bump from the right front fender, breaking his right femur. When the cab came to a halt, the right rear tire was positioned precisely atop Devlin's legs, the weight of the car splintering both of them. The driver disappeared into traffic, immediately invisible in the nearly solid stream of yellow vehicles on the avenue. Tony screamed and dropped to one knee at Devlin's side, imploring passersby to call the police.

An intense search failed to turn up a single cab with even the slightest evidence of an accident similar to the one that, as far as five orthopedic surgeons could say, irrevocably ended Devlin's romance with terpsichore. He would be lucky to even walk again, one physician suggested.

The cost of his treatment and eventual rehabilitation would be astronomical, but Dallas assured Tony he would cover everything. He even offered to create a position for Devlin in the dance department at Sanctuary College, so he wouldn't have to worry about finding a job in New York City—ever. Devlin could keep his pride, and Tony could fly down to Florida whenever he chose.

"Do you have everything you need, Dev?" Tony said, feeling Devlin's forehead for any trace of fever.

"Juice, water, chocolates, comic books, *Daily News, Colt* magazines," Devlin said, gesturing to the items splayed across the bed. "Everything but your tight little ass beside me, but I'm probably not quite ready for that yet."

"Get ready by the time I get back or I'll be *very* disappointed."

"Sure, babe. Anything you want. Now give me a kiss and go. You can't afford to miss that plane."

Tony leaned down to kiss him, and Devlin pulled him closer with his right arm. At that moment, they heard the triple strikes of the limo's horn.

"So go already," Devlin said.

"Val, you *will* look after him like I asked?" Tony asked.

"Don't worry. He'll be in good hands," Val said. Devlin smirked. Tony pouted. "Perhaps that wasn't the best phraseology. His wish will be my command."

THREE WEEKS LATER, Val met Tony at the airport.

"You look fabulous. I love November tans. And your hair looks incredible. Is it natural?"

"Bitch. You know I never color my hair. So how's Dev?"

"He's fine. He'll be up and about in no time."

"Actually, I sort of liked having him laid up. You know how insecure I am. When I'm away, I worry all the time that he'll be tricking out. But this time . . ."

"Tony, there's something . . ."

"God, Val, I met the cutest guys there. You were right, the lifeguards are *un*believable. I went surfing with three of them and I swear, they were about to rape me right there on my board. And I mean they were *gods.*"

"So did you?"

"No. Not with Devlin in bed, laying there all helpless with nothing to do but wait for me to come home. So he's making progress? I can't wait to see him. Has he been doing those isometric exercises I gave him? He really shouldn't let his upper body just shrivel up on him. It will be twice as hard for him to get back into shape if he does."

"Tony, there's something we need to talk about."

"About Dev? What? Oh, God, he got gangrene or something?"

"Do you think I would have failed to call you if he had gangrene? Australia is far away, but it's still on the same planet."

"So he's okay?"

"He's fine. We *have* moved him to my place, however."

"What? Dallas isn't reneging on his promise to take care of him, is he?"

"No, Tony. But I'll be assuming responsibility for Devlin's medical bills . . ."

"You? What for?"

"This is hard to say . . ."

Val told Tony how Devlin always needed attention and complained about how bored and lonely he was. Dallas was never around, so Val canceled his bookings and moved into Dunstan Hall. He had a second bed brought into the room so he could be available if Devlin woke up and needed something during the night.

"We were very close, physically, what with the bathing, and the rub-downs, and the exercises. And the . . . touching."

"Touching? Touching *what* for God's sake?"

"I had to help him with his catheter. . . ."

"What's that?"

"It lets him, as he so colorfully puts it, drain his lizard."

"You touched his dick? You *touched* Devlin's dick? Dallas hired a nurse. Couldn't she have done that?"

"Dev was embarrassed. He didn't want a woman to see him . . . down there. He was very vulnerable. As you can imagine, we developed a new level of intimacy, Tony. I'm sorry. I really am. I fought it, but it was so irresistible . . . rubbing lotion into his poor, dry skin, washing his hair . . ."

"He has hair?"

"Just a little. Chestnut. It's stiff like a toothbrush."

"So you had sex with him? How could you?"

"I don't know, Tony, it just . . ."

"No, I mean, he's in a cast from his hips down. How *could* you?"

"Oh, well, *I* wasn't in a cast."

Tony was practically speechless. Yet again, his life had changed in the blink of an eye, the same way it had when Connecticut deserted him and when Mitch had betrayed him. Or when his mother had died twelve years ago. He was completely alone in the world, with no one to turn to. Oh, there was Dallas, of course. There was *always* Dallas. He would cluck and coo and flutter around Tony like a mother hen, trying to make him feel better but succeeding only in making him feel claustrophobic. (Dallas had grown so large that Tony was nervous riding in the limousine with him. If they took a turn too fast and Dallas's weight shifted, it was entirely possible that Tony would be crushed.) Tony appreciated everything Dallas had done for him, taking him in when he had no place else to turn, giving him a home, providing stability. But there was a difference between security and *maximum* security, and lately Tony had begun thinking of Dunstan Hall as a prison.

He couldn't *believe* Devlin had dumped him for Val. Well, in a *way* he could. Val could give Devlin anything in the world he wanted—and there was *a lot* that Devlin wanted. All Tony could give him was his love. The entire time he had been in Australia, he had thought of nothing but coming home to Devlin. He had been so homesick it had practically ruined the trip. When he wasn't working, he stayed in his hotel room and wrote letters and postcards to Devlin. He'd missed several good parties and a couple of interesting sightseeing excursions Tuxedo had organized for the boys. Every model on the trip, every single one except Tony, had had a fling with some Aussie hunk. He'd had plenty of opportunities; he knew for a fact that at least three of the guys on the trip ended up having flings with men he had turned down. And now he had nothing to show for it.

Somehow, the pain was different now than it had been when Connecticut had left him. Thinking about that still made him sad—he wasn't sure he would *ever* fully recover. But he had only himself to blame: if he hadn't fucked around with Zen, if he'd been a better, stronger person, he and Connecticut would still be together. He loved Connecticut so much that if he had shown up on the steps of Dunstan Hall at any time in the past two and a half years—even in the past nine months, when he was with Devlin—he would have taken him back in a heartbeat. But this thing with Devlin seemed mean, cruel, calculated. Evil, somehow. *Wrong*. It made him wonder how he could have ever loved Devlin in the first place. Was he that stupid? That *blind?*

Of course, there was Val to consider. Was he evil, too? Or had he just been taken in by Devlin? Tony wasn't sure what hurt the most: losing his *boy*friend or losing his *best* friend. It was definitely too close to call.

# 19

TONY DREW BACK the sapphire moiré draperies and peered out his bedroom window, up Fifth Avenue to the Metropolitan Museum. The clouds were low and swiftly moving, the color of pewter, and what light passed through them was dull and diffuse. Colors were vibrant in the curious light, but flat. Nothing glowed; nothing shone. Taxis in particular were garishly hued, jaundiced, almost sulfurous. Passersby looked ashen. And the usually inviting Metropolitan looked more like a Nazi mausoleum than a temple of the Muse.

He let the stiff fabric wash back over the window with a whisper. Picking up his leather date book, he confirmed what he already knew. February fourteenth. St. Fucking Valentine's Day—the fourth anniversary of his breakup with Connecticut. Dallas always said he was reading too much into it, but Tony was convinced that Connecticut knew *exactly* what he was doing when he chose this day to flee Gotham. For Tony, Cupid's arrows would forevermore be dipped in strychnine. Case in point: St. Valentine's Day 1973, the blackest of days two years ago, when he met that soulless little whore at Fusion and plunged headlong into disaster.

But he knew that for Dallas the significance of St. Dick, as Dallas called Cupid, was far greater than that of St. Nick. Alfred had told him how, several years ago, Dallas had filled his new, heart-shaped, rose marble Jacuzzi with yellow plastic ducks roiling amidst the bubbles. Each little quacker held a piece of expensive ruby or diamond-and-ruby jewelry in its belly. Dallas invited his friends over and allowed their kept boys to bob for the ducks much the way they would for apples at Halloween, naked, their hands bound behind them.

For tonight's observance, Dallas had a noted Broadway set designer rig up a system of pulleys so two sex techs could swoop down in harnesses, naked save for their "wings," and refill wineglasses. At the end of the meal, the hovering hunks were to be lowered to about five feet off the ground so the diners could floss with their pubic hair. And what would the door prizes be? Monogrammed silver cock rings from Tiffany for the guests? Blow-Pop buttplugs for the harem girls?

Tony shook his still dampish hair from side to side and finished blow-drying it. It was going to be one hell of a day: a Hallmark shoot with Victor at a borrowed Central Park West town house, followed by lunch with the Malone boys at Tuxedo's Midtown home away from home, where they would meet Wolf, a new face Tux had somehow smuggled out of East Germany after seeing him in a *Time* magazine article on the persistence of the Berlin Wall. Then class with Stella at three; a massage, mud bath, facial, and his standing appointment with Rudy at Flagranté; and an anything-but-quiet dinner at home.

Tony scooped up his Burberry coat, selected a pair of leather gloves, folded a favorite cashmere scarf over his arm, and headed downstairs for breakfast. Dallas was already seated at the table, silhouetted by the odd light filtering through the Tiffany tryptych, *The Garden of Eden,* that encompassed most of the room's west wall.

"Good morning, gorgeous, you look positively radiant, as usual," Dallas said, his mouth full and his enunciation on the soggy side. "And happy St. Valentine's Day to you."

"Humbug." Tony sat down, shook out his blood-red napkin with more rigor than necessary, and placed it on his lap. Alfred stepped up to the table and poured him a cup of coffee.

"How could I forget? Our annual observance of *la mort de l'amour.* Well, I'll have no tears in this house today. Besides being St. Valentine's Day, this is also the day I sign with J. F. Mamjjasond. Your mama is working in the motion picture industry again!"

Tony laughed in spite of his bleak mood. Somehow Dallas always managed to crack him up, even when he was on the verge of buying a five-pack of Gillette Blue Blades to practice scrimshaw on his wrists. Tony was glad Dallas would be working again. He was a born enter-tainer, and he really wasn't completely alive without an audience. *Caligula* had bombed at the box office, and Dallas hadn't worked since. But earlier that week, Dallas received a phone call from his attorney, Mort Saloman, who said the Dutch producer J. F. Mamjjasond was ready to sign him to the three-picture contract they had been discussing. Dallas was ecstatic. In the first film, he would play the role of Fatty Arbuckle. In the second, Dallas was cast as an intergalactic villain who was so fat he had to be moved around his home-planet fortress on a bed of helium balloons. Finally, Dallas was to portray the Buddha in his later years. *That* would be a challenge. Dallas could think of no one less contemplative than himself, but on the plus side, he *would* be stationary throughout most of the film.

Tony sipped his black coffee and ate half an unbuttered English muffin. He drank only enough orange juice to allow him to swallow his handful of vitamins.

"Darling, what *do* you use for energy during these terribly long days you have?" Dallas asked.

"I'm just not hungry in the morning, Dal." Tony popped the last crusty morsel of muffin into his mouth and delicately sucked the crumbs from his fingers. "Everybody's doing meth anyway."

"I worry about you, Tony. I really do."

Tony pressed the linen napkin to his lips and stood up without comment. He brushed at a few errant muffin crumbs on his trousers, then leaned over and gave Dallas a kiss on the top of his head. The bristly red hair tickled his nose. "Gotta go! I'll see you around eight."

"Eight? You haven't forgotten about lunch, have you? '21.' Today."

"Lunch? Today?" Tony said. He stopped and pivoted where he stood, his leather soles squealing against the marble floor. Dallas had the look of a child restrained only six inches from an ice-cream cone. Tony hated to disappoint him.

"I forgot, Dal. I don't think I can make it. I've got this shoot with Victor this morning, and you know what a perfectionist *he* is. I could be there till who knows when. And once I escape his clutches, I'm supposed to show up for a lunch Tuxedo's throwing for his latest Aryan god."

"But I'll be signing with J. F. over lunch," Dallas said. He had momentarily relinquished his hold on his cutlery. "It would mean so much to me if you were there to toast my return to the big—or should I say *wide*—screen."

"Okay, I'll call Tux and cancel. But I have no control over Victor, so who knows when we'll be through. What time were you shooting for?"

"One o'clock. And let me handle the call to Tuxedo. I'll tell him it's all my fault." Dallas beamed as Tony raised his right hand and, without turning around, wiggled his fingers backward in a parting gesture.

"Are you dressed warmly enough?" Dallas shouted as he heard the front door open. No answer. Tony never had responded to his mothering. He picked up his knife and fork and heaved a sigh. It hadn't gotten any easier to say good-bye to Tony. He looked down at the empty plate in front of him. Seizing the small silver service bell, he rang. "Hot coffee," he bellowed. "And I'm going to need half a dozen blueberry pancakes if I expect to wait until one o'clock for lunch!"

Dallas hoped working would distract him, would ease the crushing boredom and sense of isolation he felt when he was home alone. It had been different when Tony was doing *Hair* and they had the whole morning and afternoon to spend together. They would go shopping or spend the morning at galleries and museums, followed by long lunches at Tavern on the Green or some greasy spoon or ethnic spot Tony had fallen in love with. The nights were still lonely, but Dallas often went to the Biltmore to wait for him backstage.

Now he frequently didn't see the boy from breakfast until Tony made his way up the stairs in the wee hours of the morning. And then there were those out-of-town trips. Who knew what went on in those dressing rooms or those location shoots in Barbados and Palm Springs? When would the day come—and come it would—that Tony would return home flushed with lust and excitement over a new man—the *perfect* man—with whom he wanted to spend the rest of his life? Someone who would make Connecticut Jones and Devlin DeSchuys nothing more than unpleasant footnotes to his emotional life. He simply *had* to go back to work, to have something to fall back on when that time came.

There had been only one obstacle to his film comeback: his weight. He was, of course, completely unsuited for the ingenue roles he coveted. There were, in fact, few parts for an actor of his physical type. Then too, suppose he had a heart attack or stroke in the middle of the shoot? Dropped dead on the set? Even if he didn't die outright, the film might have to be put in mothballs until he recuperated. He just wasn't a big enough star for most producers to risk it.

Dallas's weight had quadrupled since he had done *This Zulu Is Crazy* nearly fifteen years ago. In a slow but inexorable metamorphosis, he had gone from moderately overweight to morbidly obese. So complicated was the process now required to extricate him from the house that he rarely went out at all, unless it was at Tony's request. When his discussions with Mamjjasond began some months ago, he tried any number of diets, but at his weight, noticeable results would come only when the pounds lost were in the triple figure range. Desperate, he had even contemplated getting his jaws wired shut and subsisting on the latest wonder food, liquefied Japanese sea kelp, in three delicious flavors: bland, unpalatable, and downright rank. But when his doctor informed him the operation also would render him unable to suck cock, he refused on the spot. He could do without one of his great passions, but not both. Still, he managed to lose a little weight by instructing his kitchen staff to cut by half the amount of food presented to him, no matter how he railed against them, even if he threatened to fire them.

Almost as soon as he had finished eating—the staff had bravely refused requests for thirds on the blueberry pancakes—Dallas began the laborious process of dressing for lunch. At eleven-fifteen he summoned Jorge and the car. It had begun to snow, and he wanted to have plenty of time to arrive at the restaurant and supervise the configuration of a suitable seating arrangement. The Fleetwood pulled up to the restaurant at noon amid flakes the size of half dollars.

J. F. Mamjjasond materialized at the table at one sharp. "No, no, Dallas, please. Don't get up," he said as he saw Dallas quivering behind the table like a *blanc mange* with thyroid problems. Despite the great power he wielded in the world of international cinema, J. F. Mamjjasond was an unprepossessing man, the antithesis of charismatic. He could enter a room entirely unnoticed, like a wraith, without intersecting the trajectory of a single sidelong glance. He was a lean, rangy man, made elegant by the cut of his European coats and suits. His attire was always monochromatic, tone-on-tone white, charcoal, or black. No one knew his age with any certainty. Some claimed to have proof that he was a contemporary of Griffith, Chaplin, and Pathé; others argued he was too young by twenty years to have worked during the Silent Age.

Mamjjasond sat down in a chair facing Dallas, who took up most of a banquette designed to hold four. They ordered cocktails, and at 1:20 the maître d' brought a white telephone to their table. It was Tony. Dallas could hear the exasperation in his voice.

"I'm really sorry I'm late, but just about everything that could possibly go wrong has. At any rate, we're done. I've just got to change and get this crap off my face, but I should be out of here in ten minutes and at '21' in, what, twenty? Twenty-five tops."

Dallas was unperturbed. "No problem, but do you mind if we start without you? I'm ravenous! I practically starved myself at breakfast just so I could enjoy lunch."

"Sure, go ahead. I'll probably just have something light—a clear soup and a salad, dressing on the side—whatever they've got."

"Fine, I'll arrange it. And Tony, please be careful. The streets are awfully slippery, and the snow is really coming down."

Dallas hung up. He conveyed the news to Mamjjasond, who nodded and lit a cigarette. "I've got all the time in the world, Dallas. All the time in the world." He didn't even look at his watch, Dallas noted. Good sign.

Dallas used the time to sign the contracts, since Mort Saloman had already given them his seal of approval. He ordered two *filets mignon* and a bottle of cabernet from his private stock. He usually ate three filets, but he wanted Mamjjasond to see how hard he was trying to cut down.

Uptown, Tony changed and dashed for a cab on Central Park West. A dry, gray snow was falling, the color of dull nickels, and it appeared to be accumulating rapidly. The cab wasn't even making a block a minute, and with almost thirty blocks to go, he would never arrive by two. When they finally crossed West 54th Street, they came to a complete stop. Tony glanced at his watch. Two-ten. Each click of the meter felt like a pinprick. All around them, horns honked like migrating mallards.

Tony knew it was folly to proceed in the cab, and he decided to walk the rest of the way to the restaurant. Tony looked at the meter, opened his wallet, and threw a couple of bills at the driver. "I'm out," he said, slamming the door behind him. He jumped over a curb still full of the detritus of the last snowstorm and walked briskly south and east.

The wind was driving the snow almost horizontal, and those people who hadn't had the sense to wear scarves were clutching their coat collars to their necks with one hand while carrying briefcases, purses, or shopping bags in the other. As Tony turned the corner at West 52nd Street, he could see what must have been blocking traffic. A policeman stood in the center of the street, waving an ambulance forward with one hand while fending off traffic with the other. A long, steel gray Lincoln Continental followed the ambulance like a wraith. Tony continued walking, his head down, until he approached the wrought-iron grape-vine-and-*fleur-de-lis* entrance of "21."

Beneath the awning, the maître d' and a corporate type in a dark suit were talking to a policeman, who tried to make notes on a small white pad that was being barraged by kamikaze snowflakes. Every few seconds the maître d' looked at the man in the suit, as if seeking approval. Each time, the businessman nodded, and the maître d' continued talking to the cop. Tony figured a patron had been run over in front of the restaurant or maybe just slipped on the icy pavement.

Inside, there was a sensation of . . . what? Not gaiety. Excitement of some sort, but brittle, almost hysterical. Voices had risen an octave above the normal hum, and no one was paying the least bit of attention to the food on their plates. A long row of wide-eyed waiters, staring at a space in the center of the dining room, broke ranks as their captain silently clapped his white-gloved hands, then fluttered them as if he were shooing pigeons. Maybe, Tony thought, something really interesting had occurred. Perhaps a betrayed spouse, crazed with grief and jealousy, had shot a cheating husband, a lying wife, while he or she dined with a paramour.

Tony waited a few minutes in the reception area, until he saw the maître d' back at his station, delicately patting his forehead with a snow-white napkin folded into quarters. When Tony approached, the maître d', obviously unsettled, hid the napkin in a pocket. *Never let them see you sweat.*

"Excuse me," Tony said. "I'm supposed to meet Dallas Eden here for lunch. Can you direct me to his table?"

The maître d' looked at him oddly, Tony thought, as if he had asked to be seated at the right hand of God. He squinted at Tony and furrowed his brow as if he were trying to place his face. Then he ran a finger down a list of reservations.

"Yesss, I see. Mr. Eden's reservation *was* for three. But my dear boy, that was for one o'clock. It is very nearly two-thirty."

*Don't* my dear boy *me, you ass,* Tony thought. He hated these guys with their pencil-thin mustaches and Berlitz accents. "I called to tell him I'd be late, and I know he wouldn't leave without me. Now just show me to his table, if you don't mind."

"I'm afraid that's impossible," he said without a quiver. "Mr. Eden is gone."

"Are you sure?" Tony was dumbfounded. It was inconceivable that Dallas would leave without him.

"Young man, one can hardly miss the comings and goings of a man of Mr. Eden's . . . stature."

"Did he at least leave a message for me?"

"I'm afraid he said nothing before he left. Nothing at all." And with that, he turned his attentions to a man in a glen plaid suit and a woman young enough to be his daughter. "Welcome to '21', and may I say ma'm'selle is looking quite spectacular this afternoon."

Tony stalked out of the restaurant and headed to Stella Adler's studio. He was seething. This was a first. Dallas had never left him stranded anywhere. And it wasn't *his* fault the snow backed up traffic for blocks. It took him almost the entire length of his walk to realize that he was less angry with Dallas than with the little faux Frenchman. But he was worried, too. It was more than merely uncharacteristic of Dallas not to wait for him. Dallas planned his whole life around him, for godsakes. What could have happened that would have made him leave in such a goddamned hurry? Tony had broken out into another sweat by the time he reached the studio, and he remained damp, perplexed, and preoccupied during class.

By the time he arrived at Flagranté, he was tired, tense, and truculent. He spewed vitriol at the young woman shampooing his hair, first because the rinse water was too cold, and later because she had allowed a stream to trickle down his back. He stiffed her. He was impatient in the mud bath, and later, when some of the apricot-lime face mask leaked into his right eye, stinging like hell, he excoriated the attendant. At last he placed himself entirely at the mercy of Gunnar, the masseur with a voice at least as soothing as his hands, and he grew more relaxed with each pull, pat, and pummel, until he had very nearly fallen asleep in the warm, dimly lighted room. He took a Nordic plunge to wake up and to close his pores before heading for Rudy's chair.

Tony asked Rudy to turn on the TV that was recessed into the wall, so that he wouldn't have to make conversation. The picture materialized, but no sound. The *CBS Evening News with Walter Cronkite* was on, and Leslie Stahl was speaking silently with a picture of Patty Hearst superimposed behind her. Then Walter Cronkite was back on screen, and over his left shoulder was a picture of Dallas that must have been at least fifteen years old. Tony hurriedly asked Rudy to turn up the volume.

". . . as Eden, son of silent screen legend Eve Eden and sole heir to the J. L. Dunstan department store fortune, died of a heart attack today while lunching in a New York restaurant." Cronkite cleared his throat, and the picture changed to one of Dallas in khakis and pith helmet. "Eden had a brief Hollywood career of his own and received his only Oscar nomination for a supporting role in an otherwise forgettable 1962 Bob Hope film, *This Zulu Is Crazy*. He is perhaps better known for his stand-up comedy act and his appearances on a variety of television quiz shows. He was also an extraordinarily generous patron of the arts, and his palatial homes in New York and Florida are said to comprise one of the most eclectic private art collections in the Western Hemisphere. Dallas Eden was forty-five." Walter Cronkite looked down at his notes for an instant, as if to pay homage to Dallas. "And that's the way it is, Friday, February 14, 1975 . . ."

Tony jumped out of the chair, and Rudy accidentally nicked his ear. The cut drew blood, and Rudy was immediately at Tony's side with a fresh white towel. Tony brushed him aside. Still wearing his cape, he walked briskly toward the glass elevator, stopped, turned once in place, grabbed his stomach, and doubled over. Dallas, dead? Impossible. And then Rudy was beside him, guiding him back into the chair.

"Tony, I'm terribly sorry. This is dreadful, truly dreadful. Mr. Eden was a wonderful, kind man. With so many friends. You'll see. You won't have to face this alone." Rudy adjusted the cape around Tony's neck. "Terrible thing. A crime. But you must let me finish cutting your hair before my next client arrives. Mrs. Firestone does not like to be kept waiting."

Tony nodded dumbly. His mind was blank. The salon had dissolved into white noise. He thought he could feel every individual, discrete hair being cut. Tony found himself slowly shaking his head side to side in disbelief until Rudy clamped his palm firmly on Tony's crown. The roar of the hair dryer was almost unbearable. When the noise stopped and Tony opened his eyes, he saw that Rudy was at the counter talking to Claire, the receptionist, *sotto voce*. The woman shuffled through some papers and handed one to Rudy. He scanned it, looked in Tony's direction for an instant, then nodded and handed it back to her.

Rudy came back to do the final comb-out and spray of Tony's hair. "Tony, you must accept the heartfelt condolences of myself and all of my staff." *Pssssst, pssssst, pssssst.* "We were all very fond of Mr. Eden, and we will miss him terribly." *Pssssst.*

"Thanks, Rudy. I appreciate that. I really don't know *what* I'm feeling. I haven't even cried yet."

"That's all right, Tony. You're in shock." He patted a few stray hairs into place, and stepped back, swiveling the chair to view both sides and the back. What a remarkable head of hair this young man had. "Please do let us know the details when the arrangements are made. And, oh, Tony, please stop by Claire's desk on your way out."

Tony nodded and brushed at some short, golden hairs that had found their way to his sleeves. He thought for a moment that Claire must want the address of Dunstan Hall so the shop could send a card or flowers. But certainly, they already had that. Perhaps she wanted to express her condolences personally. He'd always liked Claire and usually spent some time talking to her on each visit, unlike most customers, who treated her like little more than a cash register. But when he got there, Claire had other things on her mind.

"A terrible loss, Mr. Alexander, to all of us," said Claire, shaking her head, her eyes downcast, her petite, faintly freckled hands clasped in front of her on the desk, her modest gold wedding band flashing once.

"Thank you, Claire. I can't imagine what my life will be like without him."

"Just so, Mr. Alexander." She paused and coughed. "Now, how will you be taking care of today's visit?"

"Taking care of *what?*" Was she actually saying what he thought she was saying?

"Today's *visit,*" she said, flashing a coolly neutral smile but sounding like a schoolmarm. *"Today's charges."*

"But Dallas always . . ."

"I understand that, Mr. Alexander. But now that Mr. Eden is gone, we can't very well, you know. . . . We wouldn't want to make a claim against the estate for something as inconsequential as a spa visit and cut, would we?" She placed the bill on the counter. Tony picked it up and felt the anger rising in his throat. This wasn't about the money. It was about the gall of asking him to pay on the spot as if he were going to leave town in the next boxcar to Passaic or Hoboken, penniless and disgraced just because Dallas was dead.

"Do you honor the American Express card?" he asked, his palms just the slightest bit sweaty.

"Why, yes, we do, Mr. Alexander," Claire said. "At Flagranté, we honor just about any form of payment you can imagine."

Tony walked the few blocks to Dunstan Hall oblivious to everything and everyone. From the sidewalk, he could see that the mansion, its windows usually ablaze, was dark and silent and apparently as lifeless as its owner. Was everyone already gone? In the bitter cold, beneath the winking, star-filled sky, he felt as if he were a survivor of the *Titanic,* watching helplessly as the doomed liner slipped beneath the sea forever. All that grace and beauty gone in an instant.

No lamps burned at the gate, and the recessed lights along the path to the door had also been extinguished. Tony could see lights in Jorge's rooms above the garage and in the fourth-floor servants' quarters. The harem, however, was completely darkened. He had difficulty finding the lock, and once in the foyer he tripped over the umbrella stand before finding the switch plate. From there he illuminated each room ahead of himself, penetrating slowly into the interior like an explorer tracking the source of the Nile. He thought he heard music. Strings. He cocked his head and listened. The study? As he approached the double doors, he could make out the piece. Mendelssohn's *Octet.* He knocked once and swung open the right-hand door slowly. Jacketless, Alfred sat at the great mahogany desk, carefully organizing documents he had removed from a stack of pleated, buff-colored folders. He'd looked up expectantly at the sound of Tony's knock.

"Mr. Alexander," Alfred said, rising. "So good to see you. I've been concerned all day. . . . I take it you've . . ."

"Yes, I know. Heard about it less than an hour ago. I was in Rudy's chair at Flagranté when the story came on the news."

"How perfectly awful."

Tony walked to the bar and poured himself a generous scotch on the rocks. He leaned over Alfred's shoulder, staring at the official-looking documents spread across the top of the desk: stock certificates, bonds, and other fiduciary instruments; significant quantities of foreign currency left over from Dallas's trips abroad; keys to homes, cars, boats, and safety deposit boxes; deeds, guarantees, and receipts; photographs of insured valuables; and a thick document typed on onionskin paper. "So how are *you* holding up?"

"I think I am . . . maintaining, sir," Alfred said. He looked at his pocket watch and then, uncharacteristically, used his right sleeve to mop his brow. "But to be honest, I don't really know. Right now I'm concentrating on this paperwork for Mr. Saloman. He'll be here momentarily."

"Then we better turn some lights on outside. I practically broke my neck coming in."

"I'm terribly sorry about that, sir, but I couldn't be sure I had reached all the guests for tonight's party. I had the service call everyone on the guest list, but you know there are always those whom Mr. Eden invites without letting me know. I presumed that with the lights out, no one would bother coming to the door."

"My dad always did that on Halloween."

"I was hoping anyone who arrived not knowing the circumstances would think Mr. Eden had moved the party to another location. I don't think I could really stand there and tell them the party was canceled because the host had choked to death earlier in the day."

"Choked to death? Walter Cronkite said he had a heart attack."

"That *is* what Mr. Eden's doctor told the gentlemen of the press. Actually, he choked to death on a *filet mignon*. In polite society, I believe it is referred to as a café coronary. Mr. Mamjjasond called me from the restaurant just moments after it happened. He said Mr. Eden had ordered two *filets mignon* for lunch. He had eaten the first and had begun on the second when he laughed at a joke Mr. Mamjjasond told. Then Mr. Eden reached for his throat and tried to stand up. He didn't say anything, just fell forward on the table, splitting it in two, and crashed to the floor. It wasn't until the rescue personnel tried to give him oxygen that they discovered his windpipe was blocked by a large piece of meat. And what of you, sir? Jorge told me you hadn't arrived at the restaurant by the time the ambulance left for the hospital."

Tony quickly recounted the events of his afternoon, ending with the embarrassing incident at Flagranté. "I'll never set foot in that place again, even if Rudy *is* Mr. World Coiffure 1971! Sounds like some drag title to me, anyway."

"I'll match you tit for tat on that one, sir. You should have been here when Dunstan Incorporated showed up at the door. Didn't even knock. They had *passkeys!*" Alfred told him a cadre of Dunstan top brass had invaded the house even before the boys at the morgue had had a chance to determine which side of Dallas was up. The household staff was assembled and sacked with the same speed and goodwill the Romanovs suffered at the hands of the Bolsheviks. Live-ins were expected to vacate their quarters within forty-eight hours, and as they left, their luggage would be searched in the presence of a New York City detective.

"That stinks, Alfred."

"Oh, please don't worry about us, sir. Mr. Eden provided generous severance packages for all of us in his will."

The thought of Dallas's will had not occurred to Tony. "You've seen his will?"

Alfred straightened a sheaf of papers and placed it on the desk precisely parallel to another set. "Why yes, Mr. Alexander. In fact, I was one of the witnesses to the most recent document. In any event, thank you for your concern, but rest assured there are no soup lines in my future."

The doorbell rang.

"That must be Mr. Saloman now, sir. And by the way, Mr. Alexander, you've received numerous calls of condolence."

Alfred handed Tony a stack of messages written on sheets of Eve Eden's personal stationery—two gracefully entwined *E*s enclosed within a delicate, gold-embossed wreath of laurel. He recognized a few names. He wasn't sure about the rest and would have Alfred return their calls. He sat behind the desk to quickly call Tux while Alfred took Mort's coat in the hall and equipped him with the ubiquitous cocktail, but Tux's line was busy. While he waited to redial, Tony spotted a stack of correspondence addressed to Dallas from Columbia University. As he reached for it, Alfred announced the lawyer's arrival.

Mort Saloman looked tired and picked over—like he'd just emerged from one of Dunstan's famous basement sales; in fact, he'd just left a four-hour meeting in the Dunstan Corporation boardroom. Most of the board members were in their seventies or eighties now, being contemporaries of Dallas's father, and they had long viewed the lifestyle and habits of the last living Dunstan with universal opprobrium. That afternoon the board had seen Dallas's will and his funeral arrangements for the first time, and they asked Mort many difficult and embarrassing questions. The board was aghast to learn of the existence of the harem and the amount of money Dallas had, to one director's unintentionally insightful way of thinking, "pissed away on it." Ignoble, said one board member. Ignoble, hell, shouted another. Loathsome. Then came the questions about Tony's presence at Dunstan Hall and his relationship to Dallas.

"Alfred, I need to talk to Tony alone for a while." Mort slid his glasses to the top of his head and rubbed his eyes with his fists.

Tony glanced over at Alfred, who gave the most imperceptible of shrugs.

"I understand, sir," he said. "If you need me, ring."

Arrayed on the desk in front of Mort was the real-life Monopoly game so meticulously organized by Alfred that afternoon. Mort waved Tony over to his side of the desk.

"Awful business, isn't it? Forty-five years old. What a shame. Somehow you expect fat people to die sooner, but this just seems like such a waste." Mort pushed himself away from the desk and gestured toward a chair to his left. Tony pulled off his sweater and sat down. The fire in the fireplace, although initially welcome, was making him sweat. He'd been offended when Mort called Dallas a "fat person," and was suddenly uneasy being alone in the room with the lawyer.

"Tony, I'm sure you know Dallas cared for you a great deal. He wanted very much to be a part of your life, every day, and for you to be a part of his."

Tony wasn't sure where this conversation was headed. There was something odd in Mort's voice, a tentativeness perhaps, combined with a lawyerly precision, that made him nervous. It was impossible to tell if his remarks were intended as the prelude to some joyous proclamation or if they were somehow meant to soften an imminent blow.

"As a measure of his esteem for you . . ." Mort stood up. " . . . it was his intent to make you his sole and incontestable heir."

"What?" It felt as if a small bird had flown from his stomach to his throat. *Sole and incontestable heir?*

"But," Mort said in as strong and steady a voice as he could muster, "unfortunately, he never actually put those sentiments on paper."

"What does that mean, Mort?" Tony's fingernails bit into the butter-soft leather armrests. "In English."

"In English, Tony, it means that you won the Irish Sweepstakes but lost your ticket. Dallas made no provisions whatsoever for you in his will. I know he *wanted* to—we discussed it right around the holidays last year—but there just didn't seem to be much urgency about it, and we were waiting for a few significant developments—things that would have accrued in your favor—to fall in place before we wrote the new will."

"So I'm getting nothing?"

"Nada."

"Zip?"

"I'm afraid that's right," Mort said, draining his glass. "I suppose this wouldn't be the right time to suggest that it's the thought that counts?"

Tony said nothing.

"But it is ironic—I mean even the sex techs are in the will."

"The harem? What do they get?"

"Perhaps I've already said too much."

"No, tell me." Tony got out of the chair and came around behind the desk.

Mort flipped through some papers. "Bingo. Whoever the last four sex techs were, they were each to get a sum . . . here it is," he said, pointing to a paragraph about three quarters of the way down a page, "to ensure that they would be paid by the estate since in all likelihood the Dunstan people would not honor their contracts."

"But that's twice or three times what they made in a month."

Tony stood up and paced the perimeter of the room. When John Dunstan had been alive, neither Dallas nor Eve Eden were allowed in this, his inner sanctum, "The Dutch Masters Room." The three Rembrandts were now too valuable for even Dallas to display casually, but there were several incomplete sketches for *The Night Watch* mounted on the south wall, and a number of yellowish winter landscapes by Van Der Meer and Breenbergh, a jaundiced little girl by Verspronck, and two masterworks by Frans Hals.

"Let me get Alfred. He'll warm some towels for you, get you some steamed milk."

"I'm fine. Actually, I can take care of myself quite nicely," Tony sat down in one of the leather wing backs. "Alfred said the staff had forty-eight hours to leave. How long do I have?"

Mort walked back to the desk and sat down. "I asked for a week, Tony. I did. I tried to reason with them. You've lived here for four years, I said. You were a stabilizing influence in Dallas's life. But no dice. I got you seventy-two hours. The clock started ticking at 4 P.M. today. You must be ready to leave on Tuesday immediately after the funeral."

"Jesus Christ, Mort. That's the best you could do? I'm not even sure I could pack everything by then."

"You're lucky you got what you did. The sex techs were evicted on the spot."

"Yeah, but how long does it take to pack your shaving kit and a change of jockstraps?"

"Believe me, Tony, you're going to *want* to be out of here long before seventy-two hours have elapsed. I guarantee that by 8 A.M. tomorrow the place will be crawling with officious little twits from the Dunstan front office, poking their pseudo-aristocratic noses into Dallas's business—and yours, if you're still here."

"God, I feel like Jackie O. being kicked out of the White House while JFK's body was still at the Capitol." His nose was running and he wiped it with his shirtsleeve.

"Just a few more items. I have been asked by the Dunstan people to have you answer these questions. I'm uncomfortable doing it, but it has to be done, and I think you'll find it easier to talk to me than the corporate types."

"OK, shoot."

"Did you have any joint checking or savings accounts, certificates of deposit, or other financial instruments with Dallas? If so, we'll need your signature to close them."

"Neither Dallas nor I are that stupid."

"Do you claim ownership of any works of art, statuary, or archaeological material within these walls for which you do not have provenance, documentation, or full legal title?"

"No."

"Are you in possession of any watches, rings, or other jewelry given to you by Dallas and individually worth in excess of five thousand dollars?"

"Who knows? Dallas was always giving me all sorts of tacky shit I never wore. Some of it was okay, when he stuck to diamonds and onyx or malachite. But a lot of it was shit. I have no idea how much it's worth."

"You'd better let me have a look at it. For example, that watch you're wearing tonight is worth at least eight thousand. I suspect that some of the 'shit' Dallas gave you is worth that or considerably more."

"I didn't mean anything by that, Mort. It's just that his tastes and mine were very different. Growing up a Florida cracker, I'm just not that big into jewelry. This thing is worth eight *thousand?*"

"Be that as it may, they will confiscate anything over five grand. I'll take the Rolex and anything else that might cause trouble. You can pick it up at my office Monday. Do you have your own safe or is your stuff in Dallas's?"

Tony undid his watch and laid it on the desk. "My safe's in my room. Do you honestly mean to tell me that they intend to search *my* luggage?"

"Tony, they perceive you as nothing more than a gigolo, a hustler. Until I explained the situation to them, they were ready to kick you out with the harem boys. I wouldn't put it past them to get a court order to conduct a full body search."

"What do they think I'll do, stick the Ramon Novarro commemorative dildo up my ass? If one of them even tries to put a finger in *any* of my orifices, they'll have a different kind of body search on their hands: somebody's gonna have to search for *their* bodies in the East River!"

"Tony, I would recommend that you cooperate with them. If you give them any trouble, who knows what they might do. And they are holding all the cards."

"Okay, okay. Look, it's been a long day and I just want to hit the sack. Are we about through? Or are you going to fingerprint me?"

"One final question and then we'll open your safe."

"What is this, the Spanish Inquisition?"

"Tony, I need to know. . . . The Dunstan people are going to ask me. Do you intend to challenge the will in whole or in part?"

"Fuck no, I'm not going to contest the will. *In whole or in part.*"

"I think that's a smart move."

After Mort left with his jewelry, most of it worth far more than he ever imagined, Tony put on a tape, sat in the Jacuzzi for half an hour, and, hair still damp, went down to the kitchen to scout for leftovers. It had been nearly eighteen hours since he had last eaten, here at home, with Dallas. It seemed more like a week. He found the lights on and

Alfred standing over a cutting board slicing through what looked like a Dagwood sandwich on Jewish rye.

"Sandwich, sir?" Alfred said, gesturing to the one he was cutting.

"Thanks, Alfred. No onions?"

"None indeed, sir." He placed the sandwich on a plate with a Kosher dill spear and handed it to Tony. "Ale, sir? I heartily recommend it."

"Sure. Why not?" Tony pulled a bar stool over to the island where Alfred was working and watched him construct another sandwich from stacks of cheeses and cold cuts in waxed paper. "Kinda spooky, isn't it, Alfred. I mean without Dallas."

Alfred paused in his sandwich making and cocked his head to one side. "Yes, sir, it is 'kinda spooky' without Mr. Eden here. Terribly sad, terribly empty. Mr. Eden was such a presence, in so many ways, that I've come to think of him as a part of this house, a fixture, if you will. 'Kinda spooky?' Indeed, sir. Yes, indeed."

For a while, neither of them spoke. Both were famished, and they split another multidecker sandwich and polished off two more ales apiece. Tony suggested they retire to the study, where the good scotch was kept.

"So what will you be doing now, Alfred, retiring?" They'd settled on the couch, and Tony had propped his slippered feet on the brass-inlaid Regency center-table in front of them.

"I'm afraid so, sir."

"Why afraid so? Won't it be nice to be your own boss for a change?"

"I've had a great life with Mr. Dunstan and Mr. Eden, each in different ways and different times. My own life will be considerably less interesting. The last seventeen years with Mr. Eden were so spontaneous, so unexpected. One never knew what little dog-and-pony show he'd drag home with him. Yes, I will genuinely miss the old pervert."

"Alfred, that's awful!"

"That I'll miss him?"

"No, calling him a pervert. Like Mort earlier, calling Dallas fat. It's disrespectful."

"But true. On both counts. He *was* fat, was he not? And definitely perverted. Before you moved in, naked young men and boys would wander the halls at all hours. It was a house rule: no clothing allowed at any time. You cannot imagine the scenes of lust and depredation I encountered in this house."

Alfred started a fresh fire, scenting it with handfuls of dry pine cones, and they continued to talk and drink for hours. Alfred consoled Tony on the loss of his fortune and told him had circumstances been different, he would have happily continued his service to him. Tony got up, a bit unsteadily at first, and sat in the chair behind the desk. A stack of letters from Columbia to Dallas, which he'd noticed earlier in the evening, caught his eye, and he reached across the cluttered expanse of desk and grabbed them.

"Alf! What the hell are these letters?"

"I wouldn't know, sir. Are they of interest to you?"

"I don't know."

"They obviously are, sir, or you wouldn't have asked about them."

"I had a friend once who worked at Columbia. That interesting enough?"

"Would you like me to have a look at them? Perhaps I can determine if they have any relevance to you. I'm sure Mr. Eden wouldn't mind."

Tony gave Alfred the letters and sat down beside him on the couch, sucking on the ice cubes in his otherwise empty rocks glass. The two-inch-thick stack of letters was bound with a pale peach satin ribbon, which Alfred removed and laid full-length on the armrest. He fanned them out and checked the cancellation date on each one. They were arranged chronologically from early 1970 to mid-1971. Alfred selected the earliest one and opened it.

"Well? Whatta they say, Alfie?"

"Perhaps it would be best, sir, if I read all of them first to see if they are related to one particular subject or a variety of things and, if so, to see if one or another might be of special interest to us."

"Huh?"

"Let me read them first, sir. Then I'll let you know."

"Oh, okay." Tony poured himself another drink.

Alfred slipped on a pair of rimless rectangular reading glasses and quickly scanned each letter, slowing only when he encountered an obviously pivotal or unusually obtuse paragraph. Finally, he removed his reading glasses and replaced them in his left breast pocket. "I honestly don't think there is anything in this correspondence that could be of interest to you, sir. They pertain solely to the establishment of a distinguished professorship at the university."

It took a beat or two for Alfred's remark to sink in.

"Holy fuck!" he said "Give me those things!"

Tony grabbed the stack of letters and read them. Dallas apparently wanted to anonymously endow a distinguished professorship in behavioral science in honor of the work of the preeminent researcher Dr. Hans Selye. The correspondence from the university, often poetic in its praise of Dallas's selflessness and generosity, addressed the substantial nature of the gift and its stipulations. At one point, the executive vice president for development complains, in the most inoffensive possible way, that based upon the stipulated criteria of age (Dallas wanted a young, American researcher who would continue to make vital contributions for many years) and achievement, there might be but one or two possible candidates in the field, and perhaps none at all. The tone of the letters soon becomes more optimistic. A suitable candidate is found and interviewed and, in light of the unlikelihood of finding even a single competitor, wooed and won. After a gap of six months, an extremely apologetic and overwrought letter reluctantly informs Dallas that the young researcher who had accepted the position amidst great fanfare had left the university without notice or explanation, apparently to return to his previous position.

Tony stood up and, before Alfred could stop him, tossed the letters into the fire.

"Oh my, sir. That may not have been the most prudent action. Am I to understand, that this correspondence is somehow pertinent?"

Tony drained his glass and sent it crashing into the fireplace. So, it was Dallas who had upset the applecart, who had uprooted him and Connecticut and dragged them to a city where Connecticut could not long survive. Dallas wanted Tony near him, and what Dallas wanted Dallas got. And isn't it convenient that the morning after Connecticut left town, Dallas was right there to pull him out of the wreckage of his life? He wished that Dallas was right here, now, alive, because he'd like to slice his blubbery ass up and throw it into the stinking fire one quivering little piece at a time.

# 20

EARLY THE NEXT MORNING, Tony received a phone call from Stephen Loew, the city's most prestigious funeral director. So sought after were his services, it was rumored that some of his clients accelerated or prolonged their death throes to assure themselves a place on his chronically overbooked schedule. Much of his reputation rested on the shoulders of his two makeup artists, whose work was exceptionally flattering. However, Loew was best known for the elaborate sets, *tableaux vivant*, and general theatricality that characterized his services. Loew asked to see Tony at three that afternoon. It was urgent, he said.

The funeral home was just a few blocks away, and the day was brilliant, if cold, so Tony walked. He found the address, a stunning Greek Revival town house, but there were none of the obvious indications it sheltered a funeral home. No elegantly scrolled signs, no burgundy draperies in the window, no black awning, just the small, simple brass plate on which was engraved the street address and the names of the funeral directors: Loew & B. Holde. As Tony entered the foyer, a faint chime in the distance announced his arrival. The precise tapping of stiletto heels caught his attention. Turning toward the sound, he was greeted by a dead ringer for the Breck girl.

"Hi," the young woman said, smiling and angling her head a few degrees to the right so that a great curtain of blonde hair brushed her shoulder. She extended a slender, tan arm bereft of ornamentation. "I'm Nancy McGill. And you must be Anthony Alexander. It's a real pleasure to meet you. I just love your work."

Right, Tony thought. His oeuvre of cologne and bluejean commercials would one day qualify him for a lifetime-achievement Clio.

"Um. I'm pleased to meet you, too. I guess," Tony said.

"If you follow me, I'll take you to Mr. Loew." Nancy might have

been the host's assistant on some Faustian game show, leading the bereaved onstage for the Big Deal of the Day. Behind which door would
their loved one find salvation? In which box lurked the eternal booby
prize? She led him through interior rooms that were tastefully furnished
with pieces that were contemporary without looking trendy. They
stepped into a room that was a seventies take on Art Deco—just the
right proportion of chrome zigs and Lucite zags. "Please make yourself
at home. Can I get you a drink?"

Tony nodded. "Scotch rocks."

While Nancy was mixing it in a nearby alcove, a tanned and meticulously well-groomed man in his late thirties walked into the room. He
had the bland good looks of a TV anchorman.

"Toneeeeeeeee," the man said, his arms extended. Tony stood and
proffered his right hand, which the man smothered with both of his—
large, brown, muscular.

"Stephen Loew. I am so sorry to hear of your loss. Mr. Eden will be
sorely missed by the entire arts community. He was a man with a heart
as big as . . ." he paused, gave in to a closed lip smile for an instant, and
began anew an octave higher. "But we're all terribly honored to be the
ones to give him the big send-off. I've had calls from a veritable who's
who of Hollywood wanting to know details of the arrangements. I daresay there won't be enough first-class seats out of L.A. between now and
Tuesday to handle them all."

You had to give him credit, Tony thought. He was relaxed, warm,
and genuinely friendly, if a bit histrionic; not at all clammy or obsequious. He looked more like a . . . horse fancier . . . than a mortician.
For him, this was all going to be a fabulous party. Tony guessed that a
large part of his cheerfulness derived from the fact that because he dealt
only with the deceased of considerable means, he didn't have to pry insurance money from grieving widows' hands.

Stephen Loew sat down on the sofa, close enough to reach out and
touch Tony's right knee when he wanted to communicate sympathy or
emphasize a particular point.

"I don't know if you are familiar with our services, Tony. Most of our
clientele are associated with the performing arts in some fashion—theater, film, television, opera, music, dance. We like to think of ourselves
as 'funeral directors to the stars,' and we take that aspect of our work
very seriously. We don't merely display a loved one's remains, we script
an entire last act. Scenery, choreography, soliloquy—it's all there."

*Get to the point, queen,* Tony thought. *Are we expecting Wotan and Brünhilde, or what?*

"Several years ago, at the time of his mother's death, I discussed his own arrangements with Mr. Eden. He felt the need to do so at the time, but who could have guessed he would have followed so quickly?"

Tony gave him points for saying "death," not "passing," or "leave taking." He sensed that somewhere beneath all the frippery, Stephen Loew still knew what he was packing and shipping was dead meat, pure and simple.

"The moment I learned of Mr. Eden's death, I set the wheels in motion. So there is really very little yet to be done, save one infinitesimal detail I need your help with," Loew said.

"Yes?" Tony wondered whether to tell Loew that he wasn't sure he would even attend the funeral; to tell him, now, to save his breath. But he was curious.

"As I mentioned earlier, ours is a theatrical clientele. Dramatic, so to speak. Yourself as . . . an aspiring actor, must know the importance of catharsis."

"I'm familiar with the term, yes." Tony didn't like the way Loew had said "aspiring actor." He was a recognized name in the modeling industry, not some waiter at Lüchow's who spent every free minute sitting by the telephone.

"I understand there are no relatives—even distant relatives—surviving Mr. Eden. Is that correct?"

"As far as I know." Shouldn't *he* know?

"I thought so." Loew reached for the glass of white wine Nancy had brought him, sipped it and made a show about savoring it, as if to say he sucked the pleasure out of every precious moment of life. "Then we do have a slight problem of . . . staging."

"Staging?"

"Of course. You see, in order for this funeral to be successful, there must be catharsis. Obtained, of course, through an outpouring of grief."

"I'm afraid I don't really understand your point, Mr. Loew."

"Stephen, please," Loew said, reaching into his jacket for his cigarettes, a European brand Tony knew Val sometimes smoked.

"Stephen. I don't know much about the death business, but isn't that what *all* funerals are about?" Tony said, setting down his drink to telegraph his sudden vague uneasiness.

"I was a drama major before I got into this profession, Tony, and as I've said, I like my funerals to be well staged. You always have, of course, the star: the deceased. And there are the supporting players: the family, the minister, the pallbearers, the mourners, the woman who faints on cue. And of course there are the extras: the fans, the hangers-on, the curious. In Mr. Eden's case there will be the proverbial Hollywood 'cast of thousands'—though perhaps less because of his own career than because of his mother's. Did I tell you Lillian Gish is coming? Lillian *Gish!* She worked with Eve Eden at the very birth of the film industry."

"I didn't even know she was still alive," Tony said.

"Oh, very much alive. More alive than most of us." Loew took a long, slow drag and let most of the smoke come out of his nostrils. "You know, show business types just *love* funerals, especially when they are unexpected. Let me tell you, stars know how to let it rip! But without a family, with no survivors, there is no one to direct the grief *toward*. It's like Laurel without Hardy, Martin without Lewis, Dick Van Dyke without Mary Tyler Moore. It just doesn't *work*. Something's missing. The grief remains bottled up and everyone leaves feeling, well, emotionally . . . constipated." Loew squinched up his nose to demonstrate his distaste for the word.

"So I can assume you are looking for some kind of emotional *laxative?*"

"Exactly," Loew said, sending a thin stream of blue smoke out of his mouth at precisely a forty-five-degree angle.

He certainly knows how to put smoke through its paces, Tony thought.

Loew smiled. "I *knew* you would understand. Word has it that you are *quite* bright."

Tony was offended by the statement. He understood, of course, that he had been the subject of hot dish ever since he moved in with Dallas. But he never would have guessed people were talking about his intelligence.

"And this, I take it, is where I come in?" he said, his jaw set.

"Precisely. In situations where there are no survivors, I usually request someone take responsibility for playing the role of the most bereaved."

"The most bereaved?" Tony leaned forward and picked up his drink. He rested his elbows on his knees and turned the glass in his hands. "There's a *name* for this kind of thing?"

"Yes, of course. The primary mourner. Usually played by husband, wife, or companion. In cases of a younger, unmarried person, their mother or father. The most bereaved receives the condolences of those who are . . . the *lesser* bereaved. It helps them get it out of their system, to . . ." and he smiled fleetingly and made a graceful flourish with his cigarette, "to continue the metaphor."

Tony didn't like where this was going. "You're not suggesting that *I* should be the most bereaved?" he said. "Certainly there are other people who have been friends with him longer than me. Hell, even Alfred would be a better choice. He's been with Dallas's family for maybe forty years."

"This isn't a matter of years, Tony. It's a matter of the heart. You've been his . . . *companion* for the last several years, is that not correct?"

"I've lived with him, if that's what you mean."

"There's no need to be coy about this, Tony." Loew leaned forward conspiratorially. "I mean, we know the score, do we not?"

Tony stood up sharply, bumping a knee on the coffee table. Loew's wineglass toppled and shattered.

"*We* most emphatically do not, Mr. Loew. It's true I've lived with Dallas for the last four years, but I have *never* slept with him or performed any sexual acts of *any* kind with him or in his presence. Our relationship was something else entirely. In addition, I should tell you that I have recently received some news that does not predispose me to play *any* part in Dallas Eden's funeral. If I do choose to attend, I am more likely to be the least *possible* bereaved person in the entire fucking room."

Loew had stood up in the middle of Tony's diatribe and attempted to put his arm around his shoulder, but Tony pulled away, stepping down to the far end of the sofa, his arms folded across his chest defensively. Loew sat down, this time on the couch, and patted the space next to him as if to encourage a puppy to jump up on it.

"Tony, please, sit down. I'm sorry I misconstrued your relationship with Mr. Eden. But that *was* the gospel according to Dallas. Everyone I know was given to understand that you were Mr. Eden's most favored lover. The most exquisite details were revealed. Of course, I understand from Mr. Saloman that you are not in Mr. Eden's will, and I know it must be hard to deal with that, but . . ."

"I don't give a good goddamn about the money," Tony said, sitting down hesitantly and as far from Loew as he could. "I just found out that Dallas was responsible for something that hurt me more than anything else ever has. And while I would never wish anyone ill, I can't even *pretend* to be sorry that he's dead. I'm not that good an actor."

Loew sat silently, his forefingers touching his pursed lips, the last of Tony's words ringing in his ears.

"Tony, let me say again how bad I feel for having misunderstood your relationship with Mr. Eden. And I'm terribly sorry you were hurt so deeply."

"It wasn't your fault," Tony said more calmly. He felt better for having said it all, but a bit foolish for having vented his anger so intensely at this man, who, after all, was only trying to do his job. "It's just that this particular episode has always been a sore point with me. I've never really gotten over it."

Loew relaxed visibly. He cleared his throat. "I *am* sorry, Tony. For whatever it was."

"I guess I should go, huh?" Tony said, sheepishly.

"Not at all. Stay. Catch your breath. Nancy will fix you another cocktail. We can talk about it if you like."

As if on cue, Nancy appeared with a scotch in an oversized rocks glass. Tony sighed and sat down again. It *was* an excellent scotch. He was exhausted, and he thought he must look like some wino, with a haphazard shave and road-map eyeballs. In his brain, the station master was announcing the imminent return of his headache on track three.

"You're going to think I'm horrible for asking this, but what's in it for me? After what I discovered yesterday, I feel I have a right to some . . . reparations."

Loew shifted uncomfortably in his chair. He sipped a fresh glass of wine, all the while watching Tony, glassy-eyed with distraction, as he worked things out in his head. The request was a good sign. He was ready to cut a deal.

"I'm not sure there is any way I can remunerate you for making this last effort on Mr. Eden's behalf, this final show of respect for a man who has, regardless of the hurt he has caused, dramatically changed your life," Loew said. "But there is one other thing to consider. My understanding of your relationship with Mr. Eden, while flawed, is fairly widespread. I believe that the role I am asking you to play is probably one you will be expected to play by a large number of Mr. Eden's friends and colleagues. The circles in which you currently travel are, shall we say, tightly drawn. There might be considerable misunderstanding, even hostility, on the part of people who, I daresay, could have a significant impact on your life and career."

That set Tony off again. "Are you *threatening* me?"

"Not at all, Tony. I'm just trying to illuminate the new realities in

your life, to explain concepts and circumstances you might not have encountered while you were under Mr. Eden's . . . wing."

Tony settled back into the sofa. The scotch was beginning to go to his
head. What if he *did* alienate some of Dallas's friends? Why take chances?
Keep your options open. Tony downed the last of his scotch in three determined glugs. "Will I have a script?" he asked, wiping his mouth with
the back of his hand.

Loew smiled broadly, then got up and paced the floor, dithering with
excitement. "Oh, no, Tony, nothing as heavy-handed as that. It will be
largely improvisational. Of course, you'll have the opportunity to examine the set before the guests arrive, and we might suggest some blocking,
but in terms of what you might say or do . . . that will be entirely up to
you. I'd suggest looking stoic as the guests arrive, but not haughty or ar-
rogant. Then we gradually turn on the waterworks as the various eulogies proceed. I'll leave it up to you how far off the deep end you want to
go, but it's best not to get too theatrical—these folks won't be easily
fooled. Near the end of the ceremony, you'll get a grip, so to speak.
After the funeral, while we're roasting the gazelle, I'd suggest that you
look kind of . . . dazed and confused. And that you leave early—whatever you do, don't belly up to the buffet. It wouldn't do to see you par-
taking of life's earthly pleasures too soon."

"Excuse me, did you say *gazelle?*"

TONY WAS RECLINING on his bed wearing monogrammed red silk boxer
shorts and smoking a joint when there was a knock on the door. It was
not Alfred's diminutive yet firm rapping. It must belong to another of
those oafish accountants from Dunstan's making sure he hadn't stuffed
some two-thousand-year-old, gold-inlaid back scratcher into his shorts
since their last visit half an hour ago. It had been that way all day as he
sorted through his belongings and attempted to pack.

The knock sounded again, followed by someone calling his name. It
was . . . Val. Valentine Rittenhouse?

"It's open," Tony shouted, and took another hit.

"Tony, darling, We . . . I was in Paris when I heard. I came back to
New York immediately." Val entered the room cautiously.

"Why?" Tony asked, squeezing the smoke out slowly.

"To see if there was anything I could do, of course."

"Haven't you done enough already?"

It was bizarre to have Val just walk in and start talking, as if he were
returning from the kitchen or bathroom after a TV commercial. *Did I*

*miss anything?* How long had it been since they had spoken? He had seen Val from time to time at parties or on shoots. Once they had shared a silent, seemingly interminable elevator ride to Tuxedo's office. But they hadn't exchanged a civil word in more than a year. Now here he was, out of the blue. Tony was surprised he had come, but, down deep, part of him would have been disappointed if he hadn't.

"Tony, you know what I mean. Can I help with anything?"

"No. Nothing. Everything is in the capable hands of Dunstan's, as you can probably tell from the sea of blue serge downstairs. They're working 'round the clock to inventory the goodies."

"They must have been salivating over this place for years. It's like a yard sale at San Simeon. Can I sit down?" Val said, patting a tiny space at the foot of the bed. Tony shrugged. "Listen, Tony, I suspect you're in shock at the moment, but this is going to hit you really hard soon."

"I doubt it. It's not like he was my father or anything." He scratched his crotch absently.

"You're going to need a friend."

"Who did you have in mind?" Tony thanked God he was stoned out of his mind. Otherwise he might not have been able to deal with the fact that Valentine Rittenhouse was smug enough to be sitting on his bed, thinking that an impromptu transatlantic trek would absolve him from felony treachery and adultery charges. He wondered if Devlin had stayed in Paris. Knowing him, he would have.

"How long are they letting you stay here?" Val asked after allowing enough time for the sting to subside.

"Seventy-two hours. That puts me on the streets about the same time they put Dallas in the ground. Isn't that ironic?"

"Mildly. Have you given any thought to what you're doing? Where you're going to live?"

"I understand there are several comfortable nooks and crannies at Grand Central. Or maybe I'll slink away to the basement of the Met."

"It's been done."

"My point, Val, is that I can take care of myself. I am no longer the naive bumpkin you met three years ago and whom you took advantage of soon thereafter."

"I knew it would be like this."

"How else could it be?"

Val stood up, took off his coat, and placed it across a nearby chair.

"Please, don't get comfortable on my account."

"Tony, I'm sorry things worked out the way they did. I know I hurt you, and I'm sorry. I'm sorry our friendship ended. I miss you. Terribly. I think about you every day. And I'm sad. But you must know that what happened was inevitable."

"Inevitable why? Because you're a compulsive home wrecker?"

"No, Tony, because Devlin is a gigolo, an opportunist, and a cad."

"Not a cad! Anything but that."

"He used you, Tony." Val paced back and forth across the room, his arms crossed on his chest. "He looked at you as a meal ticket from the minute he set eyes on Dunstan Hall. Yes, he thought you were attractive when he met you at Fusion. He likes pretty boys like you. Like us. But you weren't meant to be anything more than a one-night stand. And then, *voilá*, Dunstan Hall. Fort Knox North. He knew where the real money was, and he played Romeo to your Juliet just long enough for Dallas to come home. How soon was it before he moved in? A matter of weeks, no? . . ."

"A month."

"And what about this sudden need for separate bedrooms when Dallas got back from Rome? Do you remember how anguished you were about that? I can't believe you never put two and two together."

"He didn't want to make Dallas jealous."

"He didn't want Dallas to know the two of you were an item. It would jeopardize his chance of hitting the jackpot with him. He was letting Dallas fellate him two days after he got back from Rome."

"That's a lie. And even if it were true, it still doesn't justify what you did."

"No, it doesn't. All I can say is that Devlin wants—and believes he deserves—money. Big bucks. Dallas's kind of money. And mine. You were never even in the running, Tony. If you had listened carefully, you would have heard the sound of a cash register the instant he stepped out of the cab that first night. So what if Dallas was a disgusting cow? It was worth it. Devlin was raking it in hand over fist. Tiffany's. Cartier's. Brooks Brothers. And then along comes yours truly. Three times the net worth of Dallas and a much prettier package. But trust me, if it hadn't been me, it would have been somebody else. As rich as you think you are, given your previous station in life, you would have never been able to keep Devlin in socks and underwear—and you know how infrequently he changes his Jockeys. He likes money that's been around for decades. Generations. Centuries."

"And you don't mind that all he's after is your money?"

"Tony, when you're as rich as I am, you can *never* be certain your lovers aren't after your money. I stopped worrying about that long ago. It ruins all the fun. After all, Devlin can't really be a gigolo if I *know* he's a gigolo, if I'm not fooled by him. I give Devlin whatever he wants because it makes me happy to do so."

"But you *do* love him?"

"The way you loved him? I don't think so. But yes, I love him. He's exquisite to look at—leg scars and all—and he drives me absolutely wild in bed. I know that he's mine forever, or at least until the bottom drops out of the toothpick market. I can't ask for much more than that."

"So you don't *really* love him. With your heart and soul."

"I can continue to eat when he walks into a room, if that's what you mean."

Tony stubbed out the roach, got off the bed, and opened the door to his walk-in closet. When he reemerged, he was wearing a wrinkled, sweat-stained Columbia T-shirt over his shorts.

"I'm going upstairs to work out."

"Tony, stop. You're only hurting yourself by acting this way."

"Too bad. I had hoped I was hurting you as well."

"Obviously, you are. . . . Don't you ever wash that thing?" Val said, waving his right hand in front of his nose.

"I like the smell of sweat, Val, even if it's just mine. But I'm serious, I want to go work out. You know your way to the door. I should warn you they're frisking everybody who leaves, so if you've got a Picasso in your pocket, I hope you've got a bill of sale."

"Give me five minutes, Tony. Five minutes of your undivided attention. Let me say what I came here to say, instead of all this petty bickering."

Tony sighed and sat down on the bed. "Christ, there's more?"

"I'll give it to you straight, Tony. I love you and I miss you. It's a cliché, I know, but you are like a brother to me."

"Like Billington?"

"*Please*. Look, I'm sorry about the way things turned out, and I'm not kidding when I say that if I knew having Devlin would cost me your friendship *forever*, I wouldn't have gotten involved. I had no idea how strongly you felt about him."

"What were you expecting?"

"The cold shoulder, maybe. The evil eye. But not *death*."

"So this is what you have to say? Okay, apology accepted."

"No, *this* is what I have to say. I think you should consider moving in with me."

Tony laughed—one quick bark—stood up, and walked to the door. "Come in to my parlor said the spider to the fly."

"Sit down! You promised me five minutes and you're going to give me five minutes."

"I can listen just as well standing."

"Tell me, then, where are you going to go? I know you well enough that even though you could afford it, you're not going to book a suite at the Sherry Netherlander until you find a new place to live."

"How can you be so sure?"

"I checked. No reservations under the name Alexander *or* Alexamenos."

"Good work. I forgot to whom I was speaking."

"So where will you be looking?"

"Downtown. The Village, Chelsea. I might inquire about the old Grove Street place."

"Sentimental or psychotic, you be the judge."

"It's nothing like that. I'm over Connecticut. It's just that it's a great apartment, and I love the neighborhood."

"Tony, for the past four years you have been ensconced in one of the finest old mansions in the city. This place is an absolute gem. For you to leave Dunstan Hall and live in the Village would be like Queen Elizabeth moving out of Buckingham Palace to take a third floor walk-up in Belfast. Neither of you would survive long. I know the types of places you're going to look at, and not one of them is going to have the square footage of your bedroom closet. I swear to God, you are not going to be able to fit even *half* of your wardrobe into one of those fire-traps. And as I recall, you've got a jewelry box the size of a Volkswagen microbus. Where do you think you're going to park that? And insurance. Nobody will insure *any* of that stuff at *any* price in *any* of those neighborhoods!"

"You think so?"

"I know so. Tony, your life is different now. As much as you think you want to, you can't click the heels of your ruby slippers and go back to the simpler life of a Village hippie. And even if you did, I suspect it wouldn't take you long to discover that you really didn't like it. Why trade glamour for squalor? Devlin is only here every other weekend, and your suite can be *completely* isolated from the rest of the penthouse, if you want. All you'll have to do is lock a few doors. Come and go as you please. Six rooms, penthouse park view, all yours. You'll have your own private entrance, full kitchen, sun deck, and two-and-a-half baths, with

Jacuzzi. I know how much you like to do it in the bathtub. And the soundproofing is of the quality of Avery Fisher Hall. You'll never hear a word . . ."

"Or a shriek of passion?"

"Honey, my bedroom is half a block away. Literally. And if you ever feel you absolutely have to get out of town when Devlin's here, I'll pay for you and a guest to spend the weekend in any city, anywhere in the world. Moscow, Malibu, Marrakech. And I won't charge you a nickel more rent than that dump on Grove Street."

"You're going to charge me rent?"

"Only because I thought you'd like it that way. I know you don't take handouts."

"This isn't a handout. It's payback. You owe me big-time, and I'm not ashamed to take what's owed me."

"My, my, you are a quick study. Rent free it is, then. And cheap at twice the price."

"Okay. Now what about utilities?"

ON THE DAY OF THE FUNERAL, dawn presented itself as an improbable parfait of rose and persimmon sky between layers of whipped cream clouds. A meteorological anomaly known as the "Siberian Express" was funneling brutally cold, dry air from the North Pole directly to the Upper East Side. Tony awoke in his bedroom at Valentine's co-op in Triumph Towers, sixty-five stories above the taxicabs, blind newspaper vendors, and canine excrement of New York's streets. He and Val had spent all day Monday supervising two movers, alas neither one even re-motely attractive, who also worked under the scrutiny of an off-duty New York City policeman. Mort Saloman was present on Tony's behalf. On Sunday Tony had seen most of the staff submit to a screening that could only be equaled by the customs office of a Third World country, and he was prepared for the worst as he descended the grand staircase of Dunstan Hall for the last time. But no one stopped or questioned him as he headed for the door. No one, in fact, looked at him. They were shunning him, too embarrassed to look Dallas Eden's reputed paramour in the eye.

The funeral was scheduled for eleven, but Stephen Loew had asked Tony to be there by nine for last-minute instructions, blocking, costuming, and makeup. While he was in the chair awaiting the makeup artist, he perused the seating chart Loew had given him. Every half-baked celebrity in the city would be there, and quite a few fully baked ones. So many two-bit stars had flown in from the Coast that Tony was certain taping of *Hollywood Squares* had been temporarily suspended. Charlie Weaver and John Davidson were expected. Soupy Sales was to be seated in the same row as the urbane Kitty Carlisle Hart and a reportedly near-hysterical Arlene Francis. Dallas always sat between Kitty and Arlene on *To Tell the Truth,* and Arlene always felt Dallas liked Kitty best because she was more slender and sophisticated. In point of fact, he did, but he would never have wanted to hurt Arlene's feelings. The list went on: Flip Wilson, Shirley Jones, Don Knotts, Gig Young, Sonny Bono, Redd Fox, Eve Arden, Gale Storm, Ann Sothern, George Gobel, Bert Parks, Lawrence Welk, Liberace, Jayne and Audrey Meadows, and of course the improbable Miss Lillian Gish.

After makeup, Tony changed into a khaki shorts ensemble and tied a red kerchief around his neck. He actually welcomed the pith helmet with a black mourning band and mosquito netting. He thought that if people couldn't see his face, he wouldn't feel so vulnerable. As eleven o' clock neared, he discreetly peeked out from behind the curtain to see the audience—and it *was* an audience, according to Loew. Barbara Billingsley was there, as were Art Linkletter, Art Fleming, and Bob Eubanks. Bob Hope sent a massive floral arrangement. The cast of *Gilligan's Island* arrived en masse, sans Tina Louise, and Bob Denver could be seen doing Maynard G. Krebs impressions at the bar. Johnny Carson had put in an appearance earlier and paid his respects—Dallas had guest-hosted for him more than once—but didn't stay for the service. Even old Bud Collier was there, and Tony thought he'd been dead for years.

Dallas was on view in a custom-made, triple-wide ebony coffin with twenty-four-carat-gold hardware and a rolled-and-tufted genuine leopard-skin interior. It had taken sixteen men working nonstop for nearly three days to complete, and the last golden screw had been tightened only two hours before. Dallas was dressed in the costume he wore in the last scene of *This Zulu Is Crazy,* when he rescues Bob Hope from cannibals by disguising himself as a witch doctor: a grass skirt, coconut breastworks, a bone through the topknot of his teased-to-hell red wig. His honor guard consisted of six muscular African studs, each precisely six-feet-five-inches tall, on call from Mode Noir, the city's most chic black modeling agency.

At five minutes till Loew led Tony onstage, the curtain still drawn. He sat to the right of the casket in a small tent on two-foot risers, canted fifteen degrees toward the house. Tony was perched in a high-backed wicker chair à la Eldredge Cleaver, a towering areca palm on either side of him. Potted pygmy date palms, spathiphyllum, groupings of obscene red bromeliads, and other tropical foliage covered most of the stage, and a waterfall and jungle noises—roars and brays, screeches and chirrups—completed the illusion. Tony was almost certain Loew had hired a Tarzan impersonator to swing in on a vine.

What looked like a pulpit or podium was constructed of tree branches tied together with vine, like something out of *Swiss Family Robinson.* Tony smiled. He'd seen that damn movie half a dozen times before he realized that what he was really interested in was seeing James MacArthur naked from the waist up. Both stage and house lights dimmed and the curtain rose noiselessly. Tony could see late-arriving guests being shown to their seats by eight finalists from the most recent Mr. New York and Mr. New York U.S.A. bodybuilding contests, clad in tasteful cheetah loincloths. They had been selected for their strength as much as for their powers of titillation and would serve as pallbearers for the half-ton casket and its contents.

Art Fleming stepped up to the podium and gave a short eulogy. "I'll give you the answer," he told the mourners, "and you give me the question." There was a smattering of applause. "The answer is, 'A large man with an even larger heart. An extraordinarily funny man. A man who lived life to the fullest. A friend.' The question is, of course, . . ."

" 'Who was Dallas Eden?' " came the somewhat self-conscious reply.

"Alas, the real question is why was he taken from us so soon?"

Tony wanted to barf. He could barely keep from snickering. Most of the remaining eulogies were just as bad. Arlene and Kitty did a duet, Arlene looking pasty and overly made up, Kitty looking as cool and crisp as if she had just stepped out of a fur vault. John Davidson recounted the advice Dallas gave him when he was offered the part of a transvestite on a television police show—"Don't forget to shave your armpits!"—before he turned the podium over to a little man who looked like a three-hour-old albino rodent in a bad sharkskin suit. It was Manny Schmaltzman, a hard-line borscht-belt comedian with pickle-barrel breath.

"I mean no disrespect when I say we have lost a giant in the industry." He raised his right arm in Dallas's general direction. "I'm not just talking films here, or television. I'm talking about the *garment* industry. Did you know there is enough material in one of Dallas's three-piece suits to make a small circus tent? I'm not saying the main tent, mind you, just one big enough for a sideshow. So I once asked Dallas who his tailor was, Barnum and Bailey?" The crowd was silent save for one shrill laugh far back on the left side of the room.

"I know Dallas is resting in peace because he's finally gotten what he's wanted all of his life," he said, gesturing to the coffin with another flourish. "A big box." A wave of titters washed over the audience like a breeze through a cornfield, but the comedian knew he had died on that one. At least half the audience was straight and the women in particular were not familiar with the reference. Tony could see Arlene explaining it to Kitty, whose eyebrows arched once she understood.

"Yes, we all love to tell Dallas Eden fat jokes, but who among you knows that despite his weight, he was still an avid sportsman? In fact he was in the 1972 Winter Olympics . . . his stomach was the men's slalom venue." A snare drum cleared its throat offstage, and for the first time the audience laughed.

"We all know how much Dallas treasured his supporting actor nomination for his role in *This Zulu Is Crazy*. That's why, at his request, we've recreated a scene from that film here today. But as proud as Dallas was of his portrayal of Dr. Dewnuttin, he has always maintained that his most challenging role came several years later, when he was the stunt double for Herbie in *The Love Bug*.

*Ba-dum.*

"Dallas loved to eat, of course, and he loved to have sex. One way or another he always had *something* in his mouth. And speaking of sex, did you know Dallas was so big he didn't have erogenous zones? He had erogenous *regions.*"

*Ba-dum.*

The service lasted more than an hour, then the guests entered the banquet room via a receiving line with Tony at its head. For a while it was kind of a kick to meet some of the people he'd seen on TV as a kid, but Tony was at a loss for how to actually deal with the mourners. Most of them didn't really know him from shit, but, according to Stephen Loew's grand design, it was important to interact with each of them. He took their hands in his own, nodded, and uttered one of a half dozen lines Stephen had suggested: Thank you; Yes, I know; He certainly will; You, too. Again at Stephen's suggestion, he refrained from eating, but did manage to swill a couple of quick scotches after he'd comforted the most disconsolate. He learned to avoid Arlene Francis if he didn't want to hear about the Golden Age of Television, and he'd swear he was groped twice, once by a man, once by the pincer-like fingers of a long-nailed woman. At two o'clock, the party was still going strong, but

Stephen sought Tony out and suggested he retire from the room. They left by a door near the buffet, where Sonny Bono and Liberace were talking as Sonny picked at the leftover gazelle in the chafing dish. As Tony passed, he overheard their conversation.

"You know, it's the damnedest thing," Sonny said. "It *does* taste just like chicken!"

# 21

▬▬▬▬▬▬

FROM THE BEGINNING, Tony's relationship with Dallas had been marked by a sense of upward mobility, but his awareness of movement had obscured any thoughts he might have had about direction or destination. With Dallas gone, Tony suddenly felt vulnerable and adrift. He feared his career would sputter, cough, and plummet into an abyss, like Wile E. Coyote when his ACME rocket died in midair above some preposterously deep, dizzying desert chasm.

He needn't have worried. Since the first day Tuxedo Malone laid eyes on Tony, he had calculated the boy's professional trajectory as painstakingly as NASA had planned the Apollo moon landing program, with each new step based on the lessons learned from the successes or failures that preceded it. But in Tony's case, there were no failures.

Tony's success until now had rested largely on his Prince Charming good looks in magazines such as *Seventeen* and in ads and editorial spreads for the leading brides' magazines. He was the perfect groom, and he had spent much of the past eighteen months in formal wear, escorting young women in white down aisles and staircases in various churches, museums, and once, for a double-truck opening in *Wedding Dreams,* on the grand staircase of the Breakers in Newport. Now, even as Tony reeled from Dallas's death and its repercussions, Tuxedo was ready for the next step: he had convinced his lover to link the future of Parker Kensington International exclusively to Tony's exquisite face and flawless body. After considerable deliberation, Parker had been persuaded to jump on the designer jeans bandwagon with his own signature line, Black Tie, and Tony was to be the sole model for a high-profile national product introduction. His face would become synonymous with Parker Kensington. Consumers might even begin to think of him *as*

Parker Kensington. And it was to be the most visible ad campaign ever to focus so intently on *male* sensuality.

Tuxedo was the creative genius behind both the product and the breakthrough marketing plan. He urged Parker to enter the designer jeans fray sooner rather than later, to stake out a larger market share and build brand loyalty. He also suggested the concept of differentiating the product by producing black jeans exclusively and proffered the name Black Tie, which won Parker over immediately. All the ads would be shot in black and white, which, Tuxedo said, would elevate them above the "tasteless sea of putrid neon" that marked virtually every other campaign currently on the streets.

In the first phase, Tony would be photographed wearing only a black tie and a pair of Black Tie jeans. No shirt, no shoes, no jacket. Victor Panache would shoot him at the city's most recognizable cultural icons— Lincoln Center, the Met, Carnegie Hall, the Guggenheim. The images would be quirky, characterized by dramatic lighting, angled framing, and slightly grainy printing. The only copy would be "Black Tie. R.S.V.P. Parker Kensington."

In a follow-up campaign, Tony would appear naked save for a black tie, a smile, and a strategically placed top hat. A pair of Black Tie jeans would be crumpled at his feet. The tag line: "Black Tie optional." Tux *knew* it would work. They would make the ad available as a poster, and Tuxedo predicted it alone would be a million seller at ten dollars a pop. The gay boys would lead the charge, of course, but millions of dreamy-eyed women would step forward next, in the vain hope of somehow transforming their cloddish husbands and boyfriends into the transcendent beauty of Anthony Alexander, all the while buying Black Tie jeans with forty-four-inch waists.

Soon, other product lines were in development. Once the public associated Tony's face and body with Black Tie, Parker would launch his line of upscale men's underwear, also available only in black. A collection of men's fragrances and grooming aids would follow. If he was lucky, if he was right, sales at Parker Kensington International would triple in two years, maybe sooner. Parker had been waiting for this for a long time— finding not only the right face and body but also the right *Zeitgeist*. Parker was sure that in Tony and Black Tie jeans, the product, the man, and the moment had converged—and he knew it wouldn't be long before every cash register in the country would be singing out his name.

DESPITE HAVING LIVED AMID THE SPLENDOR of Dunstan Hall, Tony was unprepared for the sheer opulence and drama of Val's twenty-two-room penthouse sixty-five stories above Manhattan, a thirtieth-birthday present from his parents, who had lived in it for only a year before moving to Connecticut. As he stepped out of the private elevator into the foyer, Tony was reminded of Mame Dennis's Oriental period. The space was dominated by a John Chamberlain sculpture, *Bumper Buddha,* constructed from the chrome trim of fifties- and sixties-era cars. Tony was certain the Buddha's head had once been the bullet in a 1951 Ford grille.

"Hell, if I had known this was art, I could have made a fortune," Tony said. "We had all sorts of junkers in our front yard I could've cut up and slapped together."

"It is pretty hideous, isn't it," Val said. "I've been meaning to redecorate for centuries, but stuff like this you don't just leave at the curb."

The foyer gave on to a two-story room, floor-to-ceiling glass, that provided a panoramic view from Central Park to the East River and was filled with Oriental statuary, furnishings, and art. Two tiny, long-haired dogs scampered across the marble floor, their nails clicking like chopsticks against the polished surface.

"You never said you had dogs," Tony said.

"Truth is, I *don't* have them. *They* have me," Val said, picking up a quivering furball in each hand. "My mother bought them because they matched the decor."

"They matched the decor?"

"They're Chinese, Tony. Shih Tzu. Out at the Ponderosa—that's what I call our place in Connecticut—they have retrievers and setters. Very *Field and Stream.* I begged Vera and Charles to take the Shitses, but Vera's decorator wouldn't hear of it."

"The whatsis?"

"The Shitses. Shits One and Shits Two. That's what I call them. Get it? Shih Tzu—Shits Two? Not their real names, of course. Vera very nearly had a coronary when she heard of it."

They entered the main room, where a waterfall lofted from the second floor to the first into a pool that surrounded the living area and made it appear an island, connected by a number of gently arching marble bridges. Two red dwarf Japanese maples grew on beds of moss and rock, and throughout the room, pedestals of polished obsidian supported display cases of priceless sculpture, porcelain, and jewelry. Tony threaded his way through the room carefully. Maybe this wasn't such a good idea after all, he thought. It would be even more like living in a museum than at Dunstan Hall, which itself had been no picnic, but at least Dallas had collected sturdier things. They made their way down a long corridor periodically punctuated with dimly lit alcoves displaying Chinese art in an apparently chronological progression.

"I've put you in the Chou suite. 1027 to 256 B.C. I'm particularly fond of that period because the works are a little more primitive. One might even say butch," Val said, opening double doors to a series of rooms more simply decorated than others Tony had glimpsed along the way. Throughout the first room stood intricately etched bronze containers and statues mottled with green corrosion.

"You mean to tell me these knickknacks are what, three thousand years old?"

"Give or take a century, darling. But the *real* reason for choosing this suite is that it has a western exposure. After a long night of partying, you won't be inconvenienced by the rising sun."

Tony was certain this living situation would be short-lived. A month. Maybe two. He'd missed Val. A lot. Dallas and his dusty gas bag friends had not been much company. And this arrangement certainly *was* convenient. Despite what he'd told Val with such bravado, he really wasn't up to looking for a new place to live right now. But could they *live* together? What if—Devlin aside—they just got on each other's nerves, plain and simple? If pressed, Val could be quite unpleasant. Tony had heard that once, some eight years ago, he had reportedly snatched a hank of hair from the scalp of a post deb who had stolen a potential husband from him.

But to Tony's considerable surprise and relief, he and Val were able to reestablish their relationship with ease over the course of the next several weeks. They never talked about Devlin, and when he was up for the weekend, Tony easily avoided him by staying in his suite, which was certainly no hardship, given its size and amenities. He was often out of town on shoots anyway. Together they frequented many of the places to which Dallas had introduced Tony—Broadway theaters, the Met, the Philharmonic—but he had considerably more fun with Val. Dallas had served as an ad hoc *duenna* for Tony, keeping swarms of circling men at a safe distance the way a citronella candle repels mosquitoes. They sat at private tables or small private boxes in the loges of the more cavernous disco palaces, watching the panoply from a discreet distance. Now Tony and Val plunged headlong into the smoke and sweat, into the kaleido-scopic lights of the dance floor, their bodies swaying to the throbbing undertow of the music.

Tony had been to a limited number of gay bars with Dallas, most of them aeries for chicken hawks and their prey. Otherwise, there was Fusion, of course, and its constantly mutating string of imitators, and Elyseé, a coffeehouse/bistro where he had met a number of intriguing, if generally unfathomable, men. On the other hand, the number of bars to which Val introduced him seemed preposterously large and ranged from mammoth, multilevel dance bars to specialty clubs so narrowly focused they defied common sense and demographics by managing to attract the requisite number of fetishists to keep the doors open. In the three months after Dallas's death, there were nearly a hundred tricks, including two on the same night separately and a sprinkling of threesomes or four-somes, participants in which counted as scores only if there was certifi-able oral-genital, oral-anal, or anal-genital contact.

Even Devlin proved to be less of a fly in the ointment than Tony had feared. Their first encounter set the tone for their continuing relation-ship, and while it was initially unsettling, Tony felt he had held his own. On a Saturday morning in May, when Val was in Connecticut for Billington's twenty-fifth birthday celebration, Devlin arrived and the two of them found themselves alone together. Tony was in the kitchen pouring himself a cup of coffee when he heard the elevator power up, and he walked to the foyer, cup in hand, to see who it might be, forget-ting that Devlin was due that weekend. Three pieces of expensive but well-worn luggage came flying out of the elevator before Devlin emerged.

"Honey, I'm home," Devlin called. "Are you ready for a little ceiling cha cha?"

Tony turned and walked back into the kitchen. He fought the impulse to return to his suite just to get out of Devlin's way. He rationalized that despite his best evasive maneuvers, a first encounter was inevitable; it may as well take place today. He had already douched and was looking *good*. He just wished Val had been there to mediate.

"*Antoinette, ma cherie,*" Devlin said, sticking his head into the kitchen. "*Quelle surprise.*"

"Likewise," Tony said, replacing the top to the Sweet 'n' Low bowl with more force than necessary. He glanced in Devlin's direction for a fraction of a second. He was still unaccustomed to seeing him with hair.

"Where is *mon cher?*" Devlin asked.

Tony ignored him.

"Hey, Helen Keller! I'm talking to you. *Wa-wa.* Understand?" He reached into a cabinet, grabbed a cup, and poured himself what was to have been Tony's second cup of coffee.

Tony evaluated his options. Not speaking to Devlin—simply walking out and fixing breakfast in his own kitchen—was the most attractive, but it would give Devlin the most satisfaction.

"He's at the Ponderosa. It's Billy's twenty-fifth birthday. He'll be home in time for dinner.

"Billy twenty-five already? That must make you what . . . a hundred?"

"Look Devlin, I don't have to take any bullshit off you."

"No, but I figure you will, just the same."

"And what makes you so sure of that?"

"Because you still want it. You know you do. I could have you on your knees begging for it in two minutes flat."

"Fucking me was all you were ever good for, Devlin."

"Maybe, but I was the best, wasn't I?"

Tony was both angry and aroused. Although the thought of Devlin as a person sickened him, the sex they had together was still a frequent masturbatory fantasy.

"Do you want it now?" Devlin asked. "I'll give it to you right here, and Val will never be the wiser. All you have to do is get down on all fours like the dog you are and beg for it."

Tony's coffee had grown cold, and he busied himself with making a new pot. He brewed six cups, so he wouldn't have to begrudge Devlin any of it. While he waited, he opened the small white cardboard box of croissants, delivered to the front desk daily by the city's finest *patisserie* and carried up to the penthouse by the house staff, and set one out on a bread plate with a dollop of imported black current preserves.

"Nothing for me, thanks," Devlin said, with a theatrical belch. "I ate on the plane."

Tony sniffed. Devlin was pulling his dirty laundry from his baggage and, as was his habit, tossing it on the floor to await the attention of Val's house staff, who would dutifully launder it and deliver it to the master suite. Tony, who had sat down with his coffee and croissant, found himself suddenly without appetite. Devlin's body odor had always been a particularly intense aphrodisiac, and now the tang of his soiled clothes—most of them sweaty dance and athletic wear—unleashed a flood of memories and desire that left him aroused, if somewhat ashamed of his basest instincts. Although the croissant tasted like bark swabbed with Vaseline, he finished it and his coffee before he stood up to leave.

"My offer still stands. Bow-wow!" Devlin shouted after him. "But the clock's ticking, babe."

"Asshole," Tony said as he left.

"As I recall, that was the first term of endearment you ever applied to me. . . . And you say I'm not sentimental."

IN CRUISE MODE the practiced homosexual eye is swifter and more accurate than even the most sophisticated radar. Scanning a room—even a dark, crowded, smoke-filled room—it pinpoints the number, location, and sartorial faux pas of soon-to-be ex-husbands in less time than it takes to register a bee sting. And like the eye of a lion alert to the one lame gazelle in a herd of one thousand, the eye of a gay man quickly discovers the one man in one hundred attractive enough to drag back to the den.

Tony quickly learned that if he wanted a sure thing, he should head for certain of the city's leather bars, where the evening's obligatory sex act frequently could be performed on the premises. ("Will that be for here or to go, *sir*?") He always made a quick lap of the bar as soon as he arrived, to check out the available meat on the hoof as well as to spread his own scent around the room. Then, settling against a wall, he waited for the inevitable fly-bys. Men would walk slowly past him, look him in the eyes, and, once out of his field of vision, turn around to pass him again, like tin ducks at a shooting gallery. He needed to be able to size up his suitors without appearing to be too interested; all it took was a glance—a second too long for innocence—and a stranger would be at his side unbidden, launching into the line, the script, the spiel. Name, rank, serial number. What are you into? Got any dope? Your place or mine?

Within the confines of a bar, he enforced strict time limits on personal interactions. A potential trick, of course, was first in line, timewise. Such a prospect had carte blanche until he offered Tony a moustache ride or until he said or did something that turned him off. Tony would often devote up to ten minutes to an old trick who had been exceptionally good in bed and was likely to invite him to an encore performance. Friends and casual acquaintances received less time, perhaps a minute, more only if there was something to be gained socially from being seen with them or if they were talking to or merely standing near someone in whom Tony was interested. For old tricks whose sexual performance or personal chemistry were marginal, a wink was all he could afford, and he obscured the salacious glances of his really trashy sex partners beneath the ice in his upturned glass.

Early on, Tony would go home with the first attractive man who asked him. His tricks wore anything from business suits to bathing suits (the winner of the "Big Bad Box Contest" at Circle 9) and represented a wide range of occupations, looks, and recreational preferences. But Tony realized soon enough that what really made him sweat was a hunk, a stud, a brute as big and dumb as a man can come. His parameters encompassed men who were bigger than he was, taller and heavier, broader in the shoulders. Weight lifters fit the bill, but he stopped short of competitive bodybuilders, not merely for aesthetic reasons but because there were potentially too many steroids in their ejaculate. ("A girl could get a rash," warned Val, who joked that Tony's cruise philosophy could be expressed in four words: "Stevedores, sí; toreadors, no.")

He looked for the kind of guy who might have been nicknamed Moose in high school. Facial attractiveness was a factor—a trick couldn't be a dog, and no acne scars, thank you very much—but a pretty face alone would not get Tony home. He frequently found himself drawn to ethnic faces, rugged, maybe with a broken nose. But he avoided those men who affected butch "drag"—head-to-toe leather ("Some of the heftier ones look like Barcaloungers"), mesh football jerseys, and obviously hand-shredded clothes—when they clearly would be more comfortable in that smart shift they saw last week at Bergdorf's. Sheep in wolves' clothing, he called them.

Tony rarely went home with a potential trick who spent most of the evening lamenting the lack of real men in the bar. He knew from experience that the ones who complained the loudest about their nellie sisters were the same ones who would inevitably leave their footprints on his ceiling; for example, "Marco the Magnificent," the professional wrestler whose effeminate mien seemed incongruous in his inflated physique, like a housewife driving a Mack truck. Marco verged on giddiness when they got to the penthouse, so excited was he by Val's objets d'art. ("My God, this shit's authentic!" he exclaimed. To which Tony replied, "If you like that, I've got something in my bedroom from the Wang dynasty that will really be up your alley.")

Tony had a special classification for the sleazy hunks he picked up on the streets and wharves, the ones with tattoos, body odor, and a bad attitude. He called them "critter," and when he had a hankerin' for critter, nothin' else would do. Critter were motorcycle types, studs with grease under their nails and cheese under their 'skins. Critter talked dirty, made him lick their boots, and took an inordinate amount of pleasure from seeing his pretty face impaled on their cocks. Tony was more than willing to accommodate them. But he did have one steadfast rule: No bondage on the first date.

While Val respected Tony's right to have sex with any creature he deemed attractive, he ultimately grew alarmed at the increasing regularity of Tony's sexual encounters with men progressively lower on the evolutionary ladder.

"Tony, darling, you are at the very top of the food chain. Why do you insist on being such a bottom feeder?" Val said as he followed Tony through the penthouse at 7 A.M. with a king-size aerosol can of Lysol after kicking out yet another troglodyte. "I wouldn't worry if you stuck with the queens from the leather bars. Everybody knows they're harmless. But no, you pick up some married grease monkey from Jersey who hasn't yet figured out why this little hobby of his has suddenly turned into an obsession. Just what is it about their sad little lives you want to share in? The squalor? The quiet desperation? The alimony payments?"

Tony was willing to admit he was in something of a rut when it came to his taste in men. ("That's precisely the problem," Val scolded. "When it comes to men you *have* no taste.") He suspected it was a combination of his desire to resurrect Mitch and his aversion to men who exhibited the least sign of intelligence—to make sure he would never wind up with someone as fucked up as Connecticut. He also knew—in his crotch— that a man with a toolbox could give him a hard-on faster than any man with a briefcase. But lately it seemed his tricks were utterly without charm. They drank beer and they belched. They picked their teeth and their ears (but *not* their noses—he had to draw the line somewhere), and they scratched their balls in public, apparently an important part of their mating ritual. They were insensitive and unsentimental. Almost all of them bore tattoos, invariably a bald eagle, military insignia, or heart (with inscriptions ranging from "Mom" to "Sacred Heart of Jesus"). All they were interested in was sex, which was fine with Tony for a while, but after three or four hot sessions—Tony dared not call them dates—he wanted more. He didn't ask for much: no flowers or candy, just a movie, maybe, or actually sharing a meal in a public place. Spending an hour or two together with their clothes on for a change. Talking. Feeling that he was appreciated for more than his cock and butt. Maybe one guy in five would offer to bring a pizza or Chinese takeout on a Friday night, but out of sheer force of habit he'd take off his clothes as soon as he got to Tony's bedroom, and by the time they came up for air, Johnny Carson was on and the lo mein had congealed into something the consistency of rubber cement.

It was not that these men didn't understand or appreciate the gift they had been given. There was absolutely no question that they had *never* fucked as choice a specimen and never would again. They had been astounded when Tony cruised them at a bar (some temporarily lost the ability to speak) and had *no* idea what to think when they discovered he wanted seconds or even thirds. All they were interested in at the moment were a couple of holes to plug, some infertile ground on which to sow their doomed genetic patrimony. Tony's perfection made it easier for them to view him as some kind of object, something ultimately unattainable but temporarily within their grasp. When they touched him, their feelings never went deeper than the nerve endings on the tips of their fingers or the heads of their cocks. And at the moment Tony first appeared to be getting romantically entangled, they became confused and took it as their cue to disappear from the face of the earth.

Gradually his affairs became a series of dreamlike intrusions, compressing the gamut of emotions into a week or three days, sometimes into a single night. While they were taking place, they were the most real part of his life. He constantly evaluated a lover's reactions to him, pacing off his distance from him, beaming out an emotional radar to see if he was moving closer or drifting away. He sliced each word into inflections, microscopically fine yet able to tip the balance of his emotions wildly. The result was the elimination of the scale between euphoria and depression, extremes he privileged himself with often. It became difficult to live with no midpoint, the scales swinging so furiously that his emotions blended into each other with a cyclical rapidity that caused him to pass inexplicably from laughter to tears. His attempts to dull his consciousness with drugs and alcohol only worsened the situation, because they lessened any control he might otherwise have had. Unable to work for days after an emotional crisis, he lost himself in crowds or in the shuffling, whispered dereliction of an afternoon movie, popcorn squeaking in the buttery mouths of five co-conspirators in the dark cavern of the theater. Sometimes he simply had his mail forwarded to the baths.

Tony was exhausted. He was only twenty-four and already he felt burned out. He wasn't cut out for this shit. He was just a surf bum who had somehow gotten sucked up in this whole gay New York fast-lane life he wasn't equipped to cope with but had absolutely no idea how to escape. Oh sure, at first it seemed like fun. Glamorous. Exciting. And he thought it was what he wanted, or at least he thought it was a way to *get* what he wanted: a boyfriend, a relationship, stability. Finding a boyfriend seemed to be a way out, a regular guy, the kind of guy he used to be before he got caught up in this whole sorry mess. Maybe that was why he was attracted to blue-collar men: he was looking for someone like himself five years ago, someone who would love him the way he had once loved Connecticut, simply, honestly, and with all his heart, someone with whom he could share a home and a life—an *ordinary* life. Someone who would love him not because he was pretty or had money or was almost famous but because they just liked being with him. But as time went by the possibility of being the object of that kind of affection seemed as remote as witnessing an apparition of the Blessed Virgin Mary at Seventh Avenue and Forty-second Street. He remembered the first time he saw the New York skyline, how the buildings glowed and glittered in the setting sun as he and Connecticut approached the Holland Tunnel. Without Connecticut, the city had turned gray with soot and slush, and, at least in the beginning, there were days Tony thought he just wouldn't make it. Years later, each time he met someone new, he waited for the magic to kick in the way it had with Connecticut, but by and large his tricks fell far short of the mark. All they offered was chemistry, which, in the end, had to be enough.

*Bang! Poof!*

# PART II

# 22

ON HIS FIFTH ANNIVERSARY with Malone Men in 1977, Tony received a fire engine red Ferrari Testarosa from Tuxedo Malone and Parker Kensington in appreciation for the extraordinary success he had brought to the agency and the Black Tie fashion line. Within six months of their introduction in 1974, the designer jeans had surpassed all but one competitor in market share—a position they had maintained through three years of increasingly bitter rivalry—and with Parker's planned launch of a line of actual *blue* jeans under the name Black 'n' Blue, he expected to gain the number-one spot within the next sales quarter.

The profits from Black Tie jeans had fueled a period of intense growth and diversification at Parker Kensington. Tuxedo proved prescient again and, anticipating the fitness craze that swept the nation in mid-decade, persuaded Parker to introduce a line of men's activewear marketed almost entirely on the aesthetics of Tony's abdominal and pectoral muscles. Tuxedo, Parker, and Tony grew rich.

Tony's career and financial successes, however, were not mirrored in his love life. Now and again, he would meet someone who really appeared to have potential. Not only were they handsome, butch, and at least semi–blue collar, they also were actually fluent in the English language, had paid attention (most of the time, anyway) in personal hygiene class, owned no pets (or if they did, did not have a flea problem), and had no outstanding warrants for their arrest, or at least none in the state of New York or in states with reciprocal extradition agreements. But inevitably, each of these relationships slipped away, for reasons Tony could not fathom. His romantic disappointments were always accompanied by periods of significant depression, drug and alcohol abuse, and an occasional encounter with rough trade that left him both emotionally and physically bruised enough to miss several important shoots.

In February 1978, Tony met Kevin McCarthy at the Hook—the Tenth Street Hook and Ladder Co.—a Greenwich Village bar that catered to the erotic fantasies of queens who were drawn to firefighters or, by the inevitable extension of the concept, other men in uniform. The centerpiece of the establishment was an old fire truck that had been turned into the main service bar. It was Kevin who approached Tony. He carried a fresh beer of the same brand Tony was drinking, gave it to him, and introduced himself.

"I'm Kevin. Aren't you the Black Tie . . ."

"So much for the element of surprise. . . . I'm *Tony.*"

Kevin was cute in a bashful, little boy way. He was solidly built, with wavy brown hair, freckles, and a moustache so lush it looked like a fuzzy caterpillar crawling across his upper lip. He was a tad too collegiate for Tony's tastes, with his Madras shirt, crisply pressed pinwhale corduroy slacks, and lace-up Hush Puppies, but Tony was ultimately charmed by him. Kevin sidled up to him by quarter and half inches while they talked, until Tony felt first Kevin's breath, then his lips, on his ear. He was exquisitely aware of the first moment their torsos touched and the time when, not skipping a beat, Kevin put his beer in his left hand so he could put his right arm around Tony's back, hitching a thumb into one of the belt loops on Tony's jeans. Tony could feel surprising strength in Kevin's arm and could smell an inexpensive though not offensive cologne, beneath which he detected a smoky musk. By the time they finally did kiss half an hour later, Tony was on the verge of orgasm. Had Kevin fondled him at that precise moment, there would have been an explosion of such magnitude that the buttons on his fly would have become deadly projectiles as they sang across the room, threatening blindness and worse to anyone within their trajectory.

Kevin was twenty-six and had grown up in Blairstown, New Jersey, a wide spot in the road in the northwest part of the state not far from the Delaware River. Tony ascertained that he was not married, engaged, or pregnant with another man's child. He claimed to be a firefighter—the genuine article—and lived in SoHo with his younger, also gay, brother, Tim, a commodities trader. Kevin told Tony that he hadn't been out long, roughly a year and a half, and that he had never so brazenly approached anyone in a bar as he had just done with Tony.

"But I could see some other guys beginning to circle around you, and I didn't want to blow my chance."

In the cab uptown, Kevin said he had slept with only three men in the eighteen months he had been out. Tony didn't know if he was bragging or apologizing, but he figured Kevin's inexperience would guarantee at least a six-month run, and he liked that.

Beneath his preppy attire, Kevin had the body of a lumberjack—beefy yet well defined and exceptionally limber. He was heavily freckled from head to toe, and Tony knew that this summer the markings would deepen, expand, and multiply until they spread across his muscular, coppery back like the tawny pelt of some spotted jungle cat. But his most remarkable feature was his cock. Uncut and of dimensions Tony had never dared dream, it was mottled with a patchwork of burgundy discolorations that made it look like a newborn Dalmatian puppy: smooth, blind, and wet. Tony nicknamed it "Sparky," an appellation Val later unwittingly applied to Kevin himself in conversations with Tony.

In bed, it was clear Kevin was an amateur, nothing like the sexual athlete that Devlin was and Tony was becoming. But while he was inexperienced he was not unimaginative, and he was self-confident and eager to please. *Very* eager to please. Tony made a mental note of the practices and techniques to which he would introduce him, but he'd have to make sure he didn't scare him off by looking too accomplished.

"I think it's time to teach Sparky some new tricks," he said.

Kevin became an item more or less overnight, and the fact that Tony was dating an actual fireman and not some surplus-store clone titillated the boys of Malone Men. As a couple, they received an unusually large number of invitations to cocktails, dinner, and brunch. In the beginning, Tony accepted most of them, but Kevin appeared not to like many of Tony's acquaintances, and there came a time when getting him to leave the house was as difficult as lacing Miss Scarlett into her whalebone corset. Tony finally gave up, but he only pretended to mind.

As it developed, their relationship was probably the most sane one Tony had ever had. Kevin was honest and reliable. If he was going to be late, he called, including the time he was patched through from the scene of a fire. Kevin didn't even mind if Tony called him at the station house, as long as he was "discreet." He spent most of his days off with Tony at the Towers—a month after they met he had all but moved in. Kevin loved the outdoors and told Tony his dream job would be to serve as a forest ranger in a big state or national park, living out in the woods by himself (Tony squirmed). Kevin never wanted to go dancing or club hopping, which was just fine with Tony, although they would go to the Hook once every couple of weeks to keep in touch with Kevin's friends.

The first sign of trouble came just a few weeks before their six-month anniversary. Tony was planning a dinner party—moderate by Tony and Val's standards—that Kevin decried as "the Second Coming." Tony agreed to cut the guest list in half and cancel the appearance by a well-known chamber ensemble, but Kevin still objected. It was then Tony first suspected that Kevin was objecting not to the party but to the relationship itself and its prospects.

At about the same time, Kevin was suddenly being sent to, by Tony's estimate, an unusually large number of training sessions and being loaned to fire companies in other jurisdictions that were understaffed. Kevin apologized, but in the end he missed completely any celebration of their anniversary. Finally, while they were having dinner in Tony's suite, Kevin broke the news. He had been noticeably quiet and unresponsive, despite the fact they hadn't seen each other in three weeks.

"I knew this would happen sooner or later. I guess I'm glad to get it over with," Kevin said, looking out the windows toward Central Park and sighing. "I like you, Tony—I like you a lot, but I just don't fit into your world."

"Exactly what world are you talking about? Is it somewhere other than planet Earth?"

"Don't be an asshole, Tony. You know what I mean. Listening to Val and Devlin fight about why Devlin needs to change clothes before setting *one foot* outside 'the Towers.' Putting up with those goddamned yip-yip dogs. And God forbid the dinner wine is too dry or too fruity. I *loved* that. *'Dev, I think this wine is too fruity.'* Val's the fucking fruity one."

"So you're saying you hate Val? I can understand Devlin. *I* hate Devlin. But Val? He's been my best friend for years. You don't even *like* him?"

"Look, I'm sorry this isn't going to work. We've had some really wonderful times together. You're the hottest, sexiest, most gorgeous guy I've ever been with—or ever will be, probably. But we're too different."

"So you've already made up your mind? This isn't a negotiation, it's an execution."

Kevin flinched, but said nothing.

"You've met someone else, haven't you? You bastard. You wouldn't be in such a hurry to get rid of me unless you'd found somebody else."

"It's not like it looks, Tony. Really. It wasn't intentional. We didn't meet in a bar or anything. It was at the fireman's retreat upstate. You know, the weekend you didn't go to that big premiere party because I was out of town."

"That was only last month. All this has happened since then?"

"It *was* kind of fast," Kevin said. "Look, don't do this, Tony."

"Don't do what? Don't have an emotional reaction to the news that a man I have loved for six months is walking out on me for one of his smoke-eating pals? What, is his hose bigger than mine?"

"Christ, I don't understand why you're getting so upset. You're gorgeous. Your face is plastered all over the city. All over the *country*. You can have any man you want."

"And that's certainly one of the better reasons for not feeling guilty about dumping me."

"I like you, Tony. I really do. I hoped we could be friends."

"Friends? Sure. Next time I see you, I'll buy you a drink. And one for your little pal, just to show how friendly I still am toward you."

"I don't guess you'll have the chance to do that. There was an opening up in Jeff's company and I got it. I'm moving to Elmira next weekend."

"Elmira? Correct me if I'm wrong, you said *Elmira,* New York?"

"That's right."

"It's true then. Exceptionally well-endowed men really are more stupid than the general public."

"Tony, I'm sorry."

"Fuck you, Kevin. I don't need your sympathy. You don't want this? Fine. There are plenty of men who do. You're right about that. I *can* have any man I want. So you just move to Elmira-fucking-New York. Get *married* to your pal Smokey the Bear for all I care. I hope you both *die* in a fucking forest fire!"

"You little shit. I had no idea what a petty little bastard you were. I'm sure as hell glad I found out now. It looks like I've made *exactly* the right decision."

"I'm sure you have. You'll be far better off without me and my fruity friends."

"You know, right now I wouldn't cross the street to *spit* on you—*or* your friends—you fucking asshole."

Kevin never looked back as he made his way from Tony's suite down the hall to the foyer. Tony winced when he heard the Shitses clattering across the marble floor of the living room, nipping at his heels. A minute later, Val appeared at his door.

"Honey, what happened? Sparky stormed out of here as if City Hall were ablaze! He positively traumatized the dogs!"

"He fucking dumped me. . . . For some firefighter . . . in *Elmira!*"

"You're kidding!"

"He said he doesn't fit into 'my world.' And he called you 'fruity.' "

"Bastard! I liked *him*. I think all those toxic fumes have gone to his head. Well, come have a nightcap with us."

"No thanks, I'm going out."

"Out? Where?"

Tony pulled a pair of jeans and a white T-shirt out of a drawer. He threw a bottle of lube and some poppers onto the bed.

"Oh, God! Not the Church of St. Mark, patron saint of the broken-hearted."

"Excuse me while I dress down."

"Tony, don't. Stay here. Have a drink with us."

"And let Devlin see me like this? No thanks."

"Okay, I'll send him to get take-out from . . . Cartier's. That'll keep him occupied."

"They're closed."

"For me, *never*. I have their emergency number."

"Forget it." Tony went into his bathroom, where he kept his pharmaceuticals neatly arranged in their amber bottles—all obtained quite legally by prescription. Val refused to have street drugs in the house. He threw several into a shaving kit.

"I don't like what I'm seeing, Tony."

"Fine, don't look. I'll be out of your hair in a minute."

"Will you please stop and think about what you're doing?"

"I'm *sick* of thinking, Val. I want to be so fucked up I never think again! Just leave me alone and go fuck my ex-husband, why don't you."

"Well, *that* was uncalled for. There's really no need to get ugly."

"Then get out of my way and let me pack."

"Tony, stop. This kind of behavior is beneath you."

"That's where you're wrong, Val. There is nothing on the face of the earth that is beneath me at the moment, nothing too low or degrading I won't do it, because I am a piece of fucking trash that has once again been kicked to the curb, and I intend to wallow in the fucking gutter until I die. Now get the *hell* out of my way."

On the way downtown in the cab, Kevin's words rang in his ears: *I don't understand why you're getting so upset. . . . You can have any man you want.* At the same time, he also heard his "Aunt Mina's" accusation: *You know, Anthony, you've been with us for six months and these pants still have the Alexamenos stink in them.*

Tony knew he was an attractive man—attractive *hell,* he was fucking *gorgeous.* People paid him, paid him *big* bucks, to wear their clothes and their colognes, paid him just to show up and be beautiful, to smile, maybe show them a little skin. What was he worried about? He *could* have any man he wanted in the city—and there were what, seven million people in New York? Say half of them were women. That left three and a half million men, of which one in ten was gay. Three hundred and fifty thousand—in New York City alone! He could fuck one a night for what, a hundred years? Better line up two or three a night, just to make sure he got to them all. He had guys falling all over themselves to fuck him. He knew that. There weren't enough hours in the day to fuck them all. He'd never have to spend another night alone if he didn't want to, not in his entire life. Of course, not all of them were beauties. Most of them were fucking trolls. He might find himself in a position where he'd just as soon not know who was fucking him. He patted his shaving kit and was reassured by the chattering of the pills in their plastic containers. *Thank God for Mother's little helpers.*

TONY KNEW HE WAS IN DEEP SHIT when he saw Nola Lemmons's face. Tuxedo Malone's secretary looked as if she had just heard the news of JFK's assassination. Even the chatter in the reception area was subdued, and most of the ladies-in-waiting had made face masks out of the magazines they were reading. Just as well. At Tuxedo's instruction, Val had not allowed him to change or clean up after being hauled out of an Eighth Avenue porn palace, one of two or three places Val knew he might go for "consolation," which is to say vast quantities of anonymous sex, after his breakup with Kevin. (He had actually spent the previous three days at the baths and stopped at the theater only because "it was on the way home." The fact that he was *supposed* to be on a Kensington Sportswear shoot in the Caribbean had completely slipped his mind.)

Tony knew he looked as if he had been sleeping in a gutter in New Orleans during Mardi Gras. His face and T-shirt were crusty with the dried cum of a score of men, the knees of his jeans were heavily slick with God knows what human and manufactured substances, and the hair at the nape of his neck was sticking straight out from having sat slumped in his theater seat for so many hours to facilitate the ministrations of countless eager cocksuckers, despite the fact he had been sucked dry hours previously. And he smelled *vile*. Tony thought he saw one of the aspiring models crinkle his nose. He prayed he looked so gross no one would recognize him. And then Val wordlessly left his side, sat down, and lit a cigarette as if he were a complete stranger in an airport departure lounge.

Nola directed Tony toward Tuxedo's door without a smile—without even looking directly at him—and that was when Tony knew it was over, really over. He had even lost the indulgence and affection of the woman who served as the long-suffering den mother to the gorgeous, wayward boys of Malone Men. Tony paused before Tuxedo's burnished mahogany doors and fleetingly thought about attempting to make himself presentable, but he knew it was futile. Does a death row inmate suggest they "just take a little off the top" when they shave his head for the electrodes? He knocked but there was no answer. He turned to Nola and she motioned for him to enter in a way that made her look as if she would rather have him anywhere but within her sight. *Shoo!*

He opened the door. Tuxedo's high-backed chair was turned toward the window, so Tony could not be certain he was even there. He cleared his throat, but the chair did not swivel, so he made his way cautiously to a seat facing the desk and sat silently for what seemed like hours. It reminded him of waiting in line at the confessional. His shirt was soaked through, and he was *still* sweating, a reaction to God knows what pharmaceuticals he had ingested over the past three days, when men had pushed uppers or downers into his mouth to facilitate their particular sexual needs. Tony felt like throwing up, but he managed to choke it back in the hope of clinging to his last shred of dignity. He heard a tiny squeak, a prelude to the chair's rotation, and then Tuxedo was upon him full force.

"Just who the *fuck* do you think you are?" Tuxedo's face betrayed no emotion but pure rage. No recognition. No hint of mercy. "You *stupid* fuck."

Tony had never seen Tuxedo in such a state. His unshaven face was crimson, his black hair magnificently wild.

"Parker had twenty-five people milling around on the beaches of Antigua waiting for the lead model to show up and where are you? The clock's ticking, the creative director is going into apoplexy, and the talent is getting sunburned. And where the hell is Mr. Anthony Alexander? Sucking cock at the latrines of some sleazy theater that's showing *Dennis Does Dallas* or some such bullshit."

"I wasn't in the T-room."

"I don't care if you were giving head at the concession stand, Tony. You fucked up big-time. Do you understand that?"

"Yes, Tux. I know I did."

"I'm not even going to *try* to put a dollar figure on this disaster, because I'm about to burst an aneurysm as it is and it's just not worth it. *You're* not worth it. *You* are *not* worth it!"

Tuxedo stood up and went to the bar. He took a long time to fix himself a drink, and Tony could see that his right hand looked palsied. He wrapped a couple of crescent-shaped ice cubes in a crisp linen napkin and patted his face with it. When he returned to his chair, he took two long gulps from the tall scotch and water without uttering a word.

"Am I being fired?"

"*Fired?* No. That would be letting you off the hook too easily. Fired? So you can squander anything you haven't already thrown in the toilet? I don't think so. I owe it to Dallas not to let that happen. *And*, you've got to find some way to make this up to Parker." Tuxedo took another swallow of his drink and dabbed at his forehead with the moist napkin. "No Tony, you're not being fired, but you're going to be paying for this for a long, *long* time."

Tony straightened up in his chair. He had been sure Tuxedo was going to give him the axe. He sure as hell didn't want to lose his job, and he never intended to hurt or disappoint Tux. He just didn't *think*, period. It hurt so damn much when he was dumped by Kevin that all he wanted to do was get drunk and have sex with anything that walked, crawled, or limped in his direction, just to prove to himself that he was still attractive. But of course, that hadn't worked. It never did. In fact, he realized, it only made things worse. He looked like hell and felt like shit. *Madness takes its toll.*

Oh sure, it always started out as fun. He'd get high and strut around the baths, letting everyone know the night held something special for a lucky few. Sometimes people recognized him, nudged their friends, pointed and whispered. *Black Tie guy.* It didn't seem like such a desperate thing then. He would unabashedly display himself and feign indifference when someone expressed interest. Eventually, he'd make a few selections and try not to show that he was actually as anxious to get on with it as they were, that he was ravenous, *desperate* for companionship. He allowed the first few men to linger. Talk. Smoke a joint. Profess their awe at having scored with him. Proffer their telephone numbers. Sometimes a line would form outside his cubicle like hopeful stage-door-Johnnys eager to catch even a glimpse of the great Black Tie model reclining, temporarily sated, when his tricks left. For a few minutes, for as long as he was with another man, he could forget Kevin, or Gary, or Chris, or Greg, or whomever had most recently left his boot print on his ass. He might even do some charity work among the less fortunate.

But as the night wore on into day and back into night, as the drugs ate away at his nerves and he became increasingly dissipated and significantly less selective, word began to spread that there was a fashion-model smorgasbord on the third floor. By then, Tony welcomed all comers, but there were precious few pleasantries and as soon as his partner had come, he'd push him away, turn his head, and call out "Next!" He remembered very little after that point. He'd pass out and God knows what would happen. Time passed and if he was conscious of anything it was only the presence or absence of another man's weight on him.

At some point, people would again congregate outside his door, not to gaze at him in awe but to pity him or even call him names. Sometimes when he came to, he'd be able to stagger out under his own power; sometimes he'd wake up in the manager's private room with a very worried towel boy attending him. On those occasions, he might not be able to figure out where he was immediately or to remember the name of the man whose betrayal had sent him there. When it did come back to him, he simply wanted to die. This was one of those times. He hated himself, hated what he had become, but he felt powerless to change his life. If only there were one good man left in the world, just *one*, and Tony could find him, maybe *then* things would be different.

"Tony, for most of the last five years, you have been the top model in this agency. Not just in money, but in visibility and selectivity. In *impact*. If you didn't become besotted with every grease monkey with a big wrench and a couple of hairy lug nuts, there'd be no limit to what you could achieve. None. You did so well before Dallas passed on, and I had such high hopes for you. You had looks, you had brains, and you were a genuine, down-to-earth person. You really had a future."

"I don't have one anymore?"

"Tony, I find it nothing short of miraculous that you even have a recent past. With the type of men you pursue, the kinds of places you're seen in, and your truly extraordinary abuse of drugs and alcohol, you should have been dead long ago, your throat slit in some sleaze pit, some psychopath's jism still dripping out of the side of your mouth when they zip up the body bag."

"I'm sorry, Tux, I really am. This hasn't exactly been a picnic for me."

"Do you really think I *care* how you feel?"

"No. . . . I guess not."

"Let me ask you one question: Do you think that you have what it takes to make it in this business? Somewhere inside of you where the drugs and the alcohol haven't soaked through yet, do you think there's a part of you that still wants what I'm offering and can still grab it and run with it? If you don't, if you *really* don't want it anymore, the best thing for you to do is to go back to Florida. Surf by day and be a waiter by night. You're still attractive, you'll get good tips."

"Christ, Tux, I know I've been a dickhead, but this is all I have. I *couldn't* go back to Florida."

"You haven't answered my question."

"Which one?"

"Can you do it? Are you going to be physically and emotionally able to do the job?"

"I think I can."

"That's not good enough. *Can* you? Do you care enough?"

"I will. I can. Yes, I can."

"What about drugs? What are you into these days?"

"Nothing, hardly. Pot and coke, but everybody does them."

"Uh-huh."

"Maybe a few 'ludes now and then, and some Valium."

"Okay."

"And mesc and acid, very rarely."

"Nothing else? No smack? Nothing you can't quit by yourself?"

"No. Nothing else."

Tux fixed himself another drink and offered one to Tony. "Hair of the dog?"

This was a good sign, Tony thought. Tux looked almost normal again, except for the stubble. Damn, he was sexy in stubble.

"No thanks, Tux. I think I've still got most of the *dog* in my stomach."

Tuxedo returned to his desk, sipped his drink and rifled through some papers.

"Ah ha! Here it is," he said, slipping a yellow legal pad from under some folders. "The terms and conditions of your continued employment."

Tony watched as Tux flipped over page after page of his neat, small handwriting.

"This will, of course, become a legally binding document, complete with penalties for its breach. Among other things, you will be held personally, financially responsible for any future Antigua episodes. I'll give you an opportunity to review it with your own lawyer—you're still using Mort?—and I may be open to minor amendments. But if you want to continue to work for me, you will be expected to largely agree to these stipulations."

"And what exactly are these *stipulations?*"

"The first is no bars, no baths, no toilets, no *sex* . . . for two months."

"Two months? That's a lifetime. Are you trying to kill me?"

"No, Tony, I'm trying to *save* you. From yourself. I want you to realize that it is possible not to have sex—and with it all the personal and romantic complications that you so readily bring to the equation—and still be a functioning member of society."

"But *no* sex? Not even anonymous sex? Who could get emotionally involved with what floats its way through some glory hole at Port Authority?"

"You could, Tony. Val tells me you come home from the baths with a pocketful of telephone numbers. The concept of what the baths are has totally eluded you. You could get emotionally involved with a hitchhiker for Christ's sake. And besides which, it's illegal."

"Falling in love with a hitchhiker is illegal?"

"No, asshole, giving blow jobs in the Port Authority. You're lucky you haven't been busted."

Tony sighed. He could tell he wasn't going to get any concessions from Tuxedo.

"Second, you must be totally clean and sober for *three* months. No booze, no drugs whatsoever. I've arranged for you to have a physical tomorrow with Dr. Matthews. He'll examine you for any physical problems you may be unaware of—including venereal diseases—and determine a baseline for the presence of alcohol or drugs in your bloodstream."

"Christ, Tux, I'm not a fucking *junkie.*"

"Finally . . ."

"There's more?"

"Curfews."

"Fuck curfews, when do I get to use the exercise yard?"

"A ten o'clock curfew for the first thirty days."

"Ten o'clock? Nobody even *leaves* the house until eleven."

"After the first month, 11 P.M. Midnight for the last thirty days. You will be able to go wherever you choose, do whatever you want, and after the first sixty days do *whom*ever you want, but you must be in by your curfew. If you trick, you bring him home and he's out by 2 A.M. All of this applies to out-of-town jobs as well."

"I don't want to sound like I'm not taking this seriously, Tux, but how are you going to enforce this?"

"Val has agreed to supervise your probationary period, and I or a member of the staff will be calling you every night at five minutes past curfew, at least for the first couple of weeks. After that I'll be doing spot checks, on the phone and in person. There *will* be random blood and urine tests. I encourage you to observe these rules fastidiously. You will be allowed two free throws, so to speak, but the third time you turn up late, drunk, or stoned, you're out. Unequivocally, unceremoniously, irrevocably out. For good. I won't want to see your face ever again, and, alas, it is a face I love."

"Christ, Tux, you make me feel like I'm a criminal."

"Let me put it this way, Tony. If anyone else in the agency had pulled half the shit you have—*half*—they would have been on the street. I've kept you on because I think I know the kind of person you really are—the kind of person you once were—and because I genuinely like you and also feel some sense of responsibility to Dallas. As an adolescent, you had very little or no supervision or discipline, and under those circumstances, this kind of behavior is not unusual. On the more practical side, I think you can make us both very rich if you would only work at it a little harder. We both know—or maybe you *haven't* given it any consideration—there are plenty of new faces out there, and they're all anxious for the kinds of opportunities you throw away every day. As drop-dead gorgeous as you are, Tony, every day, every year that passes brings you closer to the end of your career. There's a kid somewhere right now who's at least as good looking as you are, who will be in the right place at the right time, as you were, and who'll attempt to eclipse whatever you achieve. Make the bastard *work* for it." Tuxedo's fist slammed his desk. "Every moment not spent in front of the camera is money unearned, time unwisely spent. Your time is now, Tony. Nail it. Ride it all the way in. Blow the rest of them out of the water. Deal?"

Tony seethed as he sat there, but he knew he had no choice.

"Deal. But mind you, I'm not going to become any Christ-on-the-cross, born-again, hallelujah princess."

"I'd be disappointed if you did, Tony."

Although he initially chafed against Tuxedo's demands, in time Tony secretly welcomed them and took them to heart with a rigorous discipline that bordered on asceticism. He eschewed dick, drink, and drugs and confined himself to the intoxicating pleasures of sleep. To be able to credibly counter the inquiries of curious friends and suspicious competitors as to whom he had tricked with the night before, he kept three index card holders near his bed. The first contained slips of paper with adjectives written on them, the others, in turn, occupations and locations. Every morning he would pick one slip of paper from each box and create his dream lover of the night before. A hunky pilot from Brazil. A tattooed hustler from the Village. A nasty trucker from Jersey City. All were possibilities.

# 23

ON THE WEEKENDS DEVLIN flew up from Florida, Val felt obliged to find a
respectable date for Tony, since Devlin's venom usually focused on
Tony's unrelenting state of bachelorhood. The men Val selected were always handsome, usually charming, and occasionally wealthy. Some had
been his classmates or were the younger brothers of classmates at Yale.
In the month immediately following Tony's successful completion of his
probationary period, these setups were designed to ease him back into
the social whirl, but in a more conservative orbit.

"Val, I've told you a hundred times I'm not interested in chicken, and
I'm not interested in pretty boys," Tony whispered as they fixed cocktails for themselves, Devlin, and Rake Holt, Tony's intended *du jour*. "I
must have pointed out my type to you a hundred times on the street, but
you were always too busy window-shopping to notice."

"Is that what you were doing? I thought you were pointing out fashion scofflaws." Val put a twist of lemon into the two scotches and, holding them between his thumb and forefinger, passed them to Tony.
"Really, *Antoine,* those types have been nothing but trouble for you.
You'd think you would have figured that out by now."

"I can't help it, Val, the guys you fix me up with don't do a thing for
me. Zip! When will *you* understand that for me an Ivy League education
is *not* an aphrodisiac?"

"Still, I just can't understand why you don't *try* to appreciate my
matchmaking efforts," Val said while carefully slicing an orange to gar-
nish Devlin's whiskey sour. "At least one of the men I fixed you up with
was a bona fide U.S. Congressman."

"That raging queen? The chairman of the House Committee on
Capitol Hill Glory Holes? Don't do me any favors. Isn't he the one
whose colostomy bag broke midway through dinner at the Plaza?"

"Perhaps he wasn't one of my more inspired choices, but he definitely did not wear a colostomy bag. As I recall, he went outside for a cigarette so as not to offend *you,* and he just happened to step in horseshit from one of those goddamn hansom cabs."

"Whatever. That evening was a bona fide disaster!"

"Hush now, you don't want Rake to hear you—hand me the vermouth—he's a very sweet boy, if a little young, and he was very excited about getting to meet you. Besides, I really tried. I mean, at least he's not a *blond.*"

"Blond, no, but your sister, Mackenzie, is about three times as butch."

"I can see this is a losing battle," Val said, picking up the second pair of cocktails. "Let's just get back to the boys before Devlin has the opportunity to seduce Rake and we *both* suffer a date worse than death. He's like a jackal around fresh meat."

"Tell me something I don't know."

When they entered the den, Devlin and Rake were sitting side by side in front of the fire looking at a fashion magazine. Devlin's right arm was draped unobtrusively across Rake's shoulders. "We're just in the nick of time," Val whispered.

Almost anyone but Tony would have swooned over Rake Holt. His brown hair was short but wavy, and he had the slightest suggestion of a cowlick above his left temple. A tasteful smattering of freckles made him an ideal candidate for Coca-Cola and Kodak campaigns. He had recently signed with Zoli, and when he professed his awe at being in the company of two such well-known models, Devlin blew his whiskey sour out his nose.

"Oh, excuse me," Devlin said, mopping his chin with the back of his hand. "It must've gone down the wrong way."

"And you were doing so well, dear," Val said. "Shall I get you a bib?"

Tony warmed up to Rake during dinner, due at least in part to his liberal consumption of wine. He figured he could get off in bed with him if he could just keep the kid's mouth shut. He'd just have to make sure it was occupied. Over coffee and cognac in the living room, Rake mentioned that some friends recently had taken him to an offbeat little bar called De Milo's.

"We've been there, haven't we, Val?" Devlin asked.

"Once," Val said with obvious disdain.

"I've never been," Tony said. "It's not that place where people bring their pets, is it?"

"No, that's the Ark," Devlin said.

"I don't know about anyone else, but the mention of bestiality gives me dyspepsia," Val said. "How about some more coffee and a change of subject?"

"No wait, Val, I'm intrigued," Tony said. "What is this place?"

"I can't believe there's actually a gay bar in this city you don't know about, Tony," Devlin said. "You must have skipped a page in your *Gloomy Gal's Guide to Gay Gotham.*"

"Okay, I'll put an end to this nonsense . . ."

"Don't tell him, Val," Devlin said. "Let's just take him there. Right now. I think it's high time Tony exposed himself to the bizarre fetishes and methodologies of . . . those less fortunate than ourselves."

A conspiratorial giddiness had taken hold of Devlin and Rake, and Tony was rushed out the door in an atmosphere of deadly serious hijinks akin to that of a group of fraternity brothers taking a virgin pledge to a whorehouse. In the cab Tony tried to guess the bar's specialty.

"Does the name have anything to do with it?" he asked.

"What do you think?" Devlin asked. "I mean, you wouldn't wear a cotillion dress to a place called Spurs, would you? Well, maybe *you* would. I've heard all about your Miss Kitty fantasy."

"Boys, boys," Val said. "Let's keep to the matter at hand."

"Let's see. De Milo's. Sounds Italian. A mob-owned gay bar?"

"Child, they're all mob-owned," Val said. He sighed. "Think of your art history class."

"*Venus* de Milo?"

"Score one for the pretty boy," Devlin said. "So?"

"It's a statue. In the Louvre. I've seen it."

"Tony, dear, I do so hate parlor games. Put on your thinking cap so we can get this over with," Val said. "What is it about the Venus de Milo that so definitively sets it apart from all other sculptures?"

"It doesn't have arms?"

"Bingo," Devlin said.

"So the statue doesn't have arms, so what? Wait a minute. Is this the bar I've heard of that has a one-armed bartender?"

"That would be Rex," Devlin said.

"But surely they wouldn't build an entire theme around a single bartender, turnover being what it is. Don't tell me that everybody who works there doesn't have arms."

"It's an equal opportunity establishment, and that applies to customers as well as employees." Devlin said. "You can be missing arms; you can be missing legs. Anything amputated. I know hands and feet qualify, although I don't know about individual fingers and toes. And what about transsexuals who've had their little weenies lopped off?"

"Qualify? Qualify for what?"

"Membership," Rake said. "In order to get in, you have to be missing an extremity of one sort or another or you pay a cover charge. Nothing outrageous. Ten bucks, I think, which goes to buy wheelchairs and prostheses for needy kids."

"Well, that's reassuring," Tony said as the cab pulled up to the address Devlin had given. "At least this evening won't be completely without redeeming social value."

The entrance to the bar consisted of two pneumatic doors that slid aside as soon as someone stepped or rolled onto a rubber mat, enabling patrons in wheelchairs to enter with a minimum of difficulty. As it turned out, when they arrived at the door they discovered that, it being Thursday, "Able-bodied Night," they did not have to pay the cover charge.

"I heard of one guy who actually used to pull his arm into his jacket and leave the sleeve flapping just so he wouldn't have to pay the ten bucks," Devlin said as he walked past the bouncer. "Talk about cheap!"

"Sounds suspiciously like you, Devlin," Tony said.

"Down, Tony," Val said. "If I can't keep *him* muzzled, the least I can do is attempt to keep *you* on this side of venomous."

Inside, a short ramp led to a wide doorway strung with beads, an inexpensive, if overly camp way to create a semblance of privacy without significantly inconveniencing anyone. Beyond the beads, the bar appeared not unlike any other. The decor was dominated by a reasonably tasteful, near-life-size copy of the Venus de Milo and a number of other limbless Greco-Roman statues.

If that night's crowd was typical, Tony thought, there was a surprising abundance of young, good-looking amputees in the city. Nearly all the men appeared to be exceptionally virile. Many had beards and mustaches, though not the ridiculously well-trimmed type to be found in most S&M bars; that kind of facial hair reminded Tony of French poodles. Plaid flannel shirts appeared to be the uniform of the day, with empty sleeves neatly folded and pinned to the side or, among those minus a leg or two, T-shirts that showed off bulging arm and chest muscles.

"No limp wrists here," Tony said.

"In some cases," Devlin replied, "no wrists, period."

De Milo's had only recently become of interest to the city's mainstream gays. The artsy set had discovered it first, when Andy Warhol hosted a buffet there consisting entirely of pigs' feet, frogs' legs, and lady fingers. Then S&M devotees flocked to it because word on the street had it that amputees were especially horny, prime masochistic meat. Finally, those merely on a sexual scavenger hunt, like Rake and his friends, showed up.

Each disabled man in the bar had a different reason for being there, but most were just ordinary gay boys who'd maybe been to 'Nam and made a bad first impression on a land mine, or suburbanites who'd been on the losing side of an argument with a Lawn Boy. Motivation among the able-bodied was less complex. Curiosity accounted for most of it, with the discovery of a hitherto unarticulated fetish responsible for those who made repeat visits.

Val, Tony, Devlin, and Rake seated themselves at a tiny, circular table and ordered cocktails.

"I would never have guessed there were so many cute amputees in the city," Tony said, looking first over his right shoulder, then his left. "I've seen the ones with no legs rolling around on those skateboard things selling pencils, but they're always so creepy looking. These guys look perfectly normal."

"How very liberal of you, Tony," Devlin said. " 'Some of my best friends are cripples, but I wouldn't want to suck their dicks.' "

"That's not what I meant, Devlin, and you know it. Frankly, it sounds more like something *you* would say."

"Look," Rake said, holding up a flyer, "they've got wheelchair basketball games on Saturday afternoon and arm-wrestling contests on Monday."

"And don't forget 'Stump-the-Bartender' night on Fridays," Devlin said.

At that instant, their drinks arrived, and the waiter glared at Devlin. Although most of the help were in possession of a full complement of extremities, they were sensitive to remarks made by callous, thrill-seeking patrons and, occasionally, obnoxious guests were asked to leave. Val stared at Devlin and gave a generous tip by way of apologizing.

Across the room Tony spotted a man he thought exceptionally attractive. He was in his late twenties, possibly thirty, with black hair and a porcelain complexion. His face was lean and angular, and his otherwise perfect nose looked like it had been broken ever so slightly. The man's azure eyes were focused directly on him. Tony smiled, hesitantly, and the dark-haired man glowed like a kid who'd just been given a double ice-cream cone—with sprinkles. Tony turned away from his gaze and whispered to Val.

"Val . . . Hunk at eleven o'clock high. Don't you just love it when someone has black hair and blue eyes? Isn't that what they call black Irish? God, he makes the hair on the back of my neck stand up."

"Nonsense. You've probably just got static cling in your shirt, dear," Val said. "If I've warned you about synthetic fibers once, I've warned you a hundred times. . . . So, where is he?"

"Three tables down, to your left. Black T-shirt. Arms like sledge hammers. A tattoo. You know how much I *love* tattoos. Tits of death. Bomber jacket."

Val tried to be inconspicuous, but he knew it would be impossible to remain completely undetected. He turned slightly to his left. The man's skin was unusually white, but creamy, not pallid. He thought he knew the appropriate foundation, Creme d'Ivoire, by Max Factor. The stranger had a hint of natural raspberry blush at his cheekbones—permablush, Val called it—a trait women would kill for but rarely inherited. His eyes were most extraordinary. They glittered like gems, like sapphires in a bowl of milk. His black hair glistened as if it were wet or had been marinated in some primitive grooming product like Brylcreem, but its volume and movement belied that perception. It was naturally, lusciously, crushably thick and brilliant.

"You're right. He is quite the stud. So *this* is your type? Now Mother knows why you never bring any chorus girls home. I can see both arms. Must be a leg casualty."

"You mean. . . . You don't think he's . . . ?"

"Tony, let's just say I doubt he's in training for the Boston marathon. And if he's not handicapped, you're still out of luck. Able-bodied guys don't come here looking to score with someone who can count to twenty on his fingers and toes. That *never* happens. At least I don't think it does. They're here because they adore the freakish physique. I understand that stumps become part of the sexual oeuvre. The romp often includes stump sucking, and I'm told that even stump *fucking* is not unheard of."

"I guess that gives new meaning to the phrase 'trick knee,' " Tony said, mildly put off and hoping that what Val said was not applicable to his ebony-maned angel-stud.

A waiter approached Tony. "Excuse me, sir. But the gentleman at the far table in the black shirt sent this drink over. You *are* drinking Johnny Walker? And he asked me to give you this." The bartender handed Tony a small piece of paper and quickly turned to leave. Tony unfolded the sheet, which had been torn from a promotional note pad for Wheelchair City, in Brooklyn. In small type below a stylized wheel logo were printed the words, "All makes, all models. Manual and Electric. Trade-ins cheerfully accepted. You're wheelin', we're dealin'." A message, in a smooth, loose hand, read, "You are one gorgeous guy. I'd like to meet you."

"Val, I think I'm going to wet my pants. Look at this note. He is so *adorable.*"

"When it comes to men, Tony, I always find your enthusiasm refreshing, but believe me, he's not doing you any favors. And aren't you forgetting that you're here with Rake?"

"Fuck Rake."

"No, I expect that's going to be your job. Do I have to brandish Miss Amy Vanderbilt's *Complete Guide to Blind-Date Etiquette?*"

"Okay, okay, okay. I'll . . . I'll just go over and get his phone number. Maybe I can fantasize about him while I'm screwing Rake."

"Try to be subtle about it, then. I'll invent some story for Rake's benefit, should he even notice you're gone. You've been *such* a devoted companion."

Tony slid his chair back, then froze. "I don't know . . . I can't do it. What if he *doesn't* have any legs?"

"I can pretty much guarantee by his choice of stationery that he doesn't."

"What are you two up to over there?" Devlin asked.

"Nothing," Tony said, swiveling his gaze from the smiling stranger to Devlin and back again.

"You're not *seriously* cruising some amputee, are you?" Devlin stood halfway up and looked in the direction of the man who had sent Tony the drink. He appeared to wince. "After all, when you were dating me, you told me you were a leg man."

"Shut up, Devlin," Tony said. "Not everyone is as moronic as you."

Rake looked as if he had unintentionally swallowed a tablespoon of ejaculate.

Tony decided he couldn't walk over to his admirer now, with Rake and Devlin watching. He decided he'd stop by his table on the way out and discreetly pass him his telephone number. Meanwhile, he tried to engage Rake in conversation, but the boy was just plain stupid. Finally, after Devlin announced the most popular book among this crowd must be *A Farewell to Arms,* Val stood up and said he was leaving.

"Come on Tony, let's go. I don't think I can tolerate much more of Miss DeSchuys' sick humor." Val put on his overcoat and turned to Devlin. "Whether you know it or not, your voice carries, *mon cher,* and I think there are several extremely angry people in the immediate vicinity."

"What are they going to do?" Devlin asked. "Beat me to death with their wooden legs?"

"We're leaving." Val motioned for Rake, who looked confused, to stand up. "I'd suggest you do the same, Devlin. But you can take your own cab. *Maybe* I will have cooled off by the time you get home."

"But what about the hunk?" Tony whispered, tugging at Val's sleeve.

"Oh please, Tony, give it a rest."

Tony looked in the man's direction as he left, trying to get his attention so he could at least shrug his shoulders and somehow convey that he was being forced to leave, but the man was concentrating intently on a matchbook in his right hand.

The ride home in the cab was difficult. "Why do you put up with that kind of shit, Val," Tony asked.

"Devlin has his good points—or perhaps I should say point. Besides, you're a fine one to talk. Need I go into the gruesome details of your own relationship with Miss DeSchuys?"

"I just hoped you were smart enough to learn from my mistakes."

When they arrived at Triumph Towers, Rake said he would just as soon continue on to his place, but he looked so crestfallen that Tony insisted he come in. They had what Tony considered perfunctory sex, though Rake did not appear to be at all disappointed. At breakfast the next morning, Val was as cheerful and gracious as a sorority sister during rush, despite the fact that Devlin was "sleeping in," or maybe because of it. He didn't like being unnecessarily ugly, and he was never angry for more than eight hours. "What's the point?" he'd said to Tony once. "I refuse to furrow my brow prematurely."

Tony returned to De Milo's that night alone. The doorman remembered him, smiled, and motioned for him to enter without paying the cover charge, again in effect. The able-bodied traffic was down considerably. Tony waited until well past midnight, but the man did not appear. He returned the following night and the next Thursday, Friday, and Saturday after that. One night several weeks later, a group of regulars struck up a conversation with him. Why, they wanted to know, was someone like him hanging around this particular bar? Tony told them about the black-haired man, and some of the men recognized the description.

"Yessir, hard to miss that boy. *Gooood*-looking," one man with no left arm said. "Lives in Brooklyn."

"A real shame," said a man with an eye patch. "Something terrible. Lost both legs."

"*Both* legs? He's lost both legs? You're sure?"

"That's right," the first man said. "Above the knee."

"How much above the knee?" Tony asked. "Not that it makes much difference, I guess."

"I'd say just above the knee, wouldn't you, Rex?"

The one-armed bartender had been listening to their conversation between orders. "The only thing I'm interested in on that gentleman, as you well know, has definitely not been amputated."

"What else do you know about him?" Tony asked, suddenly queasy. He hated competition.

"Not much. He's been a regular for a while, but mostly he keeps to himself. Name's Aubrey or Andy or something like that. Haven't talked to him much. Nobody has, really."

Tony now wondered whether he should wait any longer for this guy, no matter how hot he was. Let Rex have him. *Both* legs? The reality of it was beginning to set in. He bought a farewell round for his companions and was about to leave when one of them whispered, "Jackpot, kid."

Tony looked toward the entrance. It was him all right, his hair windblown and his cheeks flushed with cold and exertion. This time he was wearing a white T-shirt—a plain old, incredibly sexy BVD T-shirt—jeans, and his bomber jacket. Damn, he looked fine. And yes, both legs were gone. But the instant Tony saw him, all of his uncertainties evaporated. He knew he couldn't leave the bar without at least talking to him.

"A double Johnny Walker Black on the rocks, Rex, and whatever it is *he* drinks. What the hell does he drink, anyhow?" Tony fidgeted with his wallet, his fingers quivering.

"Bud, I think," said Rex.

Tony groaned. He drank beer only to appear butch and hated the way a beer-drinking trick's morning breath smelled like sweat socks. But in this case he didn't care. "Who's that guy he's with?"

"Calm down," Rex said. "I'm pretty sure he's family. I've seen the guy in the chair leave with tricks while the other guy was here."

"And that's supposed to make me feel better?"

"All I meant was that they're not lovers. Here're your drinks. Go on over there and turn up the charm." Rex handed Tony a brimming rocks glass and a beer. "I'm green."

The man in the wheelchair, now at a table, had not yet seen Tony, and his companion appeared to be headed toward the bar. Tony cut him off and set the drinks down. "Excuse me," he said to the amputee, who looked up at Tony with a smile that turned the hair on the nape of his neck into porcupine quills again. "I'd like to return the favor of the drink you sent me last time I saw you. May I?"

"Sure. You're welcome. Or thank you. Or whatever," the man said. A definite Brooklyn accent. At least it's butch, Tony thought. "My name's Avery, and this is my brother, Tom."

"Can I buy you a drink, Tom?"

"No thanks . . ."

"Tony."

"No thanks, Tony. I think I'll just sit at the bar for a while." Tom winked at Avery as he walked away.

Tony sat down next to Avery and smiled, nervously. He couldn't believe this hunk didn't have any legs. Each time he looked at Avery's face, his heart soared, only to plummet when he saw the metal rims of the wheelchair out of the corner of his eye.

"I'm sorry I left without talking last time—do you even remember me?" Tony asked.

"Hell yes, I remember you. I was kind of hurt when you left."

"I really was getting ready to come over and introduce myself, but my roommate got into a snit and all of a sudden wanted to leave."

"That's okay. I've learned to expect the unexpected in this bar—for better or worse," Avery said. "So what do you do for a living, Tony?"

Tony hesitated. With most of the men he met, Tony tried to avoid the word *model*, at least initially. His profession was a frequent turn off to the burly bohunks to whom he was most attracted.

"I'm under contract to a . . . talent agency. . . . Tuxedo Malone."

"Never heard of it. So, what's your talent?"

"I have many talents," Tony said *sotto voce*, and, without thinking, he reached under the table to caress Avery's thigh. Instead he grazed the end of his stump, neatly covered with soft blue denim. He pulled back his hand instantly, hitting the underside of the table, and emitted a cry that was part pain, part shock, and part despair. "Oh my God. I'm sorry. I mean I forgot. And, oh shit, I've ruined everything."

"Hey, hey, calm down," Avery said. "This happens all the time. People aren't used to it. You should see some guys when they sober up and realize they're in bed with a naked double amputee. You know, they'd had a couple drinks too many or they were high as a kite on cocaine or 'ludes, and they end up in bed with this guy with no legs. Some of them actually scream. I mean *really* scream. One literally jumped out of bed."

"Yeah, well *that's* fucked. A guy as good looking as you. . . ."

"Every once in a while it looks like I've hit a home run with someone—you know, they're sober and they don't freak, but the number they give me is disconnected or the people who answer have never heard of the guy. I've got a rotten batting average when it comes to second innings."

"Well, I'm pretty sober and I'll tell you right now, I'd love to go all nine innings with you." Tony leaned over and kissed Avery, feeling his solid biceps with his right hand.

"Jesus, you don't waste any time, Tony. You're sure about this?"

"That's what my Louisville Slugger is telling me."

"Well then, I'd love to play ball with you."

"Your ballpark or mine?"

"It'll have to be yours," Avery said. "I have a home field disadvantage I need to tell you about. But I do have wheels."

"I've noticed," Tony said, catching himself too late and making a face.

"That's cool, man. I like it better when people can make a joke about it rather than freak out or pretend they don't notice."

Avery rolled himself over to his brother at the bar. As they talked, Tom glanced back at Tony and smiled. It was a combination "I can't believe my brother's so lucky" smile and a "Don't you dare mess with his head, you gorgeous asshole" look. Avery returned to the table, zipped up his battered bomber, and they headed for the door. His van was parked nearby. It had a custom sapphire metallic finish with silver pinstripes. A white horse with wings and the name Pegasus were painted on the side near a round custom window.

"Nice ride," Tony said.

"Thanks. It's older than it looks, though. I take especially good care of it because without it I really *would* be handicapped. Plus I've got the time to do it, not working and all. I just wish traffic in the city wasn't so hellacious. I try to make most of my trips to Manhattan at night or on weekends."

"You're from Brooklyn, right? Rex told me."

"Yeah, and believe me, there's a world of difference."

Avery unlocked a side door and pressed a button. A small platform emerged from the truck and lowered itself to the ground. He wheeled himself onto it, pressed the button again, and was lifted into the van. A swiveling driver's seat enabled him to get out of the wheelchair and behind the wheel. Tony entered the van through the passenger side door. The interior was spotless and filled with electronic equipment.

"You've got an expensive stereo system in here. Aren't you afraid it will get stolen?"

Avery started the engine. "Uptown, right?"

"Uh-huh."

"Nah, this baby's armed with a state-of-the-art antitheft system. I installed most of it myself. I'm good with electronics. Learned it in 'Nam."

"Vietnam? Is that where you . . . ?"

"Yeah."

Tony put his left hand on Avery's thigh. Avery patted it, then returned his own to the steering wheel. "Much as I'd like to, I can't hold your hand while I'm driving because of the hand controls."

"That's okay. This is fine."

Traffic was light and they made good time. Shortly, Tony leaned forward and pointed out his building a couple of blocks ahead on the right.

"You live *there?* Triumph Towers? That's supposed to be the nicest building in Manhattan. Don't like movie stars and football players and stuff live there?"

Tony laughed. "TV people, mostly. But once you've seen someone like Ocean Mackenzie walking her dog with curlers in her hair, they kind of lose their glamour."

"Ocean Mackenzie? The anchorwoman?"

"Yeah. I think she's a fag hag. Or a transvestite. I see her at all the bars."

"Where do I park?"

"Go around the block and you'll see the entrance to the resident's garage. Just pull in and we'll leave the keys with the night attendant. He'll take care of it. . . . Here we are. Turn in and stop just short of the yellow-and-black line."

A liveried attendant emerged from a softly lit, glassed-in room.

"Hello, Mr. Alexander. Have you had a pleasant evening?"

"Yeah. Thanks, Jack. Would you please see to the van? I don't believe we'll be needing it again tonight."

"Uh, Tony," Avery whispered. "I can't stay all night. I'll tell you why later."

"Oh, okay," Tony said. "Jack, I guess you can just keep it in short-term."

"Fine, Mr. Alexander," Jack said. He opened the driver's side door for Avery, and Tony could see a barely perceptible flinch.

"Thanks, but I get out the side door," Avery said, lifting himself into his wheelchair.

In the elevator, Tony leaned down and kissed the top of Avery's head. His hair smelled great, clean but not perfumey. Masculine. This guy was going to be a lot of fun.

"I've never seen an elevator with real wood walls," Avery said. "Or these little vase things for live flowers. And how come there are no numbers for the floors?"

"It's a private elevator—goes straight to the penthouse."

"I'll bet your view is incredible. How high up are you?"

"Sixty-five stories. The walls are mostly glass, so you get an almost unobstructed panoramic view from river to river."

"Sixty-five. Geez." In a city where the social strata is an almost visible architecture, Avery Mann had rarely risen above the third floor.

When they exited the elevator, only the softly glowing night lights were on, but Avery was still impressed by the interior. He marveled at the marble floors, the fountain, the Asian art, and the view.

"You *live* here? This place is fucking incredible—pardon my French."

"The first thing you should know is that I don't *own* this place. Far from it. It belongs to my roommate, who has zillionaire parents who gave it to him for his birthday."

Avery rolled over to one wall of windows and admired the view. "I know it sounds stupid, but this is like a whole different world up here. It's like . . . I don't know . . . a postcard or a movie. It just doesn't look real."

They made their way to Tony's bedroom.

"This is the thickest carpet this chair's ever been on. It's like I'm in mud—it's really hard to get anywhere."

Once Avery hoisted himself up on the bed, Tony pushed the wheelchair aside and got down on his knees in front of him. He undid Avery's top fly button and tugged at his zipper.

"Tony, I can undress myself. People think that just because . . ."

"Shhhh . . . Avery. I'm not doing this because I don't think you can do it yourself. It's part of the fun. It's sexier. I intend to strip you naked and totally ravish your hot fucking body."

"Oh. Well then, have at it," Avery said as he lifted his arms to let Tony pull his T-shirt over his head. The tang of his underarm deodorant wafted upward.

"Christ, you smell great," Tony said.

Tony made love to Avery more carefully, more deliberately, than he had to anyone in a long time. He was so beautiful, so *strong,* but so vulnerable. Tony thought he saw in Avery's eyes both a hunger and a kind of wariness, at once inviting and forbidding, and he already knew there was a bond between them, a connection forged in mutual desire tempered by pain. God, he wanted to *devour* this man and to be consumed by him in turn. He let his lips roam across the graceful planes of Avery's chest, down the length of his muscular arms. He spent an eternity just kissing Avery's hands, touching each fingertip with his lips, nuzzling his palm. And then, feeling as if he had strayed from something important, he returned to Avery's face—that *face*—made contact with his eyes again, kissed him so long, so hard, that they both gulped for air when he pulled away.

Tony laughed. "Damn, you're hot!"

"Stop."

"I mean it . . ."

Avery pulled him closer. "I said"—they kissed—"shut *up!*"

AVERY STARED UP through the skylight while Tony slept with his head on his chest. He wasn't accustomed to such luxury, and he was even less accustomed to the kind of sex he had just been treated to. Even under the best circumstances, his sexual encounters with men left him feeling dirty and abused. Most of the men he picked up had never tricked with an amputee before. They picked him up on a drunken dare, or because he was butch and good-looking enough to make up for the lack of legs, or out of some kind of a twisted thrill. Some of them, insecure or jealous of Avery's outrageous looks and chiseled body, tried to humiliate him. Occasionally a trick had good intentions, but when they got to a hotel room all he could do was whip out his dick for a quick blow job and leave while he was still dripping.

But this guy, Tony, had done everything softly, slowly. He said everything in a whisper. He made Avery lay motionless for what seemed an eternity, while he kissed, bit, licked, and sucked almost every square inch of his body. Tony had nipped at his nipples, pinned his arms over his head and buried his face in his armpits. It was so intimate it was almost embarrassing, and sometimes it left him gasping for breath. Every once in a while Tony would let his silky hair float across Avery's chest or stomach so softly that he would swear it was a feather. He could just barely feel Tony's breath on the moist tangle of hair at the base of his cock. He had to work hard not to come, because he wanted this feeling to last forever. When he finally did, he half growled and half screamed, his clenched fists pounding the mattress. His heart was thrashing like a cat in a sack on a bridge. Tony collapsed on him, exhausted. Their hair was soaked, their chests heaving in unison. When their breathing became more regular and they got goose pimples on their exposed skin, Avery raised himself on his elbows, kissed Tony on the mouth and eyes, on the nose, rolled over on top of him, and returned the favor. By the time they both were spent, it was 5 A.M. and snowing lightly. The flakes that landed on the warm windows melted with a barely perceptible hiss. Avery was wide awake, but Tony had drifted into a light sleep almost immediately.

"Tony," Avery said, tousling Tony's hair with his right hand. "I've really got to go. It's going to be light soon."

Tony stirred, but simply moved his head a bit higher on Avery's chest.

"So that's the catch, you're a vampire." Tony reached down and pulled the sheet and comforter up around his neck theatrically.

"Tony, I'd love to stay with you—this is the best sex I've *ever* had—but I can't," Avery said. "Look, I never got around to telling you, but I'm married."

Tony raised his head, sighed, and squinted at Avery with bloodshot eyes. "To a man or a woman?"

"A woman."

"That's a relief. She'll never be able to do for you what I can." Tony rolled over onto his side of the bed.

"She'll never even know the *names* for some of the things you've done to me."

"Well, if you like men, as you so obviously do, why not get a divorce?"

"I've got kids. Two boys—Christopher and Joey. I love them more than I could ever say, and they need me. They need a dad." Avery sat up and swung his stumps around so they were perpendicular to the bed.

Damn, Tony thought, he really *is* getting out of bed. He was usually able to cajole his tricks into a farewell blow job, at the very least, but he suspected that might not be the case tonight. He sighed and fell back into a pile of pillows. Lifting his arms, he interlaced his fingers, turned them inside out, and stretched. He hated it when people he really liked—and he *really* liked this man—got up to leave. All of a sudden everything got awkward and clumsy. It was like you were strangers in the bar again: a second pursuit was afoot, and this time the quarry was *really* on the run.

"I'd rather not leave, Tony. I'd rather stay here with you and fuck until my dick gets worn down to a nub . . ."

"Which would take a considerable amount of time."

" . . . but the fact of the matter is that I *am* married, my wife doesn't know I'm gay, and she's probably worried." Avery felt among the damp bedclothes for his T-shirt and undershorts.

"Where does she think you are?" Tony reached around Avery and turned on the night table lamp. He got out of the bed.

"Thanks," Avery said. The soggy T-shirt had become twisted in the sheets. "What a mess. . . . I usually tell her Tom and I are going to a card game . . ."

"Here, take one of my T-shirts, if it'll fit. You've got a bigger chest than me, but you'll freeze to death in that wet one."

"Thanks. I'll wash it and get it back to you, somehow. I promise."

"Don't worry about it. Actually, it will be nice to know you're wearing it. I may go back to sleep with this one on your pillow." Tony stood there, naked, invitingly as possible, hoping something would happen.

"When you and I left the bar, I told Tom to call her and tell her I'd be late, but I had no idea how late. This is not the way things usually work out." He stopped dressing for a moment and leaned over to give Tony a quick, dry kiss on his thigh. "Not that I'd have it any other way. You really are an incredibly beautiful man, if you don't mind being called beautiful."

"I've been called worse."

Avery swung himself into the wheelchair, wheeled over toward the dresser, and batted at his lavish hair in the mirror.

Tony threw on a lounging robe he had lifted from the Ritz-Carlton in Nice. "Do you want some coffee? It won't take but a minute."

"No, I really need to go."

"So you mean to tell me that your wife has *no* idea you're gay," Tony said. "You *are* gay, aren't you? Or are you merely bisexual? Or perhaps you're just confused."

"No. Just drunk."

"Oh right. I haven't heard that one in a while."

"Naaaa, I'm definitely gay. I guess I sort of came out in 'Nam, with an Aussie special forces guy."

"So how do you manage it? Being gay and married, I mean. It would drive me crazy."

Avery relaxed into the chair with a sigh. It was a question he asked himself every day. "I love my family. I love my life. We both come from big families, and so there are always lots of opportunities to get together and celebrate. Birthdays, weddings, anniversaries, First Holy Communions—we're both Catholic. I still love my wife, even though I only want to *be* with men. And I absolutely worship my boys. I can't give all of that up for the fag lifestyle. It's just not enough for me."

"Doesn't all of this make for a somewhat tense relationship?"

"Not really. Brandi never really seemed to like sex that much. Sometimes I actually thought she was gritting her teeth when we did it. All she ever wanted was to have kids. And me not having legs somehow gives us a great excuse for not getting all hot and heavy. We've never talked about it, but I'd have to say we're both pretty happy and comfortable with things the way they are. I mean, we still sleep in the same bed and all, and we're still affectionate, which is important for the sake of the kids. She loves me, I think, and I love her, in a high-school sweetheart kind of way and because she's the mother of my kids. I mean I *like* her, I really do, which I think means more than love sometimes. We don't fight like some so-called normal married couples we know, who take each other for granted.

"Mostly, I guess I've decided to stay with her because of the kids. I want them to have a normal, happy childhood. And I couldn't stand to be away from my boys. I'm comfortable with what we've got, and I don't see anything better in the cards. Neither one of us could live as well if we had to keep up two places—me with just my disability checks and her with what she makes as a waitress at this greasy spoon in Greenpoint. Plus she's a big help to me around the house."

Tony knelt in front of Avery and placed his hands on Avery's thighs. He wanted to get into this man's pants again, seduce him into staying for breakfast. Maybe *never* let him leave. Not just because he was so hot, but because he was genuinely sweet, even if he was a little sappy. It was something that drew Tony to married men. They were sexy, but vulnerable and surprisingly tender. Tony could feel himself falling down that all-too-familiar rabbit hole. He reached for Avery's U.S Navy belt buckle, but Avery took Tony's hands in his own with an exaggerated frown and a pout. He leaned over and kissed Tony on the forehead.

"I meant what I said, Tony. I've got to go." He picked up his bomber and struggled into it.

"I'd like to see you again, if that's possible. I know some married men have rules about that. Basically, everything's a one-night stand because they feel guilty about cheating on their wives and even worse for doing it with men."

"You *want* to see me again?"

"Are you kidding? Wouldn't you like to get together again?"

"Hell, yes. It's just that not that many people ask—other than to be polite. That's not why you're asking, is it? So my feelings aren't hurt?"

"No way. I really want to see you again."

"Great. But you'll have to give me your telephone number, because I can't have you calling my house," Avery said, rolling backward. "I mean, I don't want to have Brandi taking messages for me from you. It doesn't seem fair."

"That's okay. You got something hard I can lean against to write on?" he said, grinning.

"Pervert."

"SO TELL ME, TONY, how was he?" Val asked. He was curled up on the oversize leather sofa, his legs tucked to his side, sipping a Bloody Mary, reading the Sunday *Times*. The sun was at his back and the Shits were at his feet.

"He who?" Tony's eyes had just fluttered open. He lay on the couch opposite Val, where he had fallen asleep watching the sun rise, his head resting on Avery's T-shirt. Its scent was overwhelming. He was never going to wash it.

"Oh, please. Don't even *try* to be coy with your Auntie Val. You know very well who I mean. That legless side of beef you've been chasing all these weeks."

"How did you know it was him?"

"Just how stupid do you think I am? For God's sake, there were wheelchair tracks all over the carpeting. Even, I might add, on the Aubusson. If you're going to get serious about him, we'll just have to strip the floors down to the bare marble."

"Okay, okay, you got me." Tony pulled himself up, stretched, and poured a cup of coffee from the silver service on the table between them.

He swiveled his head to get the kinks out of his neck. "It was *fabulous*. He was a fucking animal. And he smelled great. A divine combination of Ivory soap and sweat. Want a whiff?" Tony proffered the T-shirt.

"I think you know the answer to that," Val said, peering over the tops of his reading glasses. "And what of his legs, dear?"

"What of them?"

"Didn't you miss them? Did you not find it disconcerting at any time?"

"Nope, not for a minute. In fact, the absence of his legs made several of the positions of the Kama Sutra considerably more pleasurable."

"Seriously, Tony, what was it like? He is terribly handsome, but frankly, I know I couldn't deal with it."

"I do want to cry every time I think about it, because the rest of him is so absolutely perfect. I mean he's *flawless*. Great body, perfect skin, fabulous hair. And you know, his considerable physical attributes aside, he's sweet, if a bit naive."

"I believe the word you are looking for is dumb."

"He's not *dumb*, Val, he's just not as worldly as we are, and in my book, that's a definite plus. I was 'dumb' once, you'll recall."

"You were never dumb, *cherie*. Unwashed, definitely. Uneducated. Unpolished. But unequivocally exceptional."

"Well, I'm not sure what all this guy is, but I intend to find out."

"So, what's the color scheme for the wedding? And am I the maid of honor?"

"In your case, that would be *matron* of honor—and don't hold your breath. He's married and has two kids. He says he's been dicking around with men for quite a while, but he's still living with the old ball and chain and the deductions. While he was in the bathroom, I peeked at pictures in his wallet and his sons are absolutely exquisite. One blond, one dark like him. God help the men of this city in ten or twelve years if they're gay."

"And since when have you been above home wrecking?"

"Right. I've only seriously dated a dozen married men, of whom how many left his happy nuclear family for a lifetime of ardor in my arms? Zip, that's how many. Even if they do leave their wives, once they smell the musk in the air, they're off like a wildebeest in heat. But then again, I don't know. He just seems so familiar, so right. It's like I've known him my entire life."

"Well, I don't know about your previous life, but the *rest* of your life is going to amount to about fifteen minutes if you don't hurry up and douche. We're committed to three, count them, *three* brunch appearances. And oh yes, Besotted One. Better take a toot or two unless you want to drown in your Bloody. You look like you haven't slept in weeks."

# 24

IN THE BEGINNING, it was difficult for Tony and Avery to see each other even once a week. Tony was solidly booked almost every day and had acting classes on three nights. He also had shoots in Hawaii, Mexico, and Peru. Avery had to stay home with the kids at night while Brandi worked. Tony tried to convince him to bring the boys over to the Towers or meet him somewhere for hot chocolate and ice cream with the boys, just so they could *see* each other, but Avery was reluctant to let his two worlds collide. He wouldn't invite Tony to Brooklyn for similar reasons.

"Not with the boys there," he said, when Tony offered to bring pizza over for all of them. "Besides, Brandi would know something was up. Don't ask me how, but she would. She'd smell your cologne or she'd smell our spunk."

"She would smell our *spunk?* What is she, part bloodhound?"

"I'm serious, she's got a sixth sense about these things. I just don't want her to ask any questions."

Brandi had enough seniority at the diner that she was off both Friday and Saturday nights, and Avery reserved Friday nights and all day Saturday for family activities. They frequently met Brandi's younger sister, Mandi, at the Howard Johnson's just off the New Jersey Turnpike for a Friday night all-you-can-eat clambake or fish fry. Saturdays the family spent running errands, doing household chores, and visiting both extended families. At least twice a month, while Brandi was having her hair done at Mandi's beauty shop in Jersey, Avery took the boys to a museum or some historic New York site, like the Statue of Liberty or Grant's Tomb. He insisted the boys develop an interest in learning, so they could go to college and make something out of themselves, "unlike their father."

Saturday night was Avery's "night out with the boys." Brandi understood that he needed to get out of the house and away from the kids, and these weekly card games were a perfect solution. Avery didn't appear to lose much money at them—he said he more or less broke even every time—and she liked the quiet time when the boys were finally in bed. She did her nails and conditioned her hair, heated up some Jiffy Pop, indulged herself with one Pink Lady cocktail, and watched what *she* wanted on TV or drifted to sleep reading one of her romance novels.

Avery and Tony, on the other hand, had much more energetic entertainments planned. If Val was out for the evening, Tony would be waiting by the elevator, naked or wearing nothing but a jockstrap and a pair of sweat socks. They'd go straight to the bedroom, where Tony practically shredded Avery's clothes in the process of stripping him. Their time together was a delirium of animal fucklust. When they were joined, their lean, flat stomachs moved across one another like tectonic plates shifting on a sheen of spit and sweat and semen.

They were their happiest in bed, not just because of their intense physical attraction and sexual compatibility, but because they were on a level playing field, face to face, eye to eye. They could exchange long, lingering kisses and study each other's features, something they could not do with Tony standing and Avery in his wheelchair. It was the closest they could possibly get to being equal.

"You know, keeping you happy is becoming a full-time job," Avery said one night after having sex, "and if the Social Security office finds out, they'll cut off my disability checks for sure."

Initially, they said little of any consequence to each other. Their need to touch, to be connected physically, was so overpowering—and their time together so limited—that conversation seemed wasteful. But eventually they began to fill the time between love tussles with questions for each other.

Other than his sons, about whom he could talk endlessly, Avery didn't easily reveal much about himself and his life. Eventually, Tony managed to pry out of him that he had been a star basketball player but only a marginal student in high school. He'd been offered an athletic scholarship to NYU but turned it down because he had a wife—and soon a kid—to support. Then, close to panic, he joined the Navy to get away from it all. He was only nineteen, and he needed time to figure out these strange feelings he had for men. But the Navy didn't solve that problem. Far too frequently he found himself throwing a rod for one of his fellow swabbies in the showers. He managed to control his urges through boot camp and SEAL training, where he specialized in electronics and underwater ordnance. Once he got to Vietnam, he was discreetly frisky on the rare occasions he got into Saigon on a weekend pass, until he met a member of the Australian Special Forces and began a long catch-as-catch-can relationship.

"Was he cute?" Tony asked.

"If there was one word that I would never use to describe Bryan Bond it would be cute. Brute would be more like it. I have a feeling you would have loved him."

AVERY AND BRYAN met in the bar of the Imperial Hotel in Saigon in October 1968. Avery had had a crummy weekend—some bad food on Friday night pretty much kept him on his knees straight through Sunday morning—and in the last hours of his leave he was finally feeling better and was horny as hell. He'd heard a rumor that the MPs were out in force that weekend and that the Imperial might be on their hit list, but he told himself he'd just be real careful whom he talked to and what he said. The bar was suspiciously empty—maybe the rumors were true and there'd been a raid—but he went in anyway, sidling up to the bar and cocking his head to get the attention of the bartender, Thanh. He ordered a Singha boilermaker.

"So, Thanh, where is everybody? Was there trouble last night?"

"No Ave, no trouble," Thanh said. "All talk about MPs, very bad for business. But not true." Thanh was young and had some Western facial features—he might have been half French—and was always giving Avery free beers. Avery knew he had a crush on him, but he really wasn't attracted to him. He tried to make up for the boy's obvious disappointment by leaving him extravagant tips, which he could ill afford.

They talked while Avery pulled on his beer, all the while sizing up the room. A tall black boy, too young, it seemed, to be in a place like this, stood at the far end of the bar with his eyes locked on Avery, obviously aching. Two men in their mid-thirties, both wearing khaki slacks and short-sleeved Madras shirts, talked quietly at a table. Near the back door, a pair of long, lean legs in black stovepipe chinos jutted out of the shadows. Avery stared until his eyes grew accustomed to the darkness, and he could just make out a muscular torso and the silhouette of a head topped by a severe brush cut.

"Thanh, who's that over there? Is he good-looking? And available?"

He knew it was wrong to ask Thanh for the lowdown on potential tricks, but the stranger in the shadows looked like the only way he was going to salvage a ruined weekend.

"Good-looking, yes. Very good-looking. Boom-boom, boom-boom," Thanh said, pounding his fist over his heart. "I don't know available. Never see before."

He ordered another beer, swiveled his chair a hundred and eighty degrees, and rested his elbows on the bar, gazing into the darkness. Avery saw that in the seat next to the stranger there was what looked like a cowboy hat with one side of the brim pulled up to the crown. Avery had seen identical headgear among Australian Special Forces, who frequently were extraordinarily handsome and had the reputation for being extremely butch, though they were said to lean toward rough sex and maybe even violence. Avery thought twice about the wisdom of pursuing such a trick, but when the man took his hat off the chair and put it over his crotch, he took it as an invitation to sit down.

Avery spoke first, introducing himself but withholding a handshake. The man gave his name as Bryan Bond, and his accent confirmed Avery's suspicion that he was indeed an Aussie. Bryan was lean and rangy, probably a good two inches taller than Avery but at least twenty-five pounds lighter. There was an animal rawness to him, a stripped-down, no-nonsense sensuality. The hand that clutched his Singha was brown and big-knuckled. Beneath the taut sleeves of his T-shirt, his biceps were so round and defined they looked like cantaloupes stuffed under the fabric. His face was long and angular, handsome without being pretty, and his nose bore the mark of more than one barroom brawl. A band of muscle running from his temple to his chin flexed each time he took a drag from his cigarette or swallowed a mouthful of beer, and his Adam's apple— the size of an egg—seemed somehow obscene. From the right corner of his mouth ran an inch-long white scar, as if his smile had at one time been lopsided and had been sewn up. (Avery was later to learn it was the result of an encounter with a careless fly fisherman.) His hair, what there was of it, was dark brown or black, dressed with something, probably butch wax, to keep his flattop erect.

Bryan was not the type who indulged in small talk, and Avery's attempts at conversation ended in awkward silences. They each had two more beers, alternating paying for the rounds so neither was indebted to the other. If they had a third round, a fourth would be inevitable. It would be too late then to do much of anything, even if the beer hadn't taken the edge off their lust. Avery decided it was time to make his move. He was so nervous he hadn't been able to enjoy himself, and he just wanted to get it over with, one way or the other. It felt like his bowels had been braided.

"So, Bryan," he said. Bryan looked up quickly, sort of skittish at the sound of his name. "I have a room here, and thought I might go upstairs and have a drink." He felt like he had a tennis ball in his mouth. "Would you, ah, care to join me?"

He braced for rejection or worse, an uppercut to his chin. He looked at Bryan, who was staring at him with his jaws clenched. A small band of cartilage was fluttering wildly beneath the skin where his jawbone met his skull. He raised his half-filled bottle to his lips and drained it, setting it down on the table between them with an authoritative crack. "I thought you'd never ask, mate."

Avery's room overlooked a tree-lined esplanade along the Saigon River. At first, they sat on the verandah and drank American whiskey straight up. Bryan loosened up and they talked about their units, about Nixon, about the protesters back in the States. Despite the fact they had met each other in the city's most legendary gay bar, each seemed reluctant to make the first move. Avery was aching to get into Bryan's pants but—Bryan's quick acceptance of his invitation notwithstanding—he was afraid he had made a terrible mistake. Bryan *really* didn't look gay, or maybe it was that he didn't act gay. He wasn't nervous or nellie. He didn't look guilty or afraid. Avery wondered if he was one of those guys who got his jollies by getting a quick blow job and then creaming the fag who had given it to him. It was cheaper than getting laid by a bar girl, and he could mop up the floor with the little pervert afterward.

After three shots of hard liquor, their restraint dissolved. Bryan got up to use the head, and Avery followed. Once Bryan got his cock out, it was a free-for-all. They could barely get out of their clothes fast enough. Boots hit the ceiling and landed in the bathtub as the men dropped to the cool tile floor. One of Avery's socks floated into the toilet; underwear was shredded. Their faces were a blur of tooth and tongue, lips and lobes. Avery was hypnotized as Bryan's thrusts became syncopated with the blades of the ceiling fan twisting above them. *Whsssssh, Whsssssh, Whsssssh, Whsssssh.* The urgency was overwhelming, and though they both tried to prolong the pleasure, the inevitable took over.

"Well, mate, that was great," Bryan said when they were spent, lying on their backs, breathless. He rummaged in his trousers for his pack of Luckies. "But next time let's slow down a bit so's we can enjoy it."

Neither of them got any sleep that night, and the next morning, as they drank coffee on the hotel's riverside verandah, Avery felt light-headed and vaguely nauseated. Each of them was apparently reluctant to say the words they wanted desperately to hear from the lips of the other, but eventually Avery suggested they "get together" next time they were both in Saigon, and they devised a method to send messages to each other in the field without raising eyebrows.

In honor of their first night, they always had a ceremonial drink before they attacked each other, the rules being that they could not have sex until both glasses were drained. They would sit on their verandah and bring each other up-to-date on their missions and movements since their last rendezvous, all very butch and deadpan, while their blood pounded in their temples and their cocks throbbed in their pants. Avery sometimes teased Bryan by sipping his whiskey, but quickly enough they drained their glasses to hasten the onset of the festivities. Hours later, sore and chafed and sometimes bleeding, they would soak in a hot bath together, lathering each other's hair and scrubbing backs and butts and other places that never saw soap and water in the field. After their bath, they changed the bed linens, which were filthy and sopping wet, drank, smoked pot, and talked. Most likely the sun would be up by the time they fell asleep, each reluctant to lose conscious contact with his lover. "We only have so many hours together," Avery said. "We might as well not waste them on sleep."

Once they shed their clothes, they were naked for the rest of the weekend, never venturing outside of their horny little universe. They were constantly in contact with each other's bodies, even if it were only Avery's lips pressed to a sleeping Bryan's forehead or Bryan playing absently with a lock of Avery's hair. They knew that by the mere act of touching each other they could hold the world at bay. The war was moot when they were in each other's arms. They would stay alive as long as they could stay with each other.

"That's what I miss the most when you're not with me—the peace of mind," Avery said early one Monday morning when he could count on one hand the number of hours that remained to them. It was June, and the pale red-gold light of dawn filtered through the louvered windows and painted stripes of light on their naked torsos.

"Me, I miss the piece of arse, mate," Bryan said, and he swatted at Avery's bum.

"Don't get too choked up over it." Avery sniffed, pulling the sheet up around his chin to conceal his charms. "Mate."

"Oh, I miss yer john thomas, too."

"My what?"

"Yer john thomas, man. It's British. Fer yer dick. Yer peter. Yer pecker. You get my drift."

"I'm serious, Bryan. When I'm up to my nipples in mud looking at the business end of a water buffalo and I think about you . . ."

"My face reminds you of the arse of a water buffalo?"

"You know what I mean—out in the field. I just feel . . . vulnerable, without you. When we're together we're safe, we're in the city, here, and nothing can happen to us."

"I know. I feel the same way, Ave, but you know it don't do any good to worry about it, right?" He put two fingers under Avery's chin, lifted his face until they made eye contact, and mouthed a kiss. "Now how about smiling like a good lad so's I can sit on a *happy* face?"

If Avery checked in to the Imperial first, he would occasionally go out and buy flowers from a street vendor. The women he purchased them from always made a fuss over him because he was so handsome. They clucked their tongues and called out to their neighbors about how *rucky* his *gurfren*—his *sweethot*—was. Avery smiled sheepishly and wondered what these women would think if they ever saw his real *sweethot*. The flowers were less of a romantic gesture than they might seem. They were a badge of civility, of normalcy. Bryan rarely acknowledged them, but he once brought a handful into the tub with him and placed some above Avery's ears.

Neither one of them ever spoke the word love—it seemed somehow incriminating—but they both knew they were more than fuck buddies. They liked each other immensely, the way gay boys in college develop ground-worshiping crushes on straight roommates on the crew or soccer teams. When they weren't screwing, they interrogated each other about their childhoods, families, and previous sexual experiences. Avery gave Bryan a visual walking tour of Manhattan, and Bryan reciprocated with descriptions of the Outback and the Great Barrier Reef. They talked about other men in their units who might be homosexual or bisexual, which ones were hot, and whether they might be able to arrange a three-way. Aside from planning the basics of their next liaison, they never talked about the future. It seemed like bad karma. They both knew that they might not have a future past the next afternoon, and even if they did, even if they emerged from this shithole alive, if not unscathed, they would be separated by a continent and an ocean. Bryan was always the most levelheaded.

"No *what-ifs* or *maybes,* Ave. We can't do that to ourselves. We have what we have, mate, and I'm enjoying it to the limit and doing my damnedest to remember every minute of it."

"I know. Some guys say they're afraid they'll never forget the war, what they've seen. But I won't remember any of that shit, not a damn thing. What I'll remember is the time I've spent with you."

Over the course of a year, they were able to rendezvous at the tiny pink hotel ten times. On two occasions, Avery checked in to the hotel and spent the entire weekend alone in his room, pacing, drinking, and crying when Bryan failed to show up due to sudden, confidential changes in orders. The last time, Avery went five weeks without hearing a word from Bryan, and he was certain his lover was dead, though he never allowed himself to speak the words.

AS HIS RELATIONSHIP WITH TONY GREW, Avery found reasons for his Saturday night "card games" to begin earlier and earlier. Sometimes he found himself rushing the boys through the Hayden Planetarium or the Central Park Zoo at three-thirty or four so he and Tony could make love and still have time to sample the city's nightlife together. They might just go to the movies, or if they had time to plan ahead, the theater. After Avery revealed his hidden passion for opera—the one reputedly gay trait he would own up to—they made their way to the Met for *Billy Budd* and *Don Pasquale*. They never set foot in a gay bar, not even to visit the boys at De Milo's. And Avery was always back in Brooklyn before dawn.

To his delight, Tony soon realized that Avery was just as smitten as he was. More and more frequently on weeknights, Avery asked his brother to come over and watch the kids, and Tom was usually pretty understanding unless he had a date of his own. In January, they finally had an opportunity to spend an entire weekend together. Brandi was taking Christopher and Joey to her older sister Candi's third wedding, in Pawtucket, Rhode Island, for three days.

For both Tony and Avery, the best part of that first long weekend together was being able to make love without the urgency of Avery's curfew looming over them. They spent more time kissing and just holding each other. They lit candles and smoked dope and didn't get out of bed until two in the afternoon, and then only to raid the refrigerator and the bar. They spread the food out on the bed, ate, and talked.

On Sunday night, Tony sensed that Avery seemed anxious and distracted. He figured it was just because their first private weekend was coming to an end; Brandi and the boys would be home around noon the next day. By ten o'clock, Avery was so zombified he was virtually worthless in bed. For the first time since they met, he was completely uninterested in sex. Tony asked him several times what was wrong, but Avery just said he didn't want to talk about it.

For Tony, the quality of sex and the level of interest or disinterest in his partner was an absolute barometer of the healthiness of their relationship. The fact that Avery wasn't the least bit interested in sex, that he had in fact withdrawn completely, terrified Tony. He tried repeatedly to interest Avery in lovemaking, to no avail, and succeeded only in irritating him, also a first for their relationship. Finally he just turned off the lights, gave him a peck on the cheek, and moved to his own side of the bed. Neither of them got much sleep, and around five-thirty, just when Tony had finally drifted off, Avery leaned over and gently shook his shoulder.

"Tony?"

"Umm hmmm? Is it time to get up all ready?" Tony took Avery's arm and pulled it across his chest, nuzzling his hand. "It's still dark, Ave."

"Tony, I'm sorry to wake you up. It's just that . . . we have to talk."

Tony sat up as if a chainsaw had cranked up next to his head. "I knew it, I knew it, I knew it. I could see this coming all day. Let me guess. You've decided to recommit to your wife. You just needed this weekend together to be sure." He threw the bedclothes aside, got out of bed, and reached for his robe.

"Tony, what the hell are you talking about?"

"You said 'We have to talk,' didn't you? Every time someone has said 'We have to talk' to me, we've broken up. Every single damn time. It's probably listed in the *Oscar Wilde Thesaurus* as a synonym for *arrivederci. Ciao. Au revoir, mon ami. Auf wiedersehen. Adios.* I know the routine only too well. You say you've found someone new or you want to go back to your wife, and I express shocked disbelief. You say you never wanted to hurt me, and I say 'Then don't.' You say you want to make a clean break; I say we can still be friends. You tell me what a wonderful person I am and how much you've learned from me, and I tell you I don't know how I can learn to live *without* you. . . ." Tony grabbed a handful of tissues from the night table. "So let's just forgo the niceties. You leave and I'll go count out the Nembutal. God knows I have the dosage figured out by this time. I know just what it takes to put me halfway between histrionic and catatonic."

"For Christ's sake, Tony, sit down, shut up, and listen to what I've got to say." Avery reached out and grabbed Tony's forearm. "I am *not* breaking up with you. I love you. You are the most wonderful, most beautiful man on the face of the earth. I can't imagine how or why you've settled for some legless loser like me, but I thank God Val brought you to De Milo's that night."

"Oh," said Tony, slipping out of the robe, sliding back under the comforter, and wrapping his arms around Avery. He rested his head over Avery's heart. "Then what's to talk about, baby?"

"My legs. . . . I lied to you about my legs."

Tony raised his head off and looked into Avery's eyes. He was giddy with relief. "You mean you really *do* have legs, and that somehow through yoga, trick photography, and false-bottomed wheelchairs you've been able to conceal them from me? Or maybe you're going to tell me that you really weren't six-two before you lost your legs, you were actually only five-eight and a half."

"Tony, quit. I'm serious." He pushed Tony away, gently and not too far but enough to indicate he meant business. "It's not easy to say what I've got to say. I don't want to lose you, and I don't want you to hate me for lying to you."

Tony pulled himself up so he was eye to eye with Avery and propped himself up on his elbow, his chin resting in the palm of his hand. "Okay, I'm sorry I lost it. I guess I was just so happy that you weren't going to dump me that I went bonkers for a minute. So tell me what's wrong, and whatever it is, we'll work it out."

Avery shifted so he was on his left side, facing Tony. With the index finger of his right hand he traced a line from the bridge of Tony's nose down to his lips. Tony puckered up. Avery took Tony's free hand and kissed his palm.

"Tony, I . . . I didn't lose my legs in 'Nam."

"Oh?"

"I was there. I *did* serve. You've seen pictures of me there."

"Avery, you don't have to prove anything to me. You don't have to say another word. I don't care how it happened. I *hate* that it happened, and I'd give anything for you to have them back again. But I don't *care* how it happened. Honest."

"But I *want* you to know. It's time I told you. I'm telling you this be-cause I know now just how much you mean to me. I never doubted that I loved you, but these past couple of days have shown me exactly how important you are to me. When I'm with you, I don't care about any-thing else. You are the only thing that's important to me. I love sleeping with you. I love waking up with you. I love just *being* with you. I want to share more of my life with you. I want you to meet my friends, and I don't want you to hear this story from them or from Tom one night while the two of you are having a couple of beers. I don't want you to have to pretend that you already knew. I only tell the Vietnam story to people on the first night. And like I've said, the first night's usually the last, so it hasn't much mattered."

"Okay, so what happened?"

"It was 1970. I was back from the war and it was really tough finding a job. I had my training in electronics, but what with the recession and all, there just weren't many openings. I didn't want to move in with my folks. Christopher was just finishing his terrible twos, and I didn't want to put my mother through all that again. But that's what it looked like would happen. Finally, my dad asked me if I wanted to go to work with him. I didn't want to do it. But I said okay."

"So what was so awful about that?" Tony had been running a finger over Avery's chest, tracing his pectorals, outlining the rosy aureoles of his nipples until Avery took Tony's hand in his own and held it still.

"My dad worked for the city. In sanitation."

"He was a *garbageman*?"

"Yeah. He was—*is*. And I was. I became one."

"What a fucking waste! Avery, you have so much more going for you than that."

"I'd been on the job maybe a year. Brandi was pregnant with Joey. It was winter and cold as shit. We'd had snowfall after snowfall that year and there was about six inches of ice on the streets. The snowplows never got anywhere close to the pavement, just scraped off the top layer of fresh snow. We were working near an intersection where a fire hydrant had busted from the cold. There was ice everywhere—all over the cars, the street, the sidewalks, the stoops.

"I'd just set down an empty can and was crossing the street toward the truck. I practically had to walk with my arms out to my sides to keep my balance, like a trapeze artist. I was crossing with the light—I'm positive of that—when some woman in this big old two-tone Buick station wagon doesn't see the light until the last minute and slams on her brakes. She locks up and does a big three-sixty on the ice, and the left rear fender slams me like I'm a pinball and it's a giant flipper. I don't remember anything after that, but this is what people tell me what happened. Just as I'm hit, somebody presses the compactor button on the truck, and the blade starts to come down to scrape all the trash into the compactor. Somebody said I did two complete flips in the air, some say only one, but I landed in the back of the truck just as . . ."

Tony sat up. "Oh my God! Oh my *God!*" He imagined Avery flying through the air, a smudge against the snowy sky, and heard the pneumatic arms of the compactor straining as they bit down on his legs.

"I guess you've figured out the rest."

"Did it cut off your legs right there?" Tony had both hands over his mouth, and tears sparkled in the corner of his eyes. He looked as if he had just seen Lassie run over.

"They weren't cut off then, but they were badly mangled. Tom—he was the first one of the family to get to the hospital—said when he got there my right leg was bent up behind me and the toe of my left boot was pointing toward the floor, not the ceiling. The doctors've told me there was never any hope of saving them. They were more worried about stopping the bleeding and preventing infection."

"Were you hurt anywhere else?"

"Both my arms were broken, one by the car, the other by the fall. I crushed six ribs and had a hairline fracture of one vertebrae. My nose was broken and I lost three teeth. Between intensive care and rehabilitation, I was in the hospital almost ten months."

Avery detailed the remainder of his recovery, including outpatient rehabilitation therapy that continued for more than a year. The city offered him a rent-controlled, ground-floor apartment, and a small disability income. After a two-year legal battle with the driver, he got money to pay off his medical bills and attorney's fees with enough left over to buy the handicapped-equipped van and to provide—if invested wisely—an income barely adequate to support him and the boys, with help from Brandi's job.

"This really pisses me off," Tony said.

"I'm sorry, Tony. I really am."

"Sorry for what?"

"For lying."

"No, no, no, Avery. I'm not pissed off at *you*. I'm mad at God or the world or whoever's in charge. You spend all that time blowing up things in Vietnam—underwater, no less—and come home unscathed, but then you get your legs cut off by the damn garbage truck you're working on because you can't find any other job. *And* you get stiffed on the settlement. It's not fair."

"God, I was so afraid you wouldn't understand. It's so embarrassing . . ."

"C'mere," Tony said and pulled Avery toward him. "There is nothing you could say that would make me feel differently about you. You are the sweetest, most wonderful man I have ever been with, and I would do anything in the world if I could make you happy."

"I *am* happy. When I'm with you."

"Well then, you'll just have to make sure you're with me as often as possible."

Tony kissed Avery and shifted in bed so he could curl up around him, Avery's head resting on his chest. He still sensed some tension, a reluctance to relax, so he kissed the top of Avery's head and stroked his hair. It hurt him to think that Avery had been treated so badly by the world. What a life! He loved his kids but lived in fear of losing them because he also happened to love Tony. He'd served his country but had been vilified and ignored by an uncaring nation when he returned from Vietnam. He tried to earn a decent living but had lost his legs in the process and been screwed by the insurance company and the city. But he never complained, was almost always genuinely happy, and always tried to do right by everyone—his wife, his kids, Tony. It seemed like an impossible task.

Tony was genuinely touched by Avery's story. It made him feel a little guilty and self-conscious about all the things he took for granted or whined about. (Maybe there was a little truth to Kevin McCarthy's claim that Tony was spoiled and self-centered.) All he knew is that he had never before been so happy or felt so secure in a relationship. That worried him, of course. He'd been happy before and it had blown up in his face. But he sensed that this was different, that this was real, that this would last. There was nothing in the world he wouldn't do to make sure that happened.

IN LATE APRIL, Val threw a welcome home dinner party for Victor Panache, who had just returned from an extended stay in Rio de Janeiro. He had gone for Carnivale but had become besotted with a group of five brothers, the youngest fourteen, the eldest twenty. The youths were from the *barrio,* and Victor photographed them naked in the jungles and on the beaches of Brazil. He planned to publish the results as a book, *Bad Boys of Brazil,* with ten of the most exceptional images comprising a limited-edition private portfolio "for connoisseurs only." When it came time to return, he discovered he could not leave the second oldest, Rocco, behind, and he brought him to New York under the pretense, for immigration officials, of employing him as a photographer's assistant.

When Victor and Roc arrived at Val's penthouse, Avery was already seated at the formal dining-room table. Tuxedo and Parker Kensington arrived just minutes before Mackenzie Rittenhouse, who was filling out the table in the absence of Devlin, who was choreographing a water ballet extravaganza at Sanctuary College. Tony was immediately mesmerized by Victor's companion, whose beauty was both rough-edged and, he knew, fleeting.

"Doesn't speak a word of English," Victor said, coming up behind Tony. "But he's already quite fluent in American Express!"

"Let's sit down and I'll introduce you to Avery." Avery had been reluctant to meet Tony's colleagues and friends because he was embarrassed about his disability, but Tony had gradually been building up his confidence and self-esteem.

"I trust he's the magnificent creature at the table?"

Sensing Victor's stare, Avery looked up, smiled, and motioned for them to come over. Tony raised one finger in the air.

"You like?"

"Quite a piece of work, your man! Is he one of Tuxedo's?"

"He's not Tuxedo's or anyone else's."

"You're kidding! Tuxedo's seen him and not snapped him up? I must shoot him."

"Unfortunately, Victor, there is . . . less there than meets the eye."

"Why, what's wrong."

"He's an amputee. A *double* amputee. Both legs, above the knee."

"That's a grotesque joke, Tony."

"It's true, Victor, I swear. They were . . . he lost them in the war."

"You're doing him a grave injustice, Tony, and yourself as well, if you think he is any less a man—or any less beautiful—because of his condition. In fact, there's something in his face that sets him apart from the blandly exquisite zombies we're surrounded by in this business—present company excluded, of course. He's got character. I'm serious. I want to shoot him."

"Have it your way," Tony said. "But you'd better let me be the one to explain it to him. I think he might be more inclined to agree that way. Your current level of enthusiasm would scare him to death."

During dinner, Victor monopolized Avery at one end of the table while Roc played footsies with Val at the other. Val suffered his advances as diplomatically as any host of his experience could. When the evening was over, Victor drew Tony aside.

"As you can see, I'm totally smitten," Victor said.

"Yes, Roc is *muy delicioso.*"

"Not Roc, you fool. Avery. I'm counting on you to convince him to let me do the photos. And, oh yes, I need a telephone. And some privacy."

"Sure. The closest one is in this guest bath, but you can use the one in my bedroom. Do you need a map?"

"No thanks. I once shot this place for *Architectural Digest,*" Victor said and turned to walk down the hallway. "Oh, do you, by any chance, know the number for Varig Airlines?"

Later that night, when Tony brought up the subject of Victor's proposal, Avery was confused. At first, he thought it was some kind of a joke. Why would Victor Panache want to take pictures of him, someone without legs, when there were so many other good-looking guys in the city with all of their parts intact?

"It's your face he wants. You *are* devastatingly handsome. I've always known that. It's nice to know someone else agrees with me. And watch out, he's got the hots for you."

Over the course of the next five weeks, Victor shot Avery on twelve different occasions in the studio and on location. They worked only when it was convenient for Avery, save once, when atmospheric conditions promised a particularly photogenic early-morning fog. Victor called Avery at four-thirty in the morning and asked him to rendezvous in Central Park within the hour. Avery agreed and told Brandi that Tom was having car trouble. It was the first time he had lied to her about anything related to the hidden side of his life. It seemed astonishingly easy, although he caught her staring at him as he dressed.

"What?" he said.

"Car trouble? At four o'clock in the morning?"

"Brandi, where else could I possibly be going at this hour?"

She turned her back to him, turned off the light on her night table, and sighed theatrically.

"Brandi?" She didn't answer. "What is it?" He felt bad. Guilty. He'd been gone a lot lately. He made a mental note to call Tom at the first accessible phone booth and tell him not to answer the phone until at least 8 A.M.

In early June, the photo series was hung for the first time at a small dinner party at Victor's brownstone. In addition to Avery and Tony, the guests included Devlin and Val, and Tuxedo and Parker Kensington. Twelve oversize portraits were divided between the living and dining rooms.

"They're exquisite!" said Tuxedo. "I've met Avery a half-dozen times, but I never saw this sensuality in him. It's remarkable. I must be losing my touch. So, Avery, how would you like to come to work for me? Excellent pay, a congenial environment, and you might even get to see more of Tony."

"What would I be doing?"

Tony blushed. Tuxedo laughed. "You'd be modeling, of course. These photos are really marvelous. I can't believe I was blind to your potential all this time. I have to be honest, I don't think I ever really looked at *you*. I never got past the chair, as awful as that sounds."

"It happens all the time."

"Avery," Parker said, "I'm introducing a new cologne and I think you might be just the right man for the campaign. . . . If Tux agrees."

"I think he'd be perfect," Tux said. "Parker and I always *have* had the same taste in men."

Tony shot a glance at Val, who looked away. The new product was S/X, "the essence of sex." It had been in development for some time, had gone through several marketing plans, and now was scheduled to debut in the fall. All that was needed was the imagery. It was an opportunity Tony coveted—and until this moment had assumed was his. He thought Parker had said as much.

"Are you sure you want to start Ave off on such a high-visibility campaign, Tux?" Tony asked.

"What's the matter, Tony, feeling insecure?" Devlin said.

"No, Devlin. I'm just not sure Avery's got the temperament for this business—and I mean that as a compliment. He's too nice. S/X is a big job. Complicated. Time-consuming. He might find it overwhelming for his first outing."

"Why don't you let him be the judge of that?" Devlin patted his lips with his napkin and relaxed into his chair. "Avery? You're a *big* boy. What have you got to say for yourself?"

Parker cleared his throat and set down his napkin. "If I may jump in here? I certainly didn't intend to set off a catfight. I was more or less thinking out loud. Obviously, there are some unique circumstances to consider in this situation. Our approach—and I'm sure Tux would agree—would take into consideration Avery's experience and special needs. And rest assured, the entire staff would treat him with the utmost dignity at all times. We would work on closed sets, using only the most trusted employees on our and Victor's staffs. No one need ever be any the wiser."

Tony looked like he was getting ready to say something, but Avery stopped him by putting his hand on Tony's forearm.

"I'm not all that sure of just what Mr. Kensington's saying exactly," Avery said, "but I think I get his drift—mostly."

"Bravo," said Devlin. Val slapped him on his upper arm.

"I know you mean well. But I don't like being talked about like I'm not here. It's insulting. I get treated like this all the time. People think just because I don't have legs I must be a retard or something. Nobody thinks I have the sense to make my own decisions." He paused. "Well, I do. I'm honored Mr. Kensington and Mr. Malone think so highly of me, but Mr. Panache has made us a very nice dinner, and I think we should just enjoy it and each other's company. I'd like some time to talk to Tony about this and then, when I'm ready, I'll be happy to talk to Mr. Kensington and Mr. Malone."

"Well said, Avery," Victor said, clapping his hands demurely. "Exceptionally well said."

Immediately after dinner, Tony thanked Victor and told Tuxedo they would talk in the morning.

"No hurry. Take time to think it over," Tuxedo said, rising to give Tony a hug and Avery a handshake.

Avery was silent during the ride home, and instead of meeting Tony's eyes he stared out the window. Tony didn't know what to say. He was worried that Avery might be pissed because he had appeared to object to the proposal—he *should* have been more supportive—but he had no idea of what Avery actually thought of the idea itself. Avery said nothing until they were in the elevator.

"That Devlin is a real shit, ya know? He thinks I've got beans for brains."

"Even if you did, and you don't, you'd be better off than him. He's got dick for brains, and that inevitably ends badly."

It was getting late and Avery refused another drink because he had to drive home. Tony made coffee. Avery said he didn't know what to think. His first question was how he would explain the situation to Brandi. She'd want to know just what the hell was he doing hanging around with a bunch of models and photographers. Brandi wasn't terribly so-phisticated, and it seemed to him that modeling, like hairdressing, would scream "fag" to her and blow his cover.

"Why not keep it a secret?" Tony asked. "Just don't say anything to her. It's worked so far."

"But what if she sees the pictures? What if she's reading some maga-zine at her sister's shop and she sees me there, half naked? What then?"

"Avery, listen. She's not in the target market and neither are any of Mandi's customers. S/X is going to be an upscale product. You're not going to find it advertised in *Family Circle*. And let's just say she *does* see an ad somewhere. What's she going to think? 'Oh my God, there's Avery, my husband, right here in this magazine! And my, he looks good enough to eat.' Forget it! At the very most she'll say, 'Doesn't that man look a lot like my Avery?' It's going to be a whole lot easier for her to believe that someone out there looks remarkably like you than to think her husband—and don't take this the wrong way—an ex-garbageman with no legs, has secretly been training at the Barbizon School and is now a successful fashion model."

Avery sighed and rubbed his forehead. "It *is* pretty ridiculous when you stop to think about it. I certainly wouldn't have believed it unless it had actually happened to me. . . . But what about the money? If I all of a sudden have lots of money, she's going to get suspicious. I've never hidden money from Brandi or lied to her about it."

"Couldn't you just put it into a savings account or something? A col-lege fund for the boys?"

"That's it! I could start up a fund for the boys, one for each of them. And I could do it at a different bank than the one we use now, so no one would ask any questions. Maybe a bank here in Manhattan. Could I use your address?"

"Of course. My lawyer can set up the whole thing. . . . So you want to do it?"

"I guess so," Avery said. "So what happens next? What do I have to do?"

"I'll give Tux and Parker time to get home, then I'll call them. If you can, call me later, and I'll tell you what they say. If not, I'll talk to you tomorrow."

The more Tony thought about it, the happier he was that Avery had agreed to accept Tuxedo's offer. It would be good for him—boost his confidence. It might even make him more secure in their relationship.

When Kevin McCarthy had broken up with Tony, one of the main factors was the difference in their lifestyles. He had said as much. If Avery felt he was more a part of Tony's world, more an equal partner, their relationship would be all the stronger. Tony smiled. It was a good thing. Avery deserved it. And more. Much, *much* more.

# 25

THE ARRIVAL OF SUMMER was a mixed blessing. Tony had hoped to spend more time with Avery, but winter fashion shoots in Alaska, Norway, and Switzerland put more distance between them than ever. To make matters worse, Devlin ensconced himself at Triumph Towers as soon as classes ended at Sanctuary. Although he was on his best behavior when Val was home, he was unrelenting in his abuse when he was away.

Brandi's sister's marriage was already on the rocks, and she and the boys made frequent trips to Rhode Island, staying for up to a week at a time. Avery was infinitely more relaxed when he and Tony were together if Brandi was out of town, but an incident in late July made him wonder just how long he could hold his marriage together. Tony had an L.L. Bean shoot in Ogunquit, and he and Avery took Tony's little-used Ferrari out of the garage and drove up a couple of days early to enjoy the peace and quiet. On the return trip, in a steady downpour, they passed Brandi and the boys in the breakdown lane along westbound I-95 just outside New London, Connecticut. They'd had a flat tire on their way home from Pawtucket. The instant he recognized the van, with its distinctive Pegasus icon, Tony swerved across two lanes of traffic to get to the shoulder.

"Are you crazy, Tony? What the hell are you doing?" Avery had seen the van, too, with Brandi standing behind it looking helpless and the boys hanging out the back doors.

"I'm going to help them change the tire," Tony said, rolling to a stop. He'd have to back up a good half mile or more. "Look, the flat's on the traffic side, which is dangerous. Does she even know how to change a tire?"

"She doesn't even know where the jack is."

"So, we've got to help. If not for her sake, for the boys."

"Tony, you can't do this. She can't find out. . . . I mean, we've got my wheelchair strapped to the back of the goddamn car!"

"Don't worry. I'll park far enough away . . . right about . . . here!"

"But what if . . . ?"

"Ave, she doesn't know me from Adam. She'll just think I'm her Angel of Mercy. Now where is that cute L.L. Bean umbrella they gave me?"

"No, Tony. We can't. I just can't risk it. If you really want to help her, get off at the next exit and send a tow truck out to her."

Tony could see how distraught Avery was and reluctantly agreed. They exited five miles later and were back on the road in twenty minutes. Avery slumped in his seat, threw a straw hat over his face, and kept it there for some time, saying nothing. When he finally emerged, it was clear he'd been crying.

"Ave? What's wrong? Everything's okay. That was a perfect idea— getting a tow truck."

"I can't go on living like this. I want to be with you. I want us to have our own place—away from Val and Devlin. I want to get out of my marriage while there is still some goodwill between Brandi and me. I know she knows something is going on. I don't think in a million years she suspects it's with another man, but she knows something's up. She knows I'm hiding things from her, and she gets real unpleasant about it. Like money. I've been spending some of my modeling money on the kids—not enough to be really obvious, but apparently enough to be suspicious—and she's pissed because she doesn't know where it's coming from. She notices how much more time I spend away from home—with you, although she doesn't know it's with you—and wants to know where I'm getting the money for all the babysitters. We argue about almost everything but the old cap-off-the-toothpaste complaint. Hell, sometimes I think we argue just for the sake of arguing.

"And then there's the boys. I've yelled at Christopher and Joey more in the past two months than during their whole lives, because I'm frustrated and mad at myself and I feel trapped. It's not fair to them. I love them too much to continue taking everything out on them. Kids always think everything is their fault."

"What do you want to do?" Tony asked. "You know I'll do anything to be with you."

"I've been thinking about it. I can't do anything right away. I need to see how this S/X stuff shakes out—you know, exactly what the money situation is long term. If it looks like I'll be able to make a decent living, I'll ask her for a divorce and give her alimony and child support. I want joint custody of Christopher and Joey. You won't mind having them live with us part of the time, will you?"

"Hell no, Ave. But do you think she'll agree to joint custody?"

"I don't know. This probably isn't gonna go down easy. If Brandi finds out I'm gay, it's a good bet she'll use it to keep the boys away from me. But with the kind of money I'll be making, I can hire a good lawyer—a great lawyer—to see that doesn't happen. All this will take time, but if everything goes okay, I think I can get the ball rolling after the first of the year."

Tony dropped Avery off at home in Brooklyn instead of going back to the condo for one last roll in the hay. Avery was worried about Brandi and the kids out on the expressway, and he wanted to be home in case she ran into any more trouble and called. When the van pulled up in front of the house an hour later, he rolled out to meet it. The boys were excited by their adventure and jumped up and down beside the wheelchair after hugging him.

Brandi looked bad—tired and angry. She didn't even say hello before she attacked him. "You should have had these tires checked before we left, Avery. We had a blowout. Coulda been killed. If you'd skip one of your all-night *poker* games and didn't come home and go to bed all day, maybe you'd have the time for all the little chores you used to be so good at."

"I'm sorry Brandi, I really am. I'll get new tires this week. I promise."

S/X WAS INTRODUCED in October, and it was one of the most successful launches of a men's fragrance in industry history. Victor deserved much of the credit. The photographs were stunning, among his best. Avery looked, by turns, aloof, alluring, exotic, enchanting, and downright steamy. His hair was wild and full, and the stylist coaxed a lock or two down across his forehead, which had the effect of making him look like he had just gotten out of bed after a night of cataclysmic sex. His chest was bared, oiled, and spritzed with water and glycerin. His nipples were so provocative they were nearly obscene. But it was his gaze, innocent yet seductive, that ultimately provided the magic. Victor had somehow captured that moment when strangers' eyes meet for the first time and their personal histories are rewritten.

Retailers reported that S/X displays with Avery's likeness were disappearing almost as soon as they were set up. Bus shelters stood bereft of

S/X posters, cut out with nail files, knitting needles, and Swiss Army knives by the hundreds. No one was more surprised by the success of the S/X campaign than Avery. He worried at first that the high visibility would make it more likely that Brandi would recognize him, but Tony reassured him that it made that notion even more implausible. Avery said he felt like the pauper in *The Prince and the Pauper,* and he waited to be unmasked, but he planned, too, for his new future.

The completely unexpected success of the campaign had Parker worried, too. He fretted about the impact on S/X sales if someone found out that Avery had no legs. Tuxedo assured him he had nothing to worry about. Other than the most trusted staff at Parker Kensington, Malone Men, and Victor's studio—longtime employees who wouldn't dare risk their exceptionally comfortable positions by violating the confidentiality to which they had agreed—only one person, Valentine Rittenhouse's lover, Devlin, knew the truth. On the street, no one ever imagined that the good-looking but obviously handicapped young man in the wheelchair was also the wanton sexual athlete in the torrid S/X advertisements.

ON THE NIGHT of their first anniversary celebration, Tony and Avery donned matching tuxedos accessorized with red velvet ties and Mackenzie plaid cummerbunds, all custom tailored for the occasion. Avery bought boutonnieres made of sprigs of holly and white rosebuds. A month earlier, when they were trying to figure out how to mark the occasion, they split the responsibilities down the middle. Neither was to tell the other what the plans included. Avery was put in charge of entertainment and surprised Tony with tickets to *Evita!* Tony arranged for a late dinner at Windows on the World. The evening was perfect: the show was spectacular, and Tony didn't experience a single awkward moment as Avery navigated his way around the theater. He used to be embarrassed if Avery ran over someone's toe or blocked an elevator door, and for a long time he imagined everyone was looking at Avery with pity in their eyes. But recently, Avery's wheelchair had become almost invisible to him; it was as natural as a piece of clothing. When Avery got naked to go to bed, he got out of his wheelchair just as he got out of his clothes.

Tony thought Avery looked a little queasy as they rode the elevator to the restaurant. Avery had never particularly cared for elevator rides (Tony had learned to distract him as they ascended to the penthouse at Triumph Towers), and this one did seem like it was going to go on forever. Instead of going directly into the restaurant, Tony paused near a window to give Avery's stomach a chance to catch up with the rest of him, but he continued to look uncomfortable well into the meal. He picked at his food but nearly emptied the wine bottle single-handedly, and he continued to gaze out the window toward his home.

"Ave, something's bothering you, and it's going to ruin the evening. Can't you tell me what's going on?"

"I was just looking across the river to Brooklyn—it looks beautiful from way up here. All the lights."

"So what has Brooklyn-by-night got to do with anything?" Tony asked.

"I don't know. I guess it's just that this time last year, I would never have imagined myself looking down on home from the World Trade Center. It's been a helluva year, that's for damn sure. Meeting you, falling in love. Just *that* changed my life. And now all this S/X stuff. All the money, seeing myself everywhere I look. It's almost more than I can deal with. I guess I was just wondering how the hell I ever ended up here."

"You don't want to be here?"

"No, Tony, that's not it. I wish this night would never end. But maybe what I mean is how did I ever get so lucky? I mean, some guy with no legs from Brooklyn, with a wife and two kids, in love with without a doubt the most beautiful man in the world, who actually loves me back. In a million years I would have never thought I could be this happy."

"Then what's wrong?" Tony asked. He put down his fork and took a long sip of his wine, never taking his eyes off Avery. At that moment a waiter hovered on the periphery. Tony dispatched him with the movement of one finger.

"I just wonder what I would do if I ever lost you. If you ever stopped loving me. I mean, I'm not such a great catch . . . for someone like you."

"Is that what's bothering you?" Tony put down his fork and patted his lips with his napkin. "Avery, you are the best thing that has *ever* happened to me. The best. You're strong and kind—and good to me. You love your kids and take good care of them, better than many fathers, gay or straight, in a wheelchair or not. You're the most generous person I know—and the least phony. So don't you ever even *think* there will come a day when I won't love you and want to be with you."

Tony paused and leaned toward Avery.

"You know, I was thinking we should buy that little farmhouse we saw in Connecticut this summer if it's still on the market. Wouldn't it be great to have a place of our own, where we could get away for weekends? Some place that's close to the beach and away from the crowds. Just think how beautiful it would be in the fall. Maybe we could find a place with an old apple orchard just for the hell of it, or we could grow pumpkins if they're not too much trouble and just give them away to the neighbor kids. We ought to be able to find someplace like that, don't you think? Peaceful and quiet, far away from the city. And private. Our own place. I love Val, but I feel just a little inhibited by him, even when he's not there."

"I know what you mean. He can be a little tight-assed sometimes."

"And we could bring Christopher and Joey out sometimes and find someplace to go horseback riding or go down to the beach or go sailing." Tony wasn't sure exactly what had brought on Avery's anxiety attack, but he could tell that he was beginning to relax. He figured talking about the future, especially including the boys, had helped.

"Horses and the beach. Apple trees to climb. A limitless supply of pumpkins to carve? The boys would never want to come back to Brooklyn. I'm not sure Brandi would like that," Avery said, finally lifting his fork to his lips. "But what the hell. It would be great for them."

Tony reached his right hand across the table and lightly covered Avery's left. Avery jerked it backward just a fraction of an inch, but then relaxed and smiled a crooked, bewildered, ecstatic smile. Tony couldn't imagine what Avery was going through: the strain of living with Brandi, hiding from her not only his homosexuality but also his relationship with Tony, even his new career as a model. It must take an extraordinary amount of effort. And yet, except for moments like this one, Avery never let on that he was scared or worried. He always arrived at the Towers as excited about seeing Tony as he had been when they first met, always made Tony feel as if he were the only other person in the world at that moment. Tony never questioned that it was Avery with whom he wanted to spend the rest of his life, but it was at moments like these that he understood what it was to love someone, not just to be sexually attracted to them—and Tony was nearly consumed by his desire for Avery—but to respect them for the kind of person they were, to try to understand their problems and make them his own. He imagined sitting across a table from Avery five years from now, ten—*twenty*—when they were no longer young, no longer beautiful in the way they were tonight, and he felt more comfortable and self-confident than he ever had in his life. In comparison, all the other men in his life, from Connecticut Jones to Kevin McCarthy, seemed insignificant, almost invisible.

"I love you, Avery," Tony said, understanding perhaps for the first time what that meant. "I want to spend the rest of my life with you. I can't imagine it otherwise."

At home, Avery said he had one final surprise.

"More?"

"I've saved the best for last. At least I hope it's the best. Sit down on the couch while I get it from the bedroom."

"I can do that for you, Ave."

"No. I have to do it myself." His wheelchair whispered down the hall, turned with a squeak, and disappeared. He was back in two minutes.

"Okay, now you have to close your eyes and put out your hands!"

"Okay," Tony said, tentatively.

Avery rolled closer to him. "Okay, you can open your eyes now. And open the package, too."

When Tony looked at his cupped hands, he saw a small package wrapped in glossy white paper, etched with silver glitter in a pattern of glistening ice-covered branches. It was tied up with a slender gold ribbon.

"Avery, this is beautiful. I mean, it's the most beautiful present I've ever seen."

"Go on, now. Open it!"

Tony's hands were trembling slightly as he worked the ribbon and bow loose, turned the gift upside down, found the seam of the paper and slid out a baby blue box.

"You didn't. You did! Oh, Ave, I don't deserve this."

"Go on, open it and look. And I don't want to hear any more 'I don't deserve this' shit."

Tony opened the box to find a gold signet ring. Tony's initials were etched in a bold, masculine typeface, almost like Roman numerals.

"I kept it simple. And wait 'til you see this. . . ." He pulled another blue box out of his pocket and opened it to reveal a matching ring with his initials. "I got each of us one. I sort of thought they could be like . . . like wedding rings, except not so obvious."

Tony leaned over and kissed Avery on the mouth.

"When I think of all the drunks, dogs, and derelicts I slept with and thought I loved and cried over, I'm ashamed. Humiliated," Tony said. "You, Avery, are the man I've waited for all of my life. I only wish we had found each other much, much sooner. I love you, Ave. And I mean that with all of my heart, with everything that I am."

"I love you, too, Tony. I may not know how to say it like you and Val do, but after the boys, you are the person in this world I love most." Tears ran down his cheeks. "Listen, give me your ring, okay? Here, take mine and look inside. At the inscription."

Tony leaned over so the lighting was better and peered into Avery's ring.

"It says 'Yours always and forever. Love Ave.' They mixed up the inscription? At *Tiffany's?*"

"No, I told 'em to do it that way. See, I thought you would wear *your* ring—the one with your initials—tonight while we sleep together, and I would wear mine. Then tomorrow we'd exchange them and wear the other person's ring. For all the time. It would be like always having a little piece of each other with us."

"Ave, I don't know if that's the corniest thing I ever heard or the sweetest thing anyone has ever done for me, but I'd be honored to wear your ring tomorrow and forever after. God, I love you. I can't even begin to tell you how much."

"And I love you, Tony. I love you and I want to be with you always. *Always.* And there's just one more thing."

"Still more?"

"I've told Brandi I'm leaving her. I didn't tell her I was gay. I didn't want to risk losing the boys. But I didn't want to risk losing you, either, you know, by not showing you how much I loved you."

"What did she say?"

"Not much, so far. This was only yesterday. Tom says to watch out, that she's going to get really mad and threaten to take the boys away from me, but you know, really, I honestly don't think she's like that. We've been through too much together."

"I'd be careful just the same. And I'd get a lawyer right away. Tomorrow. She's going to find out about your S/X money in a divorce proceeding, and you're going to want to protect that."

"Most of it's in trust for the kids."

"Still—a lawyer. Tomorrow. And Ave?"

"Yeah?"

"Thanks. This is all very sweet. More than sweet."

"It's all for you, Tony. You're everything in the world to me."

WHEN TONY WOKE the next morning about dawn, a hard rain was nicking at the windows and the bedroom was filled with a bluish light. Avery was sitting up against the headboard looking haggard, his black hair slicked back over his scalp, his overnight stubble making him look more unkempt than seductive. What Tony initially thought was sweat were actually tears, sliding down his cheeks and dropping off his chin to his chest.

"Ave? My God, what's wrong?"

For a moment, Avery seemed unaware of Tony's presence. Then he wiped away his tears, vigorously rubbed his face, up and down, with his palms, and blew his nose with a tissue he had crushed in his hands.

"Tony, there's something I need to tell you," he said.

Tony pulled himself up so he could look into Avery's eyes.

"Tony, you know I love you more than anything else in the world, and I would never do anything to hurt you."

"Don't tell me you've freaked out about Brandi."

"No, I thought about that long and hard before I did it." Avery turned at his hips to face his lover. "Tony, nothing has to change because of what I'm about to say. It will be up to you to decide."

"Is *this* what you were worried about last night?"

"Yeah, I guess it is." Avery's voice quavered. Tony was both alarmed and puzzled. "Oh, God, how am I going to tell you this?"

"You're not sick, are you?" Tony reached out and touched Avery's thigh. "It's not something to do with your legs—an infection or something? You're not going to *die,* for god sakes?"

Avery said nothing for a moment, and Tony could see he was composing himself.

"I wish I *were* going to die! . . . Tony, I know this is going to hurt you, but believe me, it has made my life hell for this entire year."

"Avery, my God, do you have cancer or something? That pesticide stuff from Vietnam?"

"No. Just listen, Tony. *Please*, just listen. . . . I've slept with Devlin." He paused, cocking his head as if to see what it sounded like once he finally released the words he'd lived with for twelve months. "That's it. That's all. I've said it."

"Ha ha. How extremely hilarious." Tony drew back from him. "What a stupid fucking thing to say. Here you had me all upset . . ."

"I'm not kidding, Tony. I wish with all my heart I was, but I'm not."

"Wait a minute. You're telling me that you actually *slept* with Devlin? Devlin DeSchuys? *My* Devlin? *Val's* Devlin?" Tony scooted away from Avery sideways like a crab. "This isn't a joke? It's impossible. Ridiculous! You *hate* Devlin!"

"I despise him, Tony. I loathe him."

"But you slept with him?"

"Yes."

"Of course, you mean you slept with him before we met and were just too embarrassed to tell me. Right? *That's* what you mean?" Tony was wide awake and sober, but he felt like a drunk. His speech seemed slowed down and slurred. He wanted to grasp something solid, but when Avery moved to reach out to him, he pulled away.

Avery, too, was suffering. His tongue felt like a rain-swollen sponge, and a quivering in his bowels made him fearful of losing control right there in bed. "No, Tony, that's not what I mean. Well, not exactly. I mean, technically I did meet Devlin before I actually met you. The first time we . . ."

"The first time? The *first* time! How many fucking times were there?" Tony put his feet on the floor and inched away from the bed backward, as if he had just discovered that Avery was a pod person or a leper. Bumping into a chair, he groped for his robe, never taking his eyes off Avery. "Avery? How many times?"

At last Avery broke down utterly. He sobbed. He wailed. Strange little clicking noises emanated from his mouth, and the muscles of his jaw quivered like a hummingbird's throat. He looked paler than Tony had ever seen him, and before long he was gasping for air. He looked up at Tony with an expression that was equal parts misery and panic. He knew that he was beyond the reach of mercy or compassion. Tony could see Avery's stomach, his trim, firm, cut stomach, heaving in and out. "Tony, I love you. Please believe me. I love you, I do. I love you. This thing with Devlin was meaningless."

Tony was rooted to the floor. "How many times, goddamnit?"

"I don't know, I don't know. I lost count. I didn't want to know. Thirty, I guess."

"Thirty? Thirty times? THREE-ZERO TIMES?" Tony screamed. "What was this, a return to your old career of picking up trash?" The room seemed tilted, like one of those photographs of everyday things shot from odd angles. Avery ran his forearm under his nose. Tony threw a box of pale blue tissues at him. "Wipe your fucking nose. That's so gross."

"Tony, if you'll please just give me a chance to explain."

"Oh, sure. This ought to be rich. Explain to me why I shouldn't be upset that you, the only man I have ever loved more than Connecticut Jones, were sleeping with the one man on earth I despise above all others. Christ, Avery, how do you expect me to kiss you when you've had his cock in your mouth? How do you expect me to suck you off knowing his mouth has been there before me? And while you're at it, do you care to explain how you can sleep under this roof in good conscience, knowing that you're screwing around with my best friend's lover? Forget about *me*. Explain *that!*"

Suddenly aware of his nakedness, Avery covered his cock with a pillow. He sat motionless, his elbow resting on his thigh, his chin on his fist, staring straight across the room as if Tony weren't even there. In contrast to Tony's livid visage, his permablush cheeks had faded to a tepid dusty rose.

"My God," Tony said, shivering involuntarily. "I'm going to have to soak in the Jacuzzi for three days just to get your stench off me."

"I'll be happy to explain it to you if you would just give me a goddamned minute without jumping all over me. Please come over here and sit down."

"I don't think that will be necessary. I don't think I want to hear your pathetic excuses and rationalizations."

"But last night you said that you would love me forever, that we'd be together no matter what."

"Last night? Last night? That was before I knew you were a filthy liar and a fucking adulterer. Sorry, Avery, all bets are off. It took me the better part of a decade and a million tears, but I have finally learned my fucking lesson. I have been shit upon by a man for the last time."

"Tony, let me talk to Val, then. Let me explain it to him. He'll understand. I know he will," Avery said, his voice almost gone.

"Jesus Christ, Avery, you've peed the fucking bed."

Avery looked down and saw it was true. "I'm sorry. I'll buy you new sheets. I'm really sorry."

"Fuck the sheets, asshole, just get the fuck out. Get up, get dressed, and get out."

"But . . ."

"Out. Get out. O-U-T. Get the *fuck* out of my life!"

"Okay, okay . . . my clothes." Avery looked lost, bewildered.

"Your tux is in the closet. I'll send it over to Brooklyn along with the rest of the slime trail you've left here. The sweatshirt and jeans you came in are probably on the floor somewhere, fucking slob that you are. Jesus, I hate you."

Tony left the room while Avery dressed. He tried to make coffee, but his hands were shaking so much he couldn't get the top off the goddamn percolator. He lit one of Val's clove cigarettes, inhaled, gagged, and threw it down the garbage disposal. When Avery finally wheeled his way into the living room, Tony was pacing back and forth in the foyer.

"I could have changed five times by now," Tony said. "Forget ever doing runway work."

"Have you seen my jacket?"

Tony opened the hall closet and tore the black bomber jacket off its wooden hanger with such violence that six or seven wire hangers sang out against each other before clanging to the floor. "Here's your fucking coat, asshole."

Avery wheeled himself to the elevator, his jacket folded across his thighs, and pressed the call button. Tears rolled down his cheeks, but he didn't sigh or sob. He let his nose drip onto his jacket unnoticed. His face was set, stoic; his hands were vibrating against the steel rims of the chair's wheels with nervous energy. When the elevator door glided open, he wheeled himself halfway in, then backed up.

"Tony, please. I'm *begging* you to let me stay and talk this out with you. You'll understand. I know you will."

"Just go, Avery. I never want to see your ugly fuckface again. . . . And don't pop any wheelies in the lobby. The concierge has been getting complaints about the skid marks."

Before the doors had the opportunity to close, Tony took his signet ring off and threw it at Avery.

"Don't forget your frigging ring! Maybe you can have the monogram changed."

He stared at the elevator for a moment, then picked up a Baccarat ashtray from the coffee table and threw it. It shattered against the marble walls just over Avery's head. The matching lighter followed, as did the previous night's cocktail glasses and champagne flutes. He then hurled the champagne bottle itself, which bounced off the wall but didn't break. He was reaching for a two-tone blue vase decorated with a single white water lily, an ugly knickknack he'd always hated, when Val walked hurriedly into the room in his burgundy silk lounging pajamas and coordinating paisley bathrobe.

"Tony, please," he shrieked. "Not the Ming!"

Tony spent the remainder of the day trying to make sense of what had happened. For nearly an hour after Avery left, he was so enraged that he found himself unable to finish a single complete sentence. He stomped and stammered around his suite as if suffering from Tourette's syndrome, gathering up all evidence of Avery's existence and leaving Val confused but relieved that he was hurling epithets instead of priceless *objets d'art.* Only after filling three large trash bags did he pause and appear to come to his senses.

"Avery's gone," Tony said as if unaware that Val had witnessed his departure.

"I can see that."

"For *good.*"

"I discerned that from your ritual exorcism."

"He's been fucking Devlin."

"I see."

Tony waited for a reaction, but Val said nothing. He seemed preoccupied, as if trying to figure out how that might have been possible logistically.

"It's true. He admitted it."

"Oh, I believe you. I am, however, having some difficulty understanding the precise dynamics of the relationship. Perhaps you'd like to tell me everything you know over a cup of coffee."

As Tony related the details of Avery's confession, Val calmly made notes on a sheet of cream-colored stationery: condo, Porsche, Sanctuary. When Tony was finished, Val sat quietly, his head cocked to one side, gently tapping the slender gold pen against his temple.

"I'm sorry, Tony, but this just doesn't make sense."

"It's true. Every word of it."

"I didn't say it wasn't true. But in this case, the truth is stranger than fiction. Far, *far* stranger. And this is a plot worthy of Dame Agatha herself. We have the who and what. We can surmise the where and when. What is missing is the motive, the *why.* Avery loves you—*I* believe that even if you don't. So why would he sleep with Devlin, whom he clearly despises? I don't accept for a minute that he would do so willingly. And though I've long suspected that Devlin has had any *number* of affairs since we've been together—it's just not his nature to be monogamous and I accept that—he knows better than to shit where he eats. Does he hate you *that* much that he'd do something as stupid as this just to hurt you? I don't think so. Something else is going on, and for the life of me I have no idea what it is."

After further deliberation, Val placed a check mark next to each item on his list.

"So, there we have it," he said. "Now, shall I alert the baths?"

"I don't think that will be necessary," Tony said. "I think I've learned *that* lesson."

"Well, bravo."

"Besides, I have something entirely different in mind."

# 26

TONY WAS WAITING FOR TUXEDO when he arrived at his office at 7 A.M. the next day. He knew Tux always put in a good two hours work before Nola and the parade of pretty boys showed up at nine.

"What on earth are you doing here at this hour, Tony? Nothing wrong, I hope."

Tony told him the story—or as Tuxedo quickly pointed out, *his* side of the story—in a convoluted blast of invective. Tux interrupted from time to time to untangle the various skeins of betrayal but let Tony complete the tale. When he thought Tony was finished, he straightened his tie and cleared his throat. Tony interrupted him.

"I don't want your advice, thank you very much. That's not why I'm here. You asked me if something was wrong and I told you. But I'm not looking for sympathy or solutions. I'm through with that backstabbing cripple, and I'm ready to go on with my life."

Tuxedo recoiled at the pejorative, shifted tentatively in his chair, then rose and walked over to the bar. "Aren't you being a little harsh?"

"Harsh? I don't think so. I'm allowing him to live, aren't I? I'm not going to attempt to ruin him professionally."

"I'm certainly relieved to hear that. So then, what brings you here if not a broken heart?"

Tony chose that moment to get up and pace the room. He made several false starts, all beginning with the words "I" or "You," and he crossed and uncrossed his arms repeatedly.

"I really do appreciate everything you've done for me, Tux, and I don't want you to think I'm ungrateful."

"But?"

"But now that Avery and I are history, this modeling shit just isn't going to be enough. I don't feel like I'm getting anywhere. I want more. I *need* more."

"More what, Tony? Money? Exposure? Groupies?"

"All of the above." He smiled weakly, to take the edge off his demands. Tuxedo did not appear to be amused. "Don't be offended, Tux, but I've been thinking . . ."

"I am never offended by people who think. On the contrary . . ."

"If I could get this far after being discovered by Dallas Eden, of all people, imagine . . ."

"And what was wrong with being discovered by Dallas Eden?"

"Please, Tux. Being discovered by Dallas is only one cut above being discovered by Jim Nabors."

"Dallas loved you, Tony. *Really* loved you. And everything you are today, everything, you owe to him."

"And I'm grateful, I really am. But Dallas is dead, and here I am, lounging around in a pair of Black Tie denims, waiting for my real life to begin." Tony walked back to his chair and slipped into it suddenly, as if it were the last seat in a game of musical chairs.

"And your real life would be what, exactly?"

"Acting. You know, movies, TV."

"A star on your dressing room door?"

"What's wrong with that?"

"Not a thing, Tony. And you could probably be a fine actor. Not a Laurence Olivier, I suspect, but not a Troy Donohue, either."

"Thanks a lot."

"Frankly, it's good to see that you've acknowledged to yourself that you have the ambition and self-confidence that justifiably come with looks of your magnitude. You didn't have either one of those attributes when I first met you. But you need to be aware of two things. First, I don't like this vindictive tone you've adopted—toward Avery, toward Dallas, and in a roundabout way, toward me. It's unbecoming and, in the long run, it's going to be counterproductive. Second, these days, breaking into TV or Hollywood is a lot harder than you might think, even with the kind of looks and connections you've got. There are a lot of casting couches in Hollywood, and there are a lot of pretty boys lined up to give it a whirl. If you're going to do it right—and I won't let you do it any other way—it takes a certain amount of innate talent and a *soupçon* of finesse. Now, Stella Adler tells me you're developing nicely but that your greatest strides are still ahead of you. Translated, that means you've got a ways to go. I haven't been able to get you much in the way of decent parts until now, so I haven't put much effort into it lately."

"But you have tried?"

"Directors are always looking for handsome extras for their disaster movies. You know—fires, plane crashes. Good looks frequently substitute for character development—in art as well as life. The better looking you are, the more quickly the audience bonds with your character, so when you die, they feel something, even though it's only a minor part. You would have been perfect for the scene in *The Poseidon Adventure* when the ship turns upside down and the handsome young man falls through the stained-glass skylight. Someone called yesterday looking for a male lead for *Mall Madness II: They Shopped 'til They Dropped*. If I had known of your impatience then, you could have had your choice between being sliced and diced by an air-conditioner exhaust fan or being beheaded by some loony tune with a chainsaw in the Sears hardware department. I might still be able to get you signed, if that sounds interesting."

"I'll pass."

"And there's always the possibility of becoming a game show host. You know the type, part lounge lizard, part circus barker. Of course, we'd have to get you a bad haircut and a tacky blazer."

"Tux . . . I'm serious."

"So am I, Tony. After all, show business will be far more lucrative, for both of us. And it just so happens I have a plan that will put your name, as opposed to something else, on the lips of every producer and casting director from New York to L.A. in the most dramatic way possible. It was a secret. It was going to be my New Year's gift to you, but since you've got a gun to my head, I suppose I'll let you in on it today, although Parker will probably kill me."

"What is it?"

"Parker has been so pleased with the rollout of S/X, and the return has been *so* great, that he's moving ahead with plans to introduce a new product line, a collection of men's toiletries with a more Americanized appeal than S/X, which as you know has something of a Continental flavor."

"Since when did Brooklyn become a continent?"

"I know you saw the wisdom of offering Avery that campaign, even if you wanted it for yourself, so let's not start rewriting history now. Avery was right for S/X, for what Parker wanted S/X to be—dark, smoldering, sensual—and you were not. Plain and simple. Despite what you may think, he never promised you that job and once it became clear the direction in which he was going in product development and marketing, you were out of the picture."

"Oh, that makes me feel a *lot* better. Wait, let me see if there's a part of my ego that hasn't been bruised this week and you can step on it."

"Keep your shit together, Tony. You *are* right for this campaign: blond, athletic, direct. Wholesome, but with a bit of Casanova in you. By its very nature, this campaign, which is more broadly based than S/X, is going to have an even higher visibility. You are going to be astounded. I just wish I could have told you under the circumstances I had planned, which was the big New Year's Eve party at the Waldorf I told you about."

"Oh, right. Ave was looking forward to that."

"He knew the plan, Tony, and he was delighted for you."

"Big of him."

"The new line is called 'Me.' The flagship product will be cologne, but later Parker will introduce shaving components, shampoo and conditioner, facial cleansers and moisturizers, deodorants, soaps. The products and packaging are all going to be clear: gels, liquids, and the like. There will be no artificial dyes and the fragrance in the cologne and aftershave will be very, very light. The idea is that 'Me' lets you be yourself. And your role will be to make purchasers think that 'Me' lets them be *you*."

Tuxedo went to the walk-in closet and rolled out a presentation platform about the size of a card table. He stopped in front of an easel. Both were draped in black velvet.

"Come over here, Tony." He waited, then removed the cloth from a scale model of Times Square as it would look on New Year's Eve. He pressed a button that lit up the ceremonial ball and a miniature billboard about the size of a postcard standing on end.

"As I said, this was supposed to be a surprise. We just happened to use some existing photos from a shoot with Victor about six months ago. I'm sure you'll remember the one. That billboard is ten stories tall, Tony, and it will remain sheathed, as it is here, until midnight. When the ball completes its descent and the '1980' lights up, the canvas will fall away and . . . *Voilá!* Tony Alexander, from the waist up, naked, staring directly out onto the two hundred and fifty thousand revelers—and millions more watching at home—with only the words 'Use Me' in evidence. No product, no other reference whatsoever, until the following week, when we replace it with a duplicate ad that includes an inset of a bottle of cologne. It will look like an invitation to use *you*, Tony. A monumental come on. The world's biggest personal ad."

"Great. I'll probably get calls from Paul Bunyan and the Jolly Green Giant."

"We're having similarly dramatic rollouts in Chicago, San Francisco, and L.A., with different tag lines: 'Choose Me,' 'Try Me,' 'Buy Me.' Overnight, your face is going to become as familiar as Mount Rushmore, compounded by the mystery of just what all this is about. And then, Tony, the sky's the limit. I already have an exclusive interview set up with *People* magazine. This is going to change your life, Tony. You are going to be *the* face of the eighties."

A WEEK HAD PASSED since Avery departed in a rain of crystal and other friable objects, and Val was still waiting for the other shoe to drop. But Tony had neither threatened suicide nor ensconced himself at the St. Mark's Baths.

"Don't get me wrong, Tony, I love the way you're handling this, but I'm worried that you're seething inside and at the slightest provocation will erupt like Vesuvio. There's still an awful lot of irreplaceable glass in here."

"Can we please not talk about this, Val?"

"Have it your way. It's just that this is so startlingly different for you. So, dare I say it, *adult*."

"It *is* different. The only thing I can figure is that *I* was the one who walked out this time. I do feel empty, but nothing else. Absolutely nothing else."

"Fortunately for me, I don't even feel empty. Just a bad taste in my mouth, probably the result of all the crow I've had to eat. Oh, I almost forgot, I picked up something for you at the desk—a telegram—how very quaint. *Quelle dramatique.*"

Val rifled through his briefcase and retrieved the small envelope.

"Any idea who it's from?"

"Couldn't tell, darling, and believe me, I tried."

"Do you think it could be from Avery? How long has it been down at the goddamn desk?"

"Whoa, Flicka. Easy."

"I was just wondering."

"Right, like the condemned man wonders if the governor's called yet."

"Okay, okay, just let me read it."

The telegram was from Tony's Aunt Thalia in Tampa. It read: SOUTH
BEACH HOUSE SOLD. STOP. DEMOLITION JAN. 4. STOP. PLEASE REMOVE BE-
LONGINGS. STOP.

"That's Aunt Thalia. Ten words exactly. But I wonder who bought it
to demolish it? Why would you do that?"

"Dev said there's been a lot of construction going on in South Beach
lately. Condos and the like."

"Who'd be crazy enough to build condos in South Beach? No
Southie's got the cash for a condo. And it's got such a bad reputation
that nobody else would want to live there."

"But that's where you're wrong, Tony. When developers come in and
bulldoze everything, the reputation goes with it. They launch this big
p.r.–marketing blitz and everybody forgets their chic condo tower was
once a slum."

"South Beach is not a slum. It's not Southampton, but it's not a slum.
Nobody was ever on welfare that I knew of."

"Relax. All I'm saying is that every day there is less and less beach-
front property in Florida and that would make your old, unexploited
hometown very desirable. Your father, if he were smart . . ."

"Which he is not."

". . . could very well be a millionaire now."

"Great, maybe he'll be able to drink himself to death faster."

"So are you going to go?"

"Hell no. Why should I? I'd bet you a hundred bucks that my old
man has already chucked my board and whatever else I 'owned' back
then. Plus, I don't want to see him."

"You don't even want to see the house you grew up in one more
time? Besides, if your father's already sold the place and it's scheduled
for demolition in what, a couple of weeks, it's probably uninhabitable.
He won't be there. He's probably already bought some nice place in
Sugar Mill Beach."

"Nah, he'd probably move back to Tampa to be with the family."

"So go. Look, I have to be in Sugar Mill Beach the week after
Christmas to unburden myself of Sucre sur Mer—meet with realtors and
lawyers and such. I want to make sure Devlin is off the premises and
that he hasn't vandalized the place. I had even thought about driving
north in Devlin's Porsche . . ."

"Whose Porsche?"

"Right. *My* Porsche. It would be a lot more fun if you came with me.

We could do a 'Route 66' number. Drive home leisurely or even zip down to Key West for a long weekend first. How far is that?"

"Seven or eight hours if you're lucky and there aren't any accidents on any of the bridges."

"So, what do you say?"

"I'll think about it."

# 27

AVERY WAS DOING FINE until he ran over Joey's rubber ducky with his wheelchair. It emitted a wheezy quack when it compressed and again when it popped back to its original shape. He bent down to pick it up. The bottom of the toy was still wet from Joey's bath an hour before, and it left a bright puddle, iridescent with soap residue, on the worn pink-and-gray checked linoleum. The duck was yellow with a baby blue ribbon around its neck. Avery pressed it to his mouth and kissed it, then clutched it to his chest. He cried, silently at first, shivering like an unlucky ice-skater pulled from a barely frozen lake. And then came the sobs, little choking noises, staccato at first, then melding into long, high-pitched whining exhalations and rattle-throated inhalations.

He had to wonder if he was doing right by the boys, leaving them like this. Brandi loved them, but he figured he loved them more. Of course, he knew Brandi would take good care of them, and with him out of the picture she'd probably be remarried within the year—to someone who wasn't a cripple or a fag. It would be better for everyone.

He shook his head. He couldn't think about that. Didn't have time. Brandi and the boys were having their usual Friday night HoJo fish fry dinner with her sister Mandi, even though they had just seen her three days earlier on Christmas. Avery had said he wasn't feeling well and they should go alone.

*Fine,* she had said. *There's leftovers in the fridge.*

They'd be home by ten, ten-thirty the latest. Joey got cranky if he was out any later than that, and Brandi, he knew, was in no mood, not after the tension of the past two weeks. And there was that big snowstorm on the way. It wasn't really expected to blow in until midmorning, but Brandi was already worried about it.

He dropped the duck into his lap and looked around the bathroom. Faucets tight in the tub and sink. Shower curtain straightened out to dry. He had already checked the rest of the house the way he did before he left the house or went to bed. Gas burners off on the stove. Mr. Coffee unplugged. (Brandi was deathly afraid of fire, and she'd heard somewhere on the TV about coffeemakers that just burst into flames while everyone in the house was asleep, killing everyone in the resulting inferno.) Windows closed and locked—he always double-checked them. It wasn't solely for security; being on the first floor, they had burglar bars. It also was to make sure they weren't losing any more heat than necessary.

He wondered what Tony was doing tonight. He'd probably be at a party somewhere, or more likely parties, plural. He sure got around, him and Val, and after all this *was* the last weekend of the 1970s and that was worth celebrating. Avery could picture tonight's party, in one of those great old brownstones that instead of being cut up into three or four apartments had actually been joined with its neighbor, creating huge open spaces suitable for the construction of atriums and the display of brightly colored, oversized modern art. The scent of fresh garlands of pine or spruce, tied with bows of real satin or red velvet, would occasionally surface between clouds of marijuana smoke. Tables large and small would be swathed in gold lamé and laden with foods neither he nor Tony particularly liked: oddly colored fruits with spines or hairy rinds, strong cheeses, unfamiliar vegetables that tasted like bark, pale green dips that looked like pus. Caviar and hard-boiled eggs.

There'd still be mistletoe everywhere, so the fat old men who were giving the party—and their ancient guests specially disinterred for the occasion—could slobber over all the handsome boys just back from "the Islands," wherever the hell *that* was. He'd been with Tony for a year and he still hadn't figured that out, exactly. It was the kind of party Avery hated, and he didn't think Tony especially liked either, but Tony would insist on going, "just to be seen."

Maybe if he hadn't blown it, the two of them would be just sitting in front of the fire in Tony's suite or taking a Jacuzzi together, drinking champagne and making a complete mess of the bathroom with their water fights. Maybe they'd *still* be unwrapping Christmas presents. Tony loved giving presents—far more, it seemed, than getting them, which appeared to embarrass him. Last year, when they hardly knew each other, Tony had bought gifts for Brandi and the boys. He was so cute picking out gifts for Chris and Joey at F.A.O. Schwarz; it was al-most as if he was buying them for himself. He would have made a great step-dad.

Avery was tempted to call just to see if he was home, now, this minute. It was still early. Of course, Tony would hang up as soon as he figured out who it was, but Avery would at least know where he was this one last time. And that was something. Just hearing his *voice* was something, that first innocent hello, before he got wary and started ask-ing who it was. Avery had called a couple times to try to explain things, but Tony cursed a blue streak and slammed down the receiver.

For a couple of days, he'd staked out the lobby of the Towers on the off chance that Tony might relent if he saw him, that somehow bells would ring, birds would break into song, and he'd glide effortlessly across the marble floor, a breeze ruffling his hair, like in a Clairol com-mercial. They'd embrace and all would be forgiven and forgotten. Right. And his legs would grow back on the spot and they'd break out their dancing shoes and walls would slide back revealing the Rockettes kick-stepping themselves into a merry frenzy. But Tony never appeared in the lobby, which was unusual. Between business and pleasure, Tony was always coming and going. Avery figured one of the doormen prob-ably had recognized him and, to be polite and helpful, called to tell Tony he was waiting in the lobby. "Tell him we're not taking any charity cases today," Tony'd say, and then he'd slip out through the garage.

Other than those futile trips, Avery had spent most of the past two weeks in the apartment. Brandi had noticed and commented on it. *Why don't you take the boys out for some fresh air?* she'd say. And he'd say, *Yeah* or *In a minute,* and never move from his place by the window. Even the thought of Christmas, his favorite holiday, failed to cheer him up or take his mind off his problems. Buying a Christmas tree had been a nightmare—almost unbearable—and he had to fight not to be short with the boys, who were home from school and wild with boredom and anticipation of the holiday.

Avery sighed and looked around the cramped apartment. It was *tiny.* There wasn't even a wall between the living room and the combination dining room–kitchen, unlike Val's place, where the kitchen seemed to be hidden behind a fake wall or rotating bookshelf. The first few times he had been there, he hadn't been able to find it by himself, and there were times he doubted even Val knew where it was. This place was a dump. On the income he was now making as a model, he could have easily moved the family to a bigger apartment, one with separate rooms for the boys. At the very least they could have redecorated. But he couldn't let on to Brandi how much money he'd really made without revealing its source. Maybe it was because he felt he hadn't really earned it, because it was such an obscene amount, at least for someone like him, who used to work all year on the garbage truck for what he made on a couple of shoots now. Or maybe it was because he considered the money somehow "tainted" because everyone involved with it was gay. So he'd paid off all their bills and started bank accounts for Christopher and Joey, bought a few new things for Brandi—though nothing really expensive— and socked the rest away. Brandi would be shocked when she found out how much was there. Carefully managed, it would easily last her three years or more if she wasn't extravagant, and by then she would be remarried.

Of course, all of it would come out if Devlin followed through with his threat—the money, the modeling, and, eventually, the men. He would be ruined. That's why he had to do it. He had no choice. He hoped the boys would forgive him. He didn't think Brandi would care all that much. He *knew* Tony wouldn't. That's why he wasn't leaving a note. He'd worried for a time that Tony might be upset, that he might blame himself, but he knew that wasn't true. Tony wouldn't care. He wouldn't read a note. He'd spit on it. Avery thought Val would understand—he had promised to do everything he could when they met last week at the Oak Bar—maybe he should address the note to *him*. But in the end he decided it would be more embarrassing to his family if the police found the note and read it, or worse, leaked it to the press. Better to let everyone draw their own conclusions. Hell, most of his friends and relatives would think it had to do with his legs, even after they heard all the stories. *He just wasn't the same after he lost his legs.*

As soon as Brandi and the boys had left, he got his Navy-issue revolver out of the box with all his old uniforms—cleaned, oiled, but unloaded. He would never keep a loaded gun in a house with kids; he hadn't even had bullets for it until last week. Earlier in the evening, he'd taken a single bullet out of its box in the van and put it in the breast pocket of his red plaid flannel shirt. It was his final fashion statement; he thought maybe the blood wouldn't show up as much on red. Now he took the cartridge out with his right hand and loaded the damn thing. Unbeckoned, tears dropped from his eyes, as clean and clear as the droplets falling from a melting icicle.

Late at night the week before, he'd practiced with the gun unloaded, getting used to the cold, acid tang of the barrel. He'd looked things up in some medical books at the New York Public Library, trying to learn enough about the brain to insure that the blast would kill him, not just turn him into a vegetable that would be a drain on Brandi and the boys for as long as he clung to life. He finally decided to angle the gun almost parallel with the floor so he wouldn't just blow the top of his head off. He wanted to get rid of the brain stem, too. That seemed like an important part, a place where a lot of things joined, sort of like a cloverleaf on the interstate. He reminded himself not to stick the barrel too far into his mouth, figuring the shallower it was, the wider the area of impact would be. Yeah, it would work all right. He'd seen plenty of head wounds in 'Nam, and you'd have to be pretty incompetent—or incredibly lucky—to eat a .45 and survive.

He had given a lot of thought to where he would do it. If he did it in the living room, the boys might see his body if they walked in ahead of Brandi. Anyway, there was upholstered furniture or drapes or carpeting everywhere. The new yellow sofa was safely covered in plastic, but the black velvet painting of the Virgin Mary might get splattered with gore. There were family pictures on the wall and little china figurines of boys and dogs on the end tables. And Brandi would never forgive him if he blasted his brains out on the breakfront: the bullet might exit the back of his head and shatter the glass into smithereens.

The bathroom was clearly the best choice. He could lock the door—when he didn't respond to Brandi's knocks, she would know something was seriously wrong and send the boys to their room—and it would be easier to clean up afterward. He would roll his chair in backward until the wheels hit the tub. Then most of the blood and brains and stuff would explode out onto the white tiles around the tub. It would look bad, sure—red on white—but you could hose it right down the drain. Maybe a sympathetic female police officer would give Brandi some cleaning tips. *Remove that little screen thing from the drain before you start, honey. It'll go much faster. That's it. It should screw right out.* The kitchen ran a close second, but for privacy and overall ease of cleanup, the bathroom couldn't be beat. Of course, Brandi would never take another bath there again, but she'd probably move out anyway, move in with her folks tomorrow, unless they got snowed in.

Avery said a Hail Mary and an Act of Contrition, and then he was ready. He made the Sign of the Cross with his right hand, then positioned the gun on his tongue, his teeth tentatively biting down an inch from the end of the barrel. Somehow, it didn't feel quite right. He slid the gun another half inch into his mouth, his teeth scraping along the barrel. Better.

Avery never thought he'd find himself in this position, with cold steel in his mouth and his own finger on the trigger. In Vietnam he had spent every minute of his time, every ounce of his strength, every bit of his cunning, to stay alive, to avoid the guns, the bombs, the mines, the booby traps. Now here he was, ready to do in one second what Victor Charlie hadn't been able to do in a year. But he couldn't make it without Tony. He really couldn't. Even when Bryan went missing and he finally resigned himself to the idea that he was dead, he didn't feel this lost, so totally and completely alone. It was bad enough that they had broken up, but Tony's intense hatred baffled him at the same time it made him despair of ever reconciling with him.

Avery knew he would never love anyone as much as he had Tony. He hadn't felt like that about Bryan. Sure, Bryan was hot and handsome, and sex with him in their tiny little room at the Imperial Hotel in Saigon had spoiled him for years after he got back to the States. He was so strong and hard and sure of himself. And he was eager to please, not just to get his rocks off. But their relationship was mostly about sex. He liked Bryan. He loved him, yeah, and worried about him, and he was sure Bryan had felt the same about him. But with Tony it was full-blown love. He was aware of every minute he was away from Tony, and every minute they were together he was acutely aware of everything Tony said or did, every glance, every smile, every touch, almost as if he were sitting back and watching Tony in a movie. He never wanted the evening to end. If he woke up first, he would slide up next to Tony and try and put his arm under his neck without waking him. He'd pull back the covers and marvel at what he saw. And when he could stand being alone no more, he would kiss Tony lightly on the ear, the forehead, the nose, the cheek, the nipple . . . until Tony woke up.

Avery was hard. He had a gun in his mouth and he had a hard-on for the man who had forced him into this position. He stared into space, conscious of his erection, the last he would have in this life. It felt good. It felt sad. He was surprised that his arms and hands were so steady but they were, steady and sure. Okay, here goes. His finger brushed the trigger.

He thought it somehow appropriate that the blast would probably destroy his face, the face that, in his new topless S/X ads was being cut out of bus stop kiosks by men and women. This face, this giver of wealth, had earned him more money in six months than he had made in all the years since leaving the Navy, though to be fair he'd been on disability most of the time. This face is what had attracted Tony to him, or at least that's what Tony said. So in a way, this face was responsible for what was about to happen. It was fitting that it would probably be unrecognizable after the blast. He smiled wryly. Closed coffin, for sure.

But then he thought about what it would be like for the boys not to be able to at least see their dad one last time. If you blow off the back of your head, does your face sort of fall off? Or do your ears hold it in place like thumbtacks? He pictured the scene Brandi would find, his blood and brains all over the walls, his face sort of melted like a rubber Halloween mask.

He couldn't do it. He'd have to find a less messy way. He sat in that wheelchair, in that room, and his hands started shaking and the gun began to quiver, and he cried again, surprised at how much it hurt to say good-bye, even more surprised there were any tears left. Finally, he became aware that his eyes were focused on the silver surface of the medicine chest mirror. He almost jumped out of the chair.

He reached up and swung the door open. The first two shelves were full of the usual unguents and elixirs—Vicks Vap-o-Rub, Bactine, Crest, Speedstick. But on the top shelf, as remote as possible from an assault by Christopher and Joey, were the small amber plastic containers that held his medications—pain pills in a variety of strengths, muscle relaxants, anti-inflammatory tablets, sleeping pills, antidepressants. The more potent ones had been prescribed for his pain right after the accident, but he had used them sparingly, afraid of getting addicted. The doctor had said at least one of them contained morphine. Unfortunately the precautions he had taken to keep the pills away from the boys also put them out of his reach. He would have to use the gun to knock them off the shelf and into the sink. Using a hand towel, he dried the basin and made sure the drain was plugged, just in case a bottle opened or broke, spilling its contents onto the ivory porcelain. He would hate to see those pills, as valuable to him now as diamonds, roll down the drain into oblivion.

One by one, the bottles tumbled into the sink, their contents chattering like beans in a maraca. None overshot its mark, but two opened on impact, spraying the seeds of his destruction like unstrung pearls on a marble floor. He congratulated himself for having plugged the drain. He gathered the errant tablets and capsules and put them back in the bottles, mixing the two varieties together. Placing the six bottles in his lap, he unloaded the gun, put the bullet in his pocket, and, disentangling himself from the bath mat, rolled down the hall to put the gun in the closet.

Avery remembered that some of the pills had a bad taste, so he couldn't just take them with water. From the refrigerator he took the translucent plastic jug stained purple with Kool-Aid; the boys loved the stuff even in winter. He would have preferred orange juice, but it looked like they were all out. He picked out a tumbler from the dish drainer; the glass was decorated with thin bands of color ranging the entire spectrum. After filling the glass, he opened the first bottle and spilled its contents into his left hand. There were only seven pills and they were small. Probably wouldn't pack much of a wallop, but there were still five more bottles. One at a time, he took the pills, washing each down with the weak, sweet liquid. It occurred to him that at this rate he'd probably be bloated before he came anywhere near getting the job done, so beginning with the next handful—twenty-two sleek black capsules—he doubled and tripled up. Nineteen red-and-white capsules disappeared in four gulps, followed by seven olive-drab tablets in two swallows. The white tablets with the numbers on them were about as big as a nickel, and he had a hard time getting more than one down as a time. He ran out of Kool-Aid after swallowing eleven of them, with twelve more to go and another whole bottle yet. Just out of reach, the bottle of good Russian vodka Tony had given him stood next to the toaster. Straight vodka? Why not? Maybe Tony would find out that it was his gift that finished Avery off.

# 28

IN THE EARLY MORNING DARKNESS, the city arrayed itself in the whites and cool blues of a fresh snowfall. As Val and Tony waited for a taxi in the gilt-and-marble Triumph Towers lobby, a silver Greyhound growled past like a bright-eyed monster lumbering through an Irish mist. A diesel semi snorted at a stoplight. A taxi sped by, full of purpose. When the Towers doorman blew his whistle, a second cab stopped abruptly, like a dog brought up short on its leash.

It had been snowing heavily since 3 A.M., and by now the streets were so bad the cab driver was reluctant to take them to LaGuardia. He was a slender young man with a couple days' growth of beard on a face pocked with bluish acne scars. The unintelligible name on his hack license suggested an origin within the Fertile Crescent, and while his English was rudimentary, he had quickly grasped the entrepreneurial spirit of his host country.

"If I am going airport and stick there, I lose very much money, yes? Forty, maybe fifty dollar," he said over his shoulder, his big woody teeth glowing in his burnished face. "You give; I take you."

"That's extortion," Tony said, reaching for the door handle.

"Hush, Tony, I'm sure our friend is a family man with many children to support," Val said. "Am I right? Many children?" He mimed holding a baby.

"Yes. Very, very many. And hungry always."

Although Val was not all that excited about spending the next forty-eight hours in Gatorland with his soon-to-be ex-husband, he would have gladly paid five hundred dollars just to get to the airport and get the goddamn trip over with. Instead he gave him three twenties. "Drive," he said, and settled back in the seat.

They made it with only minutes to spare, checked their bags at the curb, and fought their way through the excited fluidity of the airport. A sense of urgency hummed in the air as travelers ran through the terrazzo-floored ticketing area, worried about reaching their destinations or being trapped at the airport, unable to get back to the city.

Having decided to accompany Val only the night before, Tony was ticketless, but he expected no problems. There was always *one* empty seat in first class. The airlines did it to taunt the coach passengers, who would covet the unused legroom each time their knees bumped their tray tables. Tony used his face, his charm, and a pinch of guile ("I have to get to Florida for a kidney transplant") to make his way to the front of the line at the ticket counter.

"I need a first-class ticket on flight 666 to Atlanta, with connections to Daytona Beach," he said, smiling capaciously at the overweight, gray-haired, and obviously harried queen behind the counter. He pushed three one-hundred-dollar bills toward him.

The ticket agent punched some numbers into his computer and glanced up at Tony with a hangdog look. The flight was sold out.

Tony did not even blink. "Well, silly me. Here's my boarding pass now," he said, slipping a fourth portrait of Ben Franklin across the cool, polished surface.

"Sir, we are not allowed to accept gratuities."

"This isn't a gratuity, bitch, it's a bribe. Bump somebody."

"There's nothing I can do, sir."

Val stepped up next to Tony. "How very butch of you, Tony. But now that you have established who is the bigger queen here, don't give the poor dear a heart attack. We'll get a later flight."

"Later, hell. If we don't get out of here now, we won't get out until New Year's Day. It's already impossible to get back to the city. I am not about to sit around the goddamn airport for three days eating Twinkies and drinking battery acid *au lait*."

"But darling, think of the T-rooms! Thousands of men await your legendary ministrations. It will be standing room only, except, of course, for the select few who will be privileged enough to sit on your lovely face."

Tony turned back to the ticket agent. "Maybe you'd like the opportunity to play a little pocket pool with me in the men's room on my return flight. I can deal with that."

"Sir, there really is nothing I can do. You can go to the gate and fly standby if you'd like."

"Standby? Fuck standby! Here's another hundred bucks, and if that isn't good enough, I'll talk to your supervisor and tell him you expressed an interest in personally inspecting my carry-on luggage, if you get my drift."

It was beginning to dawn on Tony that the man was powerless to give him somebody else's seat without risking his job and that the altercation pained and frightened him. He knew the guy *wanted* to like him; he saw the soft-edged look in his eyes that he had come to recognize among strangers as admiration or lust. But anger of such an intense magnitude and unknown origin had welled up inside of him that he knew if the argument progressed, he would have no choice but to grab the fool by the collar and bring him nose-to-nose with his furious new persona. Then, at last, it looked as if they were finally making progress. The agent returned his gaze to his computer screen and tapped in a few letters and numbers.

"Your name, sir?"

Tony told him.

"Right, Mr. Alexander, I see your reservation now," the man said, raking the five one-hundred-dollar bills toward himself. "I believe it was obscured by one for a Mr. Currier."

"That was some show, darling," Val said as they left the ticket counter. "Are you auditioning for *Psycho II?*"

They arrived at their gate in a sweat. Val had worn tweed and Tony a chocolate suede, mid-calf Australian cowboy coat. The young agent at the check-in desk smiled effortlessly as he took their tickets, and familiarity bounced through the air like radar. He told them their flight would almost certainly be the last one out for some time, and he winked. "If it *is* canceled and you gentlemen need a place to stay . . ."

"Thanks, but our husbands would be furious. Come on, Tony," Val said, pulling him toward the jetway. They were the last passengers to board, and the flight attendant closed the door behind them. Val asked a woman to switch seats so he and Tony could sit together.

"This is totally undignified," Tony said, settling into seat 2-B. He mopped his brow with his cashmere scarf. "And completely unnecessary. If that ninny from Ninevah hadn't run over that dog on Fifty-ninth Street, we would have been here half an hour ago fighting over the man in 4-C."

Val turned his head and looked over his right shoulder. The face was familiar. A professional athlete—too compact for football but quite possibly a baseball player. "You're right. He would be a catch. Or possibly a catcher. I think he plays for the Yankees," he said. "But really, you've got to ease up on the cabbie. It was a white dog. It was white snow. They don't *have* snow in Mesopotamia."

"Did he have to pick it up and put it in the trunk?" Tony said, fiddling with the air-conditioning nozzle. "On top of our luggage?"

"I think he was being civic-minded. He wanted to get it off the street."

"Civic-minded? Really? Then why did he drop it off at the Red Crescent Restaurant and Lounge? I think poor little Snowflake will be reincarnated this afternoon atop a bed of couscous and dates."

A flight attendant came around taking preflight drink orders. She was not particularly pretty, but she was groomed to within an inch of her life. Tony ordered a Bloody Mary, Val a Virgin Mary.

"I swear, Tony, this drinking before noon is not a good sign."

"Relax, Val. We're on vacation, remember?"

"Right—some vacation."

When the flight attendant returned with the drinks, she also carried the January issue of *Gentleman's Quarterly,* folded open to a spread Tony had shot months ago in a tiny Alpine village. "Here are your drinks, gentlemen. I'll be back for the glasses before we take off. And um, sir, I was wondering . . . actually we were *all* wondering, if this isn't you? We knew you looked familiar when you stepped on board, but then Ginny found this magazine and, well . . . we wondered if you might sign it for us?"

Tony forced a smile. When people first began recognizing him, he enjoyed the attention. He got better seats in restaurants. His fellow New Yorkers actually gave up cabs for him if there was the least uncertainty over who had grabbed the door handle first. In bars, his drinks were stronger, and they were often free. But now such attention was wearisome at best and rarely came without strings. His admirers had become brazen and usually wanted something more than his electrifying smile in return for their deference: a picture, an annoying conversation, a roll in the hay. Small articles of his clothing—a scarf, a single glove—would be missing when he left a plane or restaurant. He felt violated. Now he generally refused to acknowledge requests for autographs, a lock of hair, a sample of his sperm. Politely, yes, but firmly. Today was not the day to make such an inquiry. He smiled as broadly as he could, as if preparing for a professional dental prophylaxis. "Not unless I get to sit on the captain's lap," he said.

"Oh, Tony," Val said. "Give us all a break and sign the damn thing. If you don't, I'll demand they suspend cocktail service for the duration and you'll have to fly dry."

"Bitch," Tony said to Val, whisking the nineteen-cent pen from the flight attendant's hand and signing his name directly over his face. "You know how I hate this sort of thing."

"Get real, sister, you're the one who's been begging for a three-picture deal with MGM. You just *pretend* to hate it so you can bask in it a couple of seconds longer while they grovel."

Tony settled into his seat and listened to the hydraulic groans and whines of the jet as the pilot raised and lowered its flaps and other flight surfaces. "It sounds like the Tin Man doing calisthenics," he said.

As soon as they were aloft, Tony put on his stereo headphones and tuned to the classical channel, which was playing the waltz from Gounod's *Faust*. The throbbing of the engines became as faint as his heartbeat, until it seemed as though the plane was propelled by the music itself. Lulled by the vodka, he drifted into a half sleep, his head resting against the side of Val's unreclined seat. God, it felt great to get out of New York. The past two weeks had been hell.

Half an hour into the flight, Val shook Tony's left forearm.

"Tony, we have to talk," he said.

"About what?" Tony removed his headset. "Which taxidermist we'll use to mount Devlin's head?"

"No. About you and Avery."

"Nothing to talk about. It's history. Finished. *Finito,* as Dallas was so irritatingly fond of saying when he got back from *Roma.*"

When Tony put the headset back on, Val yanked the plug out of the armrest. It quivered in his hand like a snake about to strike. "You stupid little self-centered bitch. You *are* going to listen to what I have to say, even if I have to tie you up with your seat belt."

They both felt the attention of the entire first-class cabin focused on them. The man in 4-C stared, open-mouthed.

"I believe this is where I shake you and tell you to get a hold of yourself," Tony said.

"That won't be necessary," Val said, settling back into his seat. "Listen to what I've got to say if you want to. If you don't, read a fucking magazine or beat off into the air sickness bag. But do me the courtesy of not using the earphones, so I don't look like I'm talking to myself."

"Okay, if it means that much to you, I'll listen."

The plane was banking. They were turning left over Richmond, and bands of light spun through the cabin like spokes on a celestial wheel.

"Fine. Thank you." He paused to compose himself. "You know what a good man Avery is. Oh, he may not be as worldly as we are, but I actually think that's a plus. The heart of the matter is that he worships you—*worships* you—and he has from day one."

"Okay, I married an angel. So what else?" Tony toyed absently with the overhead light switch until Val slapped his hand.

"That leaves you—and Devlin. We will dispatch with Devlin first. He is an ill piece, a cur, a plague, a scourge, completely without merit, except for that hot little body and that crooked metronome I so love playing with. I should have listened to you long ago, which is precisely why you should listen to me now. Good or bad, none of us can see our loved ones clearly, but trust a friend to give you a dispassionate description of the man you love."

"I don't think I want to talk about this anymore."

"Why do you think I chose our little plane ride to bring this up? Nowhere to run. So shut up and listen, queen. Unlike Devlin, the only person you've hurt is yourself. Your own incredible neediness has undermined almost every attempt at happiness you have ever made. You scare off potential husbands with your intensity. You've got the dick of Don Juan and the emotional maturity of Gidget. Every time someone dumps you, you're devastated. Your career means nothing. Your friends mean nothing. You get drunk, you take drugs, you spend a *week* at the St. Mark's Baths . . ."

"I have *never* spent a week at the baths. A long weekend, maybe. Four days, on occasion. But *never* an entire week. I know that for a fact. Those damn cubicles are so small I couldn't get a week's worth of luggage *into* one."

"And then what happens? We have to fly you to Barbados for a week to dry out. That's two weeks, maybe three, you lose when some bruiser steps on your toes with his work boots. Do you know how much you lose in bookings over three weeks? To say nothing of momentum? And how many times does this happen in a year? Twice, at least, maybe three or four times."

"This isn't about money, Val, and besides, none of this has happened in a long time."

"You're right, it hasn't. And there's a lesson there. But I'm trying to show you how self-destructive you've been and could possibly be again. I don't think this whole Avery business has sunk in yet, and honey, I *know* I don't want to be around when it does. You'll make Hiroshima look like a convention of fireflies."

"So what? It's my life."

"My point exactly. It *is* your life. Your *life*. Honey, you have a reputation in this business that's held you back. Someone with your looks should have been crowned emperor of the New Holy Roman Empire by now. Instead, you're a modestly successful model . . ."

"I am not *modestly* successful!"

"If you're more than that it's because you're Tuxedo's favorite and were Dallas's before that. Just look at this past year. Without a doubt, it's the best year you've ever had. You signed three long-term, very lucrative contracts. And why? Because you were with Avery. You didn't drink yourself into a stupor or pull a Karen Ann Quinlan every couple of months. We didn't have to scrape you off the orgy room floor at Circle 9 come Sunday morning. I can't begin to tell you how happy I was that you were settling down and getting on with your life. And Tux finally knew his prayers to St. Jude were not in vain."

"So what am I supposed to do? Forgive Avery? Pretend this never happened?"

"Yes to the first, no to the second. Yes, by all means forgive him, because there's really nothing to forgive. He was a pawn, a victim of Devlin, just as we all have been at one time or another. And no, don't pretend it never happened. Talk about it. Reach some resolution. Then be done with it. Put it behind you. You're always talking about how some trick has the biggest this or the biggest that. The biggest arms, the biggest tits, the biggest dick. But when you finally find the man who's got the biggest *heart,* you toss him aside."

"I thought you didn't approve of Avery."

"I have to admit, I was skeptical at first. A legless ex-garbageman? Married, with two kids? *Puh-lease.* But over the past year, I've seen what kind of a man he is and how much he really loves you. It's left me praying that someday I would find a man as good as him."

"You want him? Fine. You took sloppy seconds on my previous ex-husband. No reason not to make it two in a row."

"If I thought there was a chance I could have Avery for myself, he'd have an ironclad divorce with sole custody of the boys, a handicapped-equipped Lamborghini, and a winter home in Key West by now. But I know he could never love me, or anybody, the way he loves you. *And,* I have never seen *you* as happy as you have been for the past year. Are you going to let Devlin take all of that away from you? That's letting him win, and the only thing he wants more than to have Avery for himself is for you *not* to have him."

"Fuck, no. I don't want that. But I haven't heard one concrete piece of evidence that Avery really deserves a second chance."

"You want 'evidence?' I'll give you evidence, you shit." Val self-consciously passed a pinky over his lower lip to get rid of some lip balm that had clumped up, deposited it on a napkin, and inhaled deeply. "Last week, Avery called and asked me to meet him at the Oak Bar. He told me everything. This whole mess started the first night we took you to De Milo's. Remember how obnoxious Devlin was being?"

"How would that be any different than any other night of our lives?"

"You know what I mean—telling stump jokes, making bad puns. He knows my sensibilities, and he knew it would sicken me. He was betting that I would leave and take you and your date with me. And he was right, of course."

"Unfortunately, the bastard usually is."

"The three of us had barely passed through those tacky beads at the door when Devlin was all over Avery, for whom he had fallen head over heels on sight. That's right—Devlin's in love. He sat down at Avery's table and introduced himself. At this point Avery didn't know *what* to do. He had been instantly smitten with you and wasn't much interested in Devlin. Oh, there *was* a connection, but it was pure fucklust."

"With Devlin, when isn't it?"

"Avery even asked who you were, but Devlin fed him some line about how you were the biggest fairy in the city and ran around in pink tights with holes cut in strategic places in case you wanted to work the T-rooms on the subway."

"That's pretty fucking rude."

"Hell, you got off easy. I'm surprised he didn't throw in mulatto teenage addicts and a German shepherd in a sling."

Tony raised his hand to signal to the flight attendant that he wanted another drink, but Val pulled his arm down and waved her away.

"Party's over, girl. You need to hear and remember everything I say. Plus, it's going to be one hell of a long day, and I don't want you passing out and leaving *all* of the work to me."

"If I'm even speaking to you when we land."

"Finally, Devlin put his charm to the acid test."

"He picked Avery up? That very night? That was a short infatuation."

"They apparently tore up a room at the Plaza, which Devlin uncharacteristically paid for. Avery said the sex was really good. No surprise there. It's what Dev does best, second only to breaking hearts. So Avery agreed to meet Dev again the next weekend. And who can blame him? The man is a wizard."

"The man is a *lizard!*"

"They kept this up for a couple of weekends, always prior to Devlin arriving *chez moi,* and the scene just kept on getting wilder. Avery said he fucked Devlin five times in one night and he was still begging for more!"

"Hold it. Stop right there. You are asking me to believe that Devlin DeSchuys, the man whose sphincter has but rarely kissed the head of any man's cock, got fucked by Avery not once but five times in a single night and was begging for more? Do you have any idea what this does to Avery's credibility?"

"It gets better. Pretty soon Devlin was groveling naked before Avery in his wheelchair, begging him to . . . well, no need to get into that, I suppose," Val said. "This goes on until you and Avery finally meet. After the first night with you, Avery didn't want to have anything more to do with Devlin. He said he felt cheap and dirty."

"Haven't we all?"

"He told Devlin he wanted out, but Dev wasn't having any of it. He told Avery about his relationship with you and said if you ever found out he was fucking around with Devlin, you'd dump him in an instant."

"Bull's-eye!"

"So Avery played along with Devlin for the past year, just to hang on to you. It was blackmail. Emotional, sexual blackmail."

"Then what finally made him come clean?"

"Astute question. Devlin got more and more obsessed with Avery. He started flying up in the middle of the week, just to see him. He canceled so many classes the dean of arts and sciences finally had a chat with him. Then Devlin told Avery he was the only man he had ever loved, the only man he ever *would* love, and that he wanted him all to himself. No more sleeping with you. This, of course, makes *me* feel like shit. I knew Devlin was most attracted to my money, but I thought he loved me a *little.*"

"I'm not going to . . ."

"So he gives Avery an ultimatum: break up with you or he'll let the cat out of the bag. Avery knew all along that there was absolutely no question about it—he wanted you. He knew it would be better if you heard it from him, and he agonized for weeks about how to tell you.

Finally, the emotion that got stirred up on your anniversary made him spill his guts."

"And the rest is history."

"Tony, Avery loves you. He never felt anything for Devlin but fear. You've got to give him a second chance. He's completely blameless. Everything reverts to Devlin, who, sadly, doesn't even know how to treat someone he actually loves."

"I don't know, Val. He waited a whole year. Why didn't he come to me sooner?"

"He was scared. He couldn't be sure what Devlin would do. Or how you would react. He was hoping maybe Devlin would lose interest or that some other solution would present itself. And he figured the longer you and he were together, the stronger your relationship would become and the less likely it would be that this whole mess would destroy it."

"I can't think about this now. I swore after Kevin that I was not going to let myself be hurt ever again, that if one more man screwed me . . ."

"Figuratively, of course."

"Oh, go fuck yourself! I promised myself if one more jerk fucked with me, I would just throw in the towel, forget the whole thing, become a goddamned *monk* if I had to."

" 'There are no tomorrows for this heart of mine.' "

"What?"

"Miss Karen Carpenter. 'Goodbye to Love.' "

"Oh, please."

"All I can say is that you picked a fine time to suddenly become discriminating. Avery is not responsible for what Devlin did. You can't make him the fall guy."

"I just don't want to get hurt again."

"What's wrong with that argument, *mon pauvre petit,* is that you *are* hurting—you just won't admit it. And *that* is a prescription for disaster."

As usual, Tony thought, what Val said made perfect sense. *The bitch!* If what he said were true, then Avery deserved another chance. Hell, if what he said were true, Tony should probably hire someone to kill Devlin. Val might even go halfsies on the hit man. Still, things would have been a whole lot less complicated if Val had kept his damn mouth shut. Tony had just about convinced himself that he would never fall in love again. Hell, he'd never even *look* at another man. It wasn't as far-fetched as it might seem. Initially, he had been stunned a year ago when

Tuxedo had forbidden him to have sex for sixty days, and the first couple of weeks had been hell. He had felt desperately alone, unwanted, unattractive. (Of course, it didn't help that he was still recovering from Kevin and detoxing from what had been perhaps the most debauched four days of his life.) But after that, after he had gotten over the hump (or getting humped), his outlook had changed. He felt positively liberated. It had been like adjusting to a new, rather severe diet regimen. For a while, he experienced cravings and found it difficult to understand why he had been forced to deny himself the one thing that gave him pleasure. But then after a couple of weeks, he actually felt better and could begin to see the wisdom of Tuxedo's restrictions. His sexual hunger pangs diminished. He felt better about himself than he had in years. He was more relaxed, less compulsive. He got more sleep. He didn't wonder what every guy on the street was thinking about him, whether they wanted to have sex with him. He was almost sorry when it ended.

This time, it would be *permanent,* or at least for six months to a year, which is about as permanent as many of his relationships had been. He didn't know exactly how he was going to do that. Maybe he could take injections to lower his sex drive. Or maybe he should invest heavily in porn. In the meantime, he'd really focus on his career and hope that would do the trick. Tux had already begun setting up a trip to L.A. to meet with movie producers and television executives. He was confident the spread in *People* would at the very least land Tony a guest spot on *Dallas* or *Knots Landing* next season, possibly even a recurring role. Tony would move to California and start fresh. He'd make Val come too and tell anyone who asked that they were a happily married couple. That would keep him out of trouble.

But now this, this . . . revelation. Of course, he'd have to forgive Avery—and pray that Avery could forgive *him.* That would be the easy part. What would be more difficult would be allowing himself to be vulnerable again, to fall in love with Avery all over again, this time knowing what he was getting himself into.

He barely spoke to Val for the remainder of the flight and was so preoccupied he got separated from him twice while changing planes in Atlanta. By the time they landed in Florida, he thought he was getting a migraine.

# 29

"GOD, NO MATTER HOW OFTEN I COME HERE, I always forget how rinky-dink this airport is," Val said, scanning the Daytona Beach terminal over his sunglasses. "I think they've got better facilities in the Yuca-tán."

"I know. It looks more like a bus station than an airport," Tony said. "Although when all I wanted was a one-way ticket out of South Beach, I thought of this place as the gateway to the Western world."

"I'll take care of the car, and I've got a call to make to Tropicana Towing. You find a Red Cap for the luggage. And while I know how difficult this will be for you, do not offer to take him to the men's room under any circumstances."

"Don't worry, I probably went to high school with most of them."

"Which, I presume, means you've already had them?"

"No, Vicious. As you will recall, I didn't become a slut until *after* I met you," Tony said, turning toward the baggage claim area.

"Oh, wait, here are our baggage claim tickets. Meet me at the Hertz counter."

"I'm going to pick up some Lifesavers and gum at the newsstand. Can I get you anything?"

"See if they have any self-help books for gay divorcées. And get a newspaper, too. I'm sure I'm going to want to get out and see a movie tonight. Something I missed in New York last year."

After a considerable delay, the luggage appeared on the frayed conveyor belt. Tony made sure everything was there and told the porter to meet him at the rental car desk. He walked across the terminal to the newsstand, his boots clicking authoritatively. His winter clothes were stuffy, and he could feel sweat trickling down the small of his back. Tony picked up copies of the Daytona Beach *News Journal* and the

Orlando *Sentinel*. There *had* to be a decent movie within fifty miles of Sugar Mill Beach. He tossed a roll of cherry Lifesavers and a pack of Dentyne onto the square of green rubber next to the cash register that looked like a miniature welcome mat.

"Will that be all, sir?" asked the cashier, a small, brown woman with a deeply creased, splotchy face.

"Yeah, that's it," Tony said. As she totaled his purchases, his eyes drifted to a stack of just-delivered tabloid newspapers next to the cash register. The string holding the papers together had been cut, but the vendor hadn't had time to place them in the rack yet. Tony scanned the headlines. "Husband serves wife at church BBQ," "Blessed Virgin sighted in Calcutta sewer," and "Topless Hunk is Bottomless, Too—Exclusive Photos Page 26." Tony reached for the top copy. Were they really going to print nude pictures of a man in the *Babbler*? Before he could flip to page twenty-six, the woman announced his total. He was embarrassed to be caught reading such trash but did want to see the purportedly bottomless hunk. He figured it would probably be some cheap trick—a statue, maybe.

"Go ahead and put this on there, too," he said, folding the paper beneath his left arm and reaching for his wallet. The cashier sighed as she rang up the additional item. He took his change and crossed the room to meet Val and the porter.

"Tony, what on earth are you doing with that journalistic offal?"

"There's a naked man inside."

"Why didn't you say so? Who is it, Burt Reynolds yet again?"

"I'm not sure. I'll let you know in the car."

Outside, the sun glittered off the rows of baking cars, and the heat hit Tony and Val in the face like a steaming barber's towel. The Red Cap followed them to a cream-colored Lincoln Continental sedan; Val always demanded a pastel-hued car in tropical climes. While the Red Cap stowed the luggage, Tony flipped to page twenty-six of the *Babbler*, a pastiche of heavily inked type and fuzzy pictures.

"Here it is. The headline reads 'Don't give this halved hunk Hush Puppies for the holidays.'" His eyes, scanning the page for the promised flesh, instead fell upon a photograph, blurry from over-enlargement, of what appeared to be a group of men beside a pool. One of them was in a wheelchair.

"Oh my God, Val. Look at this." Tony couldn't lift his eyes from the page. His left hand reached out blindly for Val's shoulder.

"Unless it shows actual, unsheathed dick, I'm not interested. Let's just get to the condo and out of these dreary winter clothes. Come on, get in."

"No, Val, I mean it. Look at this! There's a picture of Avery in here, *sans* legs, thank you very much, and they identify him as the S/X cologne model. And we're in the picture, too. Listen to this, 'The *Babbler* has learned that beefcake model Avery Mann, whose S/X cologne advertisements have led millions of young women to think he's twice the man than most, is actually a double amputee whose handicap makes him considerably less.' Damn!"

Val grabbed the paper from Tony, glanced at the picture, and shoved it back in his direction with disgust. Tony found his place and began reading again. "'The *Babbler* has received this authenticated photo from an anonymous source showing Mann poolside in Key West, Florida, earlier this year. According to our source, Mann lost his legs several years ago in a trash-truck tragedy. The significantly studly garbageman was hit by a car and tossed legs first into the business end of the truck's trash compactor. Just a few inches higher, we're told, and the raven-haired cologne pitch man would be a soprano. Mann was unavailable for comment.' It goes on, but what's the point. This will ruin him, professionally."

"I daresay it will have an adverse impact on his personal life, too. I don't know what's worse—the fact that they've told the world about his condition or the revelation that he was once a garbageman. You've *got* to get on the next plane to the city."

"You don't think he might do something stupid, do you?"

"He's lost the love of his life, his wife learns he's a highly paid fashion model—read *fag*—and his adoring public discovers he has no legs. You're a bright boy, Tony. *You* do the math."

"How could they have found out?"

"There is only one possible suspect—Devlin. We took that picture last February at a tea dance at Villa Testosterone, remember? I think it was my birthday. You and Avery were celebrating your two-month anniversary. We asked that cute bar back to make it a Kodak moment, and he almost fell into the pool while he was focusing my Leica. *This* was Devlin's trump card—the real reason Avery couldn't have come to you earlier. I'll bet Dev gave Avery a deadline to break up with you, and when he didn't hear from him, it was off to the *Babbler* with the evidence. He knew he wasn't going to get Avery for himself, so he set out to destroy him."

Tony slapped the hood of the Lincoln with the tabloid. "That little shit. He's even more twisted than I imagined. What are we going to do?"

"What *can* we do?" he said. "You're going home and beg Avery for forgiveness—whisk him away to some tropical love nest and worship him night and day. Meanwhile, I'll be kicking Devlin out of the condo as planned. And for good measure, I will also make a visit to the office of the president of Sanctuary College. As God is my witness, they won't renew his contract, even if I have to endow a new performing arts center."

They unloaded Tony's bags from the car and returned to the terminal. While Tony made the rounds of the ticketing agents, Val bought every copy of the *Babbler* at the newsstand, threw them into a trash receptacle, and poured a cup of vending machine coffee over them.

"I checked everybody," Tony said, "and we are shit out of luck. Nobody's flying any farther north than D.C., thanks to the storm. That queen at the gate in New York was right. The Delta agent I talked to said we *were* the last plane out of LaGuardia. An Eastern flight after us skidded right off the runway and they closed up shop."

"We've got to do something. Call him. Send him a telegram. But you have *got* to make contact with him."

They returned to the car and drove to the condo. At thirty-six stories, Sucre sur Mer was the tallest building between Jacksonville and Fort Lauderdale, but it was unremarkable for any other reason. It was a tower, plain and simple, with neither flute nor filigree to distinguish it from a child's sand castle molded in a milk carton. Still, it had sold out quickly, and a second, identical building was now under construction. They left the car with the valet and made arrangements with the concierge to have their bags sent up.

"Real estate," Val said to Tony in the elevator to the penthouse, "is the only time I like to be on top." Val turned right off the elevator and stopped before a door labeled P-3. He took out a single key attached to a gold, heart-shaped ring and unlocked the door with exaggerated care. "He just *hates* surprises," he whispered to Tony, and swung open the door silently.

An unexpectedly successful mixture of Polynesian furniture and expensive European antiques filled the condo, which also was full of oversized plants and beautifully filtered light. On a floral print sofa lay a stunning, if barely post-adolescent, boy, naked and uniformly brown from head to toe. Tony noticed he was nicely hung and uncut, which had always been a big turn-on for him. The boy, brow furrowed, lips moving, was reading a superhero comic book.

"Chicken," Val whispered to Tony. "How predictable."

"Yeah. Tasty but nonthreatening."

At the sound of their voices, the cherub tossed aside the comic book and jumped off the couch. "What the fuck? Where's Devlin?"

"Calm down, angel baby," Val said. "We're not here to hurt you."

"Right. Just to evict you."

"This place is paid for, so you *can't* evict us," the boy said.

Val turned to Tony and said, *sotto voce*, "Well, he apparently knows the score on the financial end, if nothing else."

"Just who the fuck do you think you are?"

Val took a few steps further into the living room, picked up a pair of black rayon shorts between his thumb and index finger as if they were tainted and tossed them to the boy. "We're anxious to get this over with. I suggest you put these on and go fetch your master." The boy blushed at having his nudity pointed out and stepped into the shorts, but it was clear they belonged to Devlin. They slipped down his hips until they were snagged by his cock like a clothes hook. "And you would be?"

"Monk."

"Monk? Monk! As in Thelonious Monk? Or Chipmunk?"

"Like monkey. It's a nickname."

"Indeed it is," Val said. "And a very apt one."

"It's a shame he's so cute," Tony said in a stage whisper.

"You still haven't told me who the fuck you are and what gives you the right to barge into our home."

Val slipped out of his coat and fluffed his hair in front of the gilt bamboo mirror, leaving Monk to dangle.

"Does the name Valentine Rittenhouse mean anything to you?" He turned to look at the boy, who said nothing. "Devlin's never mentioned someone by that name? No? Well, my hot monkey love, *I* own this abode you so facilely call home, and everything in it, right down to the Mr. Coffee and the solid gold finials on the ivory dildo collection. I am your lover's primary wife, so to speak, and you and I have a great deal in common. Devlin has been screwing us both, literally and figuratively, with *this* gentleman's true love. Got the picture?"

Monk looked confused. He shifted the shorts higher.

"You've lost him," Tony said. "Try again without so many thees and thous."

"We're fucked, honey. Both of us. Devlin needs me only for my money and you only for your . . . attributes! His heart belongs to another."

"What do you mean?"

"Oh Jesus, it's worse than I thought. Listen carefully, child. Read my lips if you must. Devlin has been cheating on me and on you with another man he actually claims to love. Fortunately, this third party had the good sense *not* to fall in love with him. Now, Monk, as delighted as I am to make your acquaintance, I'd advise you to take this opportunity to gather up your wits—or the half of them you possess—your clothes, if any, your comic book collection, and your toiletries, and *hit the FUCK-ING road!* I guarantee you will not want to be within five miles of ground zero when the proverbial shit hits the proverbial fan. And speaking of shit, just where *is* the so-called man of the house?"

"He's out exchanging some Christmas gifts at Dunstan's," the boy said, hiking up the shorts again.

"Typical. He's *never* satisfied with what he's got."

"He should be home soon."

"Home. There it is again. How charming to hear it coming from a little stray like you."

Tony thought he saw tears in Monk's eyes, and he touched Val's arm. "Maybe you shouldn't be so hard on him, Val. It's not his fault. And he's so young."

"And so endearingly stupid. But please mind your own business, Tony. He's just lucky I haven't sent him hurtling to his death from the balcony."

Monk disappeared into the master bedroom, closing and locking the door behind him. Val shouted, "I want to hear packing noises, Mr. Monkey—drawers slamming, hangers ringing. And please don't use the phone. Our need is significantly greater than your own."

"I've never seen this side of you before, Val," Tony said. "It becomes you."

"Mary, this was just shadow boxing. Stick around for the main event." Val stepped into the large, bright kitchen. "Go ahead and see if you can reach Avery. I'll make us some Bloodys, since it *is* after noon."

There was no answer at Avery's home. Tony hung up and tried again, to be sure he had dialed correctly. Still no answer. He tried again five minutes later with the same result.

"He's not picking up?" Val asked. "But it *is* ringing? Not off the hook?"

"Apparently not. I suppose I could just let it ring, but if they *are* there that would be pretty annoying."

As they sipped their cocktails, Val was calm enough to touch up his nails with an emery board. Tony felt as if he were in the waiting room of the dentist's office, dreading what was to come, yet anxious to get it over with. As he got up to freshen their drinks, the bedroom door opened and Monk emerged wearing a pair of purple, tie-dyed jams and an oversized, faded, aqua tank top. He carried a box that had once held a portable RCA color television and placed it near the door. He returned to the bedroom and brought out two Publix paper sacks stuffed with clothes and finally dragged out a surfboard that had seen better days.

"You surf?" Tony asked.

"No shit," Monk said, without looking at him.

"I only asked because I surf, too. Or used to. I was pretty good at it."

Monk said nothing but balanced the nose of the board against the wall.

"Tony, don't go soft on him because he's surf brethren. I need you in my corner. Besides, he's not interested. He obviously prefers the strong, stupid type."

Tony gave him a sour look, quickly followed by a guileless smile. Monk *was* hot. He was the kind of guy he had fantasized about having sex with when he was a teen surfer.

"Where will you go, Monk?" Tony asked. Val sniffed.

"I guess to my parents' house in Titusville, at least for now. I don't really get what all is happening, and I don't know what Devlin will do."

"Devlin will *do* nothing," Val said. "I am the one who will be doing the doing. So consider this good-bye. All sales final. No refunds, no returns, no exchanges. Now finish up in there."

Monk had been back in the master bedroom barely two minutes when the front door opened.

"Val! What a pleasant surprise. I wasn't expecting you this weekend," Devlin said. "And Lady Antonia as well. To what do I owe this honor?"

At the sound of Devlin's voice, Monk ran into the living room. "Dev! Dev! They say they own this place," he said. "They're trying to kick us out."

"You're certainly looking well," Devlin said to Val, ignoring Monk.

Val poured himself another drink from the pitcher. "I've made a batch of my patented Bloodys, if you'd care for one."

"A beer," Devlin said to Monk. The boy ran to the refrigerator, removed a can, and opened it.

"Well trained," Tony said.

"So you've met my houseboy?"

"Live in, I see," Tony said.

Devlin smiled. Tony, by Val's side, also poured himself another drink. Val motioned for Devlin to sit down on the sofa. Monk disappeared into the bedroom again, but left the door ajar.

"You may as well come clean, Devlin, Avery's spilled the beans," Val said. "And the gravy train has left the station."

Devlin's face was expressionless. It was as if his facial muscles had gone slack. "Spilled the beans? *Vis a vis?*" he managed to say, finally.

*"Vis a vis* my ass. Or more appropriately *your ass,* darling. He's told us everything. The night you met him after we left De Milo's. The assignations at The Plaza. Your twisted ideas about love and sex. The begging, whining, and groveling. Yes, he was quite specific about the groveling. Am I right, Tony?"

"Yes, quite. Unmistakable groveling."

"And finally, the threats, the sexual blackmail."

"Oh really? Then where *is* Mr. Purple Heart?"

"Excuse me?" Val said.

"You know, Mr. War Hero. Mr. 'I Left My Legs in My Lai.' Get it? 'Me Lie?' I thought for sure he would be the star witness for the prosecution."

"Devlin, is it too much to ask you to evince a little dignity, for once in your life? Do you have even the slightest idea of the pain you've caused Avery? And Tony?" Val said.

"Like I care about Tony. You still haven't told me why the legless one isn't among us. Wheelchair in the shop? Oh! Sorry, that just slipped out."

"I don't know why I'm surprised, Devlin, but I guess I thought that now that everything was out in the open, now that we've discovered Avery is the one person in your twisted fucking life for whom you actually feel something other than contempt, you'd drop the pretense of being disgusted by his condition."

"Old habits die hard, I suppose. So where is the little charmer?"

"If you must know, Devlin," Tony said, "if you'll lie awake tonight tossing and turning, I'll tell you. We broke up."

"Could you be more specific?"

"As to what?"

"As to, my dear, who broke up with whom? That's usually the way it works, isn't it? One partner dumps the other. That's the way it worked with you and me, wasn't it?"

"I broke up with him, Devlin. I was the one who walked away this time."

"You were the only one who *could* walk away! And am I to assume that you wouldn't take him back?"

Tony said nothing.

"Not even if he begged you on his hands and stumps?"

"You know, Devlin," Val said, "you really are the most pitiful excuse for a human being I have ever encountered. Here you are, your heart is broken—and don't tell me it's not, because beneath your stoic facade it's clear you are fucking hemorrhaging—and you're still making stump jokes about the only man you ever really loved. It's clear to all of us you *do* love Avery—or at the very least you're obsessed with him, which may be as close as you'll ever get to knowing true love. You're probably even thinking that when all this blows over, you'll still have a chance to get him for yourself. Well, I am so very pleased to be the one to tell you that Avery hates you. He fucking despises you! He slept with you out of fear—not love, not even out of lust, however hard you may have tried to delude yourself. He loves Tony, and he would do anything to keep you quiet. What you did to him is the moral equivalent of rape. And the sad thing is, you will never know who Avery Mann really is. You will never know his tenderness, his capacity to love. You claim to love him, yet you haven't the slightest idea who he is, how strong he is, how brave. Despite your exclamations of love, he is nothing more to you than a piece of meat that somehow, God knows why, tasted so good you couldn't let go.

"And let me tell you one more thing. You are never going to have Avery for yourself. *Never.* If it is the last thing I do on this earth, I am going to get Tony and Avery back together, because they're good for each other and they belong together. You've hurt four people here, Devlin, and I'm going to do my best to fix the two who are hurting the most. You must know I stopped caring about you the moment I learned of your treachery. And believe me, I'm less hurt than I am angry for not listening to what Tony said about you years ago. Thinking of the time I have wasted on you sickens me."

"Was it something I said?" Devlin asked.

"I'm glad you think this is funny, Dev, because life as you know it is going to change very rapidly and very dramatically. To wit: you have forty-eight hours—beginning *now*—to get out of this place. I'd advise you to mind the deadline. And since it's a holiday weekend, I'd advise you to make your reservation with Hertz as soon as possible."

"You're taking back the car? You gave that to me. It's registered in my name."

Val sighed, stood up, and went to the kitchen for ice. "The Porsche," he said over his shoulder as he filled his glass, "is already gone. The seat was probably still warm when my friends from Tropicana Towing removed it from the garage as soon as you parked it. I called them from the airport and they staked the place out. Yes, it is in your name, but I have all the paperwork from the purchase and the registration, *and* I have the car. With the legal counsel of Rittenhouse Inc. behind me, I can have that car registered in my name in three states and the principality of Liechtenstein in the time it would take you to write down the vehicle identification number."

"Greed is so unbecoming of you, Val."

"Greed has nothing to do with it, Devlin. I would rather see that car compacted into a hunk of scrap the size of a refrigerator than to let you continue to enjoy it. I may, in fact, do just that, as the thought gives me unexpected pleasure. I don't give a shit about the money. I don't think you've ever really grasped that. All I care about now is seeing you unhappy, uncomfortable, inconvenienced, and adrift. Should you ever come back to New York and attempt to get any job other than, perhaps, towel maven at the Ninety-second Street Y, you will find doors closing in your face harder and faster than if you were a Jehovah's Witness peddling tracts at the St. Mark's Baths on a Saturday night."

"I still have my job at the college."

"I wouldn't be too sure of that, my pretty."

"You can't do *that*. You can't have them fire me."

"You still don't understand, do you? *I* can do any fucking thing I want. If I have to *buy* the damn school just to be able to fire you, I can. Trust me, I can. And I will. Though I doubt *that* will be necessary. A new arts center will probably suffice."

Devlin said nothing, but it was clear he was shaken. Tony could almost see the gears turning, and for the first time, slipping. He had never seen Devlin look so blank, so helpless. Monk emerged from the bedroom and sat down on the sofa next to him.

"I guess I still have my little monkey, don't I? I can live with that." He hugged Monk with one arm.

"Yes, I'm sure you can. And I am equally sure the little monkey boy will *love* living with you in some seedy transient motel in Cape Canaveral. Forty-eight hours then, my little lovebirds, until you fly the coop. Tony and I will be staying in the guest suite, so try not to fuck too loudly, will you? Have that much decorum."

Val walked into the larger of the two guest bedrooms and flopped dramatically onto the bed. Tony followed and shut the door.

"Did you notice that he never once said he was sorry, never even tried to deny or explain or make excuses?" Val asked. "It was never about me; it was never about Avery. The only thing he thought about was his own tired ass. All he wanted to do was to see what he could salvage. His car—I really do intend to have it compacted, now that I thought of it. Remind me to call Tropicana Towing after my nap and have them make the arrangements. I'll ask them to put it in his parking spot with a geranium on top . . . or a big, white, funeral lily. He will shit. He will absolutely shit!"

Val stretched out on the bed and kicked off his shoes.

"That felt good, you know. Really good. I've never been so angry in my life, but I carried it off, didn't I?"

"A soliloquy worthy of Miss Joan Crawford in her pre-Technicolor days."

"No self-pity?"

"Not a drop, Val. It was quite remarkable."

Tony continued to dial Avery's number every few minutes, pacing between tries. Within minutes, Val had fallen asleep. From the living room, Tony heard Devlin and Monk talking, sometimes in voices just above a whisper, sometimes with Devlin's voice rising in misdirected acrimony toward the boy. But after a while, things quieted down, and Tony heard the master bedroom door close. They were probably screwing. That was Devlin's answer to everything.

He put down the phone and decided to take a shower. He felt absolutely nasty from the trip. While he conditioned his hair, he ran the water as cold as he could stand it and adjusted the massaging shower head so the spray felt like hundreds of straight pins piercing his flesh. It was the only way to keep himself awake. After he dressed, he woke Val.

"Hey, Sleeping Beauty, your chariot awaits. That is, if you still want to go down to shantytown with me."

"What? Go where?" Val rubbed his eyes. "You smell good."

"Always a kind word. I thought we'd go to South Beach and check out my house. Who knows what we'll want to do tomorrow. I feel a major bender coming on, now that the dirty work is out of the way."

Val sat up.

"Uh! The heat really got to me. And those cocktails. Did you get through to Ave?"

"No. And I'm beginning to get worried."

Tony returned to the phone while Val cleaned up, but there was still no answer. Suddenly he thought about calling Tuxedo and got through after three tries.

"So, any news?" Val asked as he emerged from the bathroom thirty minutes later, gently towel-drying his hair.

"I finally decided to call Tuxedo . . ."

"Christ, why didn't I think of that?"

"He had good news and bad news. The bad news is that Tuxedo hasn't been able to get Avery on the phone, either, and the city is virtually paralyzed from the blizzard. It's impossible for him to get to Brooklyn to find out what's going on."

"I doubt Tux even knows where Brooklyn is," Val said. "And the good news?"

"The phone at Tux's answering service has been ringing off the hook with requests for interviews and offers of modeling jobs for Avery. People are outraged about the *Babbler* piece and want to hire Avery. Some of them even want him to pose *in* his wheelchair. And the Disabled American Vets want him to be their national spokesman. He's got enough work to keep him busy for a year, but Tux won't let him take it."

"Why not? He'll need it for the forthcoming divorce. I'm sure Brandi became a clawing bitch the instant she smelled money."

"Tux doesn't want him to become identified as a disabled model. He says it'll pigeonhole him, and after the novelty wears off, he won't be able to find work. Instead, Parker's going to offer him an exclusive three-year contract."

Val finished dressing and asked Tony to drive, since they were headed into the *terra incognita* of South Beach.

"It's impossible to get lost on the island, Val," Tony said as he eased the Continental into light southbound traffic. "There's one road in and one road out."

The residential sections of Sugar Mill Beach south of Edensgate had not changed dramatically since Tony had last been there, but as soon as they reached the unincorporated limits of South Beach, an entirely new landscape emerged. The estuary had been dredged and was now spanned by a four-lane viaduct. Instead of taking a hard left, the main road continued straight ahead, gleaming silvery white. Tony slowed and took the left anyway and shortly afterward a right onto the now little-used Old Beach Road, partially covered by drifting sand. A sign about a quarter of a mile in warned that the road would be closed and demolished early the next year. Access to the monolithic condominiums that lined the beach like giant gravestones would be only through feeder roads off the extension of A-1-A.

"Christ, this looks like Daytona now. Worse," Tony said, cruising slowly past piles of brick, limestone, and granite on the eastern boundary of the road. "It's a moonscape."

"Darling, don't hemorrhage," Val said. "Surely it can be no worse than what was here before."

"We should be getting close by now, but I don't recognize a damn thing. Wait, I think I see it, up ahead. Jesus, there ain't much left of it."

"Tony, darling. *Mr.* Anthony Alexander, *sir.* You have been on Florida soil for less than six hours and you are beginning to slip into *dialect* already. Didn't the late Mr. Dallas Eden spend a fortune playing Rex Harrison to your Audrey Hepburn so you could speak the Queen's English?"

"No, that was so I could speak English to *queens.*" Tony suddenly stopped the car in front of a large sign advertising a condominium development. "Here we are. Jesus! 'Villa Adriana . . . four hundred luxury condominiums, Opening Spring 1981.' Doesn't that amaze you? Eight hundred people will be living on land once occupied by my mom and pop and myself. That's more people than ever lived on the entire island. Pop must have really cleaned up."

"If he were smart. And sober. Conditions you have led me to believe were rare," Val said. He stepped out of the car, took in the vista before him, and gave a low whistle. "Oh, Tony, you poor child. Now I see why you're so fucked up: you grew up in a ghetto."

"It didn't always look this bad, you snot. There used to be a couple flower beds around here, at least while my mother was alive."

They walked toward the station, their glove-soft leather shoes squinching in the hot sand. The gas pumps were already gone, and a deep, ragged hole was all that remained of the underground storage tanks. The corrugated tin overhang had been crumpled like a piece of aluminum foil and the big plate-glass office window had cracked and was taped to prevent it from shattering. Inside the office, the old cash register was open and up-ended on the grimy green-and-white tile floor. Like the mysteriously vanished crew of a derelict ship, Demetrios had simply walked out and left everything behind—maps, telephone books, fan belts and water hoses, an air filter, and a decrepit black telephone that was so old the cord between the body and the handset was made out of some kind of frayed fabric instead of plastic.

"Tony, this phone is very *Maltese Falcon*. I must have it."

"Sure, take it."

"I'll have it gold plated and put into my bedroom. God, it weighs a ton!"

"He didn't take *anything*."

"What's to take? He had a collection of vintage motor oils? Hubcaps, maybe? Hood ornaments?"

"Come on, let's check out the house."

"By all means! Who knows what treasures await us there? A Victrola? A stuffed alligator? A *live* alligator!"

"Very funny, Val. Years from now, when the National Register of Historic Places calls you to help them rebuild the childhood home of Hollywood legend Anthony Alexander, I want you to remember these details just as they are today."

"The National Register of *Hysterical* Places, maybe."

They walked out of the office and made their way up the overgrown path to the house. Behind the station were the cannibalized hulks of three Studebakers and Tony's Econoline van. A large sign, black letters against a neon orange background, announced that the house was CON-DEMNED.

"This is embarrassing, Val. Perhaps bringing you along wasn't such a good idea. The dish you'll have on me."

"Don't worry about me, darling. I have more respect for you with every step I take."

The house was filled with damp, sour, unexpected smells, as sudden, startling, and acrid as smoke. Tony traced each one of them to its source—a mildewed rug, a damp horsehair couch, a stagnant pool of water in the Florida room.

Val screamed from the kitchen. *"Eeeek!* I mean Eureeeeka! I've found the fabled burial ground of the noble German cockroach! They come to Tony's tropical hideaway to die."

"So they're dead?"

"Oh, quite dead."

"Then what are you screaming for? Come on, come see my room."

Val followed the sound of Tony's voice to his small bedroom.

"Couldn't afford a mattress pad, I see. My, you were a lusty young man."

"Hey, here are my old surfing magazines. This was about as close to porn as I got as a kid. And look at this old *Life* magazine from the week after the Kennedy assassination. See this stain here on his head, this magenta-looking thing? I never knew where it came from and always thought it was some sort of religious symbol, stigmata I think it's called, and that I had been singled out somehow to receive some kind of message from god or JFK."

"And this was *before* your first encounter with psychotropic drugs?"

"I was twelve."

"So are you saving it or what? As much as I don't wish to appear bored by your squalid childhood home, I must tell you I have never been one for rummage sales or secondhand shops."

"Okay, okay. Let's see." Tony glanced around the room, opened closet doors, pulled out dresser drawers.

"I want to take these. Don't look. They're kitsch, but they belonged to my mother. I hid them here so my father wouldn't break them in one of his fits."

"Hummel figurines? And all little boys, I see. Oh, Tony. I'd hate to see what your life would have been like if Dallas Eden hadn't needed gas on that fateful day. You'd be sitting in the living room, toothless, swilling Brand X beer from a longneck and watching reruns of *The Gong Show*."

"Well, you're right about the toothless part. I would have ground them all down out of frustration." Tony threw the surfing magazines on the floor. He wrapped the four figurines in T-shirts he had pulled from a dresser and placed them in a pillowcase and put the *Life* magazine under his arm. "Okay, that's all I'm taking. They can bulldoze the rest."

# 30

A NEW BAR, THE CAROUSEL, had opened in Sugar Mill Beach to accommodate the increasing numbers of gay college students who wanted to combine spring break on Brevard and Volusia county beaches with visits to Walt Disney World, a little more than an hour inland. Located on the second and third floors of a singularly undistinguished building on Tropicana Boulevard that had once been a USO club and later a Fred Astaire dance studio, the Carousel was designed to be inconspicuous. Painted the color of sand, the building most closely resembled an abandoned warehouse, and no flashing sign or tasteful canopied entrance alerted passersby to the presence of the largest gay bar between Jacksonville and Fort Lauderdale.

That night, while Tony blew joints on the balcony, Val suggested a visit to the Carousel, if only to get out of the condo.

"How do people live in these cracker boxes?" Val asked, leaning out the sliding glass door. "I've got to get out of here. Come on girl, throw on some bar drag and come with me. The Carousel is no Agence Seize-Neuf, but with enough booze and the appropriate supplicants it can be mildly diverting, and I can promise you plenty of both."

"Surprisingly, I'm not interested in either," Tony said, finishing the joint and flicking the roach off the balcony. "I'm too worried about Avery."

In the weeks since he and Avery had parted company, Tony had found himself uncharacteristically listless in the libido department. Even the kind of anonymous sex that was readily available to him on a daily basis had lost its appeal. Under the current circumstances, he *certainly* wasn't interested in tricking. In addition, he worried that if he went out in what essentially was his hometown, he might run into unwelcome reminders of his past, chief among them Connecticut Jones, the prospect of which left him feeling ambivalent at best.

"I'm sure Tux will call as soon as he finds out what's going on. Besides, for all we know the blizzard has knocked out the telephone lines in Brooklyn and Avery's phone isn't actually even ringing."

"I should know better than to resist. Besides, it might be a hoot to pass out fashion citations. I guarantee they would all be felonies."

"That's the spirit!"

He went inside, showered, and dressed in the scruffiest jeans he'd brought and a plain white Jockey T-shirt. Within an hour they had parked the Lincoln on Tropicana, a block south of the bar. As they approached the entrance, Val pointed out the heavily barred and shuttered second- and third-floor windows.

"The shutters were installed a couple of months ago, after a bunch of South Beach boys threw rocks through the windows," he said. "The cops caught them at the Krystal, but all they got was the equivalent of a jaywalking citation because it was 'just' a gay bar. Devlin said it got pretty scary. For weeks afterward, until the novelty wore off, these guys and their ilk would cruise Tropicana in their pickup trucks and hurl bricks and bottles at the queens going in. The bar hired a rent-a-cop and warned everyone not to walk to their cars alone. Dev and I actually started taking cabs so we could get out right at the door. Of course, the police never really did a thing. The harassment has tapered off of late, but there's no telling what those Neanderthals will do next."

"I wouldn't worry. The only thing shorter than a Southie's attention span is his dick," Tony said. "They've probably already forgotten where this place is."

Val opened a door in which plywood had replaced the full-length pane shattered by vandals. Inside, stray nuggets of broken glass glittered in the corners and crunched underfoot. The interior was garishly lighted and painted an aggressively offensive hue best described as Campbell's Cream of Lima Bean. To the right, a newly framed-in doorway offered a view of lumber and Sheetrock, sawhorses, rolls of insulation, cans of paint and thinner, and barrels full of excelsior cradling ornate light fixtures. Strips of tape stretched diagonally from the corners of the doorframe created a largely symbolic barrier to would-be intruders.

"The bar owners were building a restaurant in there, but I've heard they've put it on the back burner until things quiet down," Val said. "Isn't that the way of the world? The queens try to do a little urban renewal, and the rednecks shit on it."

A narrow stairway with worn rubber treads ascended to a mid-flight landing, then zigged back up another half-flight. When they reached the second floor, Val tapped another unpainted piece of plywood the size and shape of a door, which reverberated with a muffled disco bass line. "The dance bar is in there. They used to have someone taking cover charges here as well as the next flight up, but they got greedy and closed this one so they wouldn't have to pay two doormen."

"This place *does* get better, doesn't it? I feel like I'm touring the Bates Motel," Tony said.

"Trust me," Val said, beginning to climb the third half-flight of stairs. "You know how small-town gay bars are—they always look better inside than they do on the street."

"Unfortunately, so do most of the patrons."

The cover charge was two dollars, and Val paid for both Tony and himself with a ten and told the doorman, a boy barely old enough to drink legally himself, to keep the change. The kid gushed his appreciation and gave each of them an extra chit redeemable for a well drink.

"Two dollars?" Tony said as Val opened the door, letting music and smoke escape from the dark interior. "No wonder they had to let the other guy go. At that rate, it's hard to believe he was earning his keep."

"Well, girl, prepare for The Effect."

"Right," Tony said, tousling his hair. "Check faces."

"Faces on stun."

The Effect was a phenomenon Tony and Val encountered each time they entered a gay bar outside New York. Best characterized as a temporary decibel modulation of varying intensity, The Effect occurred as mouths dropped and conversation stopped when they first entered a room. It was followed by exclamations, fey screams, and, in Southern venues, the sudden desire to possess white gloves and a fan. The Effect varied in intensity based on the size of the city and its distance from New York. They pushed through the door. In the center of the huge main room, a carousel's stationary seats, ornately carved with swans and rose-choked cherubs, were arranged around a circular bar, which was topped by a red-striped canvas awning stitched with tiny flashing lights.

"So? What do you think?" Val asked.

"I'm stunned!" Tony said. "It's so . . . so . . . *overstated!*"

"Yes, isn't it though? Dev told me they got the decor from some defunct circus theme park in Winter Haven. Stay here, I'll get us something to drink." Val let the four red chits flutter to the floor and made his way to the bar. When he returned, they made their way across the cavernous room to a narrow hallway, fifteen feet long, its walls papered with circus posters. Val turned to Tony. "When this place gets cooking, it takes twenty minutes to get from the main bar to the show bar or the dance bar downstairs. That's why it was so stupid of them to close that dance bar entrance. I'd advise you to decide where you want to spend the bulk of the evening and stake a claim."

They reached the other side and entered a room filled with small round tables, most of them already occupied. The exposed brick walls were bereft of ornamentation, other than that surrounding the wall-to-wall stage, above which hung the inscription "Cabaret Carousel." The proscenium was decorated with cherubs and rosettes, gold ribbons, and baby bluebirds. A faded rose velvet curtain, fringed with gold tassels, bore the name of the Strand Theater, a former Tropicana Boulevard landmark that was demolished to make way for an upscale mini-mall. At the far right side of the stage, a placard announced a musical revue, "Dragstravaganza—An Operetta for Four Drag Queens and Soloist," starring drags *de la maison* Apricot Nectar, Angel Divine, Diet Patty, Heather Honey, and Tiffany Twisted. The emcee was the queen bee of East Central Florida drag, Desdemona Jones.

"I do so hate drag," Tony said. "And they take it so seriously down here!"

"Did I tell you Devlin choreographed this show?"

"You're kidding!"

"He's got *such* a promising future."

"Then by all means we must see the midnight show!" Tony said. "In the meantime, show me the rest of the dump."

A staircase led down to a room the same size as the drag bar but with a less spacious feel, since the ceiling was considerably lower. The carousel theme had been carried through, with the disc jockey's booth camouflaged behind the ornate hand-carved-and-painted screens that once hid the carousel's machinery from view. Another striped canvas canopy hung over the dance floor, shallower than the one upstairs, and a standard-issue mirrored disco ball was suspended from its peak. In the D.J. booth, the light man worked hallucinatory wonders, strobing to the beat of the music, giving the impression of motion, and creating artificial lightning and rain.

A familiar song came into the mix, and the dance floor got more lively, with people shrieking and making jungle bird calls.

"Shall we dance?" Val asked.

"Nah, this song was passé months ago. That's what I find most annoying about the queens in small towns—not merely that their music is so out of date, but that they still squeal when the disc jockey plays it. I can almost tolerate their lapses in musical taste. It's their enthusiasm I can't stand."

"How very New York of you, Tony."

"Hey, somebody's got to have standards. Let's go back upstairs to the cruise bar. We might still be able to get a good seat for the flesh parade."

"So you're interested in sex again?"

"Who knows? Besides, what else is there to do in this dump?"

Upstairs, they secured the last available booth along a mirrored wall. Val caught the attention of a waiter and ordered a second round of scotches for both of them, tipping him enough to ensure that thereafter even the most inadvertent twitch of his right hand would result in another round appearing at their table instantly. As Val's swizzle sticks accumulated, Tony wished he had agreed to dance with him, if only to keep him distracted.

"I've never seen you put away *anything* like this before, Val—scotch, coke, cock," Tony said. "Where's your renowned Rittenhouse restraint?"

"You're the last one to be lecturing about restraint, love. In your case, *restraints* would be more like it."

"I just don't want to have to nurse you through a hangover tomorrow. I've already had way too much fun for one trip."

"As if I haven't been your personal Florence Nightingale on any number of occasions," Val said, splashing some of his drink onto the table as he gestured.

"That's not what I meant, Val. I just don't want *you* to suffer through being sick. You have such a low tolerance for discomfort. And you've got enough to deal with."

"It's all *been* dealt with, darling. You were there, were you not, when the ax fell. This is a *celebration,* not a wake."

Tony could not believe what happened next. Devlin and Monk were making their way across the room toward their table, the boy clinging to his lover so tightly it would be difficult to run a string of floss between their torsos.

"Flaming asshole at twelve o'clock high," Tony said.

"Mind if we join you?" Devlin asked Val.

"What the hell do you think you're doing?" Tony said. "Shouldn't you be home packing?"

"Shouldn't *you* be cleaning out the gutters of Manhattan with your tongue? That *is* what you do when you're without a man for more than a couple of days, isn't it?"

"Fuck you."

"Boys, boys, please. I am so weary of your bickering," Val said. "Tony, let them sit down. There's no harm in having a friendly little drink together. We're all adults."

"Well, three out of four . . ." Tony said. He sighed and started to move over to Val's side of the booth, but Devlin shoved Monk into Tony's path and sat down next to Val himself.

"How cozy," Tony said, seething. He knew what was going on. Devlin was going to do his best to get Val to take him back. It would be hard but not impossible. Beneath Val's embittered resolve, Tony saw loneliness, vulnerability, and yes, a lingering affection for Devlin. To say nothing of lust. Devlin, having been without doubt Val's butchest and most sexually experienced lover, had probably awakened and satisfied yearnings in him that would be difficult to gratify elsewhere, given the refined circles in which he traveled. The mere fact that Val was here, in Florida, proved that he was still vulnerable to Devlin. If he had truly wanted to have nothing further to do with him, he would have sent some minion to Sugar Mill Beach to evict him and seize the Porsche. It was Tony's realization of this that had, the night before, made him agree to accompany Val. He wanted to provide as much support as possible for the Forces of Good. But with Val as drunk as he was, he just might acquiesce to Devlin's omnipotent sexual heat. And in the morning, waking up next to him, it would be easy to decide to give him another chance.

"Why don't the two of you run along to the dance floor," Devlin said, dismissing Tony and Monk with a wave of his hand. "Val and I have some things to take care of."

They both objected, but Val, rolling his eyes at Tony, shooed them away.

"Go on, go. I'll be okay. Dance. Have fun."

"Oh, and Tony?" Devlin said. "I've asked the bar backs to pick up all the little wadded-up telephone numbers off the floor and give them to me after the bar closes. I'll let you know how many of them are yours."

Tony practically shoved Monk out of the booth and stood up.

"I ain't dancin' with you," Monk said. "Dev said you were the sickest faggot in New York City and had done things that would turn my stomach."

"He should know, he taught me *all* of them."

Once they were away from the booth, Tony grabbed Monk by the crook of his left arm. Monk pulled free with exaggerated violence and glared at him.

"Look, Monk, Devlin's a moron and a gigolo. He doesn't care if you live or die. You're a good kid. Young, handsome, nice build. In other circumstances, you and I could probably be friends. Just some advice from me: you could do a lot better than Devlin. A whole lot better."

"Like you, I suppose?"

"To be honest, I wouldn't mind, but that's not what this is about. Hard as it may be for you to believe, my intentions are completely honorable. The best thing for you to do is to get out of here, now. Go home. Not to the condo—to your mom and dad. Forget about Devlin, because tomorrow he won't even call you before he leaves for the airport to fly back to New York with Val."

"That ain't true. He don't want that rich pussyboy. He told me he was just going to try and get the car back."

"He won't stop there. I guarantee it, because there is a lot more there to be gotten. You have *no* idea."

"You're just jealous 'cause I have him and you don't. I know you want him."

"You couldn't be more wrong. And the truth is, you *don't* have him—and never will."

"Yeah, well fuck you, you stupid cocksucker. Just stay out of my business."

Monk turned away and headed for the bar. Tony watched him disappear into the crowd. He hated that the kid despised him. He sort of liked the little fucker. Cute. Feisty. Plus, he surfed. But he could only imagine the poisonous filth Devlin had fed him. He felt sorry for the little bastard, too, because it was painfully clear how much he loved Devlin. A young kid like him was going to be hurting something awful if Val agreed to a reconciliation, which seemed more likely each minute he was exposed to Devlin's toxic charms. Even after all this time, Tony was at a loss to know what it was about Devlin that engendered such fierce love and loyalty, and despite what he had told Monk, he would be a liar if he didn't admit he still felt *something* for the man. It must be the sex, the intense, transcendental sex. He had come to realize that Devlin didn't have much of a personality out of bed, so it *had* to be some animal thing.

He got another drink and stationed himself near the passage to the drag and dance bars, so there would be a continuous flow of men passing by. Not one in the bunch appealed to him, and after fifteen minutes he moved to a darker, less-traveled area and simply leaned against a wall.

Soon, Tony saw a boy out of the corner of his eye and paid attention to him largely because he appeared to be so avidly interested himself. He was a twink, plain and simple, and Tony would not have given him a second glance in New York, but suddenly the thought of getting his rocks off appealed to him. His encounter with Monk had unexpectedly aroused him, and this boy seemed a harmless enough avenue of release. He was pretty in a fragile and probably fleeting way, and his lavender Izod set off his tan, which was a golden toast color with crimson highlights. His teeth and the slender gold chains around his neck glittered with equal brilliance. Tony kept him in his field of vision, off and on, for about fifteen minutes, but while the kid was certainly all eyes, he stayed rooted to his chair. He was seated at a table of overweight men in their forties and fifties, who were either pathetically pale or critically sunburned, and Tony ultimately guessed that nothing was going to happen. One of the older guys was acting very possessive, frequently pulling the kid toward him in a one-armed hug, which the brat squirmed out of after a polite interval. Tony shrugged and moved on. Some time later, the boy approached him near the men's room.

"You're probably the best-looking guy in here tonight," the kid said, nervously turning his gaze from Tony to the main room and back again. "Hell, you'd be the best-looking guy in here any night."

"I'm charmed." He knew his instincts about the kid's May–December romance were on target, and he wasn't in the mood to waste time listening to a lot of lies and posturing.

"As much as I'd like to, I don't think I'll be able to be with you tonight." The kid's eyes were gorgeous, the same hue of his polo shirt. Tinted contact lenses, more than likely.

"Color me crushed."

"No, really. I'm with somebody else tonight. My . . . old man, you know. I told him I was going to the john."

"I'm happy for you." Tony knew he could wreck their happy home with a minimum of effort—the kid was practically rabid—but why bother? He'd be leaving tomorrow and he didn't want to put the boy out on the street for no reason.

"Don't take it the wrong way," the kid said, sensing the edge in Tony's voice.

"I'm not taking it one way or the other."

"I thought maybe I could get your phone number."

"Not likely."

"But you *were* cruising me, weren't you. I mean, I saw you looking."

"I suppose, in passing," Tony said as coolly as possible. He forced a smile that flashed on and off like a neon sign for a cheap motel: SEA VUE ... VACANCY. He could not have cared less about the kid—really, he *was* just a twinkie—but he wondered what it was about his own look, his aura, that made the pretty boy feel the situation demanded some explanation. He made a mental note to turn down the voltage on his cruiseometer.

"Look, I gotta go." The boy smiled, hesitated a long while, turned, and disappeared into the crowd.

Tony simply looked away. He was irritated, nothing more. And he had other things on his mind. He drained his glass and plotted a course for the bar. Fresh drink in hand, he headed back to Val's booth, but pulled up short a few feet away. A waiter was opening a bottle of champagne while Val locked lips with a now-shirtless Devlin. Tony flushed, with what, anger? Desire? Jealousy?

"How fucking cheap!" Tony said, loud enough for both of them to hear, but neither responded. He'd never seen Val lose his restraint to such an extent in public, but then he'd never seen him this drunk in public *or* private. Miss Thing would see tomorrow that money and breeding were no amulets against puking his brains out through his nose. Fine, let *Devlin* hold his head above the toilet. Tony turned and walked away, his mind suddenly occupied with the ramifications of this new reality. He'd either have to find a trick or a hotel room that night, because he wasn't going to sleep at "Sac du Merde" with the Dynamic Duo banging away in the next room. He thought about having a bartender call him a cab and leaving. It would give him time to collect his things and get out of the condo before Val and Devlin showed up. If the current intensity of their ardor was any indication, that wouldn't be long. They were probably already on the verge of being thrown out—unless Val had already bought the place.

Then Tony intercepted a cruise from a beach bum type halfway across the room. When their eyes locked, the kid immediately brought his thumb and forefinger up to his mouth and sucked in. He tossed his head in the direction of the door.

*What the hell,* Tony thought. *It can't hurt to smoke a joint with him.* He smiled, nodded, and set down his glass. When he caught up with the boy, he wasn't disappointed. Although his sun-bleached, chestnut hair was cut in a fashionable shag, his integrity was saved by the fact that it was not rigorously groomed. He was wearing ragged jams and a black Ron Jon tank top—torn downward from the neckline to reveal a full, smooth chest—under a loose, faded, floral print shirt, unbuttoned, that he had probably gotten at a thrift store. A necklace of small white shells clung so tightly to his neck that it undulated when he swallowed. Tony found it curiously arousing. The kid had a couple days' growth of beard, and Tony intuitively knew it was the type that would feel soft and fuzzy, not scratchy. They didn't talk, but the boy smiled and took Tony's right arm and guided him to the door. Tony winced at the sudden brightness of the staircase but was glad to see that the kid held his own without the cosmetic assistance of bar lighting. They waited until they were down the stairs and on the street to introduce themselves.

"My name's Kip," the boy said, offering his hand. He bounced semi-urgently as he walked. "You are one hot man—obviously not from around here."

The cool night air was a welcome relief from the smoky interior of the bar.

"I'm Tony, and you're pretty wonderful yourself." He winced. He didn't want to lead the kid on, but it just sort of came out.

Kip blushed and fell self-consciously silent. He led them around the corner and down half a block to a one-way street jammed with parked cars. He suddenly turned right into an alley and came to a stop in a slightly recessed doorway. Music and sporadic applause drifted on the night air.

"That's the bar, right up there," Kip said, pointing with the joint he was about to light. When the match flared, Tony noticed a nice little dimple in Kip's left cheek at about the place his smile ended. Kip took a hit and handed Tony the joint. "So. Where you from and how long you here for, guy?" The words squeaked out as he gradually exhaled, until *guy* was almost a falsetto.

"New York. And just a couple of days," Tony said before he toked. He was relieved that Kip hadn't recognized him from his modeling work. Maybe he didn't own a TV or read magazines. "Gotta be back in the city for New Year's Eve."

"Figures. Someone as amazing as you would have to be from New York."

Kip turned the joint around and offered Tony a shotgun. When they

were through, Kip pressed his lips against Tony's. Instinctively, Tony responded, enjoying the roughness of Kip's lips, parched from sun and salt
water.

"Whoa! We better not get carried away out here," Kip said.

"What's wrong?"

"Nuthin'. It's just that we've been having some trouble with some
redneck kids from South Beach—that's the next town down. They've
been throwing bottles at gay guys, slashing tires, breaking windows.
Makin' out in public is just askin' for trouble."

Tony said he'd heard about the situation, but chose not to tell Kip he
knew only too well the location of South Beach. It was just as well, anyway. Might as well not start something he couldn't finish.

"Listen, you wanna get out of here?" Kip asked. "We can go to my
place in Cocoa."

"That'd be nice, Kip. You're a hot little man. But I can't tonight."

"Huh? Why not?"

"It's a long story. One you really don't need to hear. I probably
shouldn't have come out here with you. I've got a boyfriend back home
in New York, or at least I hope I do."

"Oh. You guys having a lover's quarrel?"

Tony could see the kid deflate right in front of him.

"Something like that."

"Oh. I hate gettin' caught up in shit like that."

"I'm sorry. I shouldn't have come out here with you. But you're too
cute for your own good."

"So you wouldn't consider . . . ?"

"No, really. It's more complicated than you can imagine. And I'm really worried about him tonight. I just came out tonight to get my mind
off things."

"That's cool. I can handle that. You wanna maybe just hit the diner
or something? Just to talk?"

"Not the diner." *Christ*, Tony thought, the S.C.D., where he went
with Connecticut the first night they met. *That's all I need.* "But maybe,
I don't know, maybe we could just take a walk on the beach or something."

"Sure, that'd be cool."

"I've just got to go let a friend know I'm leaving. He pulled a stupid
stunt tonight, but I'd be a jerk if I just left him."

"Okay, cool." Kip leaned into Tony and kissed him again, something
halfway between a peck and a serious kiss. Tony worried maybe he was

making a mistake spending any more time with him. He'd only break the kid's heart. Suddenly, the volume of the music increased and they heard voices in the street. This time Tony pulled away, his heart pounding, thinking it might be a car full of South Beach goons with the radio turned up.

"Relax. It's just the first shift of drag queens leaving," Kip said. "See that door they just came out of? That goes right up to the drag bar. The ten o'clock show is kind of an amateur hour—really big hair, the records always skip, and at least one bitch per night gets her wig ripped off, which is pretty funny because most of them are practically bald underneath. The late show's too professional. Looks like the damn Miss America pageant. I usually go to the early show. That is, when I go at all. I'm not that big on drag, period, but you know, you get friends who've never seen it and they want to go. I always take them to the ten o'clock. It's pretty funny, especially if you're stoned."

"I'd have to be stoned for either one of them."

"Look, Tony, while you go talk to your friend, why don't I get my truck? I know a little stretch of beach just down the road where we can smoke a joint and talk undisturbed. I'll meet you right out front of the bar, you know, to be on the safe side. Everybody's being a little extra cautious."

"Okay, thanks. That'd be great."

They finished the joint and Kip crushed the roach into the sidewalk. He tied the clip, a homemade contraption of copper wire and a couple of turquoise beads, to the drawstring closure of his jams, and they walked back to Tropicana. Tony turned left while Kip went right.

"Oh, Tony," Kip shouted, walking backward, "it's a black Chevy van. I'll double-park out front, so don't be too long. But don't freak if I'm not there. I'll just circle the block if I have to move."

"Okay, I'll be right out. Promise." Tony returned to the bar and made his way to the booth. Val was now alone, disheveled, with a shit-eating grin on his face.

"There you are, my little fisher of men," Val said and waggled his champagne flute theatrically. "Nothing in your net?"

"I have had a nibble, but I'm not really interested. Not tonight." Tony didn't sit down. "So where is Devlin, King of the Apes?"

"I must ask you to refrain from describing my husband with such malicious epitaphs."

"Epithets."

"Tomayto—Tamahto."

"You're kidding about the husband business, right? . . . Christ, you're *wasted.*"

"Well, perhaps a smidge."

"I saw the two of you going at it half an hour ago, but I thought you were just having your way with the condemned man. You're not *really* taking him back?"

"He explained everything to my satisfaction."

"This I've got to hear."

"We've agreed not to discuss it outside the marital bed."

"And isn't *that* convenient?" Tony said. "Fine. Dig your own grave. So where is he now?"

"He's giving the wee one cab fare, so to speak."

"You're buying off Monk. How compassionate."

"Don't be tiresome."

"I've got to go. Got someone waiting for me downstairs."

"Oh?" Val smirked.

"It's not what you think. And, listen, if I can't get a flight back to New York tomorrow, I'll be moving into a hotel."

"A girl must do what a girl must do." Val emptied the last of the champagne into his glass and signaled for another bottle.

"You don't need anything more to drink, Val. As it is, half *that* bottle is on the banquette."

"That's sweat, darling. Just as delicious and not a single calorie."

Tony hesitated, grasping for something with which to strike out at Val.

"I may as well tell you now that unless you wake up tomorrow and realize what a terrible mistake you're making, I'll be moving out of the penthouse as soon as I find a new place."

"Not practical. Not necessary."

"It is for me." Tony knew it was pointless to argue with Val—the men he loved could do no wrong, and he had obviously let Devlin back into his heart. The man was a cad, but he was an expert cad, and once you were under his spell you were lost. Tony had to give Avery credit for not having succumbed, despite having slept with him for a year.

The fanfare that announced the beginning of the "Dragstravaganza" erupted from the next room, sounding like the theme from *Shaft* as orchestrated by Barry White. The lights in the cruise bar flickered off and on, and Tony thought it was a way of urging drag lovers to their seats. As he turned to go, however, the bar was pitched into total darkness, save for the quavering votive candles on each table. One heartbeat.

Two. Three. And the lights stayed off. Several anemic emergency lights hummed on, and the two bartenders found a couple of flashlights under the bar.

"This happen often?" Tony asked Val.

In his condition, it took Val a couple of beats to discern what *had* happened. "I wouldn't know," he said cavalierly. With some effort, he lit a cigarette. "It's probably just a short circuit from some drag queen's makeup mirror."

When the lights surged back on a few seconds later, everyone quickly returned to their cocktails and conversations. Tony remained vaguely unsettled.

"Something about this place gives me the creeps, Val. Why don't you come with me?"

"Honey, this place has given me the creeps since the first time I set foot in it, but you know I've never been one to let something like an utter lack of fashion sense among the indigenous population ruin my evening. Run along if you must, but first steer me toward the drag bar. I promised Dev I'd watch his show."

Tony was irked. It would take five minutes to maneuver Val to a table in the next room. He had a good mind to just haul Val out of the bar, drive him home, and have Kip follow them. The temporary blackout had left him inexplicably agitated, on edge. He didn't know why he was reacting so strongly to a simple power failure. After all, he'd seen that the circuit breaker box was exposed and vulnerable; some drunken queen had probably spilled her go-cup into it. But it would be a good excuse to get Val out of the bar and away from Devlin. Alone, he could sober him up, talk some sense into him.

Then the lights went out again—and stayed out. The music died and with it the background roar of the air-conditioning. High-pitched conversations bubbled up throughout the room, punctuated by occasional whistles, nervous laughter, and shouted jokes about forgetting to pay the Florida Power bill. One of the bartenders fashioned a makeshift megaphone by cutting the bottom out of an empty popcorn cup and told the crowd that in all likelihood a circuit breaker had blown. Someone was on his way to fix it at that very moment. A call went up for a round of drinks on the house, but the gorgeous bartender in the black tank top dismissed it with a self-conscious smile and a wave of his hand.

"Look, Val, why don't we just get out of here? Looks to me like the party's over."

"Oh, all right, but I'm not leaving without Devlin. Besides, he has the keys."

"To the Lincoln? That was fast."

"Well, I'm certainly in no condition to drive. And he came in monkey man's car."

"Forget about him. My new friend will drive you home."

"I'm not going anywhere without Devlin. I may have forgiven him, but I still don't trust him, especially not while that little slut is on the premises. They have *chemistry*, Tony. But by all means, *do* run along."

"No, I'll wait for you. Go find Dev."

"Do you really expect me to wander around a darkened bar alone like a drunken sailor? Come with me. Please? It won't take a minute. A true friend would do that for her drunken older sister."

"Jesus, Val." Tony sighed. He wondered how long Kip would wait but figured he was so smitten, he'd come track Tony down before he left. "Where do you think he might be?"

"He said his child bride was waiting for him in the dance bar, although it's been a while. I've lost track of time. If he's not there, he's probably backstage tending to the showgirls."

Tony sighed, ran his fingers through his hair, and tossed his head. "Okay, come on." He extended a hand to Val and helped him up. "Jesus, girl, you can barely walk! You are *not* going to be a pretty picture tomorrow."

They crossed the room and threaded their way through the passage to the show bar with Val's left arm thrown over Tony's shoulders. The tables were almost completely filled, and the audience was waiting idly. In the sulfurous blush of the emergency lights, Tony could see dozens of latecomers lining the walls two and three deep, eyeing like vultures the occasional empty chair at an otherwise occupied table. Tony knew it would not be long before the crowd grew restive. Queens had a short attention span, and if the lights and music and air-conditioning did not crank up soon, the girls would become bored and uncomfortable, then rowdy and insufferable.

"Tony, I've got to sit down or I'm going to be sick," Val said. "Be a dear and find that old whore for me."

"You must be sobering up if you're calling him an old whore. That's a good sign. Okay, sit down here." Tony lowered Val into a lone chair along the back wall, scorned by other patrons because its upholstered back was missing. "Don't leave without me. Got it?"

"Got it. Don't leave without you."

"I mean it, Val. If I come back and you're gone, I'll break your fucking neck."

"Right. Break my fucking neck."

The air was growing thin and stale without recirculation, and Tony's T-shirt was damp with sweat. He left Val to look for Devlin downstairs on the dance floor but was deflected by a steady stream of bitchy would-be dancers groping their way up the staircase from the pitch-black cavern below. All Tony could make out in the darkness at the foot of the steps were a handful of neon-chartreuse and Tang-orange glow-in-the-dark necklaces, a disco accessory that had come and gone in New York at least a year before.

"Eeeek! My shoe. I've lost one of my shoes," a man in head-to-toe gold polyester screamed, stumbling forward. "Some bitch stepped on my heel and the straps broke!"

"I told you those platforms would kill you some day," his companion said.

"This is fucking ridiculous," Tony said, turning his back to the stairs. "I'm going to just drag Val's ass out of here, Devlin or no Devlin."

A noise like thunder shook the floor beneath Tony's feet, and a surge of people from behind knocked him to his knees. He stood up quickly but was swept forward with the crowd, traveling most of the ten or fifteen feet back to the passageway with no effort on his part. People pressed in from all sides, and Tony drew his arms up against his chest to buy an extra couple of inches in which to breathe. Against his will, he was being funneled into the passage to the cruise bar and the front door.

The potential for panic was in the air, and Tony wondered what he should do. He found himself thinking about the day he sat in on Connecticut's class at Columbia, the really grisly one with the photographs of dead bodies in burned-out nightclubs and theaters. What was it Connecticut said about mob behavior in a fire? Everyone tries to go out the same door they came in? They would jam up against each other, just to use an escape route that was familiar to them, even when there were other ways out, and they would trample or get trampled by the same people they had been talking to or dancing with minutes earlier. Tony wasn't actually certain there even was a fire or emergency, but he sure as hell wasn't going to stand asscheek to asscheek with a bunch of queens wearing highly flammable nylon shirts and burn to death with them. He decided to try to find the door Kip had told him about, the one the drag queens used.

With some effort, he put his right shoulder to the wall and tried to slow his forward motion. Nothing happened. He decided to crouch, sliding down the wall until he was curled into a ball. He'd crawl out of here on his hands and knees if that was what it took. All he could see were shoes: dancing shoes, running shoes, sandals. He raised his arms to protect his face, but he received several kicks to his legs, hips, and stomach, so hard he knew they would bruise. Maybe fleeing doggy style wasn't such a good idea; the likelihood of getting trampled suddenly seemed significantly greater. At the very least, he was putting his bread-winning face five or six feet closer to the business end of somebody's Guccis—or in this crowd, Thom McAns. But then the forest of legs thinned and Tony crawled out into the drag bar. The men who were anxiously clustered around the entrance to the passageway look at him as if he were nuts. Where the hell did he think he was going? He smiled sheepishly when he stood up and wiped his forehead with his arm. His T-shirt was soaked through and his hair sopping wet.

Tony circled around the knot of people in search of Val. The two of them, he decided, could make a quick retreat through the back door. But when he got to the spot where he had left Val, he was gone. The chair was still there, overturned, with one leg bent, and Tony found one of Val's custom-made loafers nearby, his monogram plainly visible on the insole.

"Christ! That stupid fucking asshole! He just doesn't listen." Tony tossed the shoe aside. "Well, fuck it. Let him find his own way out."

Tony set about finding the performers' door. He walked toward the stage as casually as possible; he didn't want to attract attention or set off a stampede. To the left of the stage was a small door between two huge potted palms, covered with faux brick paneling in an only marginally successful attempt to make it blend in to the walls. The brass knob was clearly visible, and when Tony tried it, the door opened easily. He made his way down the stairs in near total darkness, the only light filtering in from the shuttered windows on each landing. On the second floor, Tony could hear an otherworldly sort of swooshing sound, and the temperature seemed to have risen twenty or thirty degrees in the few seconds it took him to descend one flight. There had to be a fire, a bad one. He had to hold himself back from running down the next darkened flight and risk stumbling—possibly knocking himself out. He reached the ground floor safely and pushed open the glass-paned doors. He ran outside into the alley in which he and Kip had been smoking a joint, what, fifteen, twenty minutes earlier?

He crossed the street and sat down on the curb. He was out of breath and shivering in a cold sweat. It seemed chilly, although it was probably at least sixty degrees. The sky above the bar was glowing orange, and in the distance, he could hear the sound of fire engines, like wolves howling in the deep woods. This place was obviously a firetrap. The whole place would go up before long. He shuddered. And then he thought about Val. He *couldn't* leave Val in there—he was much too drunk to think straight. When Tony made his decision to leave Val behind, the seriousness of the situation wasn't clear and he hadn't really looked for him that hard. Now the certainty of Val's excruciating death exploded like a flashbulb at point-blank range.

"Val, you stupid shit!"

Tony hesitated. Maybe Val, like him, had been swept into the passageway and was already at the exit door of the cruise bar. Maybe a stranger was helping him. Maybe he was already out. Or maybe not. He could be on the floor somewhere, in some dark corner Tony had missed when he looked for him previously. He couldn't just leave him in a burning building.

He stood up. He wanted to get someone to help him—*where were the fucking firemen?* There was no time to wait. The building might go up any minute, any *second* now. He would have to do it alone. He told himself it would be okay. He had been down those stairs in less than half a minute. He could go up to the third floor, look for Val, and if things got dicey he could be out of there in a flash. But when he crossed the street and pulled on the doors, they were locked. They were meant to serve as exit doors for the performers, opening from the inside out only when their handles were depressed to prevent patrons from skirting the cover charge at the front door.

"Jesus, Mary, and Joseph! Fuckin' Christ Almighty!" He looked around him for a rock or a piece of construction trash from the new restaurant, but there was nothing. Finally he saw a temporary No Parking sign, its post embedded in a five-gallon drum of concrete. He ran to it. It was too heavy for him to lift, but he could tip it and roll it toward the door. The first time, he struck the aluminum doorframe, but the second time he shattered the glass in the left-hand door. He kicked out most of the remaining pieces, bent down, and slid inside. As he did so, the right side of his face stung. He brought his hand up to his face and felt something warm and wet. *Blood?*

The staircase was hotter now—ten times hotter, it seemed, in just minutes. But he figured it just seemed that way because he had been outside. And the swooshing sound had turned to a roar. He took the steps two at a time in the dark, and burst through the door into the drag theater. He could not believe what a difference a few minutes had made. The room was virtually empty, except for a knot of people still struggling around the passage to the cruise bar. He heard terrible screams coming from that room—real, serious, intense screams. It would be impossible to find Val in that hellhole, but he could see what appeared to be three or four bodies scattered on the floor and near the wall. He could at least check them out and see if any of them was Val. If not, he would get the hell out of there.

Tony could see sheets of dense gray smoke slithering eerily up the walls and across the ceiling. He remembered that Connecticut had said toxic gases were a major cause of death in fires, so he stayed low to the floor, crawling the way he had seen soldiers do in movies as they made their way from foxhole to foxhole. Right arm and leg first, like a crab, left arm and leg next.

The first body he came across was the little blond-haired boy in the lavender polo shirt—the one with the sugar daddy. Tony wondered where the old man was now. He was pretty sure the kid was dead—trampled—because his head appeared to be crushed and he was missing several teeth. Tony quickly went from one inert form to the other. He approached the fourth man with a silent prayer. It *had* to be Val. Most of the man's clothes had been torn off, and Tony could see only the back of his head—but the hair color looked about right. Tony grasped the man's shoulder and turned him over. The face was so bruised and swollen Tony barely recognized Val, and he couldn't be sure he was breathing.

"Well, at the very least, your parents will have something to bury. That's better than nothing." The room was rapidly filling with smoke, and now flames were shooting up the walls and across the ceiling. "Got to get the fuck out of here."

Tony raised Val's arms over his head and tied his wrists together with his own blood-spattered T-shirt. He made his way back to the exit door, pulling Val behind him as he crawled. He got up on his knees at the door, opened it, and was blown backward by a furnace-like blast of hot air. He shoved the door shut with his left shoulder.

"Oh, Christ!"

He looked around the room, figuring it would be the last thing he would ever see. Dying in a fire—wasn't this supposed to be Connecticut's nightmare? His eyes settled on the rose-hued stage curtains from the old Strand Theater. Hadn't they made a big deal of that place being fireproof? Even the curtains? He heaved himself up the six stairs to the stage, hoisting Val next to him. He lifted the curtain and pulled them both through.

The area was slightly hazy, as if an entire chorus line had been applying spray-on underarm deodorant or baby powder. But it was slightly cooler than the main room had been, and the distant screams were muffled. Tony bent down and tried to find a pulse or some evidence Val was breathing. It was hard to say, but he somehow *seemed* to be alive. Tony desperately stumbled behind the stage and into a large dressing room with three windows. They were three floors up, a dangerous, possibly even lethal, distance from which to jump. There was no fire escape. He paced the room, sweating, his bowels in knots. Was it possible to rappel down the face of the building using the stage curtains? Would he even be able to pull them down? And what would he secure them to? He decided the curtains were just too bulky, but he liked the basic idea. Then it came to him. The drag queen dresses! He might be able to construct a rope out of them, lower Val down in a sort of net or basket, and then climb down himself. What the hell? It was worth a try.

After a short search, he found a closet full of costumes. Most of the fabrics weren't particularly sturdy, and many dresses were made out of stretchy materials. Those wouldn't do. He quickly separated a pile of the most promising candidates and started tying them together. He figured he needed three or four gowns for each ten to twelve feet of descent and several more to fashion a "basket" for Val to sit in. He could use various scarves, belts, and boas to tie Val into the basket.

Working as quickly as he could, he yanked on each knot twice to test its strength. When he thought he had a rope long enough, he took it to where Val lay. Creating the basket would be the most difficult part. To form a base, he lifted Val up and sat him on a throw pillow from one of the makeup benches. He made two ropes of four dresses each, crisscrossed them under the pillow with some difficulty, and tied the ends together in a knot over Val's head. He secured the basket to the end of the main rope and reinforced it by tying and retying a black cocktail dress around the core of knots.

"God only knows if this is gonna hold together, Val, but it's all we've got. We're going to owe the drag queens of Sugar Mill Beach a debt of gratitude—and a whole new wardrobe—if we make it out of here alive." Although there was no response, talking to Val made Tony feel less alone.

Val seemed to get heavier and more unmanageable every time Tony moved him. He zigged and zagged toward the windows, finally placing Val down roughly on a row of makeup tables, sending plastic and glass cosmetics containers crashing to the floor. He had to try all three windows before he found one that hadn't been painted shut, bruising his hands as he tried to loosen them. The fresh air was like an orgasm for his lungs. He searched the darkness for something to secure the makeshift rope to, in the event it slipped through his hands. He found an old, commercial sink the drag queens must have used for their hand washables and knotted a lime-green, spaghetti-strap number around the drainpipe. That done, he raised Val to the window and sat him in it, facing backward.

"Okay, Rapunzel, it's out the tower with you," Tony said, but he couldn't bring himself to ease Val out the window. The rope seemed so flimsy, so hastily prepared. If any knot failed, Val would plunge to the ground toward certain serious injury and possible death. What if he were paralyzed, a quadriplegic? What Tony wouldn't have given for some plain, sturdy, two-hundred-count white sheets with which to make his escape. But he had no choice. They would almost certainly die here within minutes if they stayed.

He eased Val's seat over the sill, carefully lifting his legs sideways so he wouldn't tip backward and fall head first to the ground. He let the dress rope play out slowly, preventing the individual knots from absorbing Val's weight all at once. The rope felt spongy, elastic, but Tony thought those same characteristics would cause the knots to compress, to pull tighter under Val's weight. He had braced his feet against the wall and leaned back, so he couldn't see Val, but he figured as long as the rope remained taut, things were going well. When it went limp, hopefully without snapping, Val would be on the ground.

Sequins and other sewn-on spangles sliced through Tony's hands like razor blades as he played out the rope, and the resulting cuts burned like hell when sweat ran into them. A quick glance to the floor revealed the string of dresses was disappearing quickly, and his worst fear was that he had miscalculated the length and Val would be left dangling and somehow fall or strangle himself. But then there was a sudden slackening of the rope, and Tony leaned out the window. Val was on the ground, nestled in a fetal position, his arms still tied to the basket supports.

Tony immediately leaped onto the windowsill himself and tugged on the length of gowns that was attached to the plumbing. It was still firm. Taking the improvised rope in his two bleeding hands, he pushed himself out the window, landing with his feet against the building. He crouched and slowly walked down the brick walk backward. It reminded him of a scene from the old *Batman* series he'd watched faithfully ten years before. His back and shoulders ached, but what worried him most was that his shredded hands, which stung like hell, might give out. He was making good progress and when he looked down, he could see Val's face clearly.

Tony's lifeline failed when one of the higher knots unraveled, and he fell the last six feet to the pavement, where he cursed himself for having tied the red sequined number to the gold lamé. The fall knocked the wind out of him, and he lay quietly on the sidewalk for a moment to catch his breath.

It was cool and quiet out here and all he wanted was to lie there and sleep. But he could still hear the muffled roar of the fire and the screams of the poor bastards inside, and he knew he had to find help for Val. He could hear the high-pitched sirens of ambulances and the blatting of fire trucks as they arrived on the scene. He stood up and in that instant knew what it was to be old: all of his joints—hips, shoulders, elbows, knees—cried out. A phantom ax was lodged between his shoulder blades, and as he bent down to extricate Val from the tangle of dresses, the pain told him he would be able to lift his friend no more that night. He would have to drag him around the corner to Tropicana Boulevard. Putting one hand under each of Val's armpits, he lifted him halfway off the sidewalk and stumbled toward the street. He knew the sidewalk was abrading Val's legs, but there was nothing he could do. When he reached the intersection, four men in slick yellow fire coats ran past him carrying a flaccid canvas firehose, the buckles on their boots and jackets jingling like sleigh bells. One of them stopped and approached Tony.

"How did you get out? What floor were you on?"

It took Tony a couple of seconds to respond. "The window. Third floor. Climbed down the rope."

"Good job, kid. Good thinking. That's a big help."

Tony just nodded as the fireman walked away.

"Get a ladder up to that third-floor window," the man shouted to his coworkers. Then he turned back to Tony. "Find a medic! Just walk out onto the street—someone will help you. Understand?"

Tony leaned against a wall and nodded. But he had never felt so exhausted in his life. He wished he hadn't stopped; it was too hard to get moving again.

Compared to the relative quiet of the alley, Tropicana Boulevard was a psychedelic nightmare. Three greenish-yellow fire trucks were parked at angles in the southbound lanes, and a fourth straddled the landscaped median, its huge, rippled tires crushing the flower beds. Dozens of firemen were spraying water on the front of the building, which was completely engulfed in flame. As Tony stumbled across the street, an inch deep in water, Val's silk boxer shorts filled with water, slid down his legs, and floated away in the gutter. For a moment Tony thought about chasing them but instead laid Val on a swath of grass and sat down beside him, unable to go farther. Tony held his head in his hands and closed his eyes, trying to shut out the shouts of the firemen, the roar of the fire. Looking up, he thought he saw movement behind one of the decorative wrought-iron grilles on the third floor—a hand waving, a face pleading for rescue—and he shivered at the thought of being trapped in that inferno and being burned alive.

Then he heard someone calling to him—at least he thought they were shouting to him—and he turned to look. A man, splashing as he ran along the gutter, waved to him as he approached. He was wearing a luminescent yellow-and-black jacket and a fireman's helmet and was carrying a square white box with a red cross on it. Beneath his left arm he cradled something that looked like a small blue scuba tank.

"Are you hurt bad?" the man said, slightly out of breath, when he reached Tony.

"I don't think so. But my friend . . . I just ran out of energy."

"No sweat, man. Let's take a look."

The medic went around behind Tony and got down on one knee next to Val. He pulled off his helmet, strained to hear Val's breathing, and listened to his heart with his stethoscope. The medic placed a clear plastic mask over Val's nose and mouth and adjusted some knobs on the blue tank.

"He's breathin'. Real shallow. We need to transport him right now. Hold this tank steady while I radio my partner."

Tony balanced the air tank on Val's chest while the medic made the call. Something about this guy was familiar, but Tony couldn't place him. Christ, had he slept with him somewhere?

"That's a nasty cut on your face, guy, and your hands look like hamburger meat, but otherwise you look pretty good," the medic said after he finished talking to his partner. "Are you having any trouble breathing?"

"No," Tony said. "I'm okay." He had been so caught up with Val that he'd forgotten about his own injuries. He reached up to touch his cheek, but the medic gently took his hand and put it in Tony's lap.

"Don't touch it, okay, guy? I'll clean it up and put a dressing on it once I stabilize your friend."

Tony felt as though he were coming down from a bad trip. The pulsing lights of emergency vehicles—red, white, blue, yellow—were like the visuals on acid. Suddenly, everything was spinning, and he had to throw up. He tried to stand up, but the best he could do was get on all fours, hang his head, and let loose.

"Sorry," he said to the medic after he wiped his mouth with the back of his arm.

The medic reached over and patted him on the back.

"It's okay, guy, I see it every day."

As he worked, the medic told Tony that badly burned victims were being choppered to the special burn unit at Orlando Regional Medical Center. Those like Val, seriously injured but not badly burned, were being sent to Sugar Mill Hospital, a small, private facility more accustomed to seeing older, well-off patients with sunburn and jellyfish stings. The remainder—those for whom a longer ambulance ride might be uncomfortable but not life threatening—were being taken to Halifax Hospital in Daytona.

"The emergency room at SMH isn't as big as Halifax's, but it's a lot closer. And it's a private hospital with a lot of good docs on staff," the medic said as he inserted a saline drip in Val's right arm. "I guarantee your friend will be on an examining table within ten minutes. That's good time and it'll make a difference. You'll be able to see someone there about that cut on your face, too. Now scoot aside while we get your friend into the unit."

The medic's partner had arrived in an orange-and-white emergency unit. Together, they quickly lifted Val onto a collapsible gurney and pushed it into the back of the orange-and-white van.

"Climb on in," the medic yelled. "Take hold of his hand and talk to him. It'll be good for him to know you're here."

Tony slipped as he clambered into the back of the truck, and the medic pulled him in. He closed the doors and slapped the Plexiglas partition behind the driver twice. They lurched forward. The van swayed and jostled as they wove through the tightly clustered jumble of ambulances, fire engines, and police cars, and sped north on Tropicana toward the hospital. Soon the din subsided, and Tony could feel himself relax.

The medic took Tony's head in one hand, and tilted it upward to get a better look at his cut. "Tony? Tony Alexamenos? How on God's green earth did you get here?"

Tony had not a clue to the medic's identity. He glanced at the small blue-and-white name tag over the man's breast pocket. It read PICKER-ING.

"Pick? Pick, is it you?"

"Well, it sure as hell ain't Duke Kahanamoku. What the hell are you doing back in Sugar Mill Beach?"

"I came back to see the old place before they tore it down. Not worth the trip."

"I reckon not, now. You still livin' in New York? Your old man said you was."

"You talk to Pops? I haven't spoken to him in years."

"Almost every day until he moved over to the Gulf Coast. After he sold your place, he helped me with a down payment on a three-bedroom at Sugar Mill Estates II. We've got a view of Mosquito Lagoon, and when they're finished with the sanitary landfill, they're going to turn it into a park for the kids, with a baseball diamond and everything. I figure by the time they do, my slugger will be just the right age for Little League."

"You've got a kid?"

"Two girls and a boy."

"Damn, Pick, you never *could* keep it in your pants. Do they know how it started—the fire?"

"Arson. I know some cops, and they say some Southies threw Molotov cocktails from a pickup truck. Mostly they just hit the brick walls and flamed out. I think all they wanted to do was scare the fags, but one or two sailed right through the doorway, I guess as people were coming or going. Pure dumb luck. They exploded at the bottom of the stairs and that was that. That staircase acted just like a chimney. That cut off the main escape route pretty damn quick. Them that survived had to run through two floors of flame. Bad off, all of 'em. I know about burns, and believe me they probably wish they *was* dead. They was buildin' a restaurant on the ground floor, so there was lots of combustible material just laying around there, too. Lumber, paint, solvents, that kind of shit. Bad stuff. Almost instantaneous combustion and high heat. The fire spread so quick it probably looked like the damn *Hindenburg*. . . . You done good back there, Tony. Saved his life. *And yours*. No question."

"Then he'll be okay?"

"I can't make no promises. A lot of times the smoke damage isn't real obvious for a couple of hours, but unless he got some really, really bad air in there, he ought to be okay. We'll know soon enough. I've seen some worse off who pulled through."

Tony cradled Val's head and whispered into his ear. He cheered him on by saying things like "Just hang in there," and "It'll be okay," which sounded stupid, clichéd, but were all he could manage. Meanwhile, Pick monitored Val's vital signs and deftly cleaned and dressed the cut on Tony's face.

"What do you think, Pick?"

"Nothing life threatening."

Tony coughed and Pick gave him a drink of water from a small thermos.

"Maybe not life threatening, but potentially *lifestyle* threatening. You know, I make my living off this face. How bad is it really?"

Pick wiped at Tony's face with several white pads soaked in antiseptic, removing soot and embedded cinders. Once or twice Tony winced when the alcohol-based solution came in contact with raw flesh.

"I honestly don't know, Tony. Tell you what, though, I'll page a plastic surgeon I know. That'll be a helluva lot better than having some resident stitch you up. Then when you get back to New York, you can see your own man."

"Thanks. I'd really appreciate that."

When they arrived at the emergency entrance of Sugar Mill Hospital, a handful of men and women in green scrubs were waiting for them, gawking down the driveway like commuters looking for a bus.

"We must be the first unit from the scene," Pick said. "That's good for you guys—especially your friend. I guarantee it will be nuts within a half hour."

When they stopped, the driver jumped out and opened the back doors. He and Pick quickly slipped the gurney out of the vehicle and rolled it into the ER through pneumatic glass doors, followed by the swarm of medical personnel. One nurse detached herself from the group and accompanied Tony inside, asking him about his injuries. She put him in an examination room, quickly looked at his hands, and removed the dressing Pick had just put on his face. Tony saw her wince. At that moment, Pick stuck his head in the door.

"I've gotta go, Tone, but I've called the plastic surgeon, and he's on the way. No guarantee I'll see you again tonight, but call me and let me know how things turn out. I'm in the book."

Within half an hour, a doctor had examined Tony and pronounced him fit except for his obvious external injuries. By the time a nurse had treated and bandaged his hands, Pick's plastic surgeon had arrived. Like the nurse, he seemed taken aback by his first glimpse of Tony's wound—or perhaps by its awful juxtaposition with the breathtaking nature of his unblemished side. But all he said as he set about his work were the words "Nasty little bugger." Tony explained how his face was his fortune and begged him to perform some medical miracle that would restore it to its original seamless beauty.

"At best, what I can do tonight is some very basic work to minimize the damage and prevent infection," the surgeon replied. "It's clear you'll have to undergo several additional surgeries, the results of which are unforeseeable at this point. I *will* say that it is a very clean cut, smooth and of roughly even depth. That will help."

Afterward, Tony was released from the emergency room and told to go home. He asked about Val but was told he was still being treated and no definitive information was available. Tony insisted on staying until he could actually see and talk to Val.

"That may be quite some time," a nurse said.

"Fine. Just make sure you come find me."

The trauma area waiting room had filled up since Tony had arrived and been whisked to the treatment room. The dirty, ragged smell of the fire, of smoke and charred, wet clothes, was everywhere, largely overpowering the antiseptic tang of the green-and-white hospital corridors. To ward off the narcotic effects of the painkiller the nurse had given him, Tony paced the darkened hallway from the emergency room to the snack bar, where he periodically purchased black coffee from a vending machine. It tasted of metal and medicine.

"Tony!"

Someone across the room was shouting his name.

"Tony! Over here!"

It was Kip. He plunged through the crowd to where Tony was leaning against a wall. He looked completely unscathed.

"Tony, thank God! I hoped you'd be here."

"Kip?"

"I've been looking for you! Are you okay? Shit, your *face,* man! And your hands."

"Kip?"

"Yeah, it's me. I waited for you like I said, and then these assholes drive by and start throwing flaming bottles at the goddamned bar. I got the hell out of there, but I got their tag number. I gave it to the cops."

"What are you doing here? Are you hurt?"

"Nah. I was looking for *you*. I was *worried* about you."

"Well, I'm okay. I'm here to see about my friend."

"Christ, you're a fucking mess. Here, take my shirt." Kip slipped off his floral print shirt and gave it to Tony. "Go ahead, put it on. Give me your coffee. I'll hold it for you."

"I can't take your shirt."

"It's okay. Really. Thank God you're safe."

Tony grudgingly slipped into the shirt. Kip handed him his coffee and then buttoned the shirt for him.

"There. Guess you'll need someone to dress you until you get those bandages off your hands," Kip said.

"I guess so."

"Would you like to come back to my place. I'll make you some *real* coffee, not this machine crap. Or better yet, we can smoke some dope."

"You want me to go to your place?"

"Sure. You can just kick back, forget about all this shit. I'll take good care of you."

"Kip, you need to just go home. I appreciate that you were worried about me, but I'll be okay. You just need to forget about me."

"Okay, man, but let me at least give you my phone number. Maybe you can call me sometime, you know, if things don't work out with your boyfriend or something."

"Fine. Okay."

Kip gave Tony a peck on his undamaged cheek. "You are a hot man, Tony, even all bunged up like you are. Call me!"

After Kip left, Tony gave in to exhaustion and found an empty seat in a less crowded corner of the L-shaped waiting room. The coral-colored, molded plastic chair was anything but comfortable, but he discovered that with some contortions, he could lean his head against the cool windowsill and at least rest his eyes.

He didn't think he had fallen asleep, but when he opened his eyes, the room was much less crowded. Only a dozen people still paced the waiting area, and a handful of others were sleeping in chairs, but by and large the panic and mania had subsided. Tony closed his eyes again and tried to find a more comfortable position. He wondered how much longer he would have to wait for word about Val. After a few minutes, he was aware of the person next to him getting up and sensed someone new—smelling crisply of cologne, not smoke—sit down.

"I can't believe this fucking place," the new arrival muttered under his breath. "Nobody knows a fucking thing about what's going on."

Even with his eyes closed, even after eight years, Tony recognized that voice. Whiny and self-centered. Impatient. It was Connecticut Jones. There was no mistaking it. Tony cringed. He had just survived a life-threatening disaster—and hardly unscathed—and all he wanted to do now was see Val and go home to sleep. Connecticut Jones was the last person on earth he needed to deal with. In addition to all the unresolved emotional issues, he looked like hell. In his reunion fantasies, he imagined he had just won the Oscar for Best Actor when he ran into Connecticut, a mere gawker, outside the Dorothy Chandler Pavilion. But his curiosity got the best of him and he sat up, slowly, and opened his eyes. Connecticut's face bore a few more lines and wrinkles and the cloud of black hair was hovering artfully over a receding hairline, but he was still handsome in a way that thrilled Tony.

Jesus Christ! The shit that had come down since the night they had first met. It was hard to believe he was the same person. He was practically penniless then, and *scruffy!* Hair halfway down to his ass. And *young*—underage—couldn't even get into the Boy-O-Boy legally. He had only had sex with—what?—a half dozen guys when he met Connecticut—Mitch, Dick and Duane, a couple of others. There had been times since then when he had been with that many guys in one night—hell in one *hour* at the baths! Connecticut had been so cute then, so shy; they had talked for *hours* at the S.C.D. before he even *hinted* that he was gay. He'd been pretty innocent himself. He couldn't believe how quickly he had fallen in love—and how deeply. For nearly a year after they met, he didn't draw a breath without thinking of Connecticut. And then it was over. He hadn't allowed himself to think about that final night in the Grove Street apartment in a long time, but now it all came back to him: the way the idea first took shape, the panicked denials, the utter despair when he finally acknowledged the truth, and then . . . the darkness. He had been down that road any number of times since, and until this moment he thought that each time it had gotten worse. But that wasn't true. *That* time had been the worst. The other times had gotten progressively more dramatic, but *that* night, that night was the very fucking worst. And now, here he was right next to Tony, still handsome—and more tan than Tony ever remembered him getting. Maybe he was loosening up, going to the beach more, having some fun. Maybe he had changed.

What to do? Quietly change seats? Insist he be allowed to see Val *now?* Just go home? No. He had to talk to him. He had to.

"Connecticut?"

"Do I know you?" Connecticut said with more distaste than surprise.

"Well, I've looked better, but it's me, Tony . . . Tony Alexamenos."

Connecticut shot out of his chair. "Tony? Jesus H. Christ! Tony Alexamenos? What the hell are you doing here? Oh my God, look at your face!"

"It's okay, really. I'm here with a friend who's much worse off."

"Tony? Oh, God, Tony. I can't believe it's you. You were in the fire? Are you okay? Jesus!"

"I'm fine, really. Except for this new zipper running down my cheek." Tony reached up and barely let his right hand graze the bandages. "Were you there? Inside?"

"No. I'm just here to pick up . . . a friend." Connecticut sat down and turned toward Tony. "What on earth are you doing here? In Florida, I mean. And how the hell did you end up at the Carousel on this night of all nights? God, this is *awful*. How could this happen?"

Tony explained the circumstances of his presence in Florida and, unfortunately, the bar, briefly mentioning Val and Devlin but instinctively leaving out all references to Avery. It seemed surprisingly easy to sit there and calmly talk to the man he had once loved so much, so many years before. It was almost as if the intervening years had never taken place. He felt a kind of love, but for some reason he couldn't feel the pain, the anger. Maybe, he thought, he was so devastated by the night's events that Connecticut's betrayal seemed trivial in comparison.

A nurse appeared at the swinging double doors that led to the trauma area, surveyed the waiting room, and walked toward Tony.

"Mr. Alexander?"

"Yes?" Tony said.

"You may see your friend now, but just for a few minutes. I'll take you to him."

Tony stood, all the while looking at Connecticut.

"And Dr. Jones? Your father has been stabilized, but we're going to keep him overnight for observation. We should have him in a room in a few minutes, and you can look in on him then." She turned to Tony. "Mr. Alexander? This way please."

"Your *father?*" Tony mouthed as the nurse led him away by the elbow.

Connecticut just gritted his teeth and nodded.

"Will you be here when I get back?" Tony asked.

"Sure. You too. Wait, I mean. If you get back first," Connecticut replied. "And Tony? It's good to see you. . . . Even like this."

Val was conscious but groggy. His left leg was encased in plaster and suspended in traction. Tubes in his arms and crotch pumped or drained fluids into or out of his body. His face was even more swollen than Tony remembered it, and it was so swirled and mottled with orange, red, blue, and black markings that it looked like a scale model of Jupiter.

"We think he'll be fine," the nurse told Tony in a whisper. "He's got a collapsed lung, and as you can see, a lot of bruising. We suspect he was trampled. The bruising will fade over the next two or three weeks, but the swelling should subside well before that. We'll want to monitor his pulmonary function very carefully tonight."

"It would be advisable to move him to a private room before his parents get here," Tony said. "Your best available suite. They'll want a private-duty nurse here at all times, starting now. His mom and dad would never forgive me if he were left alone for a minute. Not even a *minute.* You take care of that, and I'll stay here with him."

"I understand. I can call a service right now. In the meantime, don't let him get emotional. Encourage him to sleep. With all the medication he's on, he should be out like a light by now, but he's been waiting for you. He's asked for you many times. Now that he knows you're here, he'll probably stop fighting the sedative."

The nurse left the room. Tony returned to Val's bedside and took his left hand in both of his own.

"You look like hell, girl. You're going to have to put Max Factor on retainer for *months.*"

Val convulsed slightly and Tony heard a gurgling-sucking sound.

"Sorry. I guess you should try not to laugh. I'll do my best to be as humorless as most of my tricks. Oops, there I go again. So, do you know where you are and what happened? How do you feel?"

Val cracked his lips, which were dry and showed signs of having bled. At first nothing came out, then a few raspy words. "Some water?"

Tony poured him a glass from a blue-and-white bedside pitcher. He held the glass to Val's lips gently.

"I feel like Popeye during a spinach famine," Val said, weakly.

"Well, you're going to be okay. No *GQ* covers for a while, but before long you'll be just fine. No permanent damage that I can see. Really."

"That's a blessing."

"Do you want me to call your parents? They should probably know as soon as possible, and I imagine in a couple minutes you're going to be too out of it to talk."

"I suppose it's inevitable."

"Should I be honest with them about what happened? I mean the bar and all?"

"Sooner or later, I'll have to tell them I'm gay." He motioned for more water. "This is the perfect setup. They'll be so glad I'm alive that they'll forget about the gay business until much later. It will become a mere footnote to the current unpleasantness."

"Consider it done. I'll be the epitome of discretion."

"I need another favor. Bring me my silk lounging pajamas. I feel like one of those Viet Cong orphans in this rag. And my Vuitton slippers. Are you up to that?"

"Sure. I'll bring your entire makeup case, too, although with those bruises I'd stick to the earth tones for the first few weeks."

"And what of Dev?"

"I don't know. I haven't been back to the condo yet, but I do know he wasn't treated here. They posted lists from time to time, and I read every one to see if I recognized any names from the old days. There are a couple of other hospitals I can check, though. I'll let you know as soon as I find out. Do you want to see him when I find him?"

Tony waited for an answer, but none came. Val's eyes were closed and he didn't speak again for a while.

"Are you still awake? Can you hear me?" Tony said.

"Yes. I'm thinking. Something I should have done long ago. You know, he just *left* me . . . left me there when the other queens started to rush the door." Tears streaked his swollen cheeks.

"So you found him after I left you?"

"He found me. I told him I had to wait for you, and he sat down with me. But then all hell broke loose and he got up to leave. I reached out for him—I was so drunk I needed help to get up—and he just pushed me down to the floor and walked away. I think he told me to wait for 'Miss Thing.' I presume he meant you. People were really getting jammed up and I saw him literally pick people up and throw them aside, out of his way. I was drunk, but I know what I saw, and I'll never forget it."

"He was finally showing you his true colors."

"Then something—or somebody—fell on me, and that's all I remembered until I woke up here. You *saved* me, they said. I'd marry *you*, my guardian angel, if it weren't incestuous."

"Thank God for small favors."

Val laughed and gurgled again. Tony shushed him and squeezed his hand.

"What's that on your face? No sequins, so it must be utilitarian. A bandage?"

"It's nothing. A scratch. Don't worry about it."

"When it comes to *that* face, *nothing* is nothing. Can you show me? Peel back the bandage and let me see."

Tony did as he was told, lifting back the gauze like a flap.

"Oh, Christ, Tony. We're going to have to bring out the big guns on this one." Val sank back into his pillows. The energy of this small effort was all he could muster. His head turned slightly to one side, and his eyes closed.

"Great. The first queen who sees my face faints," Tony said. He brushed a spray of Val's hair away from his forehead, and leaned down and kissed him. A soft knock on the door startled him. It was the nurse.

"The temp agency is sending someone right over," she whispered. "Is he asleep?"

"Yeah. He pretty much crashed all of a sudden, though. Is that okay?"

"It's fine. I'll check him. Why don't you go home and get some rest? I'll stay with him until the night nurse gets here—promise. He won't be alone. Not even for a minute."

Connecticut was pacing the waiting room floor when Tony returned. He was clutching a large white plastic bag to his chest, and Tony swore he saw a bright red wig and some sequined cloth protruding over the lip.

"Is your friend going to be okay?" Connecticut asked.

"So they say. Poor thing. He's such a pretty boy, but now he looks like Quasimodo. Worse off than me at the moment, I guess, but nothing *he's* got is going to scar." Tony touched his bandage. "I have to call his folks, but I thought I'd wait until morning, since it doesn't look like he's going to die or anything. Give them time to wake up and at least have a cup of coffee before they get the news. I bet they'll charter a med-evac jet—they're worth billions—and fly down to take him home this afternoon, if he's okay to fly. I'll probably catch a ride back with them."

"Really? So soon?"

"Yeah. I mean, what's there for me here?"

"I was hoping we . . . I just thought you might stay on a few days."

"For what?"

"I don't know. The police might have some questions."

"Fuck the police. They already know who's responsible. Besides, I can't be associated with any of this. We're launching a big campaign and I wouldn't want to ruin it, even if it may be my last."

Tony was ready to leave the hospital and had assumed all along that Connecticut would give him a ride. But suddenly he felt a bit self-conscious. "Listen, would you mind giving me a ride back to my place . . . Val's place?"

"Sure. Absolutely. Maybe we could get some coffee. Talk."

"With this pain medication they gave me, I'm going to need something stronger than coffee if I'm going to stay awake. Oh, and I've got to pick up some things for Val and bring them back here so he has them when he wakes up. Is that okay?"

"Sure. I don't think *I* could fall asleep if I tried."

Tony followed Connecticut out to his car, an arctic blue Cutlass Supreme coupe with a white vinyl half-top.

"Still brand loyal, I see," Tony said.

Connecticut eased the Cutlass onto Tropicana Boulevard with the soft, slightly wet feel of a new car on new tires. In a minute they were gliding past the sleeping neighborhood of Sugar Mill Estates. "It's so quiet. I don't know what I expected . . . people on their front lawns or something, watching the fire. Here all these people died, but most people in town just slept right through it."

"They're better off not knowing."

"So what the hell was your father doing at the bar, looking for you?"

Connecticut thrummed his fingers on the steering wheel rim. "Not exactly."

"What then?"

"This probably isn't the best time to talk about it, Tony."

"Don't tell me *he's* gay?"

Connecticut said nothing, just drove northward on the pristine carpet of concrete.

"Oh my God, he *is* gay! That must inhibit your cruising big-time!"

Connecticut sighed and rubbed the back of his neck with his left hand. "I don't go to the Carousel anymore. I go out in Daytona or Orlando. The P-House, mostly."

"This is just too much." Tony couldn't keep himself from smiling, even though he knew it was rude. Plus it hurt like hell. "How did you find out?"

The dimly lit interior of the car seemed pregnant with possibilities. Tony recalled another time, a similar car, a place not far from here.

"I knew you'd react this way," Connecticut said, his eyes now aimed straight ahead.

"What way?"

"You're *gleeful.* You're glad my father is gay."

"I'm not. I couldn't care less if your father is gay. I mean, if that's what he wants, fine. And it's good to know your tricks can now spend the night in the same bed with you."

"That's precisely what I mean. You think it's some sort of poetic justice that he's gay because I worked so hard to keep *my* gayness from him."

"Connecticut, really, it doesn't make any difference. I mean yes, it is ironic. But really, what *I* think isn't important."

"Still, you're not denying that you're taking pleasure in it. I find that ghoulish, in a way." In the green glow of the dashboard lights, Connecticut's face seemed set, unyielding. He didn't speak again until the pale obelisk of Sucre sur Mer rose ahead of them.

"We're here," he said.

# 31

ALTHOUGH THE FRONT DOOR WAS UNLOCKED, the condo appeared to be deserted.

"*Someone* has to be here. Unless Devlin or Monk—that's his little surfer-hunk boyfriend—forgot to lock it when they left," Tony said softly. "I wouldn't be surprised. They haven't got a complete brain between them."

Tony felt around in the darkness for a rheostat and turned on the lights in the living room. "Voilá!"

"Tony, this place is absolutely stunning."

"I call it Swish Family Robinson."

"More like Swiss Family Rockefeller."

"God, it's as quiet as death in here. I need to put on some music. Any requests?"

"Some Mozart would be nice."

"Not exactly what I had in mind." Tony knelt in front of the stereo cabinet and rifled through the tapes. He plucked an Eagles cassette out of its case and slipped it into the player. It picked up, loudly, in the middle of "Hotel California." He adjusted the volume. They heard the squeal of bedsprings and the thump of feet on the floor. The door to the master bedroom opened tentatively.

"Dev? Is that you?" Monk stood in the door, naked, again, pillow-haired, his face streaked with tears. "Oh. It's you."

"And I'm so glad you survived the night, too, Monk," Tony said.

"I'm sorry. I just thought you were Devlin. I've been up all night waiting for him."

"There's hope, yet," Tony whispered to Connecticut.

"Stop it."

"When was the last time you saw him?" Tony asked. "Were you in the bar when it caught fire?"

"No. Dev told me to go to my folk's place for the night. He wanted to work some things out with . . . well, you know. He said it would be easier if I wasn't there. I was supposed to wait till I heard from him. He said it might take a day or two, but that he'd call me."

"Obviously, you didn't go home."

"It was still early, so I went to the diner for a Coke and some fries. Then I went to Playland to shoot some pinball. When all the fire trucks came racing down Tropicana, people said the Carousel was burning, so I went to check it out. I couldn't find Dev outside, so I went to the hospital. He wasn't there. I drove over to Halifax, but he wasn't there, either. They told me he could be at Orlando Regional, but as upset as I was—and pretty high—I was afraid I wouldn't make it over to Orlando in one piece, so I came back here to wait for him. Or at least a call."

"Well, would you mind waiting for him with some clothes on? I've got a friend with me." Tony said. He headed for the guest bedroom. "Come on, Connecticut."

"Sure. Sorry," Monk said. He disappeared for a moment, his head reemerging around the edge of the doorsill. "Say, what happened to that Val guy?"

"He's in the hospital. And I'm sorry to inform you that he'll live."

"I never wanted him to *die*," Monk said. "Is he burnt bad?"

"He is neither burned nor permanently disfigured in any way, but don't worry, *if* Devlin is alive, Val is no longer interested in him. He's all yours, but sans car, cash, and condo."

Monk stood in the doorsill, clearly working hard to absorb what Tony had said. It was the *sans* that threw him. He retreated into the bedroom without another word.

"Weren't you a little hard on him?" Connecticut asked. "I thought he was being relatively reasonable, for someone of his age and circumstances."

"I suppose, especially considering that he gives me a great big woody every time I see him." Tony made a low growling sound and gnashed his teeth. "Maybe that's *why*. Doesn't help that he's usually naked. It's Devlin I'm *really* mad at, but since it's impossible to get a rise out of him, I take it out on little Monkey Man. Twisted, isn't it. Yet so like a queen."

"Jesus, Tony, I've never heard you call yourself a queen. Of course it's been eight years and you *have* been living in New York."

"At heart, Connecticut, we're all queens, in the worst sense of the word. It's an occupational hazard."

"Of modeling?"

"Of being gay. Now, I've got to get Val's stuff together. So in the car you were telling me about your father," Tony said, packing Val's bag.

"You're not going to let go of that, are you?"

"You obviously don't know who you're dealing with."

"Oh, all right. I probably *should* know better. . . . It was about six months ago. July Fourth weekend. We went to the Carousel to see the show . . ."

"We? You have a boyfriend?"

"Colleagues in town for a conference at Sanctuary."

"And you took them to a drag show? How daring!"

"My life has not been totally frozen in ambergris, Tony. I've made *some* progress. We had a few drinks and went into the show bar. My friends were from up north and they hadn't ever seen drag. The emcee was this outrageous Desdemona Jones character. You could immediately see she was ancient by all the makeup she was wearing, and before she said even one word she looked straight at me, and I could tell she was my father."

"What? Desdemona Jones is your *father?* Your father is a *drag queen?*"

"It makes sense—Desmond–Desdemona."

"Did he recognize you?"

"There was never any doubt. Our eyes *locked.*"

"I'll bet you shit yourself."

"Actually, I calmly excused myself from the table, went outside, and had a nervous breakdown. I got in the car and was halfway to Miami before I even realized what I was doing, so I just kept going. I ended up in Key West without so much as a razor or a change of underwear. I just checked into a hotel and stayed drunk for three days."

"So what happened when you finally picked yourself up and dusted yourself off?"

"As soon as I got back, I moved out of the house and bought a condo. I couldn't look him in the eye, let alone bear to be under the same roof."

"I'm sure the whole thing was as much of a shock to him as it was to you. Have you ever talked about it?"

"No. Not until tonight. I didn't speak to him *at all* until a month ago. My mother had no idea what was going on. I mean, she knew *something* was going on between me and him, but not what. She was devastated, heartbroken. She called me two or three times a day wanting to know what was wrong, why I never came by the house. I told her I was just busy. Finally, at Thanksgiving, I agreed to go up to Ormond Beach for dinner. My father acted like nothing had happened, but he never left my side. I don't know if he was trying to show me affection or policing what I was saying to my mother."

"He didn't call you aside to explain the drag business?"

"Christ, Tony, who do you think we're talking about here? The fact that we had a Thanksgiving dinner with two-thirds of the family tacitly acknowledging each other's gayness and nobody blowing their brains out is miracle enough. You want revelations? Forgiveness? Not in the household of Desmond and Mollie Jones and their precocious prodigal son."

"As bad as your experience with your dad was, I can go you one better," Tony said.

"I can't imagine your father would ever turn gay, let alone become a drag queen."

"Not quite. But he called me one night in New York, drunk, and asked if I was 'queer.' So I told him. You want to know what he said? He said, 'So do you take it or do you stick it in?' Nice, huh?"

"He actually used those words?"

"Verbatim."

"He certainly seems to know a lot about the mechanics of gay sex."

"Or the sex of gay mechanics."

"You don't think . . . ?"

"No, Connecticut I was just joking."

Tony thought it was sort of poetic justice that after everything Connecticut had done to conceal his homosexuality from his parents, his own father turned out to be gay—and not only *gay* but a drag queen. It was even more ironic that Connecticut now seemed to be the one who was being judgmental, shunning his father. Yet of all the people Desmond Jones could have called for help that night, he chose Connecticut. And Connecticut had come. Who could tell? Maybe they would start talking to each other again, understanding each other, become friends.

Tony knew that would never happen with his pop. It was too late. And besides, they had never had a relationship in the first place. There was nothing to build on, nothing to salvage. Tony couldn't recall even a single instance in which he had so much played catch with the old man. After the phone call in which he came out to his father, Tony got an unlisted number and he had never heard from him again. It must be going on five years. He had kept in touch with his Aunt Thalia and had told her he was an actor, which would make more sense to her than if he had said he was a "model," which she wouldn't really have understood and which sounded too faggy. But he never told her that he was rich and even sort of famous, so he didn't know if Pops was aware of his success. Probably not, or he would have found a way to ask Tony for money. Tony had felt a little guilty about the money, but now that Pops had sold the house and the station to developers, he was set for life. Hell, he even helped Pick out with his down payment on a house, which was more than he had ever done for Tony.

IT WAS NEARLY FOUR A.M. BY THE TIME Tony finished filling Val's Louis Vuitton overnight bag with survival essentials. With Connecticut's help, he took a quick sitz bath, careful to keep the bandages on his hands and face dry, and changed clothes. When he and Connecticut left, Monk was pacing the balcony off the living room, smoking a joint. He glanced in at them but said nothing.

"Poor kid's got it bad," Connecticut said as they waited for the elevator.

"I know. I almost wish for his sake that Devlin's all right.... Almost."

"You're heartless, Tony."

"Believe me, he deserves it."

"Maybe Devlin does, but not this little kid. He'll be devastated."

The nurses at the hospital discouraged Tony from looking in on Val, so he left the bag at the desk. Meanwhile, Connecticut inquired about his father. A few minutes after they left the hospital, heading back to Sucre sur Mer, Connecticut pulled over to the side of the road.

"Why are we stopping?" Tony asked.

"Didn't you say something about wanting to see Edensgate before you left? This might be your only chance."

"Edensgate? Where?" Tony looked out his window across a vast expanse of recently graded soil, as flat and featureless as a football field. In the moonlight, he saw a large white building surrounded by bulldozers and other heavy equipment, hunkered down like giant sleeping reptiles. "Jesus Christ! What the hell have they done? This used to be all trees. You couldn't even *see* the house from the road. Why on earth would they do something so stupid?"

"Parking lots. The Dunstan Corporation is turning it into an attraction—someplace tourists can come when it rains at Disney World."

Tony opened his door and stepped out.

"What are you doing, Tony? Come on. There's really nothing else to see."

"I've gotta get a closer look."

Connecticut sighed and followed him, leaving his door slightly ajar. They stood in front of the spiked, wrought-iron gates and surveyed the carnage. The gravel driveway had been widened and paved at the expense of one row of oaks, although the others remained as a lopsided concession to environmentalists. Much of the lawn, too, had been paved over, and a black cape of asphalt was drawn tightly around the house so that only a dark stain lingered like lipstick where shrubbery once kissed its walls.

Two signs flanked the gate. The smaller one, black letters on a yellow background, said only "Dead End." The other announced the opening of "Eden's World, the restored home of Eve Eden, enigmatic star of the silent silver screen. . . . See the sumptuous mansion built by tycoon John Lindsey Dunstan for the love of his life . . . the Greek mosaics and Italian frescoes from authentic Classical and Renaissance sites. . . . See the private screening room where Miss Eden spent her waning days reliving her luminous film career. . . ."

"What bullshit," Tony said. "Dallas told me she never watched her movies. Ever. And *he'd* be spinning in his grave if he knew the feet of the unwashed were going to tread his marble floors and Persian rugs."

"A physical impossibility, I'm sure."

"What? Walking on Dallas's rugs?"

"No, him *spinning* in his grave. I'm sure his coffin is a tight fit." Connecticut turned away from the gate and walked toward the car. He reached the door, turned, and waited for Tony, damping down his impatience.

"Look, the gates have been knocked off kilter—probably by all the heavy equipment. I can squeeze right through. You, too, if you've kept your girlish figure."

"No way, Tony. It's trespassing."

"It's not like I'm going to break in to the house or anything. I just want to take a look around."

"What about the car? It's bound to attract attention. At the very least, I'll get a ticket for being in a no-parking zone."

"Look, if you don't want to come with me, just say so. Call a cab when you get home and tell them to wait right here at the gates. But do you actually think that with everything that's going on in this little burg tonight the cops are going to have time to ticket somebody for parking on the shoulder of Tropicana Boulevard?"

"Okay, okay. Christ! I should know better than to argue with you." He reached in and turned on the emergency blinkers, then closed and locked the door.

They made their way up the driveway, Connecticut hugging the side that was sheltered by the surviving oaks in the hopes that the moon shadows might conceal him from whatever security guards might be patrolling the property. Tony thought the house looked at least twice as large and somewhat menacing with no landscaping—like a mausoleum. As they passed by it, Tony pointed out the servants' entrance, which now looked rather like the tiny door in Wonderland that could not accommodate a giant Alice. Soon they reached the back of the house, where the pool, a significant insurance liability with hundreds of tourists strolling by daily, had been filled in and replaced with a still-unfinished admission center. The lawn between the house and the ocean remained largely undisturbed, but Tony could imagine a gift shop or first-aid clinic overtaking it if business was good. He noticed a grouping of white wrought-iron lawn furniture and sat down on a love seat facing the sea.

"Toneeeee," Connecticut said.

"Shhhh! *You're* the one who's gonna draw attention to us. Just sit down. This was always my favorite view. I remember when Hiroki and I hung white Japanese lanterns in the trees all the way down to the beach for a party. When we lit them, they looked like little floating moons."

"We're going to get caught, Tony. I know we're going to get caught."

"Will you relax? Trespassing's a misdemeanor. Christ, I've come back from shoots in Turkey or India with a couple of keys of dope and the Customs boys at Kennedy never batted an eye—as long as I batted mine first. Of course there were more than a couple 'pat downs' and I seem to remember a rather lengthy, terribly exciting strip search. So calm down. If we get 'caught,' which we won't, let me handle it. Most of the rent-a-cops I've met have been gay. They like working at night and carrying a gun. Faux butch. I'll slap them across the face with my nightstick a couple times and they'll forget the whole thing. So sit back and enjoy the night air and the moonlight. It's *almost* romantic."

"Great, now you're smuggling drugs. Every time I get used to one of your bad habits, you pick up another one." Connecticut sat down next to Tony. "But you're right. It *is* romantic."

"I said almost."

Connecticut draped his arm across the back of the love seat, encircling Tony's shoulders. "So, Tony, do you ever . . . well . . . think about us?"

Tony turned to look at Connecticut, head cocked. "As something other than a textbook recipe for disaster?"

"Is that what you think we were . . . a disaster?"

"Let's see. Virtually no sex for the last month of our relationship. Then I come home to find an empty apartment, without so much as a note to explain. And all of this on Valentine's Day. Jesus, Connecticut."

"I swear to God, I didn't realize that until I was getting off the New Jersey Turnpike and the attendant at the toll plaza wished me a happy Valentine's Day. Tony, I nearly died. I pulled over to the breakdown lane and . . . broke down. I did. I cried all the way to Maryland. I almost turned around and went back."

"Well, that's good to know. All these years I've been convinced the timing was intentional, although in my heart of hearts I knew you weren't enough of a romantic to be *anti*-romantic enough to break up with me with that kind of panache. Still, it's nice to know you at least *thought* about coming back to the city. Do you know what the worst part of it was? It was so *premeditated*. How long did it take you to get your ducks in a row? To change jobs? To rent the truck and hire the movers? And yet you slept in the same bed with me the whole time. All the while, the gears were turning. For all I know, the one time you *did* make love to me that month you might have been wondering simultaneously which would be cheaper, Ryder or U-Haul."

"It wasn't *all* about you, Tony—good *or* bad. I *hated* New York. It was too crowded, too dirty. Bodies were found floating facedown in the Hudson."

"You think it was the Garden of Eden for me?"

"You survived. You *flourished*."

"Maybe. But *that* year, *that* winter, it wasn't any less difficult for me. You were always busy, always distracted. I didn't have a fucking soul to turn to for companionship except Zen, and we both know what came of that."

"Don't blame *me* for Zen, and *don't* criticize me for doing my job. As I recall, you never got home much before two or three, once you took the *Hair* job. Was I supposed to stay up and wait for you?"

"I know, I know. Look, I don't want to fight, especially about shit that's eight years old," Tony said. "All I'm saying is that daffodils didn't unfold in my path in New York, either. But I put up with it because I was there with you."

"What do you want me to say, Tony, that leaving you was the biggest mistake of my life? Well, yes, it was. I realized that some time ago. I regret what I did to you, and *how* I did it, more than you'll ever know."

Tony was speechless, an exceedingly unfamiliar position.

"Surprised? Yes, I'm sorry. Very, *very* sorry. I was a real shit. But if it makes you feel any better, I've been paying for it ever since."

"What? What do you mean?"

"I haven't had a successful relationship since I left you. Your friend Zen might call it karma. An anthropologist friend at Sanctuary calls it bad *juju*. My psychiatrist say it's because I never learned *how* to have one, and he's probably right."

"Don't feel bad. You're not alone."

"You? You can't possibly have trouble meeting men."

"Meeting, no. Hanging on to, yes. I don't think I've ever walked into a bar and not gone home with one of my top three draft choices. And I usually had to settle for numbers two or three only because bachelor number one was already spoken for, recently diseased, or so strung out he couldn't tell my ass from a hole in the ground, which wouldn't have been fun for either one of us. But the *good* guys, the guys I fell in love with, always bolted after a couple of months. Val says I smothered them."

"Someone with your looks? I just thought . . ."

"Don't sound so surprised. After all, *you* walked out on me."

"Oh, Tony. I am *so* sorry."

"So you say."

"I *never* stopped loving you, Tony. Ever. It was just that I was so afraid of getting hurt. You were so young, and *so* beautiful. Some nights I watched you sleeping, and I swear to God, it was like watching an angel, a god, especially with your long blond hair, which, you know, I kind of miss. I worried every night that you wouldn't come home from the theater, that you'd go home with some young hippie stud I could never compete with. I was nervous and jealous every minute I was away from you. And then my nightmare came true."

"I told you, Zen didn't . . ."

"Wait. Listen. I *knew* back then how upset you were about that. I knew you loved me. But I just couldn't let go of it. Every time we made love after that, I felt him there, Zen, in the room, watching us, crouching on my chest like an incubus while you drifted off to sleep afterward. So I stopped making love to you. It wasn't because I was mad at you. It just hurt too much—it made me feel too vulnerable. I knew I'd go crazy if I didn't get out of there. I was ecstatic being with you, but I was scared shitless about what it would feel like to be without you—and Zen gave me a taste of that. I figured if I cut and ran, it wouldn't hurt as badly as if *you* left *me,* which I knew was inevitable. It sounds stupid now, I know, and I don't think it worked, because I can't imagine hurting any more than I did. . . . *do* . . . right now."

"Do?"

"Yes."

"You mean . . . you still . . . *love* me? Like . . . *that?"*

"Don't let it go to your head, you little shit."

"I'm not. I'm not. It's just that I used to dream about this—day-dreamed . . . you know—about seeing you again and having you tell me that you loved me. But it's so strange to really be here and hear you say it."

"What happens next in your dream?"

"Nothing. Just that."

"Don't you ever dream about us . . . being together again?"

"You mean having sex?"

"I mean having breakfast."

"You're kidding!"

"I'm not."

"Why haven't you said anything sooner? I mean, I *am* in the Manhattan White Pages. Along with the stalls in most men's rooms, coast to coast."

"I hope you're kidding. About the men's rooms. But that's exactly why I couldn't just call you up. You're so successful now. You're sur-rounded by gorgeous men. You travel all over the country . . . around the world. I figured you long ago had found someone and settled down. And if not, I just didn't think I could compete with all the other men who were interested in you."

"So why say something now? I sure as hell hope it's not because I've got this big gash across my face and you figure no one else will want me."

"Tony, that has nothing to do with it, believe me. I don't care about that. In fact, I hope they're able to fix it."

"You still haven't answered the question. Why now?"

"Because the opportunity presented itself. You're here, I'm here. That's right, I'm actually capable of a spontaneous act. And because I've never loved you more than I do at this minute. I could have lost you in that fire, Tony. I don't want to lose you again."

Tony sighed but didn't say anything. He had dealt with Connecticut for so long as an absence it was difficult now to deal with him as a presence. After a moment, he stood.

"I need a couple of minutes alone," he said and turned to walk toward the water's edge. It was ironic: the one thing he had wanted most for so long had been set before him, and yet there wasn't a single cell in his body that tingled with joy or delight or yearning. Was he in shock from the fire? Had something died inside him tonight? No. He hadn't lost the capacity to feel emotion. He *was* in love, deeply in love, just not with this man. Of course, given his uncertainty about Avery's willingness to take him back after treachery as vile as his own, Connecticut's offer of a bird in the hand was somewhat tempting. He'd be taken care of. But it was not enough, and he was willing to bet that what he had with Avery was strong enough to survive his own insecurity and meanspiritedness.

Ten minutes passed as he sat in the cool, damp sand, his legs drawn up, encircled by his arms. The ebb tide waves that made it to shore were miniature, and they expired with sighs as diminutive as those at the culmination of a kiss. Eventually, he heard the squeal of Connecticut's rubber-soled shoes approaching on the dry sand behind him.

"Your pants are going to get wet, Tony. Here, sit on my jacket. It's waterproof."

"I'm okay."

"Come sit up here."

Tony recognized that tone of voice from years ago and acquiesced, standing in one motion, without a word. He briefly lost and recovered his balance as he passed from wet, packed sand to loose and trudged to where Connecticut was sitting, safely, three yards above the tide line.

"What are you thinking about?" Connecticut asked.

"A lot of things."

"And about us?"

Tony was looking straight out to sea. In just the past few moments he had seen the horizon line begin to define itself, black against midnight blue.

"I haven't been entirely honest with you, Connecticut."

"Oh. I see. Is it your friend Val? He's more than a friend?"

"No."

"But there *is* another man."

"Sort of. I won't be sure until I get back to New York." Tony gave Connecticut a Cliff Notes version of his relationship with Avery, sanitized, initially, to exclude Avery's disability and marital status, and ending with their breakup.

"You know what they say about being blinded by rage? I never really knew what that meant—not in my gut—until the day Avery told me about him and Devlin. And of course level-headed me, voted most likely to have a psychotic episode, I went *ballistic* with Avery. I slapped him, I punched him, I tore the bedclothes. I practically knocked him out of his wheelchair . . ."

"Wait a minute, he had a wheelchair? You beat up a paralyzed person? You *dated* a paralyzed person?"

"Not paralyzed. No legs. They were amputated after a car accident. The whole problem was that I wouldn't listen to what he had to say. I got mad and pissy and acted like the spoiled bitch-goddess I'd become. I threw him out, so I didn't hear the whole story until much later . . . not until the flight down here, in fact. But when I was trapped in that fucking bar, all I could think about was Avery. Not you, not any of the many men I fucked and sucked in eight years in New York, not even the ones who stayed around long enough to actually remember my name or how I liked my eggs cooked. And I prayed to God—and I don't even really believe in God anymore—that I would at least live long enough to apologize to Avery. They could have pulled me from the ashes, burned beyond recognition, and I wouldn't have minded the pain or the dying if I could just have gotten on the phone to Avery and told him what a fucking moron I'd been."

"Jesus, Tony, I've got to meet this man."

The earth was gradually warming under the force of the new day's sun, and the sand flushed pink as the ribbons of sunrise pushed the night sky slowly westward.

"The funny thing, Connecticut—and until this moment, I never looked at it this way—is that what I was, what I had become, was *you*. I treated Avery the same way you treated me. I was selfish, self-centered, and hurtful. Remember what you told your class the day I sat in and you showed those awful pictures from those fires? 'Save yourself,' you told them, 'Save yourself.'"

"It's true. It's the only sensible thing to do."

"Maybe, but if I had listened to you, Val would be dead right now. And I'm not sure I could live with myself if I thought there was even the most remote possibility I could have saved him and I hadn't tried."

"The truth is, Tony, *both* of you should be dead."

"But my point is bigger than that. I think you've adopted 'Save your-self' as a motto. I think a lot of people have. Maybe gay people espe-cially. I don't know. Even now, you telling me that you love me and want to be with me—when I'm scared and scarred and vulnerable—that seems kind of selfish."

"That's pretty cold, Tony. That's not what I meant, and I think you know it. And what you did to this Avery person doesn't exactly qualify you for beatification."

"I'm not pointing a finger at you. And believe me, I know I'm not a saint. I wasn't willing to sit still for a few *minutes* to listen to what Avery had to say. Instead, I was thinking about what Val might think, about what the whole damn shark pool at the modeling studio would think—and I don't really even *care* about that gaggle of giddy queens. The only one I *wasn't* thinking about was Avery, even though I supposedly loved him more than anything in the world. That 'love' turned to anger and hate in one second—*one second*—what the hell kind of love is that? And as a result, I hurt a really good man—and he is, he's a *really* good man. The best man I have ever met. I know it sounds stupid, but it may be that all of this shit tonight—the fire, the scar—is God's way of paying me back."

Tony stood up. He was tired of talking, and he turned his back to the sea. The sun was far enough above the horizon that it carved shadows into the soft earth where bulldozers had worked the day before. Edensgate was bleached white, like the bones of an animal in the desert. Tony felt the first flushed breath of morning on the back of his neck and he knew it would be a long, tiring day. Connecticut followed him with-out a word; when they got to the driveway, he walked down the center of the road, oddly less self-conscious now about trespassing than he had been in the dark. They slipped through the gates and got into the car, its emergency flashers anemic in the full sun. It was so quiet, Tony could hear them pinging on and off.

"So there's absolutely no chance that I . . . we . . . you don't feel *any-thing* for me?" Connecticut said as he buckled his seat belt. "I can't hon-estly say if I'll be here again later if you and Avery . . ."

"Look. I don't want to hurt you, Connecticut," Tony said, "but com-ing face to face with you, I realized I've told myself so many lies about *not* loving you that I've come to believe them myself. I've probably lied to myself about love too much to ever feel exactly what I felt for you again. You were the first and maybe that means you were the best. But I think I've come close with Avery, very close, and if it's the last thing I do, I'm going to make it work. . . . You understand . . . don't you?"

Connecticut bit his lower lip. Glancing into the rearview mirror, he put the car in gear. They traveled forward a short distance on the shoulder before he eased the Cutlass onto the road and left Edensgate behind.

"Don't you?" Tony repeated.

"Yes." He nodded. "Yes."

# *Epilogue*

NO PAIN, NO SCARS. That's what the doctors promised: Tony's face would be restored to its original beauty with scarcely a trace of visible damage and no loss of mobility. It would not be easy and it would not be cheap, but Vera and Charles Rittenhouse, after learning that Tony had saved Val's life at the expense of his face, had insisted upon underwriting the procedure and had assembled a team of cosmetic surgeons from Geneva, Rio de Janeiro, and Beverly Hills, who approached their task with the reverence of the artisans who had restored Michelangelo's *Pietà* following the attack of a hammer-wielding madman. So now, some two weeks after the fire, it was Val who sat at Tony's bedside, waiting for the anesthesiologist.

Val had recovered from his injuries fully and without incident, save one case of acute respiratory distress a day after the fire, although perhaps that had been brought on by the arrival at his bedside of his entire family. Alerted to their son's plight by a phone call from Tony, Vera and Charles Rittenhouse, Billington, and key members of the house staff were airlifted from their snowbound Connecticut estate by the Rittenhouse Freres corporate helicopter and flown south to Washington, where they chartered a med-evac jet and assembled a team of plastic surgeons and pulmonary specialists headed by President Jimmy Carter's personal physician, a Yale classmate of Charles Rittenhouse. They rendezvoused at the Daytona Beach airport with Mackenzie, who had been preparing to see in the new decade with her best friend, Marissa, at The Breakers in Palm Beach.

After their preliminary examination, Val's doctors found no cause for alarm but suggested he remain in Florida for at least forty-eight hours so they could monitor his pulmonary function and assess his fitness for air travel (in any event the runways at LaGuardia were not expected to be operating normally at least until Monday morning, New Year's Eve). As he had predicted, the fact that he had survived a fire in a *gay* bar was barely mentioned, though ultimately Charles Rittenhouse did use it as leverage to suggest that perhaps it was time for his son to retire from modeling and get serious about his responsibilities to the family business.

Lost in the swirl of the Rittenhouse retinue (Val simply rolled his eyes at the hubbub), Tony received a preliminary examination from one of the plastic surgeons, then retreated to Sucre sur Mer to await news from Tuxedo about Avery and to prepare for the return to New York aboard the Rittenhouses' chartered jet. Monk's surfboard and the cardboard box and paper bags that contained his belongings were gone when Tony and Connecticut had returned from their visit to Edensgate that morning, and Tony never saw the boy again.

When he was not on the phone, Tony watched local television news coverage of the fire at the Carousel, which reporters had taken to calling the "disco inferno." The death toll had reached two hundred and six, making it, one anchorman said, the seventh deadliest fire in American history. Most of the victims appeared to be between nineteen and twenty-five years old. Only a handful were over thirty, and there was an unconfirmed report that one of the dead boys was only seventeen and must have gained entry to the bar illegally. Tony wondered if that was the pretty boy in the lavender Izod he had spoken to and whose body he found when he was looking for Val.

The town of Sugar Mill Beach was shocked by the deaths of so many of its young men: almost half the dead were local boys. But parents throughout Central Florida and on up the East Coast were soon to be informed that their sons were among the confirmed fatalities or were missing and presumed dead, based on the fact that their cars were parked in the vicinity of the bar and remained unclaimed forty-eight hours later.

Devlin's body, or what remained of it, was tentatively identified by the inscription on his gold Rolex, which was undamaged because he had fallen on his left hand and forearm, shielding them from the flames. In his left hand he clutched damning evidence of his ultimate perfidy: a shattered table leg, which an eyewitness claimed he used to bludgeon his way toward the front of the bar in his vain attempt to escape. A week later, when he was publicly identified as the man who had beaten his way to the exit, his family, already shamed by the fact that their son had died in a gay bar, refused to claim his body. Val eventually would arrange to have his remains cremated and placed in a stainless steel urn, which he then secreted in the engine compartment of Devlin's Porsche, which was then compacted. He created a fictitious provenance for the resulting cube and donated it to the Museum of Modern Art in a package deal that also included John Chamberlain's *Bumper Buddha* from his foyer at Triumph Towers, which MOMA curators had been salivating over for some time.

Kip Slade, the surfer Tony met at the Carousel the night of the fire, became something of a reluctant hero. His information about the license plate number of the arsonists' vehicle led to the arrest of four South Beach boys (Tony recognized some of their family names), who were charged with arson and two-hundred-six counts of second-degree murder. He thought about calling Kip to thank him for his kindness at the hospital and to arrange to return his shirt but decided against it. He didn't want him to get the wrong idea.

Connecticut called late on Sunday afternoon. He said he had hoped to run into Tony at the hospital when he went to see his father and had even made a point of locating Valentine Rittenhouse's room, to no avail. Now he wanted to know if Tony might want to get together for dinner. Tony declined the invitation, pleading exhaustion; he had nothing more to say to him. (Connecticut told him his father already was planning a benefit performance as Desdemona Jones to help pay the medical bills and funeral expenses of victims of the fire, and Tony said he'd be sure to send a check.)

In New York, with phone service still out to parts of Brooklyn and Queens, Tuxedo borrowed a four-wheel-drive vehicle and made his way through the paralyzed city and across the Brooklyn Bridge to Avery's apartment on Sunday afternoon. There he learned from Avery's upstairs neighbor that he had been hospitalized for an apparent overdose three days ago.

When Brandi and the boys arrived home the previous Thursday night, they found Avery unconscious on the floor of the living room, his wheelchair on its side next to him. It was not clear what had happened until Christopher found the empty pill bottles on the kitchen sink. Brandi called 911 and left the distraught boys with a neighbor, riding to the hospital in the ambulance with Avery. As she watched the paramedic attend her husband, she tried to figure out what had made him try to kill himself. She had been devastated when he told her that he was leaving her. He said that it was for her own good, that she deserved a better man, a *whole* man, but she suspected he was leaving her for another woman, probably one of the nurses at the rehabilitation center he occasionally went to for treatments of phantom pain. That would explain his increasingly frequent absences from home. Perhaps, she thought, he had had second thoughts, or maybe the relationship had suddenly, inexplicably ended, precipitating his attempt to take his life. Maybe, she thought, her arm outstretched to touch the gurney on which he lay, *maybe* there was hope for a reconciliation.

When copies of the *Babbler* hit the streets in New York the following morning, Avery's family began piecing together the story of the life he had hidden from them for the past year. At first Brandi thought it was a mistake, that someone was playing a practical joke on readers of the *Babbler* (it was her favorite newspaper and she picked up a copy in the tiny hospital coffee shop while waiting for news about her husband).

"If your father is a famous model, then I'm the Queen of Sheba!" she told the boys as she stole a look at herself in the mirrored façade of an ancient candy machine. But as she reread the story and scrutinized the fuzzy photograph, her confusion and disbelief turned gradually to anger.

"That bastard! He was off in Key West last February while I was here in New York with the kids freezing my ass off in that crummy apartment," she told Mandi and Candi in consecutive calls from the waiting-room pay phone. "He told me he spent that weekend with his brother, Tom, and that his face was red from working with an arc welder at a body shop in Queens! I guess he'll be the one to see red when I file my divorce papers!"

When Tuxedo finally arrived at the hospital Sunday evening, Avery had regained consciousness but his vital signs were still weak. The local media, largely preoccupied with the impact of the blizzard on the city, had not yet tracked him down, though Tuxedo knew they eventually would and arranged to have him moved to a private psychiatric hospital on the Upper East Side as soon as travel conditions improved. When he first identified himself to Brandi, she practically assaulted him, whacking the *Babbler* against the breast of his fawn-colored cashmere coat and demanding to know what he had "done" to her husband. She calmed down considerably when Tuxedo told her that all of Avery's medical bills would be covered by Malone Men's health insurance.

"Well, it's the least you can do!" she said, brushing contritely at the smudge of newspaper ink she had left on his lapel. "You've ruined his life." She had to admit, however, that she had never seen such a handsome, well-groomed man up close before, a man with such perfectly manicured hands . . . and no wedding ring! (She wasn't thinking of herself, mind you, but of her soon-to-be divorced sister, Candi, whose three husbands all had been good looking but stupid and cruel.) Watching Tuxedo deal with the hospital staff, getting attention and responses she had been unable to obtain, it dawned on her that Avery had somehow— God knows *how*—gained access to a secret world of rich, gorgeous, *powerful* men, and that regardless of what became of her relationship with him, her life was bound to change. She saw a future in which she no longer slaved away at a diner in Greenpoint, a future in which she had the time and money to enroll at the International University of Cosmetology in Manhattan and to become a beauty operator at her sister Mandi's shop in New Jersey—maybe even to open up a place of her own in Brooklyn. She decided to "make nice" with Avery and this male model mafia, at least until she figured how to turn things to her best advantage.

Tux waited until Monday afternoon, when Avery finally seemed to be gaining ground, before he called Tony. No point in worrying him needlessly. He made no mention of attempted suicide but said simply that Avery had mistakenly taken one too many sleeping pills while Brandi and the boys were out of the apartment and that just to be safe she had taken him to the hospital. He blamed the ensuing confusion and lack of information on the snowstorm.

Tony, who had been packing and closing up the condo at Sucre sur Mer, was quick to read between the lines, but he maintained his composure on the flight back to New York City that evening and didn't say a word about it to Val other than to say that Tux had been in touch with Avery and that he was fine. Traffic was stacked up over LaGuardia—a lot of commercial flights were trying to get in to the city for the first time in three days—and they were still in the air when revelers on the ground were ushering in 1980. As they circled the city, Tony swore he could see Times Square, and he unsuccessfully strained to glimpse the giant billboard that would propel his career into the stratosphere.

The midnight "Me" launch was an unprecedented success. On New Year's Day, Tony was besieged with phone calls from friends (exhausted, he let his service pick them up), and Tux was inundated with inquiries from the media. Fortunately, he was able to use the holiday to buy himself twenty-four hours in which to compose an explanation for why the "Me" boy now had a six-inch gash in his million-dollar face: with the collusion of Charles Rittenhouse, he concocted a tale of a snowmobile accident on the grounds of the Rittenhouse estate in Connecticut.

Tony's reunion with Avery did not take place until Wednesday and was less dramatic than it might have been because it occurred in Avery's hospital room with most of his family gathered around him and two elderly women saying rosary novenas at the foot of his bed. Tony arrived with Tuxedo, ostensibly as a representative of Avery's friends at Malone Models. Brandi, who was pouring a glass of water for Avery when they walked in, apparently recognized him as the Black Tie model despite the bandage on his face and blushed. "I swear, honey," she said to Avery in a stage whisper, "who's going to walk into this room next—John Travolta?"

"I'm Tony," he said and handed her the large bouquet he carried. She was prettier than he had imagined, more petite and less hardened than he had expected. "I brought these for Avery . . . from the guys at work."

Avery's brother, Tom, in an orange Naugahyde chair by the window, looked up from the *Daily News* but said nothing.

"Tom," Tony said, acknowledging him.

Tom shook the paper once and returned to reading it. Tony knew exactly what he was thinking. Tom had always been protective of his younger brother, and it had taken him awhile to warm up to Tony and accept that his motives were genuine. But over the summer, he had become cordial, even friendly. And then Tony bore out every suspicion and apprehension Tom had ever harbored.

"They're gorgeous!" Brandi said. "You guys all seem to have such good taste."

"We've just got a good florist."

"Well, let me . . . I'll just go find something to put them in, maybe at the nurses' station."

Avery looked pale and more tired than Tony had ever seen him. But some color came back into his cheeks when Tony, feeling that every eye in the room was on him, shook his hand and held it in his own for a moment before releasing it. Suddenly emotional, he managed to choke out the words, "Hello, Avery."

"Tony. It's good to see you." Avery pushed himself up with his elbows and leaned forward as if anticipating a kiss, then, after an awkward moment, settled back into his pillows. "My God, what's wrong with your face? Tux said you'd had an accident, but he didn't say anything about your *face*."

"You don't know about . . . ?" Tony looked at Tom, who shook his head. "It's a long story. It'll be okay."

"I can't tell you how . . ."

Nervous—and uncertain he could control himself if Avery got emotional—Tony cut him off. "I just wanted to let you know that I'm . . . that *we* are looking forward to having you back . . . at work."

Avery looked at Tony curiously, shot a glance at his brother, Tom, and then shifted his eyes to his parents, who were engaged in conversation with Tuxedo.

"I'm . . . looking forward to *coming* back," he said. "I didn't know if you'd . . ."

"Of course I . . . *we* . . . do. We'd be *lost* without you!"

"And you'll be there . . . when I come back?"

"Always. I'll always be there," Tony said. "I'm sorry, Ave, I'm so sorry . . ."

Tom cleared his throat and stood up.

"I think it's best that Avery not get too excited, Tony. You know. . . ." He cocked his head toward the praying women, one of whom had not said a single Hail Mary since Tony had begun speaking.

"Okay . . . I understand."

At that moment, Brandi walked into the room with the bouquet in a blue-and-white plastic water pitcher.

"It's a shame to put these beautiful flowers in such a . . ." She stopped in her tracks. Avery was smiling in a way she hadn't seen in years. She started to look around the room, gazing quickly over her left shoulder to see who had entered while she was gone and elicited such a response from Avery, and then her gaze froze on Tony. His hand seemed to be resting on top of Avery's, not holding it but sort of covering it. She looked at Avery. Back at Tony. Then at Tom, who she knew was gay. " . . . in such a pitiful excuse for a . . . vase."

At the foot of the bed, the second prayer lady stopped for just a moment—*Blessed art thou among women*—the crucifix on her rosary bobbing and swinging in her palsied hands, and then she continued—*and blessed is the fruit of thy womb, Jesus.*

"I really better go," Tony said.

"Don't," Avery said. "Please don't."

"He's right," Tom said. "You've had plenty of excitement for one day."

"When are they springing you from this joint, anyway?" Tony asked.

"Saturday, I think. If I'm good."

"Well, *be* good."

THAT WAS TEN DAYS AGO. Tony and Avery had spoken on the phone a few times since, but never for long. Avery's family had practically camped out in his apartment and his boys wouldn't give him a minute to himself—though he didn't complain.

Tony's surgery was scheduled for 9 A.M. Val had been there since 6:00; Tuxedo and Parker had just left. There was a knock on the door, followed by some gentle thumps, like rubber against the wooden door.

"Here we go," Tony said, expecting orderlies to wheel in a hospital gurney.

But it was not a gurney—it was a wheelchair. It was Avery, and he looked much better, he looked like his old self: color in his cheeks, hair windblown, wearing the familiar leather bomber. He wheeled himself into the room followed somewhat tentatively by two young boys. The older one, Christopher, blond like his mother but much prettier, positioned himself beside his dad's wheelchair like a sentry; the younger one, Joey, shy and dark-haired, blushing, tried to hide behind his father. Tony had seen pictures of the boys, had heard countless stories about them, but in the entire time he had been with Avery he had never met them. That part of Avery's life had been separate, sacred, out of bounds.

"C'm'ere, Joey," Avery said over his shoulder. "Don't be bashful. Come meet your Uncle Tony."

Joey walked around the side of the wheelchair and Avery lifted him up and put him on his lap.

"Is he the one with the horses and punkins?" Joey asked, his face turned up to his father.

"It's pumpkins, Joey," Christopher said. "Not punkins."

"*Punkins.*"

"Not yet, Joey. He doesn't have the farmhouse and horses and pumpkins yet. But he will soon—won't he, Tony?"

"Yeah," Tony said haltingly. "Soon. Very, very soon."